Emma Cooper is a form⸱⸱⸱ ⸱⸱⸱s in
Shropshire with her partn⸱⸱⸱ ⸱⸱⸱nds
her spare time writing n⸱⸱⸱ ⸱⸱⸱ing
box-sets with her partne⸱⸱⸱ ⸱⸱⸱ still
makes her smile every day.

Emma has always wanted to be a writer – ever since childhood, she's been inventing characters (her favourite being
her imaginary friend 'Boot') and is thrilled that she now gets
to use this imagination to bring to life all of her creations.

The Songs of Us was inspired by Emma's love of music and
her ability to almost always embarrass herself, and her children, in the most mundane situations. She was so fascinated
by the idea of combining the two that she began to write
Melody's story. The majority of her novel was written during
her lunchtime in a tiny school office.

The Songs of Us

EMMA COOPER

H

REVIEW

First published in 2018 by Headline Review
An imprint of HEADLINE PUBLISHING GROUP

First published in paperback in 2018 by Headline Review
An imprint of HEADLINE PUBLISHING GROUP

2

Cataloguing in Publication Data is available from the British Library

ISBN 978 1 4722 5253 1

Typeset in Garamond MT by Palimpsest Book Production Limited,
Falkirk, Stirlingshire

Printed and bound in Great Britain by Clays Ltd, Elcograf S.p.A.

HEADLINE PUBLISHING GROUP
An Hachette UK Company
Carmelite House
50 Victoria Embankment
London EC4Y 0DZ

www.headline.co.uk
www.hachette.co.uk

For Us

I

Melody

Our life – no matter what happens in between – starts and ends with a heartbeat: our own personal rhythm, our own song. A song can rise and fall like the breath in our lungs; it can start with one solitary note and then expand with each verse: a family of sound. To me, however, a song has deeper meaning.

'That'll be eighty-seven pounds and sixty-six pence, please,' the supermarket cashier announces, filling me with dread.

I can see, from your point of view, that this is not terrible news. A respectable amount for a family of three's weekly shop. After all, the masculine-looking cashier clerk is not implying that I have one week left to live or that my skirt is tucked into my knickers. My problem lies with my bank balance; I know that today, 21st February, my bank balance totters along a tightrope of eighty pounds.

I hear the first bars of 'Can't Buy Me Love' by The Beatles. This may not seem a big deal. Songs are played in supermarkets worldwide; their upbeat tempos drive the dead-eyed shopper shuffle. But this is why the cashier's few words fill me with fear: I try to explain my bank balance predicament.

'Excuse me?' the slightly alarmed, suet-faced cashier questions me, as well she might. You see, I'm not explaining my situation with a droop of my shoulders and a 'life sometimes gets you down' expression.

No. I'm not just hearing The Beatles' classic: I've started singing it – theatrically. Perhaps you're wondering why I'm singing – with gusto – The Beatles to a supermarket cashier? Well, the answer is, I don't know. In fact, I've seen several different GPs in the past two years and not one of them knows. Nor do the consultants, specialists or psychiatrists (of which there have been many).

Let me tell you what I do know.

I woke up one blustery, icy January morning – nothing remarkable about that. There was nothing special about the fact that it was Grey Wheelie Bin Day, or that I was outside in my wellies, pink-marshmallow dressing gown wrapped around my Christmas-excess stomach, attempting to drag said bin up my steep drive. I say this is not special because my life, even then, was disorganised. Chaotic. Slapdash. If I had been the orderly, controlled person that I always intended to be every New Year's Day, then my bin would already be standing outside my house: a brave soldier facing the elements, awaiting its disembowelment with resolute pride. If I had been that person, I wouldn't have run out of de-icer the day before and so used boiling water to defrost the window of the car. There wouldn't have been a frozen patch of black ice right next to the kerb. I wouldn't have slipped backwards and cracked the back of my head against the path. There wouldn't have been an ear-splitting scream from my eleven-year-old daughter when she found me bleeding and unconscious twenty minutes later. My distraught son wouldn't have been filled with panic as he clumsily used his scouting skills to try to find my weak pulse and – of course – I wouldn't have been lying with my own urine freezing against my legs while my children waited a lifetime for the ambulance to arrive: tears, fear and too much responsibility shaking their gangly developing bodies, as they anxiously debated how many chest compressions they should give me.

By now, here in the supermarket, I have really hit my stride, explaining all of the things that I just cannot buy to the cashier: my voice triggering a ripple of uneasiness through the shop. I watch – as I have so many times before – the expressions, first of shock, then uneasiness, and finally amusement, passing over their contemptuous faces. Now, be honest with me: how would you react? Would you look the other way? Point and jeer? Put yourself here, now, standing in this queue behind me. A mundane Thursday lunchtime and a thirty-something, petite brunette is singing 'Can't Buy Me Love' at the top of her voice at the checkout. Not only is she not a brilliant singer – although thankfully in tune – but just look at the facial expressions and hand gestures! Now come on, you'd have a good old gawp, wouldn't you? I would! Just look at me! How is it possible to widen your eyes so much it looks as though they are about to pop right out and land, in all their spherical glory, on the grubby tiles? Oh here I go, repeatedly reinforcing the point that I couldn't give two hoots about the material things in life because it really can't gain you affection; have you noticed how my bottom is swaying like a pendulum? And just look at my index finger, wagging in front of the cashier's podgy face! Have you noticed how red she has gone? Look at her squirming in her seat, frantically pressing the button to herald someone, anyone, to take this mad woman away. You'd think with a moustache like that, she'd have a bit more compassion for the unusual. Hasn't she heard of waxing? Oh Christ, am I about to spin? Yep, here I go, hands stretched out like a demented traffic warden as I do a full turn and did I just . . .? Yep. I've just punched the air. Did you see me? I actually punched the air as I held my final note.

Silence. Not a peep from a grumpy child. Not even the

beep of a scanner. All I can hear is the last of my self-respect shattering into tiny pieces.

One Mississippi, two Mississippi, three Mississippi. And there we go. Three seconds is all it takes the British public to turn a deaf, dumb and blind eye. But I know they're there, sniggering behind raised hands, texting their friends, uploading me to YouTube (yes, that's happened – nineteen times, the last time my technologically gifted kids checked), filing it away to tell their friends over drinks tomorrow night.

Breathing heavily, I fumble in my bag and with a shaking hand – no doubt a side effect from all the finger wagging – try to pull out my bank card.

'Sorry,' I mutter, 'but could I take the beef joint back? I, um, I,' breathe, 'I don't think the card will . . .' Calm. Down.

For reasons the medical talents of this country can't explain, my 'condition' seems to be triggered by stress. That is to say, I'm not a singing, dancing act all the time. When the symptoms started to present themselves – first in the form of 'I Will Survive' by Gloria Gaynor, swiftly followed by an encore of 'Crazy' by Patsy Cline – I didn't dance at all. I just sang. My voice a captive beast, clawing and writhing out of me: desperate to be heard; desperate to escape; desperate to destroy. The dancing is a fairly new addition. Dr Ashley suggested that this might be a way for my subconscious to control the situations out of my control, by turning my outburst into a more 'acceptable act'. Quite how grinding to 'Boom! Shake the Room' in the middle of the leisure centre changing rooms makes it a more acceptable act, I don't know. Most of the time, I'm perfectly normal.

I try to give – I glance at her name badge – 'Sue' a reassuring smile.

Uneasily, she nods slowly, retrieving the beef from the packed bag, maintaining eye contact as if I'd just pulled out a gun, instead of paying a heartfelt tribute to John and Paul.

Stay calm. Breathe. She looks like a man and her name is Sue . . . Oh chuffing hell. Don't think about Johnny Cash, stay calm. I'll be fine as long as nothing else happens. Breathe. Don't think about it. As I pass her my debit card, I can hear the questions in the air and the muted comments of 'freak' shoot through with a 'lunatic' chaser. I can feel it begin to pulse through me: the urge – the release which my broken body is desperate for. Don't think about it, don't think about it. I close my eyes briefly and concentrate on the sound of my breathing. I'll be fine as long as I don't think about that song, but it's fine. See how I'm calming down? As long as I keep thinking about something else, I'll be out of here and home. My affliction nothing more than a story for others to devour.

'Really?' She smirks to the other clientele. 'Melody? Your name is Melody?'

'Mmhmm.'

I know; the irony is not lost on me. Several of the psychiatrists I have been to have implied that this may be a genuine link between my subconscious and my 'condition'. Another superior 'we're all in this together' smirk nearly sends me into dangerous territory, but I keep breathing. Keep thinking of what I'm having for tea and 'Sue' will soon be but a distant memory. Sue. Sue. Sue.

'Cash?'

Oh arses.

'Mum?!'

I stick my head out of the steam and peer around the shower curtain, head still soap-sudded and smelling of apple.

'I'm in the shower!' I call as the thud-thud sound of my daughter Rose running up the stairs penetrates my steamy orchard.

The door flings open.

'Why are you in the shower? It's half-three in the afternoon.'

'Spit,' I reply, giving myself a final blast of hot water.

'Oh. On the bus?'

'Supermarket.'

'Ouch. Complete works or just one verse?'

I turn off the taps and stick my hand out for a towel. Rose passes me a purple one which could do with a wash itself. I wrap it around me regardless, and step out on to the grey slate lino.

'Two.'

I look at her sheepishly, my pretty redhead.

'Two verses? That's not so bad.'

'Songs.'

She visibly flinches.

'Was there anyone who knows us there?' I grab a smaller towel and rub my short hair with it.

'Don't think so.'

'So why the spit?'

'Boy Named Sue.'

'I don't know that one.'

'It's about a boy who is called Sue by his dad to make him tough, which would have been fine if the cashier hadn't been called Sue and had a clear aversion to waxing her upper lip.'

'I see your point. Style?'

'Country.'

'Oh crikey. Dance moves?'

I stop rubbing my hair for a moment. Short spikes of hair stick out at opposing angles. I chew my bottom lip as I remember it all with dismay. Rose looks blank, slowly processing her vague knowledge of country music.

'Oh no. You didn't? Mum! You liiiine-danced?'

'I didn't even know I could.' I throw the towel down on the floor. 'It's amazing really.' I grab the hairbrush and tear through my hair. 'I started doing all these moves that I used

6

to do at junior school. I'd forgotten how much I enjoy pretending to throw a lasso; in fact, I Googled it and it appears that I apple-jacked, did several ball changes and duck walked.'

'Christ.'

'Don't swear.'

'"Christ" isn't swearing, "shit" is swearing.'

'True.'

The downstairs door slams and the tst, tst, tst of heavy metal through headphones announces the arrival of my son, Flynn. Another door slams as he disappears into his room. I look at Rose expectantly.

'How's he been? Did you see him at school today?' She finds something that resembles dried up yoghurt on one of the white tiles and gives it her full attention. 'Rose?'

'You might need to get some more antiseptic,' is her reply. Great. He's been fighting again.

Here is where I let you know that I'm not a bad mum. There are those of you who will, no doubt, have brilliantly behaved children who wouldn't dream of saying 'shit' or getting into a fight. Those of you who can, hand on heart, say that your children have been brought up to respect you as well as others and know the clear boundaries of what is right and wrong: the enforcement of the naughty step from age two; the reward charts that praise good behaviour and the Monopoly-and-Disney-film-filled Sundays. Allow me, if you will, to plead my defence. My children have been through emotions that most of you only experience later on in life; emotions that some of you may never have to feel. Let's start with terror. Pure, untainted, wholesome terror.

When Rose was two and Flynn was five, Dev – my husband – took them to Chester Zoo for the day. I stayed home; our washing machine had broken and I was waiting for the engineer to come out and fix it. On their way home, they stopped off for Dev to pick up some painkillers – he'd had a few beers the night before whilst watching the rugby – and some pop and crisps for Flynn. Dev had asked Flynn for a swig of the cola to wash down the pills, put some singalong nursery rhymes on to keep Rose happy and they set off, homeward bound, to be back in time for Rose's bedtime at seven. But they didn't make it home for Rose's bedtime because, at seven o'clock, Flynn was being lifted into the air ambulance with severe face and head injuries. Dev stood – holding a confused, tired and distraught Rose – as they watched the stretcher being carried off into the March darkness. Rose was unharmed, well protected by her car seat, and Dev was left with only a small cut above his right eye from a piece of the shattered windscreen. But Flynn . . . Flynn hadn't put his seat belt back on after he had passed the Coke to Dev. And when Dev looked away for a second to put 'Twinkle Twinkle Little Star' back on, he didn't notice the sharp turn to the right opposite the oak tree. He didn't know that Flynn was being catapulted forward at thirty-five miles per hour, and he didn't know that, for the rest of his life, his son would be blind in one eye and have a scar across his cheek that he would try to hide at every opportunity.

How about desolation? How many of you can say with all honesty that you have been truly desolate? Try having your father disappear. As in, without a trace.

The year of the crash was the bleakest of years. Dev had nightmares constantly and we argued over the smallest of things. The cost of hospital journeys, hospital parking charges, terrible-two tantrums. You name it, we argued about it. But there were also moments of exquisite anguish, where our devastation would turn into a love for each other so powerful it would take us over entirely: holding each other desperately through the night, whispering words of adoration to each other over and over as if we could fix each other

8

with love. And then one day he wasn't there. Poof. He was gone. Like Keyser Söze.

And then we have shame. Imagine watching your mum at a parents' evening burst into a rendition of 'Baby Got Back'. I did. I 'told' Rose's rotund maths teacher in no uncertain terms that I liked big bottoms and couldn't lie about it. As I've said. Shame.

Hesitantly, I knock on Flynn's door.

'Can I come in?'

'Not if you're going to bollock me.'

'Don't say bollock,' I say as I open the door. He's sat leaning against the metal headboard, headphone in one ear, long wavy brown hair covering the left side of his face, and dressed top to toe in this season's black.

'Let me see.' I step over the teenage debris of crisp packets and dirty clothes and reach for his hand. 'Oh, Flynn.' The knuckles of his right hand are raw. 'What happened?' He shrugs.

'The usual. Rob called me Quasimodo, so I twatted him.'

'Don't say twatted.'

'OK. Thumped . . . the twat.' I shake my head as he fleetingly smiles.

'I line-danced in Asda.'

'Cool.'

'I was really busting out the moves.'

'Don't say busting.'

'Jerking?'

'Mum, that is wrong in a whole other way.'

'MUUUUUUUUUM!' We both turn to where Rose is bounding through the door, red hair blazing behind her. 'I've been on the website and there is a person that fits Dad's description!'

'Rose,' I interrupt. We've been through this so many times: the hope, the optimism, the desire to fix the unfixable. 'Calm

9

down, remember there are a lot of people that fit Dad's description.'

'But this time it's different.'

How can I tell them? How can I tell them that Dev is dead? When I'm the only person who knows?

2

Rose

I've decided to write a diary. Is it OK to start one in the middle of the month? I suppose so. I'm the only one who'll read it. My 'counsellor' suggested it might help me to organise my thoughts, so here goes. I don't understand why Mum isn't more excited. I know that I've thought we've found Dad before but this time it's different.

Although Megan understands that I want to find my dad (I mean she should, I've been her best friend since we were three), I know she thinks I'm weird and I can see her point. When most of my class are on Instagram at break time, I'm on www.mymissingfamily.co.uk, and I get it. I do. I heard Becca Grimstone telling Ben Stone (who always picks his nose and eats it when he thinks no one is watching – ugh) that I was a ginger freak, obsessing about dead people. Stupid cow. Mum says that people who say horrid things are really just jealous of you. Yeah, right. I'm sure Becca, who's already a C cup, has perfectly formed features and is in top set, is really jealous of me. I'm ginger, way more clever than everyone else in my class and I'm not just being big-headed, I'm just saying it like it is . . . My maths teacher actually cried at our last parents' evening when she said that she felt she was 'letting me down' by not giving me even more challenging work – the government has a lot to answer for. Mrs Turner is holding on by a fine thread if you ask me, and I'M the one going to a counsellor?! Mum sympathised with her and her 'workload'; by that I mean she sang '9 to 5' by Dolly someone. Thank God we had a separate room for our appointment after the 'Baby Got Back' incident, so only the teacher saw it. What was I saying? Oh yeah, I'm also sister to – by his own admission – the most antisocial boy in school AND Becca knows that Dad left us and that my mum . . . well, there is no point even going there, is there?

The nights are getting worse. How can we tell her that the reason we look so tired isn't because we've been up all night on our tablets but because we have to listen to a soundtrack of her dreams each night? Take last night. She started quietly with 'Shake It Off'. Swifty is not one of my favourites, especially at half-one in the morning. Sometimes it's only snippets of songs, which change as quickly as her dreams. We know when she's having a bad dream because 'Wake Me Up Before You Go-Go' starts. But the worst is when it repeats. Like last night. From between two and five we had 'Don't Stop Believin''. Three times me and my brother passed each other on the landing; bed hair and irritated grumbles has become a regular thing as we try to subtly disturb her enough to shut her up. If we have a test the next day or something, we take it in turns to sleep downstairs. It kinda works, even though we have to set the alarm for half-six so we're up before Mum.

When the night songs started, Flynn told Mum when she got up that he was too tired to go to school because her rendition of 'Sweet Dreams (Are Made of This)' had gone on for hours. Mum was so upset she spent the whole morning crying and got so cross with herself that she flew into an Eminem mash-up. That was not pretty. It's worse if she doesn't know the songs very well because she makes up the lyrics and as she's not Eminem's biggest fan, the lyrics during that episode were so messed up it sounded like a middle-aged gangster mum with Tourette's. So that was that. We don't tell her.

Anyway, back to Dad. It might seem strange that I'm so obsessed with finding him when I can't even remember him, but it's like I do. Know him, I mean. Mum talks about him all the time and then there are the home videos that I've watched, like, a hundred times. Mum looks really different on them, her nails are always painted dark red and she's all sort of hair swishy (it was really long then, almost to her bum) and pretty. She's still pretty, I guess, even with her hair in a slanted bob. She's not like Megan's mum, all fake tanned and head to toe in branded gear, Mum just looks plain and pretty at the same time. Her make-up looks nice and her eyes are this weird colour between green and grey and they are wide apart, a bit like an alien, but in a nice way. Dad is good-looking, I guess, he had one of those chins with a dimple in it, Mum said she used to call it his bum chin. He had shoulder-length, russet coloured (that's what Mum always puts on the missing-person forms) curly hair. The hair is one of the things that Mum was always going on about when I've read the missing people forms that she's kept. Seriously, she has one of those old-fashioned filing cabinets in the garage with all the forms and reports and everything. It's like crazy insane stuff. He was quite tall, like over six foot, and he was quite slim.

They were proper in love. Mum and Dad. You can see it on the videos, he's always making her laugh and they are ALWAYS touching each other. Not in a creepy way, just, you know, like a hand on the knee or stroking an arm. That way. AND they danced a lot. Gran says when he first went missing, Mum spent months and months looking for him constantly.

She visited every missing persons' bureau she could and even hired a private detective. Gran said the police got a bit fed up with her in the end because she rang at least twice a day to see if anything had turned up. She just refused to stop looking. I can remember when I was six, being strapped into my car seat for what seemed like days as we travelled to London to go homeless person watching. I remember being quite scared. Of Mum as well as the homeless people. And then it all stopped. It was like she just gave up. Which is why I don't understand why she's not more excited about this one. He had a tattoo on his left shoulder of three swallows, to represent the three of us, Mum says . . . and this guy – the one on mymissingfamily.co.uk – has got that tattoo.

Anyway. That will do for tonight. I want to go online to check the school shoes in Shoehome; Mum has got to take me shoe shopping (cringe) and I want to be in and out before she gets stressed and sings 'The Hills Are Alive' like last time.

3

Melody

'Brogues? Aren't they a bit, you know? Old-fashioned?'
Inwardly, I wince at the irritated look on my daughter's face;
clearly, I have failed in some way . . . again.

Do you remember that wondrous instant when the most
innocuous of things – a little pink line – smiles at you?
That little pink line, heralding news that seeps through your
consciousness: a jigsaw of your past, present and future, a
universe of electrical currents fusing your thoughts and
emotions together, as an image of this tiny entity swallows
you entirely. Your mind becomes a collage of tiny fingers,
tiny toes, tiny hairs, tiny worries that grow in simple
synchronicity as you – and your world – expand and you
ask yourself, am I strong enough to ever contain this infinite,
consuming love? I stroke that memory fleetingly as the little
pink line pulls back her hair, bundles it into a knot and
sighs.

'Can we just get these and go? They are the only ones that
I like in the whole shop,' she announces, as I bend down to
pick up a pair of patent black shoes that are similar to the
ones that she has just grown out of. As I stand back up, I
see her glancing around, scoping the environment for threats
– not the threat of stranger danger or pickpockets: no, my
Red Rose is looking for threats that may hinder her chances

of escaping without being recognised; I'm the threat, ever encroaching upon her beautiful anonymity.

At leisure, the throbbing bud starts to uncurl from its seed. Pulsing from within my stomach, it starts to stretch in the rays of my anxiety as I realise the reason that Rose is so quick to choose the pair of shoes that she wants: she has chosen them. Already. As I start to hear a church organ introduction judder through my core, I realise that it is too late. I look at Rose with panic as I watch the colour drain from her face. She knows it's coming.

'Oh no, Mum, not now.' I watch helplessly as my vibrant Red Rose pales; she looks towards a group of teenagers jostling each other just outside the shoe shop door.

Go, Go, GO. I practise the word in my mouth before the stem can stick its thorns into my subconscious.

'Go.' With relief, I get the word out before trying to clamp my lips together, breathing in through my nose and trying to puff out through my mouth, lips pursed in a whistle pose as I try to calm myself down, but it's no use; I can hear the last bars of the introduction. Rose releases her hair and tries to let it hang over her face as she picks up her denim back-pack and slings it over her shoulder.

'And did those feeeet . . . in ancient time,
Walk upon England's moun-tains green . . .'

My voice peals out of my body and I taste the sweet relief that it brings, along with the horror and shame etched on my daughter's face as she looks over her shoulder at me with a mixture of dismay, pity and pure embarrassment. As for me, I'm standing with my back straight, my hand still clutching the black school shoe − which I now use as a conductor's baton − swishing and flicking it from side to side, à la Harry Potter. I begin to swoop a gentle figure of eight motion with my free hand, thumb and index finger pinched as I start to introduce – what I can only imagine my subconscious thinks is – the string section.

'And was the ho . . . ly Lamb of God
On England's pleasant pastures seen?'

My bottom lip starts to tremble as I register the agony in every step that Rose takes towards the door: towards her peers.

'And did the Count-en-ance Divine,
Shine forth up-on our clouded hills?'

A nudge, a snigger, and strained necks surround us.

'And was Jerusalem builded here?
Among those dark Sa-tanic Mills?'

By the time I have been brought my bow of burning gold and arrows of desire, Rose has almost made it out of the shop. With tears tracing my remorse, I continue introducing various parts of the orchestra of my mind with my patented baton.

'I will not ceeeease from Mental Fight,
Nor shall my sworrrrrd sleep in my hand!'

I see the boy who has been in Rose's school year since she was in nursery. The one who gave her the nickname 'Goldfish', a name referring – of course – to her red hair and full lips; I note with annoyance that he's turned into an attractive young man: crooked smile, bright-blue eyes and one of those perfectly coiffed quiffs that seem to be the thing at the moment. He smirks at her and nudges his less attractive, pimpled pal.

Rose adjusts her bag, keeps her head down as she veers left, past the bargain bucket of PE black pumps and almost through the door.

'Till we have buiiiiiiiiillt . . .'

I narrow my eyes.

'Jer-us-a-lem!'

Pull back my arm.

'In England's greeeeen and plea-sannnn-t land.'

And with my final note, I throw the well-aimed baton across the shop floor, past the fake designer boots, and land it straight between those twinkling, startled blue eyes.

With a maestro's flourish, I bow, but sadly I'm not met with a cascade of red roses at my feet; I'm met with a glare of hatred from my daughter before she shoulder-barges past the group of teenagers, and dives into the sea of Saturday shoppers.

Saturday night and what am I doing? Sitting in my bedroom, wearing my old fleece pyjamas covered in Scotty dogs; drinking tea and faffing about on my laptop. I double-click on the information that caused Rose so much excitement and stare again at the details.

Gender: Male
Age range: 30-40
Ethnicity: White European

Height: 1.88 m
Build: Slim
Date Found: 20/02/16
Circumstances: Male found collapsed outside shopping centre, Taunton at 1600 hours. Later disappeared from Musgrove Park Hospital. Suggested name of Tom: was wearing an inscribed silver wrist band.
Hair: Dark, clipped, approx 1cm length
Eye colour: Green
Distinguishing features: Tattoo – left shoulder blade – 3 swallows, shaded dark blue
Clothing: Headwear: woolly hat – grey
Jacket: Dark brown with logo on right chest
Shirt/Blouse: Green-checked padded shirt
Trousers: Jeans – dark-brown, good condition
Footwear: Boots – desert, brown.
Possessions: One ten-pound note, 2x£2
South West England
20/02/16 Avon and Somerset Constabulary

The eye colour is wrong; it can't be him . . . although, if he was tired or had been crying they did tend to go sea-green rather than grey/blue. Grey/blue. I'm so used to describing them like that. It's frustrating when you're filling out form after form, that you are reduced to that. You can't say that your loved one's eyes are the colour of the Welsh sea on a summer's day, or that they crinkle at the sides when he sees you walk into a room, or the way they half close if he is eating something nice, or that they water at the mention of King Kong. Grey/blue. I scratch the back of my head and wonder where the hell Taunton is, just as there's a knock on my bedroom door. What am I doing? He's dead. But even so, I can feel the old pull of hope, a rope that I hung on to for so long that it cost me my friends and ultimately, for a

19

short time, my sanity. That rope swung me back and forth into insomnia and the dark world of missing people, of permission slips and days where I forgot PE kits and lunch-boxes. My friends, mostly parents of Flynn's friends, started to keep their distance as my appearance became more unkempt, my concentration more erratic.

My closer friends, friends who I'd had my first drink with – a bottle of Tia Maria stolen from Pauline's nan's house – friends who I had excitedly told when I had my first kiss, and then when I'd first been dumped, and who I opened my GCSE results with, had still kept in touch, but both Pauline and Emily live on opposite sides of the country and so didn't see the woman I had become.

Still, we sent texts: hope you are OK, Ben has taken his first step, I'm pregnant again, we must meet up soon, oh my God, really? Are you OK? Let's get together soon . . . and we did. We went out for dinner and drinks, but I had been so nervous after not seeing them for so long that I'd sung the whole tune to *Friends* before we had left the bar and taken our drinks to the table. Pauline had always been conscious of her weight and before I knew it I was singing 'Fat Bottomed Girls' by Queen. She had tried to carry on as if it hadn't bothered her but when I started on 'Whole Lotta Rosie' I knew that I had to leave. It wasn't fair on them. I hated seeing them looking around the bar with embarrassment but more than that, I hated that I had hurt one of my dearest friends. I knew it was for the best that I no longer met up with them, no longer replied to their texts, no longer called them friends.

'Mum?'

I close the laptop and quickly shove it under my bed.

'Come in. What are you still doing up, Flynn? It's half-eleven.'

'You're, um . . .' He nods towards me; I furrow my brow in question.

'What?'

It's then that I realise that my mouth is dry and my throat is sore. I've been singing. It happens sometimes. I'm distracted in some way that I don't notice it happening. How can you possibly not notice? I hear you ask. Simple really. It's like having a song stuck in your head. For example, think about that song by Kylie Minogue, 'Can't Get You Out of My Head', got it? Can you hear it in all its glory? Good. Now notice how you are still sitting in a relaxed position. You are still breathing in and out and I'd wager that you've probably just blinked a few times too. See? It's easy to function, even with Kylie robot-dancing somewhere inside your hippocampus. You hear it, it irritates you, but you still manage to function through your day without it having any impact on the outside world. It's the same for me except I vocalise it. Damn Kylie, now it's stuck in my head too.

'Sorry. I'll go and make some camomile tea.' I stretch and smile at my boy. 'You OK?' He shrugs his shoulders and leans against the door frame, chewing on the inside of his thumb. I tilt my head then tap the space beside me on the bed. He ambles towards me and flops down, all elbows, Adam's apple and Lynx spray.

'What's up?'

'I've,' he begins, his deep adolescent voice bumbling his sentence out, 'we've, um, got a meeting at school on Monday morning.'

'OK.'

'It won't be a good one so you might want to, you know, take some of that stuff.'

By 'that stuff', he means my 'medication'. I've been trying different combinations of anti-anxiety medications. So far, I've tried celery seed, feverfew and valerian root, to name but a few. I gave up on the real stuff from the doctors; I felt like I was in a constant state of oblivion, always balancing on the brink of sleep, wobbling around the edge of life but never quite part of it. Sometimes, I have a few blasts of Rescue Remedy before I know I'm going to be in a stressful situation. It seems to help; the last time I had to ring the gas people, I only sang the first part of 'Jumpin' Jack Flash' rather than the whole of 'You're the One That I Want' that the electric company was subjected to.

'OK. Would you rather I do it over the phone?'

'Nah, I don't really care about, you know.' He gives me a lopsided smile. 'I'm already a freak. If anything, you being a weirdo can only make me look better.' I smack his arm as he starts to slope off the bed.

'I had a call the other day from a behavioural support teacher? He says he can get things in place to help you feel more settled. Maybe that's what it's about?' He shrugs his shoulders – before he changes the subject.

'Oh, Gran called earlier. Asked if you could give her a call back because she can't decide on the red-checked curtains or the—' He looks up, trying to remember the details. 'Green? No. Purple? I dunno. Anyway, something like that.'

My mum and I have always been on opposite ends of the spectrum. Her house is immaculate, mine is a mess; she is surrounded by friends, I have none; she runs, I sit. Her life has always revolved around herself; throughout my childhood, my mum's needs came before me. I'm painting a bad picture. She wasn't – *isn't* – a bad mum. I always had clean clothes, Clarke's shoes; I was polite. I've always felt loved, never felt like I couldn't turn to her and I always felt safe. But. My first school play, Mum was helping a friend move into her new house. My first broken heart, Mum had to go out, it's the opening of the new library and you'll be fine, there's plenty more fish in the sea. My engagement party, of course I'll pop in but I promised Reverend Daniel that I'd help with the bingo. She loves me but it's as if having me was a box ticked off on a to-do list: find suitable older man with means – check; have child – check; join WI – check.

My dad was well into his fifties when she had me. I barely remember him apart from the sense of a rather bland man who was mildly disappointed with life. He faded from my life and into a home when dementia set in. I can't say it had a dramatic effect on me; it was as if I was a pet. A quick pat on the head when I was well behaved, a scowl if I had displeased him.

The only thing my mum and I agree on is my kids. Flynn and Rose can do no wrong in her eyes. Birthdays and Christmas presents are always thoughtful and perfect. She spoils them, excuses them when they behave badly, blaming it on the school, their lack of sleep, the weather. They love her too. Hours of card games and jigsaw-making, which she never did with me, cementing their relationship.

After a shared bottle of wine one night, she had told me, 'It's different with your grandkids, you'll see; your mistakes don't matter because they go back after the weekend.' I wonder if she was so worried about being the perfect parent that it stopped her from *being* the perfect parent.

'OK, I'll call her tomorrow.' I smile at him as he reaches for the door, closing it quietly behind him.

'Mrs King?' I receive a limp handshake from the chinless head teacher, Mr Smythe. Honestly, is that the best you can do? I want to ask. If a fish could shake hands this would be what it would feel like. How hard is it to give a firm hand-shake? And not only is it as weak as wilted spinach, but his palm faces downwards. Now, I'm no psychologist, but surely a submissive, wet handshake is not a good sign from a man who has your child's education in his aquatic palms. As I fake-smile at his glassy, gormless eyes, I notice that he really does have a very fishy face. His mouth hangs open and his glazed eyes are too wide apart to ever be thought of as attractive. I pull my hand from his clammy – pun intended – grip and turn to the other man, who I presume is the head of year. Mr Greene grasps my hand and pumps it enthusiastically. It's a handshake that attempts to befriend me, get me on side; it says: 'Hey, we're already buddies,' but I'm not his buddy, not anywhere close. He is tall, wiry and has yellow stains under the arms of his blue checked shirt. I look around the grey-blue room and walk towards the pair of seats in front of the flat-pack, beech-toned desk.

'Take a seat,' he adds. Flynn is oblivious to the formal introductions; I hear him sigh as he lowers his rangy frame into the chair. 'So,' Mr Greene begins, stretching himself briefly on tip-toe, hands now in his pockets, before he takes his seat next to Mr Fish Face, and I wonder who is really in charge of this school.

'So,' I reply, my lips a tight line.

'I'm sure you know why we're here. Flynn's behaviour.' I hear a quiet click as the door behind me opens and shuts, allowing another person into the room. This unnerves me for a moment, knowing a new party to this little tête-à-tête is hovering outside of my view.

I purse my lips together as the word 'Quasimodo' echoes through my brain.

'Flynn's behaviour?' I ask with a raise of my eyebrows.

'I'm not sure if you are aware of this, Mrs King, but your son has assaulted one of our outstanding students.'

'Outstanding students?' I ask, puzzled.

'Yes. Rob Hunt. He's one of our reliables.'

'Reliables?'

'Yes. He has an exceptionally bright future and unfortunately . . . your son's recent acts of aggression towards him may have jeopardised his chances of being selected for the next *Star Wars* film.'

'Pardon me?' I can feel my whole body begin to vibrate; a fury of crescendos, power ballads and workout tunes explode through my body. Strands of jazz and blues go hand in hand around my head and then evaporate, my brain unable to anchor one note to another.

'*Star Wars?*' I tilt my head. '*Star Wars?*' I repeat once more, aggressively this time. Mr Greene tips on his toes again and Fish Face sits blinking.

'It's a George Lucas film,' he explains.

'Actually it's Disney now,' a disembodied voice from behind me adds. Too furious to take my gaze from Greene, I don't join in with the debate.

'You have asked me here to discuss how my son spoiled someone's chance to be a Stormtrooper?'

'He's too short to be a Stormtrooper,' Flynn puts in.

'True,' the voice agrees. Flynn sniggers.

'Can we stop talking about Stormtroopers?' I ask a little hysterically.

'Mrs King. The fact of the matter is that your son', Greene gives me a condescending look, 'seems to lack the social blocks which enable him to see a clear right from wrong.'

'Well he *has* only got one eye working,' the bodiless voice adds again from behind me. Startled, I watch Flynn bring his hand above his left shoulder to receive a high five from behind. This gesture was so relaxed, so natural, that I find my thoughts tilted towards this new dimension of my son. Fish Face and Greene give each other a strained, annoyed look.

Invigorated by this new confidence in Flynn, I pounce upon the control that I have, before these jumbled melodies find stable ground.

'Mr Greene, let me tell you about my son's behaviour.'

Again, that condescending look. What is wrong with this man? 'Let's start at the beginning of each day . . . when he spends a considerable amount of time rubbing Vaseline into his scar to help relieve the tightness that builds up overnight. That's followed by a vast amount of time taken to arrange his hair over his eye so that the left side of his face is as covered as it can be. Now let's talk about his behaviour when he gets home from school: he helps cut the grass, does the washing-up or fixes things that I can't reach because he is forced to be the man of the house. And shall we talk about his behaviour when his mother performed an impromptu rendition of Artic Monkeys' "I Bet You Look Good on the Dancefloor" at his class assembly?'

'Good song,' the floating voice contributes. I continue regardless.

'He didn't die of embarrassment and glare at me, did he? He smiled and waved, even though his peers laughed and poked fun at him. And what about the time he had to call an ambulance while he put his mother into the recovery position when he was only thirteen years old?'

'Mum—' I put my hand up to quieten Flynn.

'You talked about your "outstanding student"? My son has endured eight operations so far. Eight. He had his eyeball forced into his eye socket. He has survived a broken cheekbone and severe cuts and scarring. Have you ever had a scar that itches so much that you want to tear off your own skin, Mr Greene?'

'No.'

'My son was five years old. He survived this at the age of five. Now that's pretty outstanding, no? Do you know how difficult is it to do simple things such as cross the road when you're blind in one eye, Mr Smythe?' His fishy face blinks his response: no.

'You can't see objects until they are almost past your face unless you turn your head a full forty-five degrees. This is just one example of how difficult my son's life has been and will continue to be. You say my son has seriously damaged another pupil? Do you know how many names Flynn has been called? Do you know how many times I've had to listen to him defend his peers – when he says they are only having a bit of a laugh? Do you have any idea how much *damage* that does to my son? And then you talk about your so-called "outstanding student" . . .' I look at Flynn for his name.

'Rob C. Hunt.'

'You're joking?' I ask.

I hear a chuckle behind me as I raise my eyebrow. 'Where was I? Oh yes, Rob C. Hunt, who according to you has an exceptionally bright future? I'd like to point out that this boy's most "outstanding" and original put-down is "Quasimodo" . . . which, incidentally, we've heard about six times this year already.'

'Seven,' Flynn corrects.

'Seven times. I'd rather you spend more time assessing who the real outstanding pupils of this school are, rather than pinning your hopes on the next Luke Sky Diver.'

'Walker,' Flynn and the voice say in unison. Another high five.

Flynn has a bond with this person. Flynn trusts this person. This person knows my son. This person could help him. I calm my breathing as heavy notes start to take hold. This person – I stand and look over my shoulder – this person . . . is hot.

'I think we're done here,' I squeak.

I pull Flynn up by the arm and hold my lips tight together; he notices my composure unravelling.

'Mrs King, we haven't yet discussed . . .'

I just about hear, 'You heard her, gentlemen, she said she's done,' before the saxophone intro starts, my head filling with Tom Jones's gyrating hips. Flynn ushers me out, closing the door quickly just as 'Sex Bomb' erupts from my mouth. I look at him, my beautiful son, mortified, while I explain, in a low, husky voice, how to press my button on. He laughs, mutters, 'You're gross,' and, shaking his head, throws his bag on his shoulder and heads towards the boys' loos.

'Dum-dum, dum-dum . . . you are a dum-dum . . .' I sing as I walk down the chipped grey corridor towards the double doors, hesitating every now and then as I gyrate my hips and continue to urge any passer-by – the sixty-year-old, steel-grey haired receptionist included – to see that they are an exploding device about to have the opportunity to make me very happy indeed.

4

Flynn

My mum is amazing. I know it's not what you would expect to hear from your average sixteen-year-old, but I'm not your average sixteen-year-old. She has this thing, right, where she sings at the wrong time and she makes a total dick of herself. I mean, like that Star Wars kid on YouTube, the one where he's pretending to be a Jedi with a broom handle? That dude was tortured at school, it's had like thirty million hits or something. That kid is in therapy for the rest of his life. But Mum? She does things that embarrassing almost every other day AND it gets YouTubed. A lot. OK, so I'll give you an example. When we went to my mate Josh's birthday thing at the pizza place (she was just going to drop me off, she hates putting me in a situation where she might embarrass me, but I mean, how stressful can going for a pizza be, right?), so she dropped me off, but like a Muppet, I left his card in the car. She came in, spotted me, and waved the card, so I got up. Then, my other mate Jacob says (in the loudest whisper possible, ever), he says, 'Mate, your mum is fit,' so OK, gross, that is not a cool thing to say, like ever, but Mum heard it. I think she was kind of pleased but at the same time I could see the telltale signs: she was starting to do this thing where she looks like she needs a pee and her lips kinda clamp shut. I walked as quick as I could towards her but by then she had started singing this lame-ass song from the eighties, which basically meant she was telling Jacob that if he thinks she's sexy and that he wants her, then he should tell her, you know? It was by that Rod Stewart guy, I think . . . like I said, lame. OK, so I can see from the outside that it was funny, especially when she started doing this striptease thing with her cardy that she couldn't pull off her arm because the button got caught on her watch strap. The more stressed she got, the louder the singing and the more mixed up the lyrics became. By the time she had started calling him a whole load of sweeteners, there must have been about fifteen phone screens pointing her way. Last time I checked, that little episode has had 2,154 hits. Like I said, embarrassing. But, unlike the Star Wars loser, she doesn't go into therapy. I mean, she cries from time to time but she just has this way of looking at it. She says when Dad disappeared, next to me or Rose getting killed, the worst thing has already happened to her.

Here is what I remember about my dad. Before the accident I remember he was funny. I remember playing Lego with him for hours, we would do things like build a tower of it until it reached the ceiling. We'd lie it on the lounge carpet and we would have to call Mum in to help us lift this multi-coloured tower and hold it to see if it reached high enough. I remember Mum going away, for a night I think, but Dad made me sit at the table and make this banner that said 'Welcome Home Mum'. Each letter was a whole A4 sheet and we coloured each letter in with different patterns. It took ages, but Dad just kept making it fun, like, 'Let's see if you can draw more circles in your letter than mine. I bet you can beat me.' Everything was always a game. 'I bet I can throw this wrapper into the bin before you can run and put yours in.' I remember that when it was Christmas morning he would always make us wait outside the lounge door and then say, 'No, he hasn't been . . . back to bed,' but we always knew he had been. I remember Mum laughing. She laughed a lot. I never quite understood what Dad had said that was so funny, but she did.

I remember going to the zoo. I remember having to walk all the way over to the other side just because Rose wanted to see the flamingos. She even had a flamingo Christmas decoration for the tree from the gift shop. I had a penguin in a snow globe. I remember wanting to stay and see the penguins being fed but the zoo keeper was late and we had to go. I often wonder how different my life would be if that zoo keeper had been on time. Maybe, if he'd not stopped to give directions to somebody on the way to the enclosure, things would be different. When I was about seven, at bedtime, I would close my eyes really tight and try to make that keeper run to feed the penguins. I would imagine him sprinting with his bucket of fish: 'Sorry, I can't stop to give you directions, the penguins need feeding!' He would smile and continue running, the water in his bucket of fish sloshing over the side. But when I slowly opened my left eye and kept my right eye shut, there was still nothing but black.

I remember the accident. I remember the noise: it sounded like a horse neighing for a really long time. And I remember flying and feeling numb and weightless, but I think I might have made that bit up.

I remember Dad after the accident. Mum didn't laugh very much then. They didn't look at each other the same way. I remember feeling like I had upset him, my dad. He would look at me with this weird expression, like I was so deformed that he couldn't bear the sight of me. I heard him screaming in the night once. I started screaming too. I didn't know what the noise was that had woken me up. Mum tucked me back into my superhero duvet and said that sometimes even grown-ups have nightmares. She stroked my hair and sang 'Can't Help Falling in Love' by Elvis, until I started to drift off to sleep, but I can remember hearing Dad making this whimpering sound in the background. But the most afraid I've ever been, wasn't when I had the car accident, or realising that grown-ups have nightmares; it was when I heard Rose's high-pitched voice calling my name from outside, and seeing Mum unconscious with blood matting the back of her hair. That was the most afraid I've ever been – and the most afraid I can ever imagine feeling for the rest of my life.

What I'm trying to say is OK, being sixteen sucks and don't get me wrong, my life is a long way from being perfect. But I kinda think if I've survived my life so far, I think I've got a pretty good chance of turning out OK. Even when twats like Rob have a go now and then, I think I can handle it because I know I can handle life. Life has already given me a beating and I'm still OK. So, when Rose starts delving further into this missing person thing and she comes up with that guy with the tattoos? I start to feel something new. I feel, I don't know, defeated? Like I can handle most things you can throw at me, but that look? That look that Dad used to give me? I don't think I could handle that, and if I don't handle it . . . who will take care of Mum and Rose?

5

Melody

Christ, what now?

My hands are full of this week's essentials from the corner shop – quite when red wine and Pringles became my weekly essentials, I'm not sure. I shoulder-barge the front door open, with both my home phone and mobile ringing simultaneously. With hurried care, I put the bags at my feet, slam the door shut with my denim-clad bottom, and breathlessly answer the black plastic, wall-mounted phone that would, in all honesty, not look out of place in a retro novelty shop.

'Mrs . . . King?'

'Yes?'

'Hello, it's Summerfell Academy here? I'm ringing about Rose.'

Rose? I'm used to getting calls about Flynn, but this is new.

'Oh, is she poorly?' I ask over the repeating rings of my mobile.

'Um, no.'

Oh, I bet it's about that competition that she's got to go to. She was really upset about it, some gifted and talented thing that she had to go to last year, but this year she has to go with a kid who is horrid to her. She asked me to ring the school and request that she doesn't go, but they were less than helpful, and basically said she had to suck it up. 'She, Rose, well I've been asked to call you by the head teacher, Mr Smythe, he's asked that you come in and see him. Today, if possible.'

'Oh, um, OK . . .' I mentally kick myself for not going and picking up another bottle of Rescue Remedy, although I do have some Kalms in my bathroom cabinet. That'll have to do.

'Thank you, we'll see you at three?'

'Oh, um, yes, three.' I hang up and grab my mobile which is ringing repeatedly, swiping the screen as I hurry upstairs to the bathroom cabinet.

'Yes?' I can feel my heart rate increasing, electric-blues contracting hard-core muscles, bluegrass pumping into chamber music quarters as progressive rock exits, its increased tempo threatening ska.

'Hello, Mrs King?'

'Mmhmm.' I pinch my lips together and pull open the cabinet, holding the phone between my shoulder and ear.

'Mr Greene here, we met the other day? It's about Flynn. As we were unable to conclude our meeting the other day . . .' Patronising idiot. I can practically hear his furrowed brow and condescending look.

'Hmmmm,' I reply, desperately trying to pop off the lid of the Kalms with one hand.

'Well, we have just had a *Senior* Leadership meeting, and I'm afraid that we have no other choice but to exclude Flynn – for two days. Can you pick him up from school?'

'Fnnnt.'

'Sorry?'

'OK,' I manage to say through gritted teeth before swiping the phone screen, erasing the smug Mr Greene. I sit on the side of the bath singing the chorus of 'School's Out', wondering how I am going to be able to sort this problem out. This isn't just a slap on the wrist for Flynn; it could destroy his chances of getting into college, let alone university – and what on earth was the problem with Rose? Without realising I've changed genres, I stumble into 'Beauty School Dropout' and am declaring that my story is too gloomy to tell, a teenager not doing well, and as I stand up – pop two Kalms into my mouth – I, 'la, la, la, la, la, la' and 'doo-wopp' my way back to high school. As the final recurring gems of advice about returning to high school peter out, I glance down at my phone, ringing again. It's not a number I recognise, so I decline its invitation to answer, preferring instead to wipe away my worried tears and enjoy my own momentary silence.

Ignoring the vibrating urgency of the phone in my pocket, I slam the car door, hear its reassuring whirr as it locks and adjust my navy-blue jacket. I look up at the windowed fortress, wondering how many parents have faced this same fate. The innocent reflection of the cobalt sky, smattered with clouds the colour of putty, reminds me that spring is not quite here but has started its journey towards daffodil-warm days. I take a slow, deep breath in, filling my lungs with cool calm, and then slowly exhale my worries and anxieties. Closing my eyes, I envisage myself walking into that office with confidence and control, not song and shame. With a determined stride, I walk through the heavy creak of the entrance doors and see my beautiful boy chewing his thumbnail, dark wavy hair camouflaging half of his face, and all concepts of calm evaporate in a fog of fury. How can they have him sitting there, a target amongst the torrent of teenagers? How can they be so oblivious to the humiliation he is facing, a criminal in metaphorical stocks as the mob hurls jibes like rotten fruit? I look around as the smell of hormones, insecurity and heartache overwhelm my senses. He looks up, sees me and gives a lopsided smile, shrugs his shoulders and raises his two thumbs up at me in defeat. Digging my fingernails into my palms to shock my senses into a more coherent form, I walk over and sit next to him on the row of blue chairs, reserved for those who await their fate with the educational powers that be.

'Hey.'

'What happened?'

'Nothing.'

'Nothing?'

'Nope. Not since last time. I was in art, they called me out and stuck me here.'

'Oh. I thought maybe something else had gone on. How long have you been here?'

'About an hour . . .'

'An hour?! Have they told you they want to exclude you?'

'What?' His expression is somewhere between horror and amusement. 'You've got to be joking! Dylan pulled a knife on Brandon last week and even he didn't get excluded. That can't be right. Were you, you know, upset when they told you? Maybe you misheard?'

'Well, I was upset but, not *upset*. Mr Greene was very clear. Two days, he said.'

'Shit.' He shook his head.

'Indeed,' I agreed. 'Do you know what's going on with Rose?'

'Supergeek? No, why?'

'Mr Smythe wants to see me about her.'

'She's probably won an award or something.'

'Hmm.' I scratched the back of my head. 'Maybe, but, oh, I don't know . . . it's just it sounded like one of your calls.' He nudged my arm. 'Sorry, you know what I mean. I'm going to pop to the loo before we go in, where is it?'

'Down that corridor, by the staffroom.'

'I won't be a min, just going to down another couple of herbal tablets.'

'Druggy,' he says from the corner of his mouth.

'Reprobate,' I answer with a smile.

I wash my hands, smooth down my hair and smudge on some lipgloss, smiling as I read some of the declarations of love for the latest boy band, kindly commented on by some of the older girls about their 'musical' talents. I put my bag over my shoulder and head for the door; I don't know what makes me stop with my hand on the sticky handle – perhaps an inbuilt ability to hear your own name above the usual cacophony of school life – but stop I do.

'Rose King . . . no relation to Flynn King? The one with the singing mum?' asks a female voice. I can hear the background chatter of the staffroom – the door must be open.

'Yes.' A muted comment from inside the room makes an eruption of laughter filter through. I catch the phrase 'The Hills Are Alive'.

'What's this?' Another voice, closer to the door and male.

'You've not heard?'

More muted voices from the staffroom.

'Smythe was going to exclude her, but what with the Year Nine Gifted and Talented Challenge coming up . . .'

'Oh, right, in with a chance this year, I heard. Old Smythe has been after that new library prize since it began. Is she that bright, then?'

'Put it this way, Jim Boyle has been giving her AS-level questions to keep her from pointing out his inaccuracies in class.' Both laugh.

'Let me grab a cup of—' The rest of the sentence is lost from me as the door shuts.

Rose? Excluded? What is going on? Tentatively, I open the door and head for Flynn and answers. With a sigh, I sit down next to him as I impatiently pull out my phone and see seven missed calls from an unknown number; a text appears from the same number across the top of my phone. I skim the entire message and focus on the words 'behavioural policy' as my name is called by the receptionist and Flynn and I rise like the defendants we are.

'Just you, Mrs King, for now.' Flynn slouches back down.

'Oh, but I thought—'

'If we could address the issue with Rose *first?* Flynn, we'll be with you shortly.' She speaks with a tone implying that neither my son nor I are worthy of her attention. I narrow my eyes and decide in that instant that I do not like this woman and I would like to retract my last offer of letting her make me happy with her Tom Jones detonator. Regardless, I follow her stoic figure down the corridor – past the displays of 'Art Week' and grinning, sporty, spotty stars in frames – and around the corner to the head teacher's office. She knocks on the door, opens it and ushers me in, where I'm met with my distraught daughter. Teenage mascara pools in puddles on her school shirt, the end of which she is twisting around and around her finger.

'Mum, I—' She looks at me with desperation and guilt before silent sobs rack her body. The door is softly closed behind me. Fish Face gestures to the same seat that I was in not two days before.

'Mrs King, I'm afraid I have some unfortunate news to tell you.' I hear a noise from Rose that sounds somewhere between a moan and the pft, pft of an old car starting on a cold day.

Oh Christ.

'She's pregnant?' I ask somewhat hysterically. For a moment I see a glimpse of my daughter shine through in the look that she gives me. 'Really, Mum?' it says, the ridiculousness of my statement written on her face; as far as I know, she's never even kissed a boy.

'Um, no, no. I'm afraid it's more serious than that.'

'Drugs?' I ask, sounding slightly more hopeful. Drug addiction can be dealt with easily. Babies are more addictive and harder to get rid of.

'Um, no, no, nothing like that, but just as serious in the eyes of our school.'

'You're not', I look at her, her bewildered look mirroring my own confusion, 'running off to join the jihadists, are you?' I gulp, imagining Rose's passport stashed inside her school bag. It's all over the news at the moment, young girls being seduced by the excitement of far-off lands, until they fall victim to radicalisation. Rose's shoulders sag and for a moment I spot the ever-present look of disappointment on her lovely, freckled face.

'Oh, um, no, no, it's not that.' My mind is rifling through the most recent headlines.

'You're not having an affair with your maths teacher, are you?'

'Mum!' she interrupts. 'I've been stealing.'

Is that all?

Hold on a second. Stealing?! I close my eyes for a moment. Cool, calm air in (though the air in that room is anything but cool – it smells of horrid old coffee and basketballs). Anxiety and worries out. Stealing. Stuffy coffee basketball in. Maybe it's just a few pencils or something? Burdens and baggage out. I open my eyes and swallow down 'I Shot the Sheriff'.

'Stealing?' Rose's lip starts to tremble as she looks down, the regret and desolation clear in her eyes that cannot hold my own. My heart breaks for my clever, sensitive girl. I turn my attention back to Smythe. 'What exactly has she been stealing?'

'The thing is, Mrs King, as you know, your daughter is a bright, hard-working and reliable pupil so when she started up a fundraising scheme, the staff were one hundred per cent behind her. We all agreed when she started doing her charity table every break time, that she should be commended for her efforts. She was given the head teacher's award only last week.'

'Charity table?'

'Yes, for example, last week it was guess the name of the teddy, at twenty pence a go. One day this week, it was have your nails painted for a pound. That was a great hit for most of the girls in the school, and then yesterday we had a "throw a wet sponge at the teachers for two pounds" . . . it was a great success.'

'OK . . . what charity was it for?'

'Help the Homeless,' Rose whispers. She looks beseech-ingly at me while I try to process these thoughts.

'I'm sorry, Mr Smythe, but I'm confused. My daughter was raising money for charity but you think she was stealing it?'

'Unfortunately for Rose, one of the teachers overheard her telling a friend that she was using the money to hire a private detective to find her father. When she was asked by her form tutor to hand the funds in, she said she couldn't because she had already donated it, but, when we questioned her on the details of where and when the money was donated, well, it all became clear. Rose eventually confessed.'

'I wasn't lying, Mum. If I didn't get enough for a detective, I was going to give it to Help the Homeless. Finding Dad will help him not be homeless, right? It's not really fraud.'

'Fraud?!'

'I'm, I'm very sorry but', I start to purse my lips, 'could you, hmmmmmmmmm, give me a minute to . . .' Giving an apologetic look towards Rose, I get up and run out of the room, past Flynn, and head for the toilet. I manage to lock myself into the graffitied cubicle, pulling across the grey plastic lock before throwing up Kanye West's 'Gold Digger'. By the time I have got down, way down (which is no mean feat when you consider my confined dance studio) I feel more in control. I open the door, ignoring the evidence of my sweating exertions in the mirror, and calmly walk back to the office.

When I enter the room, the bodies have increased and now include Flynn, Mr Greene and the hot guy from the other day, who Flynn had told me afterwards was the behavioural support officer. He seems to be giving me a strange look; almost quizzing me with the need for an answer to a question that I haven't been asked. He has short, dark, slightly messy hair, taller than I had originally thought, about five foot nine, and is wearing jeans, white T-shirt and a tweed jacket. He has a touch of the James McAvoys about him.

I bend down in front of Rose and rub the top of her arms.

'Sorry, I had to, you know . . . It's going to be OK, Rose. I'm going to sort this out.' Slowly, I stand up, walk over to the wall and lean against it. I'm tired of being below everyone else's eye level. Flynn and the hot behavioural-support officer sit down and Greene assumes the same position as last time, next to Mr Smythe.

'Mrs King, this is . . .' Mr Greene gestures almost dismissively, 'Shane Thomas. Flynn's behavioural support officer. He recommended that we all speak together.' By his tone I gather that Shane had more insisted than suggested.

'To continue from where we were . . .' Mr Smythe emits the sentence from his fishy mouth with a touch of boredom, 'due to the severity of Rose's deceptions, this cannot go unpunished. That being said, it's clear that Rose is clearly mindful of her wrongdoing and is obviously very regretful. As such, we feel that missing her breaks for the next week and obviously paying the money back to the intended charity would be fair.'

Well, that seems, um, yes, fair. If I'm honest, I think we've been let off a very large hook. Relief floods through me and as I smile at Rose I can see that she's as shocked as I am. She smiles at me before quickly rearranging her facial muscles into a more penitent state.

'As for Flynn, I'm afraid we cannot be so lenient.'

Arses.

'As we discussed on the phone,' Greene interrupts, 'it has been decided that we feel that a two-day exclusion is the only option here.'

'If I can just say something?' Shane speaks in a smooth southern English accent. Not quite London geezer or Prince Harry but somewhere in between. 'How is it that an exclusion is going to help Flynn or his family? I would suggest that an action plan, within school, should be put in place. A system where he could be removed from his triggers and, as a school, we can perhaps dig a little deeper into the comments made by Mrs King last time, where she explained that Flynn is the victim of ongoing verbal abuse.'

A small smile plays at the corner of Flynn's mouth; it's clear that he knew about this plan.

'Er, well, no. We,' Greene gestures to Smythe, 'the school, as a whole, have been tolerant enough of his outbursts, and we have a duty to the parents of the other pupils to ensure that their children feel safe.'

'Oh come on,' Shane interrupts, 'he's hardly a danger. He punched a kid who has on several occasions called him offensive names! He's not a danger if we help to control the whole situation.' My mind is going around in circles. It's been a very long time since I've had anyone fighting a battle on my behalf.

'That's all well and good, and of course we will give Flynn

support upon his return to school, but as I've said, we have a responsibility to the other children's—'

'Parents. Yes, I get it, especially if that child's parent happens to be a parent governor.' He raises his perfectly formed eyebrows (does he pluck? I wonder) and gives a tight-lipped smile.

Alarm bells start ringing. How can they justify letting Rose get away with fraud and theft, and some other kid get away with pulling a knife, but exclude Flynn? Then I think of the skim-read message about the 'behavioural policy', the staffroom conversation about the competition, and now this . . . the little swine, the metaphorical thorn in Flynn's side, is the son of a parent governor. I try to dredge up the rules outlined in the text.

I'd been handed the policy the first time Flynn had pushed a boy, who was in the year above, against the school bins – James somebody. I recall it took me two weeks to get out of Flynn why he'd pushed him and when I got to the bottom of it, I found out that James had asked if he could take Flynn's photo; he'd said it was to scare his little brother on Halloween. From what I gather, James's mother didn't get a copy of the policy.

That old feeling of injustice starts to seep through my core, jangling my worries with a 'testing, testing, one, two, three' into my internal microphone. I start breathing deeply, focusing on the pictures on the wall, the certificates confirming Mr Smythe's prowess at First Aid, and move my body slightly further along the wall so I can concentrate on the small, silver-marble desk cradle (circa 1980) as I form my words.

'Could I just', tick, tick, tick . . . I watch the little balls with intense concentration, 'see if I understand the situation correctly. According to your behavioural policy, any incident where a child is guilty of physical violence in the school is . . .' I take another deep breath and focus on the rhythmic sway of the steel against steel, 'recorded into some sort of file? If this happens more than four times a letter is sent home, is that right?' I look up and can see little pink spots appearing on Greene's cheeks. Smythe just blinks insipidly. Returning my gaze to the desk, I notice a picture of Fish Face and his wife. Blimey, now there is an unfortunate-looking woman. I tear my gaze away from the startled seaside snap back to the cradle. 'And if there is another incident, the parent is called in?' I dare not look away. I go on to say that if I'm not mistaken, theft, however, is an immediate exclusion. As I'm explaining this I make direct eye contact with each person in the room. Flynn is smiling and Rose looks appalled, as she should. I'm basically throwing her to the lions. But surely, I continue, they cannot deviate from the policy in such a way. A practice that I'm sure the governors or local authority would have strong views about. Taking the smiling faces of Flynn and Shane as encouragement, I expand my case by saying I feel that the school is lacking in empathy for the plights of my children. Rose did not want to go to the gifted and talented competition, and when I raised this issue with the school, they showed no understanding. The school's total lack of compassion to my family and my children is totally unacceptable.

I take a deep breath as I begin to feel hot and breathless. Rose is now biting her lip and looking away in embarrassment. She hates it when I have to complain on her behalf as she normally excels in school, but I think this is one of those moments when I have to do what every parent hates doing, 'something for their own good'. When I look at her again I suddenly realise something is very, very wrong. She's upside down. I try to get my bearings and see my hand stroking my left leg seductively and gather that I'm bending over, peering through my open legs. I pull my head up and register the startled yet amused looks on the teachers' faces. I flip my weight on to my right side, hand sliding up from my leg, and then lean suggestively against the wall as I start to comprehend that right now, as I rotate my hips then stride towards Mr Smythe's leering face, I'm expressing my thoughts through The Pussycat Dolls' 'Don't Cha'. As I ask him if he wishes that his wife was as scorching as me, I notice that my hands are clasped behind my head and that I'm thrusting my hips back and forth in his direction; with each enthusiastic thrust, I can feel my arguments being laughed out of the room. Finally, I feel my heart rate slow as I run my finger along the edge of the desk. I sense normality returning, as I conclude my taunting of Mrs Smythe with a husky 'Don't you?' and return to my position by the wall.

'I think,' Shane looks at me, eyes glinting in the dazzle of my shame, 'that what Mrs King is saying is that, right now, as you are in clear violation of the behavioural policy, it would be unwise to exclude Flynn.' I smile as my thoughts return to normal, my heart rate slows to a gentle rumba and then finally stretches its legs and settles into a tango. 'Mrs King?'

Feeling relief at last, I reply. 'Um yes. That's exactly what I was trying to say.'

As Shane outlines his proposal of an adapted curriculum for Flynn, where he will spend time out of class, I look over at my Red Rose and think over the events that have been discussed. My girl, who has never set a foot wrong in her whole academic life, my girl who always lines up in the correct barriers in the cinema, my girl who doesn't even sneak a drink in her bag if we go to the theatre for worry of getting caught, has stolen money. Stolen money to find her father. I need to help my children. I need to give them hope of normality.

'Sorry, I don't mean to interrupt, that all sounds really encouraging . . .' I nod at Shane, 'but in light of what has happened and my concerns about the way that this school has handled these recent events,' I take a gulp of air and question my sanity, 'it seems to me that my children need a break. From school. For a week.' Rose looks at me as if I've really lost it this time.

'Mrs King, due to the changes made by the government,' Mr Smythe holds his hands out in a 'this is out of our hands' gesture, 'we don't authorise holidays within school time.'

'I see. Well, you may take it as unauthorised absence, then. That is unless you would like to risk the chance of Rose taking ill the week of the gifted and talented competition?' Mr Smythe coughs and clears his throat.

'Perhaps, yes, yes,' he nods as if it was all his idea in the first place, 'a break may be what is needed. Yes, I'm sure we could accommodate your request.'

'Fabulous.' I smile and offer my firm handshake to Mr Smythe and Mr Greene before turning and giving my kids and Shane a sly smile.

I pick up my handbag and start walking towards the door.

'Kids?' I say over my shoulder as they scramble to their feet in a flurry of blazers and backpacks. 'Thanks for your time,' is my parting shot as I close the door behind us.

'Jesus, Mum,' announces Rose.

'Don't say Jesus.'

'Sorry, I mean Christ, seriously? You're taking us out of school for a week?' she asks as we depart through the cabbage-smelling corridor.

'Yep.'

'Why?' she asks, running a little to keep up with my stride.

I stop and turn to her, stroking the side of her face with my hand. 'We're going to look for your dad.'

'Really?'

I nod with sentimental determination.

She smiles shyly at me through her pale eyelashes. I nod again, hug her briefly and continue walking.

'Er, Mum?' Flynn asks as we push the door release button.

'Hmm?'

'You know you're gonna turn me gay, right?' I elbow him in the ribs as he grins and we head towards the optimistic, uncertain sky.

6

Melody

'Takeaway's here!' Flynn jumps up from the sofa, as does Rose. I grab my purse and enjoy the comfort and sense of occasion that a takeaway so often brings. A birthday celebration, the end of a working week or simply the reward of not having to use those precious moments of your life to cook. I head to the door, open it and receive our brown-paper bagged Chinese takeaway from the balding Polish delivery man, thanking him as I hand over my pounds and pence. Behind me, I can hear the kids taking on their roles: Flynn setting the table, Rose getting out the plates and filling up glasses with budget-priced diet-cola. This makes me smile: the reassurance of the familiar, a routine of unexciting components that when put together can envelop you in a blanket of stability. Envisage just one of those components being ripped away from your life: take away the food and you're left with starvation; take away the home and you're left without warmth; take away your children and you're left without love. Take away your husband and you're left with a gaping hole.

'Pass the rice.'

'Please.' I point a chopstick at Flynn.

'Pass the rice, please,' he grumbles as Rose hands over the silver container.

'So,' I start, fake optimism resonating in my ears, 'have we all decided what to pack? We can't take too much, remember, because you'll have to carry it on the bus and then the train.'

'Can't we just go in the car?' Rose asks as she dunks a chicken ball into the sweet and sour tub.

'I can't, sweetie. What if I decide to start singing along to "Cha Cha Slide" and swerve to the right and swerve to the left?' I shake my head whilst popping some duck in green pepper and black bean sauce into my mouth. 'It's too risky.'

'But I hate going on the bus, everyone gawps at me,' Flynn complains, as he grabs the paper bag of chips and adds the contents to his already groaning plate.

'That's because they're looking at how handsome you are, my boy.'

'Mum, that didn't work when I was seven, do you really think I'm going to start believing it now?'

'Well *I* look at you because you're handsome.' I grin and a little bit of sauce escapes my mouth.

'Classy.' Flynn shakes his head at me.

'Could've been worse,' Rose adds, 'you could have been ginger too.' We all laugh at that, as she self-consciously tucks a stray piece of hair behind her ear.

'Or you could be a real freak and start singing and dancing at inappropriate times.' I skewer a piece of red pepper on to the end of my chopstick.

'And be ginger,' Flynn adds again. Rose sticks her tongue out at him as he flings a prawn cracker at her.

'Maybe we should all start wearing really gaudy outfits and jewellery?' I suggest. 'It might distract them from realising our family is a bunch of freaks.' I scoop some rice into a prawn cracker. 'We could start wearing bright kaftans or shorts in the middle of winter.'

'I know,' Rose grins, 'you could have a load of piercings, Flynn, to disguise your ugly mug.'

49

'Maybe you could do the same,' he retorts, 'and besides, I don't wear jewellery. It's not my thing.'

'Your dad would never wear jewellery either.' I sow one of the seeds of doubt about the quest we are about to embark on.

'I thought he had that bracelet?' Rose questions me with a furrowed brow. 'You told me he never took it off.'

'Oh *that*, it wasn't a proper, precious metal bracelet or anything. It was a plaited piece of burgundy embroidery thread that I used to have in my hair.'

'Really?' Flynn asks.

'Yeah, I was cool.' I raise my eyebrows and suck in my cheeks, nodding the affirmative. 'The colour matched my boots.' I flick my hair back and put on a faraway look. 'I had to cut it out in the end, though, it got too tangled up with the bell.'

'Bell?'

'Yeah, I had a bell at the end of it . . . told you I was cool.' I laugh at their appalled faces. 'Anyway, your dad used to wear it on his wrist. I could always hear him wherever he was in the house. He used to say it was so he always had melody with him,' I say wistfully. My hazy look is instantly wiped from my face as the kids start making puking noises and gestures. 'Well *I* thought it was romantic,' I add huffily.

I stack the last plate on to the draining board and sigh. What am I doing? Wiping my hands on the tea towel, I walk back into the lounge, lean against the door frame and watch them, heads tilted identically as they laugh at the same joke, both engrossed in *The Big Bang Theory*. I'm taking them away from school and subjecting them to a long, tedious (here's hoping) journey to find a father who I know isn't going to be at the end of it. Am I right in getting their hopes up? Clearly Rose needs this, but what about Flynn? He rarely talks about Dev, no matter how many counsellors he's seen. I suppose he must feel some degree of blame towards Dev for the car crash, but he's never mentioned it to anybody.

When Dev disappeared, it was almost as if Flynn closed the door on any feelings or opinions about his dad. He used to idolise him, truth be told; I used to feel left out when they played their games. Two peas in a pod.

They laugh again, as I watch Flynn kick Rose's foot off the end of the sofa. She glares at him for a moment before returning her foot, but closer to his side this time. She bides her time before knocking his foot off with a precise and firm stretch. She grins at him as he grumbles, learning his lesson and tucking his long legs under his bottom. I ruffle their hair as I head towards the laptop, perched on the dining table at the back of the room. Stroking the mouse pad, I wait for the screen to turn from black to technicolour and check the route again. Our train from Telford to Birmingham should only take about an hour, then we have a bit of a wait until the train takes us from there to Taunton. Three hours without calamity and we should arrive in Taunton by lunch-time. I reopen mytrainticket.co.uk and hover over the 'buy tickets' icon. I take another glance at my kids, willing them to say something that will either confirm or eradicate my plans, when I hear Rose say quietly to Flynn:

'Do you think he'll recognise us? Dad? If we find him?'

'He'd have to be stupid not to. How many sixteen-year-olds do you know with scars like these?' Rose tilts her head, and they look at each other. We look at people all the time. When you walk into a coffee shop you look at the person when they ask you if you want a large or medium. You look at them when they give you your receipt. But if I asked you what colour that person's eyes were five minutes later, could you tell me? Blink and you would miss it, but in that moment, I see my children *look* at each other. Laying their stories and dreams, naked for each other to see. The spell breaks as Flynn kicks her legs back off the sofa and she mutters, 'Loser.'

Am I really going to do this? Am I going to let them believe that he might be out there when I know that he isn't? What if the disappointment is too much for them? I look over again at Rose. As a child, Rose never gave up, never stopped trying to find that last piece of the jigsaw, always coloured in every picture in the book, always carefully blew the bubble mixture to create the biggest bubble. Flynn, in contrast, was happy to accept that sometimes, the bubble wasn't ever going to get bigger; instead he would blow as hard as he could, creating his own little atmosphere filled with as many bubbles as possible so he could chase them, popping them and watching them float away with a gap-toothed grin, happy to make the most of what he had. But Rose would use every last drop of mixture, each dip blown into a spherical reflection of her four-year-old face, as she tried to make it bigger and bigger until it inevitably popped; the wand patiently dipped back into the blue tube, making the next bubble more impressive, larger, and more durable than the last. Until one day, she didn't open her bottle; she gave it to Flynn, her face sad and her gesture defeated. When I asked her why she had given Flynn her bubbles, she said, 'I made the biggest bubble already, they don't get any bigger.' And then she had joined Flynn running around the garden catching as many as she could, following his lead and making the best out of what they had.

If I don't do this, Rose will never stop until she finds an answer.

I remember dragging them along with me when I was certain I would find Dev amongst the homeless. The way Rose's wide eyes would take in the mounds of destitution that littered the sides of the streets; the way Flynn would tolerate the disappointment when we didn't find him in the same way he would accept it if I told him we couldn't afford a McDonald's, but they were young then. The emotions they are going to feel now are so much bigger than the disappointment they would have felt then. They are so much more invested now that I worry they will be beaten by the reality. But if I don't take them, Rose's life could be destroyed by the need that she has to fix this puzzle. This way, if I take her, show her that this – our strongest lead yet, our biggest bubble – still isn't the answer, then maybe she will follow Flynn and make the most out of what we have.

Even so, as I turn back to the screen and start humming 'Leaving on a Jet Plane', the enormity of what I'm about to put my children through is lodged in my throat. I take a sharp breath in, bite my bottom lip and hit 'buy'.

It's for their own good, I tell myself.

Rubbing my hands together, I try to encourage my blood to warm the ends of my fingertips. I look at my watch for reassurance that the bus will arrive on time, as Flynn pulls his black woolly hat further down his forehead and the incessant 'tst, tst, tst' of his headphones demands his attention.

Rose rearranges her emerald green scarf. She wouldn't have noticed, but it is the same colour as her feline eyes. She swipes her phone with her touchscreen gloves before fighting with her scarf again. I breathe out a plume of impatient air.

Oh come on.

At last the bus rounds the corner, slows down and blinks its arrival through the freezing morning fog. Excitement mixed with fear fills my dry mouth as I give a tight-lipped smile of comradery. Rose's eyes shine with glacial optimism; Flynn's are hooded with indifference. It's still early, so thankfully we clamber on to the middle of the bus without mishap or double-takes. I think about the day ahead, of how to handle the news when we get to the hospital that reported the missing person. I will have to prepare them. Especially Rose. I know I'm hoping this will give her some kind of closure, but I can see how hopeful she is. What if this makes things worse and she starts trying to track any new leads, however small, without my help? I draw a heart on the steamed window with a zigzag through it. Who was the man at the hospital anyhow? How would he feel if he knew that a family of misfortune was travelling halfway across the country to find him? First we will go to the police. I want Rose and Flynn to see how futile it is, trying to find someone who's been missing for eleven years. After that, we will go to the hospital itself and see if we can find out any more information. I'm hoping we will find something that will put an end to this. Something concrete for them to have which will let us abandon the idea that Dev is still out there.

'Mum?'

'Hmmm?' I look down at my hands and realise that my elbows are in front of my chest and my forearms are swishing from side to side. It takes me a moment to adjust and recognise that I'm singing 'The Wheels on the Bus', and that I'm currently imitating the wipers on the bus going swish, swish, swish.

Oh, sweet lord. This is going to happen alllll day looong.

Our bodies move in rhythm to the swaying of the train, a soothing accompaniment to the brewing storm within me. Watching the bare trees stretching through the evaporating haze, my thoughts drift to another cold March morning years ago when I rushed into my college classroom. My hands were cracked and red from the cold as I held tightly to my portfolio case: a khaki backpack, decorated with band names and logos, weighing me down. I shake my head as I remember the calamity I had caused as I stumbled over a stray art box and knocked over one of the easels. Murmuring apologies, I had shuffled my way through the sniggers and perched myself on a spare desk as the plaited patchouli-smelling art tutor introduced a local sculptor. I hadn't even looked in his direction, as I was so intent on pulling out my pencil, chewing gum and bottle of Coke before finally flipping my sketchbook open and looking up. I noticed his hands first. His fingers were long and nimble as he manipulated the wire into intricate designs; the straight, lifeless steel was transformed into a dove within moments. A blue marble was placed inside a cage of silver, a bird's eye, giving it sight. Occasionally, I was distracted as its creator tucked his dark auburn hair behind his ear, the rest falling over his eyes: long dark eyelashes releasing intense, sea-green eyes. I remember the first time we spoke. I was standing at the bus stop outside college. 'It's raining,' he said. 'It is,' I replied as I did up my coat. I was flustered because I hadn't been able to think about anyone else but him since I'd watched him sculpt in class the week before. It was as if part of myself had been reaching out of my body, stretching and searching. Little sparks of energy frantically trying to find a place to latch on to, to hold, to burrow inside. When he reached for my hood and pulled it over my ears, it felt as though my body had found what it was looking for. Everything about him, the sound of his voice, his smell, the way he moved, seemed to fill me with calm. It was like we had been searching for each other across time, since the moment we were born.

The sound of the train hissing and halting at another station disturbs my thoughts. I stretch and then rummage in my bag for a drink. The kids glance at one another from either side of me – Rose from across the aisle and Flynn to my right – and I wonder if my dry mouth is a result of dehydration or if I've been entertaining the morning Birmingham commuters.

'Have I been?' I whisper across to Rose.

'No, just humming a bit, that's all.'

I grab a packet of chocolate biscuits and pass them to Rose, enough of a distraction from her phone to pause her Twittering; Flynn pulls out a headphone.

'How much further?'

'About another hour and a half, I think.'

'I've Googled Taunton, Mum, it looks quite nice.' She takes delicate bites of her biscuit. Flynn's was eaten in two bites. 'It's got loads of nice parks and stuff and a free museum, oh, and you can go scuba diving.'

'Scuba diving?'

'Yep.' She nods as though we are definitely going scuba diving after we've had our fill of the museum and the parks.

'Well,' I smile, 'we might as well make the most of a day out, if nothing turns up, I mean.' Rose wipes her crumbs away and returns her attention to her phone screen as the train stretches away.

An hour passes past the window. The grey concrete bones of the city are bound by endless washing lines, like veins stretching towards the black and white motorways, their stomachs stabbed with street lights: alien guardsmen with their shining eyes penetrating the morning smog. Flecks of greenery start to show, brown arthritic fingers leaning forward, hungrily catching stray shafts of sunlight, ignoring the invasion of hulking pylons who stand legs apart, throwing their wires across the countryside like a spider's web.

We slow into another stop and an angst of teenage girls board the train. I notice the two girls – one blonde and cute, the other brunette and brooding – looking at Flynn as they pass us. His left side is hidden against the window and concealed by hair. They sit on a table just ahead of us, all nudges and giggles, lipgloss and tousled curls. Flynn notices none of this as he flicks his screen and selects another playlist.

I take this opportunity to study him, feeling that familiar tug of parental pride and fear that accompanies the raising of that common, yet elusive, Half-Man-Half-Boy creature.

The girls are now openly looking in his direction; hair flicks, whispers and lowered lashes are launched at him. He turns towards me and asks for a drink. The love I feel for him multiplies as the girls see his left side. The flirtatious smiles change to shock and then pity. Pity is the most offensive of emotions. Pity defies its own definition. Instead of passing on a feeling of comradeship or support, it inflicts pain and judgement. Pity evokes the pained face, the sad, hopeful smile, the 'hang-on-in-there' arm rub. Pity; I roll the word around with contempt as I watch its infection cross the girls' faces. At this point his gaze is stabbed by it. Pity plunges like a knife which he yanks free, discards and dismisses. He's dealt with it before; he bears its scars and yet survives. Without a hint of a scrape, he pulls back the lid of his Coke, waits a brief moment, his contemplation sliding back to the girls as he gulps down the incident with his sugary bubbles. He burps and wipes it away with the back of his hand with confident indifference.

I feel an emotion between pride and grief, an emotion not yet named, as I wonder what goes on in his head. Is it defeat or a sensation of detachment?

We sit still inside the carriage at the next stop. And we wait. And we wait. My face feels hot and the air of frustration is palpable.

The balding conductor announces, in a manner that suggests that he's just as fed up as the rest of us, that 'There will be a short delay as there was a problem with the toilet tanking.' I neither know nor care what toilet tanking is, but I feel the air in the carriage become decidedly heavy, as murmurs of impatience ride through the compartment. Aloof strangers become partners in crime as we are joined together by our shared disapproval of Britain's public transport.

I start to fidget, smoothing down my jeans and bouncing my knee up and down.

It's fine as long as we're not stuck for too long. We'll still make it on time to catch the connecting train.

My stomach starts to contract; slowly and without pain it pokes an attention-seeking prod. The tuning of instruments echoes in my ears. The thum, thum, thum of a bass guitar followed by a bumph, bumph, bumph of a bass drum, pedal against taut skin followed by the hsssss-sst of the high hat.

Flynn rubs my back rhythmically, trying to calm me as I feel my lips closing, my throat desperate to scale its hill of la-la-la-la-la-la-la-la-las in preparation for the opening song.

Breathe in deeply.

Breathe out slowly.

Even as I repeat this, I know my battle is lost. My stomach holds its muscles so tightly that I worry I might scream out in pain. A sensation akin to bile rising in my throat takes hold.

'Mum, do you want—' Rose's sentence cuts off; her eyes widen as she looks at me, the tube of chocolates pointing in my direction before drooping, anti-climactically, along with her shoulders as she takes in my appearance.

I put my head down, with my voice calm and low, and in the words of Queen and one of their most loved songs 'Don't Stop Me Now', I let the passengers know that today I was going to have a right good time and that I felt: 'A-li-igh-hi-hiiii . . .' and that, with the notes rising steadily – the earth was turning outside in. In fact, with my voice venturing falsetto territory I continue, announcing that I am 'floating about in em-pa-thy . . .' Without control, I stand dramatically as my brain flicks through the lyrics stored within and finds them lacking. My next step is to repeat the title 'Don't Stop

Me Now' to the flabby, tracksuited man opposite. I repeat the command in short, sharp bursts of F major then start nodding my head, raising it a little as I begin grinning – telling my fellow train travelling companions that I'm having a great time, having a great time. I energetically explain that: 'I am a superstar flying through the clouds, ignoring the laws of hilarity!'

Rose half crouches her body around the chair to signal that the conductor (his face confused, amused, bemused) is starting to walk towards me. Feeling a weird sensation of panic mixed with elation I start to shimmy backwards along the aisles, stopping every now and then to tell – first a group of rugby supporters – that 'I'm a chasing car flying by, like Lady Beee-hiiiiva!' I cringe as the lady next to them does indeed have an impressive beehive. I go on to tell them that they shouldn't think about stopping me because: I'm 'burrning through the pie, yep, at one hundred decrees,' and that's why they should call me: 'Mr Bellysiiiightt!' I insult the portly gentleman sitting with beehive lady: 'I'm crying with the speed of niiiightt! I'm going to bake a super manic gal out of pooh!' I start to back away from the advances of the conductor and by the time I get to the back of the carriage, I'm gesturing with my arm straight across my chest pointing to my far right. Keeping my pointed pose, I slowly bring my arm a full one hundred and eighty degrees across the carriage, gathering the amused spectators into my party, which, I am starting to realise, seems to have people joining in. I tell the fake-tanned mother holding the robust-looking toddler with cupid curls that she shouldn't halt my fun: 'Yeah! Yeah! Yeah!'

'Ooh-hoo-hooooo!' she replies as I high-five her.

Rose is standing now, waving frantically at the red-faced conductor as Flynn stretches his neck and gives me a thumbs up, pointing to the people waiting on the platform, who are also joining in with the 'ooh-hoo-hoos'.

My ears become tuned in to the nervous laughs and tone-deaf choir who it seems are 'burning through the pie' too. Avoiding my pursuer as best as I can, I begin climbing over some of the empty seats, crossing over aisles whilst continuing to have a great time, great time. As I hit the guitar solo, my fellow band members sing out in 'boww-nns bum, bow, oooh wowey-owey-ow!' Flynn has now taken it upon himself to dramatically play the air guitar, while Rose is trying not to smile behind her hand at the ridiculousness of it all.

'Miss, if you would refrain from—' The conductor tries to contain my actions with his stern words but I reply that I am still 'burning through the pie . . . yeah!'

I have now almost made a full circle of the carriage and reached my kids, continuing to light up the sky and calling myself 'Mr Bellysight' along the way, before leaving the poor man no other option than to open the doors and make a lunge at me. I am grabbed around the waist and unceremoniously yanked a few times (I think he has underestimated my sturdy frame) through the doors of the train. Whilst this is happening (picture me if you will, still singing, legs and arms apart as I try to wedge myself Spiderman-like against the door frame) I am lucky enough to see my son, grinning from ear to ear, flick his hair off his left side, wink at blonde teenage girl and throw his bag over his shoulder before placing a scrap of paper – what I can only assume is his phone number – on to the table in front of them. As the boos and claps erupt, I am being deposited into the tiny holding cell between carriages, whilst the conductor rants at me about Rule Fifty-four of the trainspotting bible. Dramatically, and with solid purpose, he pushes the door opening button and grandly waves his hands in a manner which undeniably means that I should vacate the train without delay. I begin the leap of shame on to the platform, turning my head just in time to watch as Flynn's audacity is answered by the girl's fake fingernail pulling the piece of paper towards her, a coy smile playing at the side of her mouth as she looks up at his retreating back.

7

Rose

OK, so today didn't quite go to plan. We haven't even got to Taunton yet because Mum turned into Freddie Mercury on the train; Flynn says the lyrics were way off base this time. I think Mum is getting worse. We had to wait at Bristol Temple Meads station for ages while the bloke off the train took Mum to the office where she was bollocked by some woman in a scruffy suit (who looked like a real-life Ursula from *The Little Mermaid*) for causing disruption on the train. I watched her through the glass panel in the door. I felt so sorry for her – she kept trying to interrupt, but after a minute she just looked beaten. Like a naughty girl being told off by a head teacher. She kept biting the inside of her thumbnail and scuffing the floor with her knock-off Uggs. She hadn't been causing that much of a problem anyway. Most people had started to join in with her. I'm sure it was better than when that Cliff Rich-something sang at Wimbledon to entertain the crowds when it was too wet to play (our music teacher had told us about how singing can even fix the weather). I have to disagree. We Googled Cliff at break and we would rather have been rained on. Anyway, Flynn stormed into the office and gave a load of bollocking of his own. I caught my reflection in the glass door while this was going on. I hate looking at myself when I'm not expecting it, I really do look like a goldfish. No matter how much lip balm I put on, my lips still look swollen, and I'm so pale I constantly look like I'm in shock which – given the state of my family – kinda fits. Through the finger-marked reflection, I could see Mum pleading with Flynn to calm down, tugging on his sleeve and apologising to Ursula. It's at this point (after deciding that my attempt at a fishtail braid hadn't worked) that I slung my bag over my shoulder and interrupted to tell them the train had gone anyway.

When we came out of the station (which, by the way, looks like a miniature Big Ben from the outside) we had to wait ages for Mum to 'have a Google'. I think she thinks calling it that is funny. It's not. It's just lame. She found us the cheapest B&B she could, as the next train was hours away and we'd end up arriving in Taunton close to midnight and what would we do then? Flynn sat the whole time with his earphones in, while I had to tolerate Mum's cheery attempts at making this all a part of our adventurous day out. Then, we had to walk for ages until we found this place called Welsh Back Waterfront as we couldn't afford the taxi as well as an overnighter. It's pretty, this place. I like the view of the riverbank and the arches of the bridge that I can see from the window. The last place I can remember going with Mum is that horrible trip to London when I was little. I remember walking through Camden Market, holding on to Mum's hand as we pushed through the crowds. When I talk about that day to her, she says that was the last place she looked for him. It was a long shot; a policewoman had suggested that she try some of the big cities as that's where they find a lot of missing people. Mum says that even when she went, she knew deep down that he wouldn't be there. She just knew it in her heart, but she had to try one last time, like an itch that needed to be scratched. I remember being scared as I clung to her hand. There were people everywhere and weird smells. It was the smells that I remember the most, different cooking smells every few metres as we pushed our way through the stalls, each smell partnered with its own music and foreign accents. One stall sold just octopus; the vision of this steamy, seaside smell and creepy drawing of an octopus is as real in my memory as the feel of my mum's hand holding mine tightly, her worried face scanning passers-by.

She's thinking a lot about him at the moment, we can tell, because she; started humming that song again. The one about not being able to live, if living is without him? Sometimes she really goes for it when she gets to the bit about seeing his face as he was leaving . . . something about that's the way the story is? We don't tell her about this one either because she cries when she's singing it and then looks shocked when she notices her face is wet. Once she sung it over and over while she was cleaning the oven and she genuinely didn't know she was crying until she had finished. I walked into the kitchen to see her stand up, grab the squirty oven-cleaner bottle and squint at the back of it. She was going to complain to the company because it was supposed to be eco-friendly, and how could it be when her throat was sore and her eyes were streaming? Flynn laughed, then put on this stupid hippy voice telling her to 'Relax, lay-day, peace mother,' and she laughed and threw the dishcloth at him as he fake-screamed, 'My eyes! My eyes!' He's good at distracting her and calming her down. It's a shame he can't do it when he gets wound up himself. It's like a red mist when he loses it, and he looks scary. Dead scary. I can see why he gets into so much trouble, but he really isn't mean. He just, oh I dunno, he just doesn't handle outside stuff well.

Anyway, I'm gonna go. Flynn has finally come out of the bathroom and if I hurry I can have a quick one before Mum comes back from her walk.

8

Melody

Blimey, this hill is steeper than I thought. I can see my breath billowing out of my nostrils as I puff-the-magic-dragon my way up the frosty hill towards the summit. OK, so summit may be a little bit of an exaggeration – really it's the steep incline of the beer garden at the back of the B&B, but the reception lady said there is a pretty view from the top and, to be honest, I need a bit of time to myself to calm my thoughts. The train journey here wasn't so bad – embarrassing, granted – but the office overture was worse. Flynn. I worry so much about him. I really think he was just a moment away from punching that woman. Every muscle in his body seemed to be tensed and ready, the vein in his neck visibly pulsating, when he told her to 'get it into your fat stupid face'. I'm cringing even as I think about it, the way he spat at her about my medical condition that she would have 'no concept of understanding'. I had glanced through the door at Rose. She looked like she was watching a horror film. Her face was twisted into this look of such disgust that, to my shame, I had to look away from it. We should have just stayed at home. I stop for a moment to catch my breath and pull my collar further up to battle against the stiff wind, then pull up my boots which never seem to hold their shape quite right.

When Flynn was a baby, I remember lying in our bed, this

tiny, wondrous piece of perfection sandwiched between me and Dev, both of us marvelling that we had created something so beautiful. The room had been lit by the first light of dawn, no sound other than our breathing and the gentle tick-tock of time passing by. Time that we need more of, time that we never have, time that we chase after like some mythological prize even though we have an abundance of it day after day. We hadn't spoken a word, we had just simply lived, the three of us wrapped in a white, fabric-softened duvet of perfect time. But in that office, there was no perfection, no softness, just reds and purples and fractures: time shattering around me.

I stand at the top of the incline and look out over the River Avon, its ripples carrying away the end of the day as it captures the reflections of the sunset, turning the foaming banks into Double Dip sherbet, the lost, precious times that can never be found ebbing back and forth. The first house you buy, the exciting sound of keys about to unlock your future as you step into your own home for the first time – ours was a flat above a local Chinese – we'd laughed as we ran up the long flight of stairs, giggling before throwing ourselves on to the grubby lounge floor; lying on our backs, hand in hand as we breathed in the smell of chow mein and freedom. We'd played through the montage of wallpaper stripping and paint-splattered giggles, made up through first fights with tears and favourite chocolate bar gifts. The growing sense of belonging becoming thicker with each weekend trip to the city, overnight bags filled with cheap drink to be swigged from chipped mugs in budget hotels. Feelings intensified with a trip to the hospital after a minor car crash, gentle kisses on a bruised forehead, clenched hands stroked and whispers of worry with declarations of love becoming so concrete and real that you realise you have built yourself a home.

Like a flipbook these memories fly . . . the proposal, the hen night with pink veil and 'L' plates, the dress, the smiles, the vows, the speeches, the honeymoon – running in the rain with beach towels above our heads – the bills, the worries, the stomach bugs, the shopping, the avocado bath suite, the midnight caress, the pregnancy test, the sickness, the back rubs, the dungarees, the swollen feet, the glassy-eyed scan, the pain, the joy, the night-time feeds, the first steps, the new house, the Christmas mornings, the rows, the slammed doors, the love, the laughter . . . the crash.

My breath comes in short gasps as my mind slows, and a five-year-old Rose – with droplets of her red hair floating behind her – sings at the front of the school choir and I'm filled with calm as I watch a lonely bird swoop across the red, scarred sky while I sing along with the memory that is so clear. *'A-maz-iiing Grace, how sweet the sound . . .'* I gulp as my voice increases in volume, while I wipe away the tears that are slipping down my face, the wind turning their tracks icy cold. *'That saved a wreeeeetch li-ike meeee . . .'* The wind wipes my hair around in blurry confusion as I continue, *'I once was lost, but now am found, was blind, but now I seeeee.'* I smile, pull out a tissue, wipe my eyes, then blow my nose and pull my shoulders back, closing the flip book, and instead open a fresh, clean page.

I turn over for the fourth time and listen to the teenage snores filling this unfamiliar room with familiar sounds. Sleep ducks and dives from my grasp, scrambling away around worrying nooks and anxious crannies. I throw back the crisp, white sheets, shove my feet into my boots, grab my black cardigan and tiptoe my way into the en-suite. My mouth is dry from too many bags of cheap crisps and two overpriced glasses of dry white wine. I fill the plastic cup with tap water and I'm grateful for its icy flow down my throat as I sit on the edge of the bath. My plan for tomorrow is simple. To give them a chance to have their own experience of what it is really like, looking for a missing person, now that they're old enough to understand.

Ask yourself what it would be like to lose someone you love. Lose. Often when we lose a loved one, we mean they've passed away. But with a missing person, it means exactly that. You have lost them. Misplaced them, like a set of keys. You retrace your steps, think of what happened the day they disappeared. What colour trousers were you wearing? Where did you last see them? What day was it? A Sunday because you had a leg of lamb in the oven. You feel panic. What if you can't find them? How will you be able to cope if you don't? They are your only set. Irreplaceable. You feel anger: if such and such hadn't happened you wouldn't have been so distracted. You feel elation when you remember you had a different handbag that day. That's where they are! You feel disappointment when you open it to find nothing but an empty bag. Highs and lows that pull you up and smash you down with each crashing wave. A voyage with no end, only turmoil and storms interrupted by brief calm seas.

I want Rose to have closure. To be able to know that she has followed a credible lead exhaustively and, in turn, has all the proof she needs to realise her dad is dead. Gone. More than that . . . I want her to know that she doesn't need him in her life for it to be full. Full of joy, full of love, full of . . . I stop mid-thought and bend down towards the red bloodstain beside the waste-paper basket next to the toilet. Clearly the bathroom hasn't been cleaned properly. I scrunch up my face, wipe the drop away with a piece of loo roll, discard it in the bin, turn out the light and blunder back into a fidgeting slumber.

We start our day full of English breakfast and optimism. The train arrives on time and without soundtracks. After a swift drink in a café, we Google-navigate our way to the police station in a bubble of apprehensive accomplishment, which gives our chins a lift. The first eager daffodils nod their heads at our footsteps, before Starbucks and shopping tills flood our senses with town life. We stop outside the police station, the three of us dwarfed by the words above the door that beckon and repel us in equal measure. Right now, I'm trying very hard not to start singing The Clash's 'I Fought the Law'.

'Ready?' I question.

'Yep,' Rose replies. Flynn snorts the affirmative before I push open the doors and step inside. The office sounds of phones ringing and being answered, hums of a photocopier and closing of drawers are coupled with the smell of instant coffee and disinfectant. We walk up to the desk in front and wait patiently as two policemen – one young, fresh-faced and enthusiastic, the other older, dulled but friendly – talk quietly and seriously before a parting guffaw.

'Can I help you?' the youngster asks.

'Um, yes, no, I mean, yes, we hope so.' He tilts his perfectly groomed dark hair and smiles what I'm sure he has practised to be a helpful, approachable beam. What actually grins back at me is a can't-you-see-I'm-busy-and-really-can't-be-bothered-with-middle-aged-women-and-their-petty-complaints sneer. 'We – we've come about a missing person,' I stammer. How did I used to do this day in and day out? I've torn a strip off most of my local police force with embarrassing regularity. It once came to the point when I was told that if I didn't refrain from 'vocalising frustrations rudely and antisocially' that I might have to 'submit further questions by written means'. As I say, embarrassing.

'Hmmm. And has the person been missing for long?' He glances up at the clock.

'No, I mean yes.'

'To be able to report a person as missing,' he does little inverted signs with his fingers, 'the person needs to be absent for over twenty-four hours.'

'Yes I know but that's—'

'These things tend to sort themselves out.'

'They do?' I ask, losing my grip on what I had asked in the first place. An eighties classic from the king of pop is starting to itch. I bite the inside of my cheek.

'Mmhmm.' He smiles, nods and straightens a pile of papers on his desk.

'If of course your . . .'

'Husband.' I close my eyes briefly, but I see a white suit, dark shirt, white hat bowed in an iconic pose.

Oh no.

'Of course,' he smiles a knowing smile, obviously concluding that my husband has gone off on a jolly with his gym partner, 'if he hasn't come home within the twenty-four hours' stipulation then, by all means,' he smooths the top piece of paper and smiles at me, 'please feel free to pop back and we'll take it from there.' The king of pop starts to click his fingers, head nodding in short, sharp, precise nods in time.

'Oh, um, but—'

Not Jacko, pleeease.

'My father has been missing since 2004,' Rose interjects, 'so I believe we meet the missing person,' she mimics the policeman's inverted comma actions, 'requirements.'

'Oh. Of course, but isn't it a little late to be reporting it now?'

I notice that I'm now looking at the blue lino; my head is bowed, my fingers are beyond my control as I start to click with my right hand . . . my left moving dangerously close to my crotch.

'Sir, I don't mean to be rude,' I hear Rose's voice above

my inner radio, 'but we never said anything about reporting a missing person. We're here about a report of a man who fits Dad's description in your constituency.'

Oh Lord. I can't stop it – 'Smooth Criminal' begins.

I start murmuring a few lyrics about an intruder making a sound like a 'shendo' before pelvic-thrusting my explanation about a mark on the carpet.

I hear Flynn sigh the words, 'Oh great,' and watch him put his headphones in his ears and skulk his way to a bank of plastic chairs, as I moonwalk my way across the room, punctuating each stanza with a Jacko-esque, 'He, Hee!' with matching tip-toed treats.

'Please excuse my mother, she has a condition,' Rose says, exasperated, as other uniformed heads start peering at us. 'We're here about the—' She doesn't finish her sentence because it's clear from the look on the policeman's face that I'm putting on too good a performance to be ignored. Currently, I'm asking very loudly if someone called Annie is in good health and that I wish she would tell us if she's all right.

Luckily as I hit the falsetto wails of a man in distress and add another Jacko, 'Ooooh!' I have moonwalked, knee-jerk-kicked my way out of the room and into a corridor. I slump on to a chair, out of breath and aching. Who knew I could moonwalk?

Flynn opens the door and sits down with a grunt, still with his headphones in. He passes me a lukewarm bottle of Coke from his backpack and leans his head against the wall with his eyes closed. I sit listening to the quietened hustle and bustle of the police world, gathering my thoughts and calming my inner pop princess.

'Could have been worse, I suppose . . .' I mutter as I look at Flynn. 'I could have started singing "Thriller". I actually learnt all of those dance moves when I was at junior school, so that would have been a much longer performance.' He snorts. 'I'll go back in a min, can you pop your head in and check on Rose?'

He nods, unfolds himself and shoulder-sags his way back in. I concentrate on regulating my breathing as best as I can until he returns, an embryonic smile at the corner of his mouth.

'What?'

'What?' he replies.

'What's funny?'

'Nothing, she's just . . . man, she's something else.' He shakes his head. 'Got them all running around at her beck and call like a little ginger commandant.' He pulls the head-phones from his pocket as I straighten myself up and head towards the main part of the police station.

'Coming?' I ask him.

'Nah . . . I'll stay here if that's OK?'

Rose is sat – bolt upright – with a policewoman in the corner of the room, staring at a computer screen. The young policeman is nowhere to be seen but the older one is at Rose's side, offering her a cup of tea like she's royalty. I walk past the elbow nudges and join them.

'I'm afraid that's all we have, Miss King.' The policewoman looks up at me, her dark eyes sympathetic and tired. She pushes a stray strand of light brown hair behind her ear. 'I was just explaining to your daughter, Mrs King, that unfor-tunately we don't have any more information than the details we posted on the missing persons' webpage.'

'Would it be possible to find out who found him outside the shopping centre?' Rose asks with an authority I've never heard before.

'Unfortunately, we can't release that information, but perhaps you could try the hospital? There may have been staff that remember him.'

'Yes, I think that should be our next step.' Rose nods at the policewoman. 'Are you free now, PC Davis?' she asks her. 'I'm sure your uniform could assist us in a more efficient manner than the three of us unchaperoned?' I smile. It's so refreshing to see my normally slightly awkward daughter taking control.

'Um, yes,' she nods, 'I can take you now, just let me get some things together. I'll quickly print this off . . .'

I turn to see Flynn at my shoulder.

'Always knew I'd end up in the back of a police car,' he whispers.

'Shush.' I smile tightly at PC Davis as she returns with the missing person report, her rigid uniform breathing competence and compassion as it passes us.

Walking up the steps, I feel uneasy. Michael Jackson is long gone and Elgar's mournful cello concerto is vibrating in my core. It's content to stay hidden, nothing more than a gentle plucking of my nervous stereo system. Sometimes the music develops into something other than vocalisation. At the moment, it's making my senses thrum, which is a sensation I imagine a deaf person to feel when they walk into a music concert, the music so loud they can feel its highs and lows of emotion through the vibrations travelling through their body. I once read that the part of the brain that recognises vibrations also processes hearing music, therefore replicating the emotions and reactions between a hearing person and a deaf person. I can believe it. You know the feeling. The bass that thuds through your feet. The pulsing in your ears, the quiver in your fingertips when you touch a speaker . . . you would be able to tell if the music was happy or sad from those vibrations. Right now, my inner playlist is filling me with those vibrations; its sombre, selfish stings are sinking their barbs into me.

We pass through the gentle click of the automatic doors and step into the busy world of the sick and the well. I look at the waiting faces – yellow fear, boredom blues and sickly green grief – a rainbow of emotions in every passing minute.

I link my arms through Flynn's as we follow Rose and PC Davis through the In Patient department and into the main corridor. The cello's deep, painful notes slice through me, the slow melody taking me through its own story of hurt and loss. It quickens its pace as we turn a corner and the vibration's tempo speeds up. The melody soars higher before swooping back down.

I concentrate on putting one step after the other; the green, grainy floor becomes my focus as the peaks and plummets swirl through my body. The harmony pokes and prods, pierces and soothes my emotions as it pulls me on its journey. Finally, we arrive at a small side office. It has sliding glass windows and posters warning you against consuming too many units of alcohol, alongside a harrowing anti-smoking picture.

'Good afternoon, I'm Police Constable Davis.' She smiles a warm smile as I try to turn down the volume inside. 'We were hoping one of your staff could answer some questions about a missing person case we have? A gentleman was brought in after collapsing outside the local shopping mall on the—' She hesitates and flips open her printed copy of the report.

'Twentieth of February,' Rose interjects. 'He had dark hair, green eyes and a tattoo on his left shoulder of three swallows. He was wearing a grey hat, dark brown jacket, green-checked shirt and boots.'

'Sounds like a lumberjack,' Flynn adds under his breath.

'He was aged between thirty and forty,' Rose continues, 'and had a silver bracelet with the name Tom on it.' The volume has started to rise again and I'm finding it hard to hear the words being spoken from behind the glass. Deep, heart-wrenching notes have taken my journey low and dark, pulling me with it. I feel sorrow and anguish and I long for the opening movement to take me to the highs of its tale. The deep bass notes are reverberating inside my muscles, I can feel my legs trembling and fighting against the invisible pull of the concerto. I can no longer hear what is being said. I see the nurse pointing in the direction of a tall man in his late fifties who looks to be a porter. I see them, thank the nurse and start walking over.

I pull against Flynn's arm, urging him to stop. I'm a child in the back of a car, battling against a wave of nausea. Each twist and turn of the road takes me closer to the travel sickness that ruins the great Family Day Out.

'Mum?' I look into his worried face.

'Cello concerto.'

'Tempo?'

'All over the place. I'm hoping it's just the first movement . . . if it's the whole thing, I don't think I can . . .'

'Rose!' Flynn shouts. Rose turns and I see in her face that I must look worse than a little travel sick.

'I'll be fine,' I gasp as the notes surge upwards and my whole body feels like it is swaying, flying with blissful, aching joy. I feel a euphoric sickness as the music takes me to its climax before the smooth, cold plastic of the chair encapsulates me. Rose is kneeling in front of me and I notice PC Davis signalling for a nurse.

'I'm fine,' I gasp as the final, long, desperate note tears at me. A small, rosy-cheeked nurse turns and runs towards me, dropping as she does a cardboard box which she had been holding out for a distraught mother and tearful little girl. As the final note hangs heavily inside me, the contents of the box fall to the floor; my gaze is drawn to the detritus. The little girl shrieks with joy and grabs a battered elephant. The relief is evident in the mother's face as the feeling of good-will passes across the waiting patients like a cool breeze on a hot day. The last vibration quivers quietly away before I see it. I swat away the cup of water that's being offered to me, ignore the instructions to stay sitting down for a few minutes until I'm feeling better, ignore the worried look on my children's faces as I stand, stumble and collapse to the floor, my hands slashing through the rings, purses and mobile phones until I grasp it. Rose and Flynn are by my side as I pull myself up, not quite daring to open my hand. Open my heart, open my mind to the impossible.

'Mum?' Rose asks.

'Mum? What is it? What's wrong?'

'It's . . .' I shake my head. 'It can't be.' I look into their worried faces, first at Rose then Flynn, not knowing how to take the next step.

'Open your hand, Mum,' Flynn says.

'Mum . . . open up.'

9

Melody

This can't be happening. How can something impossible become possible? I'm trying to find some explanation as I open my hand and reveal the burgundy thread that was unravelling my thoughts. The bell is tarnished but undoubt-edly the same one that jangled its way through my teenage years and later through my years with Dev. This is not possible. But wasn't that what people said about landing on the moon? It's impossible to put a man in space and yet we did. Before that, it was impossible to make men fly and yet we did. How about transplanting part of a pig's heart to a human? Impossible, right? It worked: another heart in another person's body, pumping their blood, their life, their energy around as if it had been there all along. It became possible. I look at my children's faces as they realise what's in my palm. Rose starts smiling and nodding as if she knew all along that we would find him. Flynn's face is harder to read. He looks up at me and tilts his head to the side as if trying to find a solution to the puzzle.

This can't be possible because Dev is dead.

He has to be.

Because the only other explanation is that he left us – a detail that I have always known to be . . . impossible.

I stride forward and grasp the nurse by the arm.

'Where did you get this?' I ask desperately. She looks startled and slightly annoyed at my tone. I swallow hard. 'Please,' I add in a gentler manner. 'This,' I hold the bracelet in front of her, its gentle chime peeling away my memories layer by layer, 'belonged to my husband who has been missing for several years.' I can hear the quiver in my voice as my voice cracks. 'I thought he was dead but a man fitting his description was reported near here.'

'I'm sorry,' she smiles sincerely at me, 'I don't know. This is just the lost property box from this department. Any member of staff could have put it in there.'

'But you must know something?' I beg.

'I'm sorry, I can't help you.'

'But that's your job!' I shout. 'Helping people!' I feel Flynn's hands on my shoulders.

'I'm sorry.' He steps forward and moves me so that I'm standing slightly behind his shoulder. 'As you can see, my mum is overwhelmed. If you could find out anything about who was working in this department on the—?'

'Twentieth of February,' PC Davis adds. I'd forgotten she was even there. 'It would really help with our investigation,' she concludes authoritatively.

'Of course,' the nurse stammers, 'but it's not as straightforward as you might think. We have several shift changes – administrative staff, doctors, nurses, consultants, as well as volunteer staff. This will take time and right now I'm supposed to be taking another—' She flusters and flaps her hands.

'We understand; if you could point us in the direction of the nurse in charge?'

There is some discussion about the off duty something or other and I hear a muted conversation about it being best if PC Davis questions the nurse in charge while we wait elsewhere. I'm pulled, nudged and guided past beds and down yet more corridors. Confusion and anger grab my feet, the weight of uncertainty tangles my limbs and I feel like I'm struggling through a mangrove swamp which cuts out light and syphons the air of clarity from around me.

He is dead.

I've accepted this as fact.

He is dead.

A comfort in the years after my accident; the phrase that has stopped me from the endless maze of 'what ifs'. I've been through the five stages of grief. I indulged myself in denial for months, actively trying to find him. I withdrew from our mutual friends, their sympathetic arm rubs and oh so tactfully aware, stilted conversations pushing me further away as my denial gave way to aggressive anger. Anger reacts quickly, it sees denial as a threat, attacks it, pushes it back . . . then bargaining approaches. The most degrading of the stages. You start to believe in a God, in family long gone, in the stars, in a scrunched-up tissue . . . 'If I can get this tissue in the bin from here, they'll find him.' Then depression hits. You cry, continue to put your faith in the tissue. You tear it into pieces, scream at its box, scratch at it . . . stare at it for hours, until your body is rigid and aching, and you have no idea how long that tissue has been in your hand. Until finally, with one final throw, one last effort, you pull the last one from the box and watch, helplessly, as it falls to the floor and you finally accept that it was never going to land in the bin from this angle anyway, that it was just a lost cause. You rise, walk towards the debris – picking up the pieces along the way – before finally throwing them into the bottom of the bin, slamming the lid shut.

Once the grief had consumed me and had retreated to a dull hum at the back of my life, memories would leak into my day: the way he would hide his old Star Wars figures in a box of cereal, in my underwear drawer, under the bed covers. The cereal box, my underwear drawer and the bed covers – just reminders of my life before – left empty, barren, and asking for forgiveness.

Then when I forced myself to leave the house, to go shopping, I would be hit by memories of him standing on the back of the trolley, pushing himself around like a child on a scooter. Sombrely, I pushed the trolley around the shop, filling it – with my children in mind – with healthy food, confused as I got to the checkout and realised there were no hidden goodies, no packets of jelly babies, which he would always sneak in, no lemon curd, which used to ooze out of the edge of his sandwiches, no hidden surprises for me, which I would later be given with my cup of tea that night.

Moments later, I find myself in the hospital canteen; smells of overcooked lasagne and the scraping of chairs bring me back to my surroundings. I sip from the plastic cup of coffee and watch Flynn's ripped-jeaned knee bouncing up and down like a jackhammer. Rose is talking excitedly to him, animated hands flying all over the place. I sip the coffee again.

'Mum?' I realise she is talking to me.

'Hmmm?'

'Once PC Davis finds out who was working, she'll inter-view them, right?'

'Um, yes . . . I expect so.'

'And I bet someone will tell us something that will help us find him . . . I can't wait.'

'Rose,' Flynn warns.

'What?' She leans back and folds her arms defensively across her chest. 'What is the matter with you two?' She throws her arms up in exasperation. 'We've never been this close to finding him. What about all those months, Mum? All of those calls to the police station? That trip to London, for Christ's sake? Homeless people watching, Mum! Homeless people watching! And now we are this close,' she pinches her thumb and forefinger together, 'and you two don't even want to talk about it? Jesus!'

'For someone so intelligent you can be really dumb sometimes,' Flynn groans at her. She frowns and blinks questioning eyes at me.

'You're right, Rose.' I fake-smile my reply. 'We're just a little taken aback, that's all. It's amazing that we've found out about all this, isn't it?' I nod at Flynn. 'It's just taking a little time to get used to, that's all. You know, that he might be . . .' I clear my throat, 'alive . . . after all . . . this . . . time.' I can see tears blurring my vision; I blink them away. 'Would you mind if I take a walk?' I fumble in my bag for my purse. 'You two get some lunch, you must be starving by now. The lasagne looks nice.'

'Mum.' Flynn grabs my hand; I give his a quick squeeze.

'I'm fine, I could just do with some air.' I scrape back the chair and smile at them; Rose glares back at me. Flinging my bag over my shoulder, I walk as quickly as I can away from them, but not before I hear Flynn tell his sister the piece of the puzzle that she is missing.

'If he's alive, you moron, it means he left . . . he left us, Rose.'

For once, the song within is quiet. After Elgar had taken me on his harrowing, rapturous journey, the cello, it seems, has battered the Soft and Hard Rock into its House, closed the Garage and left it in a Trance. I hurry through the passages, around corners until the main exit doors slide into view. Christ, I wish I still smoked. Almost there. I feel my lungs swell as they do when you're swimming underwater at school, just one more effort and I'll get my five metres underwater badge . . . almost there, but then, I never could make it. I stop as an elderly lady, unsteady with her cane, stands shaking in my path. I try not to notice. I try to see the other people close by who will take her into their care but they all seem to be too busy. Too busy on their phones, too busy minding their own business to notice this frail, desperate lady who clearly needs help. With confusion, she looks around: a beige lavender-scented soul, marooned without a companion. She fumbles in her bag with her free hand. The doors blink open and shut as her watery blue eyes echo them. She stares at me and I hesitate before walking to her side.

'Would you like some help?' I hear myself ask. I feel her cold, paper-thin-skinned hand on my forearm as she leans against me.

'My husband, he was in an accident. I told him not to clean those windows but,' her voice is a tremor, more reverberation than sound, 'there was blood all over the window sill, dripping on to the roses.'

'Oh dear.' I cringe at my feeble response. 'Do you know what ward he's on?'

'Oh, um, no, I had to get a taxi. I wasn't allowed in the ambulance. Insurance or something.'

'Oh goodness. Well, I think he would still be in A&E then. Would you like me to, um, come with you?' Her eyes fill and I fear she is going to collapse. I'm not even sure how she is still upright; I can feel her exhaustion and worry through her delicate grasp. She nods and stifles a quiet sob as we shuffle our way back through the hospital.

'Do you think he'll have brain damage?' she asks as we approach the desk.

'I'm, um, well, let's just wait and see what the doctors say, shall we?'

I explain to the nurse what has happened, give the name 'Derek Summer' and guide the elderly woman who I know now to be Edith to the cold row of chairs and we wait.

'I met him when I was eleven years old.'

'Wow, that's a long time to stay with someone.'

'Oh, we didn't get together then!' she chuckles. 'My father, God rest his soul, would have had a thing or two to say about that! He was a bit of a show-off, you see. Always whistling and striding about in his finery. He was eighteen then. Even then . . . I never could take my eyes off him.'

'Mrs Summer?' A tall, reedy-looking sister smiles at us and we rise unsteadily and follow her to the sounds of steady beeps and purposeful footsteps. The blue curtains are pulled back to reveal a blur of activity.

Mr Summer is just having a red neck brace removed and a balding, tanned doctor is leaning over him as a nurse is tying a plastic apron around her tiny waist.

Edith stands still, hunched and scared. Her bony fingers dig into my arm.

'Do you have any chest pain?' the tanned doctor asks. I wonder where he has been on holiday. A good two-weeker with a tan like that, unless he's been at the spray tan. He doesn't look like a spray tanner type, though . . . too chubby.

'No,' a surprisingly strong voice replies. Her grip relaxes a little.

'Dizziness or tummy pain? Stay really still for me.'

'I feel a bit out of breath.'

'Well, what do you expect? Cleaning the top windows at your age!' Edith makes her presence known.

'Told you I would be in trouble, Doc.' The doctor looks up and smiles at her.

'Your husband has been telling us you were quite the dancer.'

'Pfft, he was the dancer, always spinning me about. Bloody big show-off. Always has been, always will be.'

The doctor turns his attention back to Mr Summer and then to the nurse.

'Can you order a scan from the head down to the hips, please?'

'What's that for?' Edith asks, the banter slipping away.

'We're just going to make sure there is no internal damage, Mrs Summer. Your husband has taken quite a bashing, but I'm confident that there's no severe damage to his spine since he's responding well to our pokes and prods.' He smiles and pulls a chair towards the bed. 'Take a seat, Mrs Summer, I'll be back shortly,' and he leaves in a whoosh of caffeine-fuelled, night-shift stubble.

I watch, entranced, as the two Summers lean in towards each other. Years fall away as they look into each other's eyes; a whole lifetime of love, loss and understanding are conveyed in that simple look.

'Ham and tomato,' she whispers.

'Cheese and pickle,' he replies.

A secret endearment, an apologetic smile, a relieved cheek stroke. The strength of a relationship there for all to see in three simple gestures. Sometimes in this life you are lucky enough to witness true love. True love is not being showered with red roses on Valentine's Day. It's not about the nine-thousand-pound wedding, the carefully thought out vows or the matching flowers and table dressings. True love is simple. It's there in the little Post-it notes, in the cup of tea when you wake up. It's there when you argue and laugh five minutes later. It's there in the bath run at the end of a difficult day. True love is selfless . . . or is it? There is no greater reward than watching the person you love be happy. Maybe the answer is in the word itself. Selfish, or selfless? If you're truly in love . . . doesn't the word 'self' kind of become obsolete anyway?

As I stand there watching a scene that wouldn't have been out of place in a Nicholas Sparks book and debate the intricacies of love, a sick feeling spreads through me . . . Have

I ever really experienced love? I've never questioned that before. I have always known that what Dev and I had was true and pure. That's why I knew with unshakeable certainty that Dev was dead, because our love for each other, through thick and thin, was a constant . . . but now? If he is alive? If he did leave us? Maybe what we had wasn't true love after all.

I wish the Summers well and do a loop to the other side of the hospital. Slumping into a chair, I survey the remains of the hospital lunch. Flynn looks up from his phone, as does Rose.

'So . . .' Earplugs are unplugged and Facebook statuses are postponed momentarily. 'Any news from PC Davis?'

'She came and spoke to us a while ago and said she'd be in touch once she's interviewed the people working that day, oh, and that she has your number.'

'Right. I think we need to stay here another night, what do you think?' Rose smiles and nods, not as enthusiastically as before but keen nevertheless. Flynn shrugs and then gives me a short, sharp nod. 'Good. Right then, let's get out of here for now. I'm starting to smell like disinfectant. I think we should go and check out the shopping centre that he was found in. You never know if it'll help.' I stuff a couple of limp chips into my mouth and swig the dregs of my cold coffee.

'Mum?' Flynn asks as he unfolds himself.

'Mmhmm?'

'What if we do find him? What then?'

'I don't know. Find out why, I guess, and ask him, well, where the hell he has been for the last eleven years.'

'He'll want to see us, though, won't he, Mum?' I pause as I push my arms through the sleeves of my jacket. 'Mum?

'I don't know, Rose. I hope so. The man I knew wouldn't

have let anything come between him and his children.' I smile reassuringly but keep the subtext to myself.

If he's alive . . . I'm not sure I knew him at all.

We arrive outside the shopping centre without drama and look around in bewilderment. There are several shop openings into the centre as well as a main entrance, and the whole place is humming.

'This is ridiculous!' Flynn throws up his arms. 'He could have been anywhere. Are you sure the report didn't say whereabouts he was found?'

Rose looks flustered.

'No, it just said outside.'

'Great.' He puts his headphones back in and sits down on a nearby bench.

'Dick.'

'Rose!'

'Sorry,' she mumbles, 'but he is, Mum, look at him!' I follow her gaze as he shakes his hair into place and pulls up his hood. 'Why is he being like this? Doesn't he want to find Dad? It's our DAD, for God's sake!'

'Sweetheart, this is a big deal for all of us and we are all dealing with it in our own way. Give him some space, he'll come round.'

I sit next to him and hand him a bottle of Coke. He takes it with a quiet thanks. I nudge him.

'So,' he pulls out an earplug, 'what's next? We start handing out leaflets? Share family albums on street corners?'

'Flynn . . . let's just take it one step at a time. We're all tired but we've got this far . . . it would be stupid not to at least try to find him, don't you think?'

He shrugs.

'It's not like he's tried to find us, though, is it? We still live in the same house for fuck's sake.'

'Oy.'

He rolls his eyes.

'For crying out loud?'

'Better.'

'Look, we don't even know that this is him. Let's just ask in a few shops around here and see if anyone can remember anything about a man collapsing and then we'll call it a day, go back to the B&B and you can YouTube to your heart's content.'

'Fine . . . I'll start in Game. I need to see if *Call of Duty* is out anyway.'

'Deal. You start there then, Rose can take the row starting with the Body Shop and I'll do Marks and Sparks to Waterstones.'

The smell inside the bookshop is like a favourite pair of fluffy socks, soothing your aches and warming your ice-cold toes. I breathe in the scent and stroke the covers of the bestsellers . . . had he been here? Did he sift through the crime novels like he used to when the kids were small? I would head off for the latest bodice ripper but Dev would always be after a whodunnit . . . I've never had the patience for thrillers, but put me in Henry VIII's court and I can be lost for hours. I pick up the latest chick-lit bestseller, *No Wonder*, which has a teal cover and a picture of a camper van on it, and head for the checkout.

'Ooh, that's a good one.' The coiffured lady behind the till, with a name badge that identifies her as 'Anita', smiles at me. 'Is that all?' She goes about the business of scanning the back and I grimace at the price.

'Um, yes, no, well, I was hoping you could help me? I'm looking for a man.'

'Oh!' She looks slightly startled at my request but then nods with understanding, tilts her head to the right and does a quick jerk of her head in the direction of a very hairy, portly man in a Waterstones shirt, rearranging the Peppa Pig display. 'Brian over there is lovely, such a sweet man.'

I feel confused at first but then conclude that Brian must have been working in this branch for longer.

'Oh, shall I ask him?'

'I think that would be wonderful!' She claps her hands together excitedly. 'He's not had much luck lately, poor thing, but, well, you never know when you might find The One.'

'That's exactly what I'm trying to do.' I nod with conviction.

'Shall I call him over? I can ask him for you if you're a little nervous?'

'Um, yes, please, if you don't mind.' I start to feel the first hint of uneasiness as Brian waddles over to us.

'Brian, this lovely lady,' she smiles at me, 'is looking for a gentleman friend.' I get a waft of Brian's lovely nature, and it is anything but sweet. I try hard not to grimace at the piece of food attached to his Moses-style beard.

'Yes, I—'

'Brian could arrange to meet you this evening, it's his night off . . . The new Italian is supposed to be a nice, intimate place for a first date.' She claps her hands together again. I want to snap them off.

Oh. Hell.

The penny slowly drops as a childhood favourite starts to unfurl.

'I think there has been a misunderstanding,' I mutter before breaking into the chorus of the eighties hit from the film *NeverEnding Story*.

'Ow-ey-oh-owey-oh-owey-oh . . .'

'Mum!' I turn apologetically to where Flynn and Rose are heading towards me. 'We're in the wrong side of the shopping centre.'

'Oh.' Rose stops in her tracks as she surveys the scene.

The hand claps have stopped and Anita looks decidedly uncomfortable as I continue with my tales about 'the never-ending story . . . oh-ey-oh-owey-oh-owey-oh!!!!'

'Sorry, she has a condition,' Flynn explains as he puts his arm through mine and grins as I wave back at the two confused and awkward looks being thrown in my direction. Luckily, I am a safe distance from them when I hear Brian's condemnation of Anita's choice 'in a suitable partner'. Apparently, he's 'not that desperate'.

Charming.

We end up around a much more bohemian entrance to the shopping centre, just one entrance into the main mall, which is part of a square courtyard. There are tourist gift shops, a vintage tea shop and various quirky shop fronts around the cobbled courtyard. As we stand next to The Retro Shop, I can't help but think about how much it would have hurt to collapse on to these cobbled stones. I notice a small family-run pharmacy and make a note to get some more Rescue Remedy and some painkillers for the migraine that has been threatening since my last performance.

'The bloke in Game said he remembers an ambulance having to get up that narrow passage a couple of weeks ago, so it must have been around here somewhere.'

'OK, so we'll do the same as before, but first let's grab a drink. I need to rest after my eighties soundtrack, bookshop debacle. And I could do with a piece of that cake.' I nod towards the slab of chocolate cake adorning the window of the tea shop. I rub my temple briefly.

'It wasn't that bad,' Rose replies as we walk towards the vintage tea shop.

'Really? Getting rejected by Brian "wasn't that bad"? He was the man of my dreams!' We giggle and Flynn groans as we walk through the door.

The shop is smaller than my lounge at home and top to toe in Cath Kidston. I order us all a piece of chocolate-orange cake and a pot of tea and smile at the shards of rainbow light reflected from the glass domes holding in the delectable delights on display. We sit quietly, apart from the moans of gastronomic pleasure that we keep emitting with every mouthful. The only interruption is a gentle tinkle of what I presume to be a wind chime and the quiet lull of conversation around us. Thinking about the cost of the trip so far, I warn myself that this is the last extravagance until we get home. An extra night is something I hadn't factored into my budget and so next week will have to be a 'beans on toast' week. The price of the tickets and the extra night at the bed and breakfast is only going to leave me – the jingle of the wind chime interrupts my thoughts and I feel temporarily annoyed – plus – I open my purse and count up the loose change – there it goes again, jingle-jingle – I snap my purse closed, put it back into my bag and pull out my phone. I swipe open the calendar app and try to work out when the child benefit goes in – it last went in on the – jingle-jingle – 17th so it's due again – jingle-jingle – I close my phone case in annoyance and watch as a blue splinter of light twists and turns on the white tablecloth. Looking up, I turn and try to see what it is reflected from. A glint. A wink. And then I know.

Know that Dev is alive, because hanging behind us, just above a small open window next to the counter, is an intricately sculpted dove, and the chimes that have been piercing my thoughts hang from it. A dove with a blue marble inside its eye socket encapsulated by two separated threads of silver. To the untrained eye, those two pieces of silver would look like nothing more than a muddle of swirls and knots, but to someone who has watched these two chaotic streams be manipulated by hand into a three-dimensional signature before, it is clear that this design is as unique to the artist as a thumbprint. But these initials, the initials that he would have written on the back of his first drawings in school, the initials he would have signed every time he asked for cashback in a supermarket, are not the same.

10

Melody

I watch, fixated, as the dove spins around in concentric circles, swooping to the right before twirling around in the opposite direction, elegantly suspended between invisible threads. The gentle chime of steel against steel rings through my ears as I try to make sense of what I can see, what I now know. Within, I can feel the low-lit club, the hazy cigarette smoke and the tuning of an electric guitar, but, regardless of the inevitable, I continue to stare at the dove, mesmerised. Did you know that there is no real separation between a dove and a pigeon? And yet, our views and opinions of these two birds are so far apart. A dove: pure, romantic, clean . . . an icon of peace, an image of trust. But then you have the pigeon: to the majority of us, they are a nuisance, a pest, that infects our daily life as they peck at the debris of chip papers and chocolate wrappers. They share the same features: slim beaks, neat, curved heads and rounded bodies. Their wings narrow in an identical way and they sing the same song. A dove coos and we smile, clink our glasses of Prosecco and marvel at the bride and groom. A pigeon coos and we find it an irritant; we shoo it away. How quickly we forget the lives they saved, the messages they carried and the intelligence hidden beneath their thick feathers. I wonder – as I stand up and listen to the electric guitar climbing its scale – is this a dove? Or is it a pigeon? I close my eyes briefly and see Prince – or the artist formerly known as – resplendent in his eighties suit, Mozart ruffles and angular guitar. I'm so lost in my thoughts and the relief that I'm feeling, that this time, as I stand up, I don't feel embarrassment, just sweet indulgence as I start to click my fingers and jerk my shoulders to that pop classic, 'When Doves Cry'.

I smirk as I face my children, asking them to imagine me and a stranger in a sweaty kiss. Rose is literally turning a paler shade of freckle at this – and then I ask them:

'My angels? Can two fixture hiss?'

By the time I'm talking about the temperature between me and my stranger, I realise that my lyrical knowledge of the verses may not be great. Oh well, it can't be helped. I shoulder-shimmy a bit more before asking them:

'Why did they heave me hanging?
Cologne in a herd so bold?
Baby I'm fussed to bemandin',
Baby I'm fussed hike my brother . . . too fold?'

My voice shoots up another octave.

'Baby I'm fussed hike my other . . .
She's got a great big hide!
Hi, baby shout at each other,
Missus what a cheese finds . . .'

I grin as I sing the name of the song, 'When Doves Cry'. I start to shimmy around the room, doing a few little high-pitched 'wiheee, hooooos!' as I go. It takes me two full circuits of the tea shop to finish this classic and by the time I return to our table, I'm spent. Rose is looking awkwardly around the room, and Flynn just looks bewildered.

'What the hell was that?'

'Prince.'

'Harry?' Rose questions hopefully. I think she has a soft spot for him, all gingers together and all that. Flynn snorts.

'YouTube it.' Flynn's fingers are a blur as he sticks his headphones in. I gulp down my tea and try to ignore the uncomfortable mumbles behind me. After a few minutes Flynn pulls out his earphones.

'Do you know that you got almost every single word wrong, Mum?'

'I didn't, I . . .'

'Even I know that, Mum, unless this Prince is completely illiterate.'

'What do you mean?'

She passes her phone and I watch myself dancing around. In fairness, I look quite good. I'll definitely get another pair of these jeans, my bum doesn't look bad at all. Oh. They have a point . . . 'Missus what a cheese finds'?

'But I know most of the words.'

'You might know them, Mum, but you weren't singing them.'

'Hmmm. Maybe it's to do with my stress levels?'

'How stressed can you be? You're eating cake and drinking tea!'

I take a deep breath and look from one beautiful face to the other.

'He's alive.'

'And you know this because?' Flynn asks sceptically.

'Jesus, you're not . . .' Rose nods at my cup.

'What?'

'Tea-leaf reading, are you?'

'What? No! I'm not insane.' We all pause a moment for the irony to sink in before erupting into hysterics. What must we look like to the outsider? I've just gyrated a whole load of bizarre lyrics to a Prince classic and my children and I, rather than vacating the premises with our heads hanging in shame and apologetic embarrassment, are laughing so hard that we are starting to make primaeval snorting sounds.

Once we have calmed ourselves, I point to the dove. I wait a moment and watch as recognition crosses their faces.

'Maybe that was bought when he was alive?'

'Nope. Look at the signature.' Flynn gets up and walks to the sculpture. He reaches out to the dove, holds it and stares into its eye. He furrows his brow and gently turns it, squinting hard, trying to make sense of the coils and kinks. The chubby, flowery-aproned lady behind the counter is giving him concerned, shifty glances. Delicately, he turns it the other way before releasing it.

'I can't make it out . . .' he says as he sits back down.

'What, that weird squiggle with the metal eye that he did?' Rose asks. 'I couldn't make out his initials at all in the one in my room and I've tried loads of times.'

'You have to kind of look at it from underneath,' Flynn tells her. 'On this one, it looks like three letters and they are definitely not a D and K.'

Before I have a chance to have a look for myself, Rose goes over to the concerned-looking lady plating up pieces of carrot cake. She talks softly and looks through her golden lashes.

'I'm sorry to trouble you . . .' I see a new-found confidence in my daughter's stance as she gathers her hair into a loose ponytail and pulls it over her right shoulder, '. . . but, could you tell us where you bought the dove? You see, my mum,' she lowers her voice, 'is, um, mentally unstable and it seems to calm her.' I try to put a mentally unstable expression on my face, then realise that after my tribute to Prince, it's really not necessary. Regardless and just for added effect, I pick up a chocolate-crumbed plate and begin licking it.

'You're unbelievable,' Flynn mutters.

'Mmmmhmmm,' I reply, trying to look as if I hadn't noticed the look of pity on the lady's face.

'We are her main carers, you see,' Rose sniffs a little, 'and it can be,' she clamps her lips together, 'difficult at times.'

'I imagine it must be.' She walks over to the dove and lifts the delicate thread from the hook. 'It was from the shop across the square . . . The Little Shop of Everything? I like the way the feathers look to be soft even though they are cold and hard.' She strokes it lovingly. 'It's just beautiful.'

'How long ago was it that you bought it, do you know? We would love to see if we can get our mum one. As you can see, she is quite mesmerised by it.'

I stare at it as I finish licking the plate. Rose and the lady look uneasily at me.

'Oh, only last month, I think it was, but I'm not sure there was another. I just adore it.'

'Yes, it is beautiful. Would it be OK if Mum, well, if she held it briefly before we leave? It would help keep her, well, stay calm . . . for a little while at least.' Rose manages a brave smile.

'Oh! I, um, yes, I suppose so . . . It is quite delicate even though it's made of sturdy material.'

'I'll be sure to take care of it,' Rose assures her and then strides towards us, sticking her tongue out of the corner of her mouth a little – a crack in her mask of sincerity. 'Here you are, Mum . . .' She rolls her eyes and pats me on the shoulder.

'Nicely done,' Flynn remarks with pride in his voice, 'although I would probably have got her to give it to us for free.'

'Shhh.' I bring the dove up to my face closely and squint at the coils and loops around the eye and notice the signature has a more angular feel to it than in his other works. Flynn is right; it definitely looks like three separate levels, three separate initials. I slip my little finger into the socket and close my eyes, tracing the shape kinaesthetically. I can see him concentrating, clipping the wire with his eyes narrowed in concentration, his hair falling into them before he flicks it out of the way. He would look up at me if I walked into the room, his concentration remaining but always a little smile of acknowledgement as I put a cup of tea – strong, two sugars – beside him. My fingers retrace the start of the first letter until I'm sure.

'It's a T.'

'T as in Tom?' Rose's voice falters a little. I nod.

'T as in Twat,' Flynn adds.

'Flynn!' His frustration is a screw slowly loosening the structure of our ship. The stable stern starts to sink and slowly but surely our balance is thrown.

'Then it's him?' I nod, not trusting myself to speak. 'But why would he change his name?' Rose's voice is a creak, as the pressure from outside starts to buckle the strong, steel walls.

'At least this means he's alive, Rose,' I furiously try to turn the rusty screws back in. 'He's alive and we can find him. We can find out why or what's happened to him.' I turn the screwdriver firmly and for a moment it holds, and our balance is restored.

'But what if he didn't want us, Mum?' she asks, as water starts to trickle around the rusty screws, turning it murky and unclear.

'Then we don't want him,' Flynn answers as we get up, give back the dove with our thanks and leave the shop.

Outside, it's started to rain. The leaden clouds burst and ricochet gun-metal grey raindrops across the defenceless shop windows. The droplets linger lethargically on our hoods as we hurry across the square and tumble into The Little Shop of Everything. We wipe our feet on the thick coir rug as incense-rich fumes fill our lungs. Pulling back our hoods, without speaking, we start to wander around the shop. It is a four-course, seam-bursting collection of colours and textures. A meal that you feast on, dip your fingers into as your primal urges take over society's niceties. We pick up items, devour their offerings – sometimes with a grimace and sometimes feeling puzzled – as we try to decipher their exotic origins before returning them to the overfilled shelves. As I head towards the back of the shop, there are delicate mirrors with sharp edges – a palate cleanser – before I sink my teeth into the luxurious artwork that drips from the walls and hangs from the ceiling. I savour the sunset landscapes, the bridges from long-lost times, before devouring the strong strokes and strange textures of the more modern pieces.

'Mum?' I turn towards where Flynn and Rose are standing, amongst swirls of soft pink material, iced with ribbons and sloping fonts that are edged by white baskets: an assortment of soft furnishings and haberdashery ready to be picked. To the right of them is a nook filled with sculptures. Sculptures I've never seen before, yet they are as familiar to me as pain is to joy.

The emotions I feel are hard to define. I clutch at relief as I pick up one of his more abstract pieces, a woman and child entwined within the branches of a tree, but relief slips through my fingers and I find anger easier to hold. I replace the tree sculpture and grab another, each with the same signature hidden somewhere within. This time it's a surrealist dagger that droops into a peach, almost as if the metal of the dagger is soft. When was this made? I wonder. Before Flynn started getting into fights, perhaps? Maybe it was as I was lying outside my house unconscious or in hospital? I pick up another, more classical piece of a man and woman together under an umbrella. Did he make this while Rose was being humiliated at her parents' evening or possibly when I had to sell my grandmother's tea-set to pay for Flynn's laptop? Resentment fills me as I look at the prices attached to the pieces before me.

Rose puts her hand on my arm and I look into her concerned eyes.

'I, I don't know this one?' Flynn says.

She looks at him and shrugs as realisation dawns on me that I'm singing Natalie Imbruglia's 'Torn' and that I am currently explaining how I knew a man who was kind and distinguished, that he showed me how to cry. I pick up a sculpture of two children facing away from each other but remaining entwined and I continue to sing. I shake the sculpture and gaze at my children, pleading with them and telling them that I've got no faith left, that I can't change how I feel – which is, apparently, stripped and frozen. As I start to take my clothes off – to emphasise that I feel bare – I fear I'm slipping on to very icy ground. As the lyrics come thick and fast, I feel like I'm slipping and sliding across a frozen pond; the raging creak tearing apart my platform. Rose grabs my handbag, which I have slid from my shoulder, and starts rummaging through it. Flynn takes the sculpture from me and tries to hold my wrists still; I warble something about 'delusion never fails' as I try to raise my arms and explain that the 'worthless sky is born'. Rose tells me – her voice an echo, like a backing singer – to open my mouth and I do. Just as I'm about to undo my jeans and fall into the deep, freezing chasm, I tell her that she's too late because I'm already, and as I open my mouth to sing the title again, she shoots Rescue Remedy into my mouth and my ode to the Australian beauty comes to an abrupt end as I start spluttering and coughing. A rescue and a remedy indeed.

I sit nursing my banging headache and swigging down the two paracetamol that Rose found in the bottom of my bag, willing myself to be calm. I'm sitting at the back of the shop on a wooden tree stump, my bottom hiding the cubist design painted on top.

'Just take deep breaths, Mum.' Rose is rubbing my back.

'Sorry . . . thank goodness you stopped me. I couldn't control it, I really was going to strip off all of my clothes and lie on the floor.'

'Let's . . . just not think about it,' Flynn says with a shudder.

'Quite. My underwear doesn't match and has seen better days if I'm honest.'

Flynn holds his hand up, making it clear that he would rather not know the state of my underwear.

'We need to speak to the shop owner,' I say quietly. 'I have to know why he did it.'

'I'll do it.' Flynn stretches. 'You two just stand with me, I'll look more amenable and less like a hired thug with you standing next to me.'

'You don't look like a hired thug!' I exclaim.

'Whatever,' he replies. 'Ready?'

We head over to where a mid-twenties, violently violet-haired woman is standing, wearing a pinafore denim dress with a sky-blue knitted cardigan over the top.

'Hey,' Flynn greets, as seems to be the salutation of choice among teenagers lately. 'So, we're really interested in the sculptures that you have over there,' he gestures with his elbow.

'Oh right, which one?'

'Oh, um, well . . . actually, we're interested in the artist?'

'Right, can I ask why? I mean,' she tucks her split-ended, shoulder-length hair behind her ears. 'His work is amazing, why is it that you want to know the artist rather than just buying his work?'

'Um, because, well,' he throws up his hands in exasperation, 'look, we think it's our dad. He's been missing for, like, ever and he used to do sculptures just like those.'

'O-K . . .' She glances over Flynn's shoulder at me.

'Are you his mum?'

'No, no, I'm not that old. I've been having a few hectic weeks and I've not had a chance to do my roots,' I apologise. Blimey, get a few grey hairs and suddenly you look two decades older.

She chews the inside of her mouth and Flynn looks over his shoulder at me with a look of bewilderment and shakes his head.

'She means Flynn, Mum, not the artist. Jesus.' Rose sighs.

'Oh, yes, yes, I am.'

'OK then. The guy's name is Tom P. Simmonds. I do have an address but, well, I need to keep the man on side if you know what I mean. I don't want to,' she holds up her hands and waves them, 'get in between any domestic dramas, but I can pass on your details if you want?'

'Oh, um, yes, please. I'll write down my mobile number and if you can tell him . . .' She slides a notepad and blue biro across the counter. 'Oh, thanks. If you could tell him that . . .'

Tell him what? I think over the prayers that I've spoken, the words that I wished I'd been able to say to him, like how proud he would be when Rose first wrote her name in joined-up handwriting. About the way that Flynn would just mow the lawn without me having to moan and bribe him like so many of his peers. About the way Rose and I sit in exactly the same position on the sofa, legs crossed, identically feet-tapping to the theme tune of whatever Saturday night television has to offer. About the way that we still have pizza and cheesecake on a Friday night just like we did when he was still alive. About the way that I'd wake up in the night and pretend he was there after I had my accident. How I would cry into his blue fleece and ask for his help, beg him for a sign to let me know that everything would be OK. I can't tell him how proud he would be of our kids; can't tell him how, for the last eleven years, I have lived with only half of myself intact.

'If you could tell him that . . . that . . . I would really like him to get in touch and that my name is Melody.'

I turn the key to the bed and breakfast bedroom door and we all blunder into the cramped room. I fill the plastic white kettle from the tap in the bathroom and flick it on. Rummaging through the paper-cased tea bags and sachets of sugar and coffee, I decide on some decaff before slumping on to the bed.

'Shane says hi.'

'What?' I sit upright, looking about as if I'm expecting him to throw back the duvet and shout 'Surprise!'

'Shane . . . he's just texted? He says to say hi.'

'Oh.' I quickly smooth my hair and pull my shoulders back, tilt my head to the side and smile. 'Tell him hi back.'

'He can't see you, Mum,' Flynn smirks.

'I know!'

I throw the pillow at him which he deftly ducks away from, then puts on a 'female' voice, flutters his eyelashes and repeats, 'Tell him hi back.' Rose makes puking noises as Flynn's fingers blur in a flurry of text messaging and Wi-Fi accessing.

'Is he, er, what is he texting for?' I ask nonchalantly.

'He's just checking in and asking if I'm, you know, all right about going back to school next week.'

'Oh.'

His phone pings and I try not to make it obvious that I want to know if it's another message from Shane. Get a grip, I tell myself as the kettle gurgles at boiling point. I pull myself off the bed and try to ignore it when Flynn snorts at whatever message he's just received.

'No way!'

'Hmmm?' is my casual reply.

'He's on a course about half an hour away from here.'

'Small world.' I give stirring my coffee the full attention it deserves. A good cup of coffee is quite an art form.

'Yes. At last, decent signal.'

'You had signal in town.'

'Yes, but I used up the last of my data on that Prince clip.'

'Oh. Well, you shouldn't use it up so quickly.'

'Do you know how quickly five hundred megabytes goes? I have the worst phone package ever.' He throws himself down on his bed, plugs in his headphones and disappears from social interaction.

'Mum?'

'Ouch!' I curse as I take a sip of my too hot coffee, then look up at Rose's pale, worried face and melting ice-blue eyes.

'Rose, what's the matter?' I put the cup down and hurry to where she is leaning against the bathroom door. She's holding her iPad tightly and I can feel her thin body shaking as I rub her arms.

'I've found him . . . he's got a Facebook page.'

'Who's got a Facebook page?' Flynn pulls out his earplugs and looks over.

'Dad, I mean Tom P. Simmonds.'

'He's on Facebook?' I can't quite keep the hysterical sound of my voice under control. 'FACEBOOK?!' Tears have started running down Rose's face and the muscles in Flynn's jaw are flexing as I take the tablet from her shaking hands.

He's. On. Facebook.

I look at the website of Tom Simmonds' sculptures and click on the 'photos by page' icon. I trawl through the pictures of sculptures and museum displays until there, in 800-pixel clarity, is Dev. Older. With very short, almost shaved hair, but unmistakably him. I swallow the bile and betrayal down. I swipe the screen with furious movements as photo after photo of his work blurs past me; faster and faster the photos travel, high-definition colour punctuated with soft black-and-white sketches, one by one a comic strip of his life since he left us, before my wide-open watering eyes, until I'm hit; winded. A-ha start to 'Take On Me' as I drink in the screen. A woman, younger than me, smiles up at him. His arm casually drapes over her small shoulders. Everything about her screams gym and manicure. This is a well-maintained woman. Eyebrows perfectly plucked; flawless, subtle make-up and deliberately dishevelled blonde ringlets . . . While I'm not knowing what I should say but saying it anyway, I drop the tablet on to the bed, and start pointing to Flynn and Rose with every backing singer repeat of the title. Rose is winding her hair bobble around and around her fingers, looking down at the quilt as I sing that we'll be leaving in a day or so anyway. At length, and after I explain that they should be safe in the knowledge that I'll be OK, I finish with the advice – and a shrug of my shoulders – that I was right to come here; it's better to be safe than sorry. Rose folds herself on to the duvet and Flynn leans against her, my dependants depending on each other.

'Let's just go home, Mum,' Flynn says with quiet determination. Rose looks up at him, her small upturned nose red with emotion, and gives him a slow, slight nod.

'OK . . . let's go home,' I agree.

II

Rose

OK, so, I know I've not written anything for, like, ages, but I've not really felt like writing anything. What's the point of writing things down if there is nothing worth writing about? I had to see this educational psychologist the other day who just kept saying 'and how did that make you feel?' I mean, as if I'm going to tell a complete stranger anything about my life, especially one who looks about eighty and doesn't even wear deodorant. How come Flynn gets to have Shane and I get to have Mrs bloody Doubtfire? I see Flynn around school a lot more. He seems to be doing OK, at least he hasn't been in any fights lately. As far as I can see, he seems to be spending most of his time doing extra art in the demountable, rather than having to sit through double French like the rest of us. Miss Knowles, the teaching assistant, is the only one worth talking to at school. At least she doesn't treat me any differently from before. Even Megan is being weird around me. She keeps making excuses when I ask her if she wants to do stuff like go to KFC after school. We used to do it every Tuesday and then go and hang out at the park behind the old community centre, but now she just gives lame excuses, which is fine, I guess. I mean, I can see why she wouldn't want to when everyone else is giving me the cold shoulder.

It's like they've all taken it really personally, like I broke into their houses and robbed their most precious belongings. It was only a couple of quid – tops – and I ended up giving it straight to the charity once I was busted anyway. I had it all planned out, I was going to sell the story to one of those magazines with all of the naff stories and crossword competitions in, or a newspaper, you know, like a long-lost family thing? Anyway, none of that matters now. Now that I know that he left us. Who would want to read about that? It's not like it's unusual for a husband to do a runner, you only have to watch Jeremy Kyle to see that it's nothing special. Lisa says the girls in my year are not worth my time, she says what I did is no big deal. She's in Year 10. I met her when I was waiting outside Mr Greene's office. She asked me if I'd really pocketed all of the money from the break-time stalls and when I said yes, she just said 'cool'. I don't like her friends all that much, I think they try too hard to be different. They all have the same drawn-on eyebrows, red lipstick and jet-black hair, but Lisa is different without trying to be. She's quiet, which suits me, because I don't feel like talking much anyway, but when she does talk she says really clever things that make you think about how crap the world really is. I've got the gifted and talented thing coming up, part of me just wants to mess it up on purpose but I know I won't. I'm weak like that – Flynn says it's just my way – being the good one. He takes the piss out of me saying stuff, like, even when I'm breaking the rules I'm still trying to be an over-achiever. Lisa asks about him quite a lot; it's nice that she takes an interest in our loser family. He doesn't like me hanging around with them, though. He calls them The Death Squad, which is ironic because he looks like their older brother.

Sometimes it feels like I have no control over my life now. Three months ago – before the trip – I had a purpose, you know? Finding Dad had always been something that I knew I could do, that I would achieve, but now I feel like I've just ruined things for everyone. Flynn says it's no big deal, and to be honest, it really doesn't look like he's that bothered, but Mum? God, what I have done to Mum? The night songs are getting weirder and more chaotic . . . she went for a week singing Kodaline's 'Pray', which totally sucked because I really liked that song AND she's taken to humming the tune as well as singing the lyrics, but what's worse lately is I can tell she's crying at the same time because her voice will break in places. There are a lot of songs I don't know but they all seem so sad or angry. Flynn sleeps through them most of the time now. He's got this app on his phone that plays background noise; this week it's been the sound of the beach which is really calming until Mum starts. Some days I go into school and feel like I'm walking in a fog and I feel sick a lot too. I just wish I could sleep. The only time I feel alive is when I close the door to the bathroom, run the tap and watch the dark, red drips swirl down the sink – and I think of the lucky parts of me that get to escape.

12

Melody

I wipe the tropical-fresh steam from my face and place the iron back on to its metal plate. I lift the silk blouse, which probably cost as much as my entire wardrobe, and hope against hope that I don't imprint a black triangular-scorched brand on to its perfect skin. It slides itself into position with a whisper and goads me with a pearlescent wink. I pick up the sleek, top-of-the-range iron and wonder when they started looking like vehicles destined for an aerospace hangar rather than the catalogue section for domestic appliances. When did they become such a masculine design? Sleek, sharp, calculated. What happened to the fundamental designs that breathed the essence of home and hearth? The metal pans filled with hot coals that would be simultaneously baking your bread or heating your water? In India they burn coconut shells instead of coal – according to *QI* – as they have so many power cuts. I spray the silk and enjoy the hiss of the iron, putting the smug smoothness in its place with a gust of the tropics; clearing the debris of driftwood folds and waved creases to leave a blanket of lustrous pink-white sand.

'Hi there! Jesus. Fucking. Christ, it's hot.' Her soft Welsh accent slices through her Chanel ruby-red lipstick. Joanna – my employer of sorts – flies into the kitchen in a burst of expensive perfume, cigarette smoke and stress. She flicks back her shoulder-length chestnut hair, dumps her Waitrose bags on to the table and rummages in her Mulberry handbag for a packet of Marlboro Lights whilst slipping off her winter white jacket and kicking her Jimmy Choos from her pedicured feet.

'Shit, is that the time?' she asks through gritted, perfectly polished teeth which are clamped around the butt of the cigarette. I look up at the Laura Ashley vintage white clock and nod from behind my Caribbean fog; the doorbell rings as I slip the blouse on to a padded coat hanger.

'For fuck's sake, they're here already. Could you be a star and grab me a couple of bottles of fizz from the fridge and replace them with those?' She nods at the Waitrose bags as the doorbell rings again impatiently. 'Smile,' she grins maniacally before stubbing out her cigarette into the sparkling glass ashtray and disappearing into the glass-tiled hallway – into which my lounge would fit twice over. Opening the fridge, I try to ignore the shrieks from the doorway of how fabulous they are all looking and how they simply must get the new designer name that I've never heard of, from the 'whatever' range. Standing on my tiptoes, I take out the bottles of 'fizz' and replace them with the three bottles from the shopping bag as requested. I put two on the kitchen side and return to the fridge, trying not to whimper with envy at the smoked salmon and specialist cheeses that jab my impoverished stomach with affluent jeers as I slam the heavy, giant American fridge door in their faces. Joanna strolls back in, her harassed gait of a few minutes ago now replaced with an authoritative glide. She arranges the bottles on to a tray with a small glass vase holding a white dwarf orchid, crystal champagne flutes and a cut-crystal bowl filled with raspberries.

She rolls her eyes at me as if this is the worst possible way to spend an afternoon and disappears into the gleaming, gilded lounge and into a world behind closed doors that I will never be a part of. Joanna, from what snippets of conversation I've had with her, is an only child from a small village in mid-Wales. She moved up here after she went to Keele University and moved to Shropshire when she moved in with her boyfriend, who is soon to be her ex-husband. She does something to do with the council or town planning, can't have children and seems to spend her life rushing from one event to another. I look around at the beautiful kitchen with its white-gloss smile and wonder . . . would I swap my life for hers?

I ease the Donna Karan black trousers on to the board. Life without my kids. Life without song. Life with money but no time. I spray the trousers, turn up the heat on the iron and roll those thoughts around my head. Life without my kids . . . life without the constant guilt that goes with motherhood. I'm feeding them too much junk food; I'm not feeding them enough junk food. Takeaway pizzas cost too much; I don't care if Tyler has them whenever he wants. I'm too busy to do things with them; I'm doing too much with them, do they feel smothered? I don't give them enough freedom; I give them too much freedom, should I be checking their phones? Should I even be thinking about checking their phones? What kind of mother would invade someone's privacy like that? What kind of mother wouldn't? I prod the thought of life without kids as you pick a scab. You know it's a horrid thing to do, but you can't help having a little peek underneath.

Life without song . . . now that I would change in a heartbeat. This thought is so solid, so permanent that I'm momentarily shocked when I feel it wobble. The idea of not having the, well, the high that it gives me; would I want to live without it? That feeling that I can scratch the itch as it drives through my body. The sounds and vibrations within, as a song takes hold . . . sometimes there is such beauty and joy when I get there that – I shake my head and swap the trouser legs over – well, I'm not sure I'd want to give it up, even with the embarrassment, the headaches and exhaustion that go with it. Christ, I sound like an addict.

Life with money? That's easy. Of course, I want life with money. Not money in its tangible form – although being able to walk into a shop and hand over a card that I know has a mountain of credit behind it would be appealing to say the least – I mean money in the abstract. The daily energy that not having it takes up: the constant looking for the best deals; checking the specifications of cheaper brands; the constant prioritising of bills and the Christmas shopping that has to start in September to be able to buy things cheap from eBay because they take a month to arrive from China. I pull off the trousers and feed them through the hanger, ignoring the bitter voice within that says the cost of these trousers could probably pay for Rose's Christmas presents this year.

I correct myself, ashamed, and remind myself that she gave me this job without questioning my 'condition', even though she had seen it in full swing, literally, as I had been 'doing it my way' when I'd got to the end of the queue to pay for the meal deal at Marks & Spencer. I remember how she had watched me with a frank, open expression and given another shopper a look of disdain when she had started to film me, not very surreptitiously. The following week I had bumped into her when I had just dropped some of the change from the parking ticket booth. I'd said thanks as she picked up some of the change for me and when I replied to her without a big band playing in my head she seemed surprised that I was, well, normal. We ended up walking together towards the same car park. As it happened, I was in a rush to pick up Rose from after school science club, so my step fell naturally in line with hers, as she was also in a hurry. She asked me if I worked up in the town centre and I explained that as I had my 'condition' it was hard to find employers, especially since I'd had hardly any experience either. Apart from a few part-time waitressing jobs, my adult life has been taken up with supporting Dev's business and being a stay-at-home mum. She asked me a little about my condition, I explained, and she offered me a job ironing for her twice a week. Sometimes she asks me to do other bits and bobs about the house but it's never in a condescending way; it's almost as if she feels cheeky asking me to, as if by not doing it herself she's showing weakness.

As the designer-labelled occupants of the wicker ironing basket diminish, the giggles and appalled gasps from the lounge increase until, as I'm finally wrapping the cord around the base of the iron and collapsing the board, they all disappear in a haze of air kisses and good wishes. Joanna turns to me, the calm façade disappearing once more to leave a slightly blurred but relieved expression.

'Do you know, I think I might have a bath?' She stretches the stretch of someone who fits in a trip to the gym at six in the morning before grabbing a skinny latte from Starbucks and power-walking to her office while most of us are still, with bleary eyes, making packed lunches.

She gives a little nod as if granting herself permission and softly treads up the oatmeal-coloured stairs. I put the ironing board and water softener away and head upstairs with the clothes to put away in her 'work' wardrobe. She has an entire room of wall-to-wall wardrobes, each with a different purpose. Work, formal, casual and one just for lingerie. Smelling a sweet, subtle fragrance, I plod up the stairs and into the wardrobe room just as I hear her phone ring. Even from here I can hear her sigh.

'Hi Dad, I—' I close the door to give her some privacy

and continue putting away the clothes in colour co-ordinated, hanger-facing-the-same-way precision. The door swings open and she stands there ashen-faced.

'Joanna? What's wrong?'

'My mum, she's had, she's . . .' I grab her hand and lead her to the day bed by the Roman-blinded window. 'She's. Fuck, I need a cigarette.' She covers her mouth. 'She's had a heart attack.' Her eyes filling, she continues, 'She's OK. I mean. Fuck. Not OK but, not dead. She's in intensive care. I've got to go. I need to pack.' She stands up and starts pulling out clothes from all the wardrobes. I take hold of her hands and keep her still.

'Go and have a cigarette. I'll pack.'

'No, I can do it, I just need—' I take the item from her hands, which is a toe-length blue evening dress with diamanté beading around the neckline, and hold it up to her. She blinks twice then gives me a small smile.

'I don't think that this is in "this year's must haves" for the hospital ward, is it?' She shakes her head, gives me a quick hug and runs down the stairs where she bangs her way through the kitchen drawers trying to find her lighter.

'Drawer by the dishwasher!' I call down to her. By her clenched-teeth reply of thanks I gather she has found it.

Half an hour later I have packed her bags, made her drink several glasses of water, booked her a train ticket and ordered a taxi to the station. Joanna, on the other hand, has been on the phone desperately rearranging appointments and deliveries, and using manic hand gestures to explain the urgency of her predicament.

The taxi beeps from outside as she slams down the phone, asking the receiver how someone so incompetent can be personal assistant to a solicitor who charges such an astronomical fee for an hour's work.

'The taxi is here.'

'But I've . . .' She flaps her hands about. 'Shit! I forgot the blueprint delivery!' She grabs my hands. 'I need to be here when they arrive. It needs my signature, they can't be passed to anyone else.'

'Well, it will have to wait.'

'Be me!' She shakes me by the shoulders.

'What?'

'Please?' She looks over her shoulder at the front door where an impatient driver is parping his horn.

'Look . . .' She rummages in her bag and scribbles her signature on to a piece of paper as thick as my duvet. 'Just answer the door.' She looks at my Primark jeans and bleach-stained black T-shirt with a barely contained grimace. 'Help yourself to my wardrobe, and just fake my signature.'

'Wouldn't that be fraud?'

'Well yes, but not really . . . You're not going to do anything with them except give them to me, so nobody will know. I wouldn't ask, but—' The taxi revs its engine from behind the door. She strides across the glass tiles, flings open the door and puts up her index finger at the driver, commanding him to wait. 'Look,' she shrugs on her paper-thin white jacket and picks up her Ted Baker luggage. 'It's not due until five, so you've got a couple of hours. Oh! Have my bath! They're Jo Malone bubbles!'

And with that, she is gone.

I stand in the vast, gleaming hall for a moment before slowly fingering the white lilies that are housed in an immaculate cut-glass vase. I head towards the kitchen where my phone is buzzing and I smile when I look at the message telling me to help myself to the rest of the fizz and anything from the fridge. Looking at the clock, I realise that I've got about three hours until the package arrives, so I take the opportunity to enjoy my peaceful, immaculate surroundings. Opening the door into the lounge, I feel like an intruder as

I run my hands along the plush fabric of the latte-coloured sofa and soft white throw. I sit down on the edge and look at the fifty-five-inch TV screen on the wall above the mounted fireplace that flickers orange over perfect white stones. No cumbersome TV stand and chaos of empty DVD cases. On top of the smear-free glass coffee table is the remnants of the afternoon picnic. I lean forward to examine a glossy, charcoal-grey wine cooler, pull out the bottle which is still ice-cold and grin as I realise that it is almost full. Feeling like a naughty schoolgirl, I grasp one of the glass flutes, fill it and lean back against the sofa as the sip of cool, effervescent liquid runs down my throat.

Once I'm on my second glass, I start to relax into my position of imposter for the day. Feeling like Melanie Griffiths in *Working Girl*, I head up the stairs with my glass in one hand and slide my fingers through the contents of the formal wardrobe. I notice a docking station on the chest of drawers next to the door and press play on the iPod. Adele fills the room and as she chases pavements, I pull out a dusky-salmon silk dress. The back is open and edged with an almost invisible fur trim. I hold it up against me and pop the hanger over my head. Watching my reflection, I stand on tiptoes and scoop my hair up into a one-handed chignon. I give myself a lopsided smile, thinking how much easier it is to look stunning when you have a wardrobe full of stunning clothes. I pull the hanger back over my head, drop my hair back into its lacklustre bob and replace the dress. Swigging the remains of the glass, I wander into the deliciously scented bathroom before sitting on the edge of the free-standing Victorian clawed bath. I swish my fingers into the water, turn the hot tap and then nip downstairs for a refill. There is a moment where I question whether it's a good idea to have another but dismiss it quickly when I look around my surroundings. How often am I going to have the chance to enjoy a liquid lunch in a situation as uncluttered by life's chaos as the house is uncluttered with junk?

Moments later, I'm submerging myself into soft, fragranced foam. A groan of pleasure escapes my lips as I lean back and sink deeper into the water. Above me is a small, tasteful glass chandelier, no cobwebs in sight, no grout that could do with the bleach and toothbrush treatment, just clean white lines everywhere I look. While Adele is setting fire to the rain, I let the past few months slowly come to the forefront of my mind. The hurt is still as raw as it was the day we discovered that Dev was still alive. I have forced all the questions that have been building up to the back of my mind, locked them in a safe within a concrete block. As Adele's fingers are staying strong, I open the heavy door of the concrete cell as a shard of light slides across the grey wall and, with a hammering heart, descend the dreary steps. Systematically, I unbolt the heavy bolts with a clunk as one by one they release the pressure on the hinges. As Adele hits her chorus and flames are descending from the sky, I turn the dial two clicks to the right, three to the left, before spinning the handle open. I take another sip of my wine and let the tears fill my eyes as I walk into the safe and let myself look at the Facebook pictures, the pain on Rose's face when she realised that her father wasn't the mythical creature she had built him up to be. Wasn't the hero coming to save us but was just a coward. While Adele talks about there being a side to someone that you might not know and a game that you may not ever win, I close my eyes and see the look of contempt on Flynn's face, the hatred that was bubbling just below the surface as he looked at the screen with Dev's smiling face and success beaming from within the thousands of tiny pixels on the screen.

As she's igniting the rain, through the sparks falling down, I remember the last time that I saw Dev, alive as it were. I had fallen asleep on the sofa. He had shaken me gently, stroked my hair from my eyes and then carried me to bed, as I tried to stay in that elusive place between wakefulness and sleep. I feel his feather-light kiss on my forehead and the soft click of the bedroom door as sleep claimed me. As the orchestra reaches its climax with desolate notes encouraging an inferno, sparks fall from the safe's roof as I walk through the memories before slamming the door, resetting the lock, climbing the concrete steps. I pause for a moment before closing the heavy door behind me. The playlist finishes and I close my eyes and then let myself slide beneath the bubbles, the sound of water rushing into my ears, filling me with liquid harmony. I hold my breath for as long as I can before I break the surface of the water with a slosh of bubbles. My face is a snowy drift and I frantically tap my hands around the edge of the bath trying to find a towel, but before I can clear my face from its covering of white slush I'm met with a shriek.

'Ahhhhhhhhhhhhhhh!' A male voice announces his presence in the bathroom.

'Ahhhhhhhhhhhhhhh!' is my reply as I try simultaneously to clear my face of bubbles and submerge my assets beneath the foam. Panicking, I grab the nearest weapon I can find in my blinded condition, which is a heavy granite soap dish, and throw it in the direction of the voice.

'Ahhhhhhhhhhhhhhhh!' is his reply as I hear a thud of contact. I open my eyes, their blurred vision clearing to show a familiar figure in the doorway who is rubbing his shin.

'Ahhhhhhhhhhhhhhhhhhhhh-gaaaaaaaaaaahhh- do! Do! Do!' He looks up as I shove a pineapple and rattle a tree. With the correct hand actions, I continue to shove a pineapple and grin coffee. Now this wouldn't be so bad, let's face it, we've all joined in with Black Lace now and then, the odd Christmas party or wedding reception. Come on, admit it,

you've joined in with grinding a bit of coffee in your time
. . . I bet you've even mimicked the actions to Superman and
brushed your hair before spraying your armpits. No, there is
no shame in joining in with a bit of novelty pop when the
occasion calls for it, but in my current predicament there is
indeed great shame, as I'm now making coffee whilst standing
up in all of my stretch-marked, thirty-something glory.

Shane grabs a towel from the heated rack and throws it
at me with wide open, surprised eyes but alas, he throws it to
the right whereas I shimmy to the left; he throws another
but I slide to the right. I climb out of the bath, the two
sodden towels sinking into the Jo Malone tepid water. By
the time I'm jumping up and down and crossing my hands
on my knees, I think it's safe to say that Shane and I are far
more acquainted with each other than we were at the last
family support meeting.

'Sign here.' I stick my tongue out of the corner of my mouth
as I scribble Joanne's signature on to the black electronic
machine, inwardly thanking the Etch-a-Sketchyness of it; it
would never hold up as evidence in court. I close the door
with a sigh of relief, smooth down the black leggings from
the casual wardrobe and roll up the sleeves of the grey
checked shirt. Taking a deep breath, I follow the sounds
from the kitchen where Shane is busying himself opening
heavy soft-close drawers with familiarity. I watch him retrieve
an array of crackers from the correct cupboard and feel
uneasy as he opens another to pull out a cheese board without
hesitation or uncertainty.

'So,' I announce with an overly cheerful voice.

'Hi! I thought you might be hungry?' he asks with a blush
rising up his throat as he arranges grapes and a range of
cheeses on to the board and carries it to the breakfast bar.

'Oh, um, yes, I am.' He rushes back to the fridge and grabs

a bottle of Prosecco, waves it at me questioningly and I nod my consent. Again he goes to the right drawer, extracts a white tea towel (who in their right mind has white tea towels?!), covers the top of the bottle and opens it with a muted *pock.*

We sit down in awkward silence, disturbed only by the glug of the wine being poured and the ticking of the clock.

We both take a deep swig of our drinks before we burst out laughing.

'I'm so embarrassed,' I blurt out as I wipe the tears from my eyes. 'What must you have thought?'

'I didn't know what to do apart from throw you a towel and when you moved to the left and then—'

'To the right . . .' Again we start laughing. Now, with the proverbial elephant in the room gone, we start to tuck into the cheese, which is so ripe it could have walked itself across the kitchen.

'So . . . can I ask why you were in my bath?' he asks, as he slices a grape in half and puts it on top of a multigrain cracker piled with Stilton.

'Your bath?' I pause with a cracker halfway to my mouth.

'Technically, yes . . . until the divorce is final, that is.' I shove the dairy-laden snack into my mouth and chew thoughtfully as I process the information that Shane is Joanne's ex-husband-to-be.

'I'm Joanna's ironer slash mail interceptor,' I explain. 'She's asked me to sign for some blueprints.' My hand flies to my mouth as I realise that he would of course know her mum. I swallow hard. 'Her mum has been taken ill, I'm afraid.' He stops chewing and looks up at me. 'They, um, think it's a heart attack.'

'Shit.'

'Indeed.'

He rummages in his pocket and pulls out his mobile.

'Would you excuse me a min?' He gets up looking flustered, and drags his fingers through his hair as he furiously taps the screen. I continue to pile on the dairy – damn, this Roquefort is good – as I hear the deep tones of a one-way conversation. He comes back, smiles a tight smile at me and then drains his glass of Prosecco in one, gives a quiet burp behind his hand and refills it. He sits down, opens a jar of Kalamata olives, spears one with what looks like a specially designed fork made simply for the job of olive-retrieving and pops one into his mouth thoughtfully.

'How well do you know Jo?'

'Erm, well, not that well really. I know that she is kind enough to give me a job even when she knows about my . . . thing. She seems nice but busy. Very busy. ' He snorts.

'"Busy" was one of the only words we could use to communicate.' He takes another swig and looks up as if contemplating whether to continue our conversation. 'She's just so . . .' He sighs. 'Her mother is ill, seriously so, and still she is bothered about whether her blueprints have come? What kind of person does that?'

'Coping mechanism?'

'I'd like to think so, but from experience I doubt it.'

'You'd be surprised what you say and do to cope in a stressful situation.' Thoughtfully, we continue to help ourselves to the food.

'Flynn told me about your week when you took the kids out.' I take another sip. 'He did?' He nods. 'And?'

'And . . . I can't tell you what he said.'

'What?!' I flick the tea towel at him as he holds his hands up in defence.

'Student confidentiality!'

I roll my eyes. 'Well, what did you tell me that for then?'

He shrugs his shoulders, smiling. 'He's doing well, you know, his art is something else.' I feel the warm glow of parental pride. 'I like him a lot. In my job you work with some kids that, you know, no matter what you do to help, they're already on a path that no matter how hard you try, you won't be able to get them off.' He shakes his head. 'But your boy, he's special.'

'I know.' I jab at another olive. 'He's had a tough time.'

'You've had a tough time.' He gestures towards me with his glass.

'We all have.' I push away my plate slightly as Shane tops up my glass. I go to cover it, realising as I do that I'm a little bit tipsy.

'Oh go on, I'll feel rude if I carry on drinking on my own, and to be honest, I'm still a bit shaken up by the intruder in my bath.' He chews his bottom lip, which I find I can't tear my gaze from, and smiles lopsidedly. Slowly, I remove my hand.

'But only this one.' I glance up at the clock. 'Flynn will be home soon so I need to get back.' He shakes his head.

'Check your phone.'

'Pardon?'

'He's not home until after eight tonight. Open evening at school and he's been asked to stay in the art department.'

'Really?' I ask, pride and confusion in my voice. Sliding off the stool, I regain my balance a bit more slowly than I would have usually and wander into the hallway to retrieve my bag. True enough, there is a message from Flynn telling me he will be late and another from Rose reminding me that she's going to Lisa's house and won't be back until later.

Shane walks into the hall carrying the glasses and gestures to the lounge. I follow him with a foggy thought that I really should be making polite excuses and leaving the house, but I can't seem to find the inclination or the words to make it happen. He flicks on the television and chooses a radio station, then the screen turns blank and the soft tones of

Ella Fitzgerald fill the room. I lower myself on to the sofa and tuck my feet under my bottom. With ease, we start to talk about Flynn's art, about Mr Greene and how we can't stand him. I ask him about where he met Joanne and he tells me about how they met at university, about how ambitious she had always been but that whereas his ambition was always about the job and the kids he worked with, hers became the job and the expensive things in life. I told him about the accident. About Dev leaving and about how much in love we had been. And I told him about finding him.

'Why did you come home? I can't imagine how you must have felt seeing the photo of him being successful with somebody else on his arm, but,' he shakes his head and pours the last of the bottle into our glasses, 'I don't think I could have walked away without knowing why he did it.'

'Why he left us?'

He nodded and then relaxed back on to the sofa.

'I couldn't bear to put the kids through any more. Rose, she, well, she'd held on to this perfect image of him and . . .' I shook my head. 'What they have to put up with on a daily basis? With Flynn it's different, he can handle my thing, but Rose? Sometimes when it happens I see real embarrassment in her eyes. I just couldn't put them through any more. If they want to see him, it will be their choice. Right now, I need to protect them as best as I can and that meant just coming home and letting sleeping dogs lie, as it were.' I clamp my lips together before poking my tongue out of the corner of my mouth, wondering if I've said too much. Shane is leaning his head on his knuckles and looking at me with a weird expression. Somewhere between amused and upset.

'What?'

'I like the way you stick your tongue out when you concentrate.'

'Oh.' I feel unsure as to whether I should stick out my

tongue a bit more or keep it sealed within my mouth. I decide to make light of his comment and the effect it is having on me and stick my tongue out of the corner of my mouth in what I have intended to be a goofy yet cute way. It's not having quite the effect I'd hoped for as I realise that a large dribble of drool is slithering down my chin. He laughs at my mortification as I grab a tissue from my bag and wipe it away with a nervous laugh. Just then my phone rings, blasting out 'Don't Stop Me Now' – Flynn must have been messing with it again.

I smile apologetically as Shane waves his hand dismissively and, swiping the screen to accept the call, I answer whilst tucking my hair behind my ears and resuming my position on the sofa – just a fraction closer to Shane than I'd been sitting before.

'Hello?' A punch to my stomach winds me as I feel the blood drain from my face, putting all of its nourishment into keeping my heart beating and my lungs working. Shane leans forward and puts his glass down on to the table with a look of deep concern.

'Hello?' The voice repeats. 'Is this Melody? Melody King?'

'It is,' I whisper.

'Hi, my name is Tom? Tom Simmonds? Sorry for taking so long to call, I've been away . . .' And with that, I drop my phone and I watch as the world tips on to its side and I feel myself falling off the edge.

13

Melody

'Mum!' I move my aching head in the direction of Flynn's voice. He is shaking my shoulder. 'Mum?' I pull my thick tongue from the roof of my mouth; it snakes across the dunes of my lips like a sandstorm. I remember half-heartedly watching a documentary about a wind in the Sahara called the Sirocco which could last a couple of hours or weeks. Sandstorms so strong that they break machinery and penetrate buildings. I feel the storm serpent twist in my head, numbing grains grinding into my ears and throat, piling heavily in my chest.

'What? What's wrong?' I stretch my hand out and fumble with my fingers until I find the cord with the light switch attached and click the room into a soft forty-watt glow.

I sit up with squinted, make-up-smudged eyes and look at Flynn and Rose's worried faces. 'What time is it?' I ask, reaching for the glass of water that Rose is passing me.

'You've been screaming.' I gulp down the lukewarm water, dampening my dry mouth and the stinging at the back of my throat. My pyjamas are wet with sweat and the bed covers are on the floor. Flynn picks up the white duvet and folds it at the bottom of the bed.

'Screaming what?'

'Just screaming,' Flynn replies, sinking back down on to the mattress.

'What, without singing?' Rose scratches the back of her head, her maroon hoody nervously tugged over her hands, just like she used to do with her school jumper when she was a nervous three-year-old walking into nursery.

'Without singing, or saying, well, anything.' She tucks her hair behind her ears as I lower my eyes and trace the line of freckles across the bare shoulder that has slipped free of her jacket.

I shake my head dismissively.

'It must have just been a bad dream. I'm fine now.' I smile at their worried faces and feel uneasiness creep up my spine as they look at each other. Bitten cheeks answered with shrugged shoulders and purposeful, questioning eyebrows. 'What? What is it?'

'Mum, we kind of know,' Flynn starts.

'That is, we can tell when you're um—'

'Having a bad dream.' Flynn leans forward and picks up a bit of fluff from the bed. 'But this wasn't like the other times, Mum.' He looks up at me through his long, dark lashes. 'You were screaming in one tone for . . .'

'It doesn't matter how long, what matters is that it was different, Mum. It was one single note, screamed, just with pauses when you needed a breath.'

'How long?'

'About twenty minutes.'

'I mean how long have you known when I've been having nightmares?'

'Not long,' Flynn says with conviction, but his flared nostrils tell another story. He's always had a tell, ever since he was three when he tried to say that he hadn't eaten all of the chocolates out of the advent calendar, but I don't push for the truth. Not this time; they need to believe that I'm not being made to feel guilty.

'Do you think you should go back to the doctors? You never made it to the last scan—'

'What, why? We've been through this so many times. I had that CT scan after the accident, remember? They've said it's neurological and brought on by anxiety, so I just need to find another way to deal with it, that's all . . . and they always say the same thing, that my condition is—'

'Unique,' we all say in unison.

'Then what is it? What's changed?' Flynn asks, concern etched across his scarred young face. I look away from him at the clock on the wall, which hangs ever so slightly off balance, and tell them that nothing springs to mind. With an exaggerated yawn I stand, then usher them to bed mumbling about a dodgy quiche I ate at lunchtime.

Once the sounds of deep sleep penetrate the house, I pull on a thin grey cardigan to take away the 4 a.m. chill. Even though it's June, I don't ever seem to feel warm. Rummaging in my top drawer, I find a battered packet of cigarettes that has been there for an age and wonder – as I head downstairs – if cigarettes have a shelf life. I slide the key into the patio door and step into an old pair of black flip-flops. As I step outside, I breathe in the dewy grass, tilting my head to the night sky which has already thrown off its dark blanket and now stretches and unpeels, revealing blood orange. I sit on one of the cold steps leading down to the lawn, pull out a cigarette, strike a match and watch its red glow. I haven't smoked properly for years, but right now, I inhale deeply and enjoy its cancerous calm. I hug my knees as I blow out a plume of smoke towards the glistening blades of grass.

I replay my conversation with 'Tom' and take another deep drag.

'Hi, my name is Tom? Tom Simmonds?' I feel the same prickling all over my skin as I did when I recognised the softness to his voice. The same voice that had told me how loved I was, the same voice that had told me lengthy jokes with the punchline so hidden within the story that a bubble of laughter would escape me even on my lowest of days – the thought and effort behind it, purely to make me smile. The same voice that had told me Rose was a girl; which had excitedly told me Flynn had crawled and had tentatively asked me to marry him. 'Sorry for taking so long to call, I've been away . . .' I shiver as I look at the end of the cigarette, turning it to the left and right as if it holds some answers. I inhale again, enjoying simultaneously the light-headedness and skittish rush that is awakening my senses which have been numbed for the last week.

Shane had reached for the phone as I sat with my fist forced into my mouth. The blood roared in my ears as the lioness within me padded slowly in circles, feeling the threat of a predator but not knowing where or when it will strike. Above the low, primal growl inside, I could hear Shane talking, familiar words, a 'sorry, she's unable to take the call, if I could take a number?' then a 'mhmmm, mhmmm, nine-eight-six-seven, got it . . .' He had finished the call then leant forward to ask me if I was OK. I'd nodded, made my excuses and left, stalking through a forest of concrete. Danger and disruption resonating with every dog bark, every door slammed, until I finally got home, bolted the door and screamed into the silence.

I grind the cigarette butt out on the step and listen to the sounds of the awakening summer as I rub the heel of my hand into my eye, acknowledging as I do that I can't go on pretending that he doesn't exist; pretending that I can live without knowing what has happened to him; pretending that I can protect my children from the past. I close the patio door as quietly as I can, make a cup of coffee and with my heart hammering in my chest, open my laptop and search for everything I can on Tom Simmonds.

Later, as I'm buttering four rounds of toast and making

steaming mugs of tea for the kids – which I hope will help them through the day – I rehearse what I'm going to say when I ring him. He had my name but didn't seem to know me, and if he doesn't know me then what happened to him? It's clear from the short interviews that I could find that he's still fully absorbed in his sculptures, but apart from that one photo, I can't find any other evidence of his life since he left us. It's clear that he has a new home, but does he have a new wife? A new family? I throw the knife into the sink with more force than I intended as Flynn grumbles into the kitchen.

'Morning!' I greet, flinching at my own jovial voice which grates through the uneasy atmosphere. He raises a questioning eyebrow in my direction before grabbing the toast and slurping some tea out of the cup.

'Did you sleep?' he asks, his own voice weary and weighted.

'A little,' I lie. 'You?'

'A bit,' he answers, toast crumbs sprinkling on to his school shirt. He runs his fingers through his hair, clearing his face momentarily. 'Can you get me some charcoal from the shop in town?' He crunches on another piece of toast.

'Why? Are we having a barbecue?' I laugh at my own joke.

'Funny,' he replies. Rose appears at the doorway, her hair pulled into a messy bun and her tie slightly askew.

'What's funny?' she asks, as she looks down her pale nose suspiciously at the slightly burnt toast.

'Nothing,' we reply.

'Oh-kaaaayyy,' is her response as she bins the toast and picks up a somewhat bruised banana instead. 'Later,' she adds as she leaves the kitchen.

'Why are you going so early?' I shout.

'I'm meeting Lisa then we're going to the shop,' is her

muffled reply as I hear her dragging her shoes out of the cupboard under the stairs.

'Oh. Have a nice time!'

'Whatever,' I hear her mutter under her breath before the door slams. I raise my eyebrow at Flynn, who shrugs his shoulders.

'What is she like? Lisa?'

'Dunno, a bit of an emo. A bit, you know, anti-social.'

'Oh. Do you think I should invite her around for tea?' He snorts into his cup. 'What?'

'Rose isn't four, Mum. Do you really think she would want her new,' he inverts his fingers, '"cool" friend around here for nuggets and chips and a bowl of ice cream?' He stands shaking his head and plops his plate into the sink full of cool, murky water.

'I just thought I should get to know her; she seems to be a big part of Rose's life at the moment. What has happened to all her other friends?'

'I've got to go.' He glances up at the clock. 'I'm running late.'

I put my hands on my hips and raise my eyebrows at him. 'Flynn?'

'What?' He avoids eye contact as he picks up his blazer from the back of the chair. 'Seriously, I've got to go.'

'Flynn!' He stops at the doorway and turns around.

'What has happened to all her other friends?'

'They don't talk to her.'

'What?'

He scratches the back of his head and sighs. 'After what happened with the money . . . they all kind of avoid her.'

'Why didn't either of you say anything?'

'Do you need to ask?' he answers, with the exhaustion of someone well beyond his years. He shrugs on his blazer and leaves the room, slamming the front door behind him.

I stand there, the smells of every other schoolchildren-filled house on a Monday morning surrounding me, but the familiarity does nothing to ease the feeling of inadequacy. I start washing up and tidying the kitchen, noticing that Flynn has left his tie on the table. I try to ring him but there is no answer so I leave him a quick voicemail and then hang up as I feel the knot building inside, the millions of fibres meticulously collecting into a complexity of threads, each one twisting and wrapping its way through my insides. It intertwines and weaves its way through me, wrapping itself tighter and tighter until, with relief, I hear the waterfall of piano notes descend from The Boomtown Rats and I consider why 'I Don't Like Mondays'. As I start to sing about a microchip overloading and explain that there will be nobody at school on this day because they are going to wait at home, I notice that − almost without control − I'm walking up the stairs towards Rose's room. As I hold the handle to the door and explain my confusion that her father didn't understand things, he always thought she did well in school, I agree with Bob that I'm not a fan of Mondays either. The door creaks open and I tread carefully into her room. I'm embraced by the smells of hair products and fruity-smelling body spray. Her wooden floor is littered with various pieces of clothing and on her chest of drawers is an array of powders and foundation which she applies religiously before leaving the house − her determination to hide her freckles evident. I start to make her bed, lifting the mattress as I start shooting:

'OOOOOOH-hooooo-hooo-hooo-hooooo . . .' I stop as I conclude the sentence; the optimism of the day is in decline because my hands have brushed a small, hard object under the mattress. I turn the small notepad over in my hands. I can't see a reason for her hiding it other than to keep something hidden. Something private. I clap it twice against my palm in time to the music and my thoughts turn to my little girl. As I continue to hate Mondays, I turn the book over in my palms before opening it and seeing her beautiful looped handwriting staring back at me. I close it immediately and learn that today's lesson isn't going to be about dark thoughts but about trust. I replace the book, smooth down the duvet and – even if her father isn't here to understand her – I am. I walk out of the room with another:

'Hooooooo-oooooh-hooooo-hoooo-hoooo,' and go the. Whole. Way. Down . . . the stairs.

I sip my coffee and stare at the phone. The phone stares back. I pick it up off its cradle, grip it tightly and then replace it. The phone continues to stare at me. This is ridiculous. It's just Dev. Tom. Whoever. I feed the scrap of paper with his scrawled number through my fingers like those fuzzy snakes you used to get when you were a kid. A cloud passes over the sun and the phone's smile fades. I take another sip of coffee. I need to do this now, I need to ring him while 'I Don't Like Mondays' resonates through me, calming my need for release. Snatching the phone up, I punch the numbers in. It rings. I bite my bottom lip. It rings. I run my fingers through my hair. It rings. I fiddle with the cord.

'Yep?'

My heart batters against my ribcage and the phone shakes against my ear. I try to speak but only a squeak comes out. 'Hello?' he asks. I take a deep breath and feel myself calm.

'Um, hello, I'm Melody? Melody King?'

'Yes?' I fidget, feeling uncomfortable, both emotionally and physically. I'm sitting on the notepad I was writing on; I pull that and my mobile phone from under me.

'I'm returning your call? I, I love your work . . .' I stumble over the words, realising that he either doesn't know who I am or is keeping up an act, making it clear that he doesn't want to know me. He laughs. A soft chuckle. I swallow the confusion.

'Well, that's nice to hear, but—'

'Could I see some more of your work?' Again he laughs. 'I really am your biggest fan.'

'Well, that's certainly nice to hear, but—'

'I've always really wanted something like that for my, um, lounge.' I'm running out of things to say, I realise, but I don't want to end the call. Hearing his voice again after all this time . . . I used to replay his answerphone message over and over when I was looking for him, leaving him countless messages; did he listen to them? I wonder.

'Really? Is that all you wanted?' he asks with humour in his voice. I clearly sound like a complete idiot. I cover the mouthpiece, momentarily fighting back the tears. 'I've been looking for you for so long.'

'I don't think it's me that you've been looking for, but thanks for calling,' he laughs and I grimace inwardly. I didn't think he would have heard that and now he evidently thinks I'm a lunatic.

'Wait!'

'Was there something else you wanted to tell me?' he asks as if addressing a child.

Yes! I want to scream how much I love him. How I've only ever wanted him, how I love the way the light used to catch parts of his hair and it used to look like they were strands of copper, about how much I cared for him, so much that I thought my body would flow over with it. I want to ask him where he has been because right now I have no idea. But most of all, I want to ask him if he's lonely, or has he got someone else to love? Maybe I could start by telling him I love him? But instead, realising I've made a complete mess of this phone call, I just say:

'I just wanted to—' but I'm left with silence at the end of the phone, as it dawns on me that he's hung up.

I'm jolted awake by hammering on the front door. I can hear sirens blaring outside and intermittent flashes of blue awaken my senses and transport me into a blue-blinded panic. I scramble from the sofa, glancing at the clock, which smiles ten to two. I must have been asleep for a couple of hours, as evidenced by the slight crust around the right side of my chin which I wipe away with my sleeve. I momentarily freeze in the face of the unmistakable silhouettes of two police officers through the small, rectangular glass pane in the top of my wooden front door. My kids. The first thing that any mother would think of in this situation. Please let them be OK. The unsure feeling of whether or not to indulge myself in this short moment in time where I'm safe from whatever news I'm about to be told, or whether to run head first and with urgency into it, pauses my movement and I stand still. Frozen by the fear of what might be. I'm not sure if I've been standing here for five seconds or five minutes, but my decision is made for me when the door is, once again, pounded upon.

'Mrs King?' A man's deep voice booms through my door, breaking me out of my frozen state and drawing me towards the door.

'Mrs King?' a uniformed woman of about forty queries as I open the door.

'Yes?'

'May we come in?' It is then that I notice my next-door neighbour – Mandy – standing behind them, relief and concern etched across her face. I look at her questioningly but she just gives me a short smile and nods, as if her work here is done, then I watch her turn and walk away as I close the front door.

They walk into the lounge. Their solid statures and stiff, heavy uniforms feel alien amongst the soft teals and greys that comfort our ice-cream Sundays, watching box sets with tucked-under legs and sticky spoons.

'Tea?' I ask.

'No, thank you,' the man booms, 'we won't keep you. Are you here alone, Mrs King?'

'Yes. Oh, please sit.' I wave in the direction of the opposite sofa and gingerly sit on the edge of the arm.

'Mrs King, we were dispatched after a concerned neighbour called nine-nine-nine.'

'Mandy?' I smile.

'Mrs Dawson. Yes. She reported screaming coming from this address.'

'Right. Oh.' Relief fills me. This is about me, not my kids. This is about Me. Me. Me: the one who cannot even have an afternoon nap without causing concern. I shake my head as embarrassed tears fill my eyes and the lady officer is crouching down by my side.

'Have you been hurt, Mrs King?' I shake my head. 'Is there anyone else in the house?'

'No.' I take a deep breath. 'I have a condition, you see, that seems to be a side effect after I had a fall a couple of years ago. It manifests itself in many ways. The latest symptom seems to be uncontrollable screaming when I'm asleep.'

'Screaming?'

'Yes. Mostly it's singing.'

'Singing?' asks the man with more than a hint of scepticism.

'Yes. Look, I'm really sorry to have wasted police time, but I'm fine really. Just a bit mad.' I grin through my tears and watch their uncomfortable, doubting glances at each other.

'Well, if you think of anything that may be causing you distress and you need anything, don't hesitate to get in touch.' The lady officer squeezes my knee and I jabber on about the weather as I quickly shepherd them through my hall and close the door softly behind them. I run upstairs keeping my lips clamped together as tightly as I can, jab the plug into the sink, blast the water into it until it's almost full and then submerge my face in the cold water, bubbles exploding from my mouth and rising in aerated anger as I sing Radiohead's 'Creep', the water muting the sounds of my fury at the injustice the world has put on my shoulders. Spent, I stand with my fringe dripping over the sink as I watch the water swirl clockwise down the plughole.

'Towel?'

I sigh. Of course he would be here. Behind me. When once again I'm a far cry away from sanity. Feeling defeated, I turn to him with my hand outstretched as he passes me a black towel from the radiator.

'What are you doing here?' I ask as I wipe my face and the mascara from under my eyes.

'Flynn is downstairs. We've not had a great day.'

'Perfect.'

I watch the peppermint tea bag swirl in the glass cup as Flynn sits quietly while Shane fusses over the ice pack over his right hand.

'Better?' he asks. Flynn shrugs.

'So, what happened?' I ask as I blow over the surface of the cup.

'Some of the dicks in my class overheard me listening to your message. Thanks for that by the way.' I detect a note of sarcasm which I'm confused by. He flinches as he shifts the ice pack.

'No problem,' I say wearily as I take a sip of my tea, still with its bag floating around. 'So what's my message got to do with this?' I nod towards his hand.

'They started the usual stuff, called me a mummy's boy,' he shrugs, 'that sort of thing.'

'Well, that's not worth you getting into a fight over,' I say, exasperated.

'Well, when they start saying shit about you shagging your mum, it kind of is!'

'What?' I say, outraged. 'Because I tell you you've left your tie at home that means you want to— Never mind. What is wrong with these kids?' I turn to Shane who is looking at the floor.

'Not that one, the other one,' Flynn says under his breath.

'What other one?'

'The one when you called to ask if it was you I was looking for?'

'Eh?'

He lets out a frustrated sigh, flicks his hair back over his eye and shifts his bottom forward, pulling his phone from his pocket. He swipes his fingers across the phone and taps it a few times.

'Message received at, eleven, twenty-four, a.m.,' announces the upper-class robotic voice. For the next few minutes, the room is filled with my voice. I am giving an emotional rendition of Lionel Richie's 'Hello'. I feel sick as the realisation hits me that this is my phone call to 'Tom'; I must have accidentally rung Flynn when I pulled my mobile phone from under me. I strain my ears and can just about hear Tom's replies to my heartfelt declarations. There is no mention of my name or my enthusiasm about his work, just verse after verse of an eighties love song. That moment when I had wanted to tell him my feelings? When I wanted to know where he was and if he was alone? Well, it seems that I did that and more. I watch as the cup slips from my fingers and shatters on the wooden floor; the golden liquid oozes across the floor creating a map of opportunity, a thousand directions in which to travel. I watch as its freedom is contained at every turn by the sharp, sinister shards of glass and that no matter how hard it tries to escape, the glass is always there, directing its course until the soft golden liquid finally gives up, staying motionless with its own reflection trapped in the very thing that it was trying to escape.

14

Flynn

Ten reasons why I hate you:

1. Let's starts with the obvious one. You left us.
2. If you hadn't left us, maybe you would have scraped the car windows that morning or bought de-icer. That's a bloke thing to do, right? So Mum wouldn't have slipped.
3. If you hadn't left, it might have been you putting out the bins, so Mum wouldn't have slipped.
4. If Mum hadn't slipped then our lives wouldn't be the joke that they are right now. And I know they say it's neurological, but it all started after that fall.
5. If you hadn't left, then Mum would be happy.
6. If you hadn't left, Rose wouldn't have committed social suicide and ended up hanging around with a bunch of losers.
7. If you hadn't left, we wouldn't always be broke and I could have a decent frigging phone.
8. The car accident. Right, let's get this straight. I don't hate you for crashing the car. I'm not an idiot; I don't think it was anything but a stupid accident. I don't hate you for the state of my face, but I do hate you for the way you used to look at me. I was just a kid, Dad, and you looked at me like I was a monster.

9. I hate you because you're a coward. What kind of dick leaves his family, makes them look for him for years, makes them think he's dead, but sets up a Facebook page?

10. I hate you because instead of being out with my mates right now, I'm grounded and sat in my room with hardly any data, writing this stupid list.

15

Melody

The phone rings and I pick it up as the cable repair man closes the door behind him. It's Shane. I can't deny that I feel myself react to the soft way he pronounces his vowels, the way he holds out the last word in a sentence sometimes, ending the word with a click.

'Hi, it's Shane.'

'Hi.' I run my fingers through my hair and look at my reflection in the mirror by the door. I roll my eyes at myself and the way that a flush is rising in my cheeks.

'So, I was wondering how you were doing?'

'Good.'

'Good?'

I wonder how much I should tell him. I mean, he's been thrown into the secrets and troubles of my life, so maybe I should just dismiss his concern and return to our professional relationship – I'm the mother of the child he works with – and leave it at that. But as I hold on to the receiver, I'm yearning to talk to him, to confide and to have him as a friend if nothing more. I stick my tongue out of the side of my mouth and remember how he had said he liked it, then shake my head at my ridiculousness. 'Do you want to come over later?' I ask, biting the corner of my thumbnail. If he makes his excuses and declines then I'll know where I stand.

'Sure, what time?'

I panic. Evening would sound too much like a date; I decide to go for afternoon instead. Coffee and biscuits, not wine and dinner.

'Three-ish?'

'It's a date.'

I replace the receiver and wonder if that was just a turn of phrase.

'Flynn!' I shout up the stairs and hope that my voice will drown out the volume of his headphones.

'What?' he shouts back.

'Wi-Fi is fixed!' I reply.

'About time!' is his heartfelt thanks.

I walk into the kitchen, open the window and close it again quickly as a bumblebee bumbles against the window pane. I knew having a lavender bush so close to the kitchen window was a mistake, but Dev had had visions of lavender-scented breezes filling the home with furniture polish perfume. I open the kitchen door instead and welcome the breeze that flows through. Sitting on the step, I listen to the sounds of summer. An aeroplane burrs through the sky as an apologetic bird's call embellishes the distant buzz of bees, punctuated with the strong melody of a more ostentatious bird. I breathe in the summer air and think about my son upstairs who has hardly come out of his room since he sat his last exam. I'm relieved, to be honest; the sooner he is officially out of that school the better. His GCSEs have been sat and his college application has been accepted; his course – a BTEC in art and design – has been chosen. It took a lot of sway to get him in with his behavioural issues in school, but thanks to Shane and the high standard of his portfolio, they've given him a place. The thing is with Flynn, he knows that he shouldn't fight, but for him, it's always protective fighting. He doesn't instigate it, and I know I might sound to other people like I'm making excuses, which I suppose I am, but he's not a malicious boy. He just wants to protect himself, and us, I guess.

Wandering back inside, I flick the kettle on and then pull open my laptop, scraping it across the kitchen table. It hums into action as I spoon the coffee into the white chipped mug, add the hot water and glug in a splash of milk. I sit myself down, click on the Facebook icon and wait. I entertain myself with the notion that I'm just having a quick look at what my friends and family have been up to. I entertain myself with the pictures of happy smiling children on day trips to the sea and I smile when someone has been tagged with a photo that eradicates all of their own profile pictures, revealing a slightly chubbier, older version of the one they have depicted. What I don't entertain is the thought that I'm only on here because I want to see if 'Tom' has made any updates on his page. My hand hovers over the mouse pad as I click on the search button before quickly typing his name and waiting for his page to pop up. There is one new post. I click on the events icon and take a sip of my coffee . . . here it is, my chance to see him; he is having an exhibition. It's only small by the looks of it, in a seaside gallery on the coast of Cornwall. I lean back in my chair. This is it, after all of this time: I know where and when he is going to be; I have to see him. Feeling a sense of closure, I jot down the details, close the lid of my laptop and smile.

As the hour hand ticks towards three o'clock, I add some lipgloss and change my top for the third time. This one shows too much cleavage. I rub my lips together and tear off the blouse and replace it with a plain, pale-blue T-shirt. That will have to do. I don't want him to think I'm trying too hard anyway. I shouldn't be trying at all; my husband is still alive. My stomach flips when I think this. The torrent of emotions floods my mind, pushing everything else aside: a landslide, a huge chunk of my stable life detaching itself, pulling away, destroying other parts as it crashes its way down.

There is a knock at the door. I open it, we go into the kitchen, I pour coffee, I open biscuits and we slip into easy conversation. I've missed this, I've missed being able to talk to someone other than the kids; it feels right that I should tell him about the exhibition, about what I'm about to do.

'Why don't you just tell them the truth?' Shane asks as he reaches over and grabs another digestive then dunks it into his coffee.

'I don't want to get their hopes up. What if he doesn't want to see them?'

'What if he doesn't want to see you?'

'I've got to see him,' I say with finality. 'I can't keep screaming in my sleep, Shane, it's not fair on them. I can't stop thinking about him, about why he left, you know?'

The end of his digestive sinks beneath the liquid. He sighs and looks up at me. 'Don't you hate it when that happens?' he asks.

I shake my head and pass him a teaspoon, watching with amusement as he tries to fish out the – now sodden – biscuit. 'How's Joanna's mum? Have you heard?' I ask as he smiles, holding up the teaspoon with the limp, defeated piece of biscuit hanging over the edge. Sadly, the biscuit gives up, lets go of the ledge and plummets back into the cup with a splosh. Shane's shoulders sag.

'Not great. Jo's been staying at a hotel five minutes away from the hospital for the past two weeks.' He admits defeat and pushes the cup away.

'Poor thing, it's horrid that she's going through this and doesn't even have the comfort of her own bed.'

'Yeah, I'm sure she's struggling with the five-star hotel amenities.' I raise an eyebrow at him. 'Sorry. I know it's awful,

I don't mean to sound callous but,' he gives a wry smile and scratches his chin, 'even in these circumstances, she'll be surrounded by . . .' he waves his hands in the air in a circular motion, like a magician conjuring his powers before levitating an unsuspecting volunteer from the crowd, '. . . stuff.'

'Stuff?'

'Luxury.'

'Oh.'

'So,' he rubs off the crumbs from his fingers with three sharp strokes of his hands and changes the subject, 'when is it?'

'The week after next.'

'What will you tell them?'

'That I'm going to see an old friend.' He tilts his head and gives me a look that shows he disapproves. 'What? It's true. They can stay with my mum for the night.'

'I'm not sure they will like that.'

'What, staying with my mum?' He puts his chin on his hand and leans it on the table, staring at me intently. 'Well, what do you suggest I tell them? I can't take them with me!'

'Why?'

'Because!'

'Because what?'

'Because I can't protect them from what he might say.'

'And who's going to protect you?'

'I don't need protecting, I just need the truth.'

The phone rings, and with relief, I leave the table and speak to the hospital about my change in appointment.

The week flies by, and the train journey to the seaside town is calm and enjoyable. I dress carefully the morning of the exhibition; as I smooth down the black-and-white maxi-skirt, I look at my reflection and wonder what he will see. Turning my head, I once again spray the loose ballet bun of my newly coloured 'ombre' hair and twirl the loose strands that frame my face. I pull a stray hair from the shoulder of my black fitted T-shirt and gently finger the chunky gold necklace that Rose chose for me. Leaning forward towards the hotel mirror, I gently run my finger underneath my eye, smudging the smoky-grey eyeliner before applying another coat of lipgloss. Will I seem so much older than he remembered me? Is there anything left of the college girl that he fell in love with? I pop my black oversized sunglasses on top of my head, put the leaflet about the exhibition into my Cath Kidston-style bag and take one more nervous look at my reflection, before gently closing the door and heading towards the harbour.

The sun is high and the salt and vinegar air cools me with nostalgic seaside memories, and I'm reminded of day trips to Wales in the summer. Dev would always order diet lemonade when we were on holiday – never when we were anywhere else – he said it was because when he was younger, it was the only time he was allowed to have it, an old family tradition that he couldn't let go of, I suppose. His parents died in a car crash when he was seven, hit by a drunk driver while on their way to Scotland; it had been a last-minute surprise, he'd said, for their anniversary. Dev lived with his grandma after that until she died just after we first got together.

I find the gallery which doubles as a tourist trap, its windows displaying seascape watercolours. I look at my reflection amongst the cool blues and warm-orange sunsets, plucking up the courage to step into the scene rather than standing looking at the view. I take a long pull on my water bottle and then walk into the air-conditioned room. The smells of oil paints and canvas fill me with familiarity, even if the scenes do not. A willowy, greying lady with paint-splattered overalls sits behind the counter. Her watery eyes crinkle with her smile as I approach. The calls from hungry seagulls beckon from outside the door; they mingle with the chatter of an excited five-year-old's demands for ice cream, becoming part of the studio as much as the tranquil canvases that adorn the whitewashed walls.

'Can I help you? I'm Janet,' she smiles, putting her brush into murky blue water inside a jam jar.

'Hello, um, yes . . . I was hoping to see some of the exhibition pieces?'

'Ah, a fan, I take it?' She gestures to an enlarged poster of the flyer that I hold in my hand. 'Tom Simmonds' is written in art deco-styled writing with a steel grey sweep across the darker grey background, which, if you look long enough, reveals itself to be a swallow.

Next to it is another poster, bolder, with vibrant reds and greens displaying looping writing with the name 'Georgie Hunter' written diagonally; a blood-red petal falls from the 'r'.

'Yes, I mean, I've seen Tom's work . . .' I trail off as I wonder who Georgie Hunter is.

'Sorry, but the exhibition isn't open to the public until five o'clock today as it's opening night.'

'Oh. OK, I'll come back later then.' I glance at my watch, which tells me I've got another three hours to wait.

'It will be worth the wait. Are you a collector?' she asks, noticing one of his smaller works clutched in my other hand. I had bought it on eBay and it had arrived last week. It had arrived without apology as it tumbled from a brown jiffy bag and into my palm. It didn't explain where it had come from, didn't creep into my life cautiously like a disgraced relative; it bounded out with a 'ta-daah!', winking in my palm as if it had every right to be there: oblivious to the way the breath had been sucked out of my lungs, and to the way I had to reach for the chair so that I didn't lose my balance completely.

It is a small metal ball that looks similar to a roll of twine, but if you hold it to the light at just the right angle, you can see a figure in a foetal position trapped inside. I'd waited for the kids to go to bed and then pulled out his old toolkit which had been sleeping beneath a cover of dust for years. I used one of his old keyrings, with a metal braid hanging from it that he hadn't completed, and soldered the ball to it, the smell bringing sharp memories and sharper needles of hope. It was one of the things that I used to help him with when he got a more mass-produced order.

'No, no, I just . . . like his work.' She smiles at me as I give my thanks and leave the cool room, heading back into the bright seaside sun.

Looking up and down the street, I notice a small café selling paninis and coffee and realise that I'm hungry. Thinking that there are worse ways to spend a few hours, I wait for the open-top, summer-song-playing cars to pass, before I cross the road and sit myself on one of the elegant cast-iron bistro chairs. I scan the menu and give my order of a brie and cranberry panini with an iced peach tea. I watch the passers-by and marvel at how quickly we adapt to our surroundings. The gentle pace of lazy summer mornings stretches into our limbs, slowing us down as we meander around the soft curves and turns that the day brings. The rapid work days – with hastily grabbed coffee and relentless deadlines – fade helplessly into the background.

I delve into my bag and pull out my phone, checking for messages, as the blonde, tanned, teenage waitress, oozing vitality and charm – places my food in front of me. Hastily, I move my belongings, as she adds napkin-wrapped cutlery and individual packed condiments. In my eagerness to help, I knock my bag on to the floor, the unglamorous contents – a half-eaten packet of Polos, train ticket stubs, a portable mobile phone charger, lipgloss and flyer – all scatter along the coastal path. Flustered, I bend to pick them up, but The Hand is already there. The Hand, with long, slim fingers and pale trimmed nails, picks the items up and returns them to their bag. The Hand holds the flyer and pulls it towards The Face. The hand that I first saw in an art college class, the hand that pushed a wedding ring on to my finger, the hand that rubbed my back when I was in labour is holding the flyer out to me, and with it, a smile.

The movement around him stills until there is no sound. Time is standing still: a dream fabricated in the late nights when I believed him to be dead and was indulging my grief. His face is freckled with early summer, his eyes their clear blue – the knowledge that he's well rested springs to the forefront of my mind – had he been tired, they would be green. This familiarity both startles and comforts me. I can feel the breeze flicking the feathery wisps of my hair around my face. I can smell coffee, warm bread and suncream, and yet time stays motionless. I can feel my chest rise and fall. I can see . . . him.

It takes a moment for me to realise that time has begun again; the cutlery is once again clinking against plates, frustrated, overexcited children are crying and seagulls continue to circle the sky. I take my bag from his grip.

'Thanks,' I say, staring at him. His face looks more weathered than when I last saw him, a few more lines around his eyes, and his hair is short – a buzz cut – and I can see the faint silver line of a scar above his ear.

'Are you going?' he asks. His voice is warm toffee that fills my ears and warms me from within. My mouth is dry and I search my sticky brain for questions to the answers that scream from my clouded subconscious. '. . . to the exhibition?' He smiles again and holds the flyer towards me.

'I,' I clear my throat, 'yes, I am.'

'May I?' He gestures at the seat and I nod my consent. I

take a sip of the iced tea; the cool jolt to my senses is welcome and I shake my head a little.

'Er, yes, I mean, please, um, yes, sit.'

He stretches out his hand. 'I'm Tom.' He smiles again and I'm torn. I yearn to throw my arms around his neck and breathe him in, to smell his neck and stroke his face, but the tearing anger wants to claw at his face and rip away the layers of deceit. Tentatively, I stretch out my hand and he clasps it. The inside of his hand is calloused and I can tell that he's been working long hours; the skin along the bases of his fingers is hard, blisters forming and hardening against the tools of his creations. My hands are damp in his grasp; the dryness of his creating balance. He signals the waitress and orders a diet lemonade. I try to hide my smile; some things don't change even when your world has changed so much that you barely recognise it. He seems so relaxed that I'm lost for a moment. Lost in time and lost for words. There really is only one thing I can think of to say.

'Where have you been?' I ask.

'Oh,' he looks down at the shopping bags around his feet, 'the market. There's a great one around the back there . . .' He points. 'I hope you don't mind me intruding on your lunch.' Again, he gives me a crinkly smile. 'But, I just wanted to know if you're coming? Tonight? I'm not always there, you see, but I will be there, um, tonight.' My heart is hammering in my chest. Is this really happening or am I still at home asleep?

'What?'

'To the exhibition? It's just that I noticed your keyring? Sorry if this is a bit forward, but it's not often I see one of my pieces adapted into everyday items. It has me intrigued as to what you might do with one of my larger sculptures.' He chuckles and seems a little uncomfortable, as if he's trying to impress me but realises it's not going according to plan. 'Are you an artist?'

'Pardon?'

'An artist – you obviously know your way around a soldering iron.' He tilts his head and gestures to the keyring.

'No, I'm not but—' This exchange makes me feel like I'm scaling a helter-skelter. I was on a solid, yet frightening edge a moment ago and now I seem to be swirling around and around this conversation as it gets faster and more out of control with every sentence. I grab on to the sides and pull myself to a stop, my fingers gripping tightly until I gain control. 'Have we met before?' I ask him, searching his face for some hint as to whether he knows who I am. I release my fingers slightly and allow myself to continue sliding at a more sedate pace.

'Sorry?' He looks uncomfortable. I lean forward and look directly into his eyes.

'Have we met? Before?' I ask again, eager for some clarity during this dizzying descent.

'I have intruded, haven't I? Goodness, I'm sorry if I've made you feel uncomfortable,' he becomes flustered, 'I just get a bit carried away when I see that someone likes my work, you see, a bit over familiar.' A blush has begun to spread across his face and his eyes look almost glassy as if he may be on the verge of tears. I'm quick to end his embarrassment as he begins to stand, looking around for his bags and trying not to return my gaze.

'No, no, you haven't intruded.' I reach for his arm and as I touch it, I feel as though I'm home; anchored . . . safe. The warmth of him, the vitality, the closeness of him envelops me. He's alive. I can see him, I can hear him, I can smell him. Think about the horrors of grief when somebody close to you has died. What would you do if you had the chance to see them again? This is not what I'd planned when I'd wished for this moment. He doesn't know who I am. I can't hold his hand in mine; I can't rest my head on his chest as I used to on lazy Sunday afternoons. My emotions are pushing each other, jostling for first place. Relief is here, relief that he didn't leave us; it exhales as happiness glows brightly and anger dissipates with an apology: sorry to disturb you, it says as it takes its leave. I watch him blink. Blood is flowing through his body, his lungs drinking in oxygen; his brain is sending signals. But. He doesn't know me. I bite my lip hard as I try to control the tears that are desperate to spill. He's lost us. He's lost our lives together. He's lost our children . . . I've lost him all over again.

He looks at me and I respond by smiling at him, gently pushing pressure on to his arm until he returns my gesture with a cheeky grin. The grin that he had when I had bought him a Mr Frosty for Christmas one year when he mentioned that he'd never had one as a child. Obviously, this was before he realised what a let-down Mr Frosty was. His lemonade arrives, a welcome distraction as he thanks the waitress. He doesn't know who I am. What happened to you, Dev?

'Do you, um, do you live around here?' I ask with as much nonchalance as I can manage. A flurry of notes rises up and down my spine, fluttering in bursts outwards: a butterfly shape of notes. I shiver.

'Yes, but I used to live in Devon. Are you cold?' He looks concerned for a minute and I want to crawl into his arms.

'No.' I take a sip of my water. 'I have a, a . . . never mind.' I shake off my explanation, hoping that the little electrodes that are igniting their way from my back and into my shoulders can stay contained. He lived in Devon. Devon. Why did I never think to look for him in Devon? I feel angry at myself for missing such an obvious clue, but then dismiss it. Why would I think that he would end up in a place with the same name as him? 'Whereabouts in Dev—' I clear my throat.

'Devon?' I'm hungry for information – desperate to know everything about the man in front of me – and I take another sip of tea to hide my eagerness.

'A small town called Kingswear. Do you know it?' I spit out my drink as the millions of nerve endings through my spine explode into a firework, fizzing inside before it diminishes and disappears. He grins at me and laughs as he picks up a napkin and starts cleaning up my spray from his legs and table. Is he serious? This can't be real. Devon King was living in Kingswear, Devon?

'Sorry, it, um, went down the wrong way. Have you lived here long then? Is this where you do your work?' He tilts his head again and raises an eyebrow and I realise what I must sound like.

'Yes, I've been here about . . .' he chews the inside of his lip and looks up, trying to remember, 'five years, I think. No, six, and yes,' he smiles at me again, 'that's where I do my work. Do you live here? Shit! Sorry, I haven't even asked you your name!' He slaps his hand against his forehead.

'Mel—' I don't know why, but I can't say it. I can't. 'Mel-lissa, and no. I live in Shropshire.'

'Oh. I've never been there, is it by Birmingham? I'm rubbish—'

'At geography,' we say in unison. He scratches the back of his head, smirks and takes several gulps of his lemonade. I notice his leg bouncing up and down, which I know means he's thinking of something important to say.

'Are you, um, here on your own? Or with friends and family?' he asks and the urge to place my hand on his face and stroke his cheek is almost too hard to bear.

'I'm here on my own. Will your family be coming to the exhibition?'

'No, I've never been, well . . .'

'Tom!' He shields his eyes from the sun with his hand and

looks over at the gallery where a tanned, toned arm is waving to him and I recognise her as the woman in the picture from Facebook. 'Time!' she shouts with frustration. I push my lips together to suppress my smile, knowing even before I glance at his arm that there won't be a watch. He can't stand the idea of sweat collecting under the watch face. It was almost a phobia.

'Be there in a min!' he shouts back. He drains the rest of his drink and stands. 'Well,' he holds his hand out to me, 'Melissa, it has been,' he scratches his cheek with his other hand, 'a pleasure.' I shake his hand and can't help but grin back. We both laugh while we continue to shake. 'Will I see you, tonight?' he asks, still holding my hand.

'You shall,' I answer, not wanting to let him go. His eyes twinkle at me and then he releases his grip, grabs his bags, turns and walks away . . . but not before looking back over his shoulder and giving me a quick, suave wink whilst simultaneously slipping down the kerb and losing any cool that was there before. He looks back at me and shakes his head in embarrassment, to which I reply with a deep belly laugh that I had forgotten even existed.

I finish my drink and pick a little at the now cold panini. The notes from earlier begin to pluck at my ribcage again; a gentle, mournful organ gives way to the finger-picked notes that rise up and down, as if 'The Edge' is climbing a hill, up, up, up then back down as I realise that I need to get out of here. I need to find a place where I feel invisible, and I notice how fitting the title of the song is: 'Where the Streets Have No Name'. The drumbeat builds – the organ still haunting in the background – and gives way to the desperate need to run towards the seafront. I need to hide; I need to rip down the invisible barriers that have contained me for so long. I can feel the clips holding my hair loosen as I run past the hordes of day-trippers, past the happy families with happy pets and happy children. I ignore their questioning glances as I sing. I head to the ocean, slowing my pace as I tell an elderly couple sitting on a bench that I love the sensation of the rays of sun on me and that I can feel the dirt haze leave me without knowing that it was ever there in the first place. I pull the clips from my hair and let it tumble to my shoulders as I spin, arms stretched and smiling. Dark, melancholy clouds have started to gather as I stride towards the pier. I need to find somewhere to stand under cover; I feel the first spots of rain – it feels so close, this elusive place where I can be free – even if only for a few moments.

Holding on to the rail along the pier front, I sing to the far-out sea that I'm still standing like a building, even after I have felt so many times that I have been burnt down. I feel the reassurance seep through me, that the next time I will feel the need to escape, that I will be able to escape with him. After all this time, there is something he can do.

The rain starts to fall and people hurry from the unexpected downpour, cardigans pulled above heads and sticky, rock-coated, podgy hands grabbed by mothers and fathers rushing to shelter. Activity erupts around me but I continue striding along the seafront; you too . . . stay with me. The road starts to flood, and the steps I descend are starting to rust. The sand's once smooth skin becomes mottled, acne-ridden; the wind becomes stronger and I'm blown by it, almost crushed by its force; the sand stings my eyes and face. I wipe them and through my blurred vision, I see Tom. Walking towards me, he grabs me by the hand. The image of him standing here in front of me seems surreal and I momentarily question my sanity.

'There's a place,' he shouts, his voice grounding me, 'high up there.' He points to some far-off point in the distance.

'A place?' I continue, and he stares at me.

'Somewhere you can find shelter,' he explains, looking up at the bipolar sky; the wind swirls around us as we are battered and blasted along the shore.

'Can you take me?'

'Sure, it's the least I can do,' he answers, smiling, as we start walking towards this distant place that I don't know – and yet, am desperate to get to – and it's then that I realise: I've stopped singing.

16

Tom

I knew it was you. I watched you from upstairs in the gallery. I watched you as you drank from your water bottle and stared at the shop front with such intensity that it was like watching my own expression when I see a piece of art that just . . . gets me. That feeling that overwhelms me with joy but leaves me breathless with the knowledge that no matter how hard I try, my own work will never match up to it.

I watched you walk across the road, the sunlight reflecting off your necklace, tiny glimmers of light dancing across your face when you looked left and right as you headed towards the café. I borrowed Janet's shopping and dashed out of the shop and across the road to give credit to our chance meeting; I could barely breathe as I headed towards you. I had no plan. No speech ready, I just knew I had to speak to you. Then I noticed *The Womb*, a piece that I'd sculpted as part of a miniature set that a solicitor's office had commissioned, and I knew it was a sign. I know I shouldn't believe in things such as 'signs', but when you've been as lost as I have, you come to accept that, sometimes, the world will give you a little helping hand every now and then.

When I touched you I knew how you would feel. I knew that your palms would fit in mine perfectly; I knew that your hair would smell of apples. I knew that I was meant to be with you. I loved the rise and fall of your breathing and that I could smell peach on your breath and the way you smiled shyly as if you knew a private joke about me.

When I got back to the studio, Georgie said I looked like the cat who had got the cream and I suppose that's how I felt. The studio went dark as I finished hammering the final nail that held the brackets for one of Georgie's larger sculptures: *The Butterfly Bomb*. It was named after a German bomb which had looked like a butterfly when its outer shell opened; they were never dropped alone, always in a swarm. But then destruction is never singular, is it? Georgie's interpretation is of the money spent on war. It's a seven-foot gun that is made of hundreds of entwined bramble bushes made from bronze. The gun bears the proverbial cross, made from clear Perspex, and contains hundreds of green silk butterflies which represent the money that could be spent on something that transforms into beauty rather than blood; the blood is symbolised by scarlet glass petals that make up the trigger. I looked out of the window and noticed that the sky was heavy with a summer storm, but all I could see was you. Even from this distance I knew it was you. As the heavy rain started falling, I watched you set your hair free and spin around, head tipped back towards the sky. I knew you would be smiling and I could see, from the way that you gestured to passers-by, that you were singing.

'I've got to go out for a min!' I'd shouted to Georgie, who was polishing the glass on one of her other sculptures – this one a bronze coffin holding yellow glass daffodils – signifying rebirth.

'But it's pouring!' she replied as I ran out and down the street. I lost you for a moment, and the wind took my breath away, but your voice travelled on it. I could hear 'Where the Streets Have No Name' being sung as if you were standing right by me, but when I caught the pattern of your skirt amongst the steps heading down to the beach, I realised you were further away than I thought. I took the steps two at a time, until I could see you walking towards me. As I got closer, I could see the grey-green of your eyes, almost translucent. You looked out of control and perfectly in control at the same time. You continued to sing until I was standing in front of you, like a siren from some seafarer's journal: beautiful, dangerous. Were you there to lure me into dangerous territory, or were you the one who needed rescuing? You were soaked and as I explained that we could take shelter in one of the old smugglers' caves ahead, I'd even slipped your hand in mine as if it was the most natural thing in the world to do. We said nothing as we walked. We said nothing when we entered the cave nor as we stood at its mouth and faced the storm. I could feel your pulse in time with mine as we watched fork lightning on the horizon. Cracks of thunder made your fingers tighten around mine, seeking reassurance. The sea rolled under the broken sky as if it was channelling the emotion in the heavens above it, just as my body was channelling the agonizing emotions between us. It was the most stimulating and contented moment of my life. When the rain stopped, you turned to me with your grey eyes searching my face.

'Is it really you?' you asked.

'Yes,' I had replied. You reached for my face and stroked my cheek; I could feel the vibrations of my stubble against your hand and then – you were gone.

I stepped out of the shower and wiped the steam from the mirror in an arch and looked at my reflection, wondering what you saw when you looked at me. Did I look older than my years? I rubbed my hand where you had stroked my face. My cheekbones still held firm even if under my eyes had started to show the first signs of wear and tear. For the first time in a long while, I'd managed to sleep for at least five hours that night, and it had gone some way to easing the bags that had started to become a permanent fixture. I rubbed the stubble across my chin with its annoying dimple, which I always cut when I shave, and then my head. I kept my hair short for convenience really; a long time ago it used to be a dark auburn colour and quite curly, but I figured I'm a bit old now to have long hair – a rock star I definitely am not.

As I stood in front of the bed and laid out three different short-sleeved shirts, all of a similar style and similar colour, I deliberated over my choice as if my life depended on it. I was choosing an outfit that I wanted you to like. Something that would feel soft against your skin. And I worried that if the fabric was too coarse it would scare you away and I would lose you. I opted for a pale-blue silk one but then worried that it would seem too flashy, so I hastily stuck on a Nirvana T-shirt with the album cover for *Nevermind* on it, and shrugged the shirt back on over the top, hoping that the floating baby would distract from it. I put on my one and only pair of stylishly ripped jeans and hoped that I didn't look like I was trying to look like a teenager, but my reflection told me that I was, so I swapped the jeans for some navy-blue chinos. I looked down at my bare wrist, missing the feel of my bracelet on my skin. I wished I knew where it had gone. The image of the cobbled floor, as I had hit it, blurred in my memory. When I had come to and looked around that hospital room, it had taken me a moment to remember where I was: that I was on one of my sales trips; that I was miles away from home in Taunton. I'd felt a panic like I've only once felt before. I felt like I was back there. Lost. Alone. I shuddered at the memory of walking out of the hospital like a criminal but I was desperate to get home; being found unconscious without any ID had already raised enough questions, and I couldn't face any more interrogations about my past – who knows what they may have found? But my main regret was that I had left the bracelet that Georgie had given me. She'd had it engraved with my name as a joke, 'So you don't forget who you are,' she had laughed. I think she had wanted me to replace the tatty one with the bell on it, telling me to let go of the past, but that was the part that I couldn't. The clasp on it had broken a few times that week; I should have fixed it, because that day, both my wrists were left bare.

I hadn't fainted since then. That feeling of being slightly out of breath and sick when the sound of the shop shutter was being drawn down wasn't particularly pleasant. I'd probably had a touch of food poisoning. I wasn't the greatest cook in the world, to say the least.

I looked at the clock, drained the last of my bottle of lager and headed out of the cottage.

The cottage was my home. It had been nothing but a shell when I had rented it from George Finnegan, an elderly man whose family had just persuaded him to go into a retirement home. It stands towards the edge of a cliff and will crumble into the sea in the next fifty years if the cliff continues to erode at its current rate. There was no central heating, only a very temperamental range – which I still have a turbulent relationship with – and the garden was a series of half-finished vegetable patches and a much-neglected lawn. There are three bedrooms, two of them with original open fireplaces and chimneys that hadn't felt the brush of a chimney sweep in many decades. The carpets had been strange swirly patterns which had long lost their original colour and had held fast to stains from times gone by. When George had died, his daughter, Grace, had offered me the chance to buy it. As I had no bank account, I didn't think it would be possible, so we came to the arrangement of my renting and buying it at the same time; when I got a good commission, I paid a lump sum. Grace's husband is something very successful in invest-ment banking and so I didn't think money was a concern. She seemed to like the idea that her dad knew who had ended up with his home, which gave her a sense of peace – I can understand that now.

The floors were now all sanded and polished, the open fireplaces clean and restored. Over the last nine years I've renovated all the furniture in it, finds from car-boot sales and junk shops, and I've discovered that I'm also quite good with a sewing machine. Everything in that house was mine. Everything in that house was me.

I turned the heavy key in the oak door, looked up at its whitewashed walls and wooden porch that runs the length of the front of the cottage, and I smiled. You would love that house. I just knew you would.

It was almost six and you still hadn't arrived. The night was going well, the storm from earlier had passed and the doors and windows to the gallery were open, letting in the sounds and smells of the seaside. I looked out of the window and smelt garlic mixed with the sea air.

'Tom!' Georgie was signalling me over to where a man, who bore a striking resemblance to Father Christmas – but in beige shorts and Jesus sandals – was looking at my free-standing statue, *Stability*, which is an oak tree that is bent over double as if in pain. Do you remember it? I shook the man's clammy hand.

'I love this piece, what is the inspiration for it?'

'A nightmare,' I replied. Nightmares. The bane of my existence. Until then, I would have four or five a night. They had become so unbearable at one point that I had survived fifty-two hours without any sleep. That sculpture was the result. I figured if I could make the nightmare into reality, I could control it somehow. Mad, I know, but that's sleep deprivation for you. I touched a cold leaf that bends with the shape of the tree; the whole sculpture bends away from the right, defending itself from the unknown, except for one single rose which leans into the direction of the pain. My nightmare.

I stayed for a polite enough time, listening to his interpretations of my work. Opening nights often bring in the amateur enthusiast, an art teacher or retired art history lecturer, as in this case. The ones who will talk your ear off but never actually buy your work. The well-dressed, quiet ones, who watch the clientele as much as the work, are normally the buyers, but that day, all I was interested in was you. I looked at the clock again: six-twenty and still you hadn't arrived. I took a glass of Prosecco from the makeshift bar and watched Georgie doing her thing. She's stunning to look at. Her thick blond ringlets, which are normally piled high on to her head, had been set free. Her tight-fitting black dress showed off her Jessica Rabbit figure, and I couldn't help but smile behind my glass as she gently and shamelessly placed her hand on the arm of a bespectacled, portly chap who, by the colour of his cheeks, had had a few glasses of Prosecco himself. Georgie is gay. But that doesn't stop her from flirting brazenly with men of a certain age who happen to show interest in her work.

Georgie saved me. When I had nowhere to go, she took me in. I'd been taking shelter under an underpass in Devon, freezing and hungry, so I'd started making sculptures out of drinks cans. I can't remember where I'd found the knife, but it would keep me busy through the long days. Sometimes I'd make enough sales to be able to pay for a bag of chips or a hot cup of coffee, but that was the extent of my income. I don't know how long I lived on the streets. She had stopped by a few times to bring me a sandwich or a drink. The day she saved me, I was unconscious and bleeding from my head.

I don't know what had happened; I just remember being hit over the head with something heavy and when I came to, all my work was stolen, and my shoes, along with the few pounds I had hidden in them, had gone. I had drifted in and out of sleep until I finally woke up in hospital. She had sat with me asking me questions about my past and then offered me a job, working in her studio. When I thanked her she had shrugged it off and said it eased her middle-class guilt.

She looked over her shoulder and gave me an exaggerated wink. I raised my glass to her in salute and then stopped still as I saw your reflection in the glass. You were standing in front of one of the open windows and as I turned my glass slightly, your face was framed by fairy lights. You hesitated before walking slowly to the opposite side of the room. My heart pounded in my chest as I dared myself to turn around and face you.

You didn't notice me at first; you seemed captivated by *Stability*. I watched as you gently reached forward and touched the curve of the tree. There were tiny wisps of hair escaping the plait at the nape of your neck, hair which I knew would seem thicker to the touch than its appearance would lead you to believe. The curve of your nose, which turned upwards slightly, was tinged with sunburn and your eyes, which were further apart than would classically be considered beautiful, were framed with a smoky grey eyeshadow. You bit your bottom lip, which was wide and full, with your top middle teeth and I remember wondering what the lipgloss that shone on them tasted like. Your dress was vivid red, a fifties-style polka-dotted affair, revealing slim, tanned legs. Your hand travelled over the sculpture and stopped short of the rose and then your whole face changed. You clamped your lips tightly together and your eyes filled with tears; tentatively you traced the stem and its petals as a tear rolled down your cheek. Your eyes turned to me then, searching for me in the room. Our eyes locked and I could see desperation in yours. Desperation that I didn't quite understand then. You had put your hand up to me as if apologising and holding me at bay. I started to move towards you but you backed away; again your eyes darted in panic. I stopped still as you continued; back you went, eyes pleading and apologising for something I couldn't understand. I tried to warn you but your panic had made you oblivious to your surroundings as you backed into *The Butterfly Bomb*. The room stilled as the high-pitched jarring sound drew everyone's attention to you. You stopped and looked up, realising that you were powerless to prevent the cross from tipping forwards slightly, releasing the swarm of butterflies. The colour of your eyes mirrored the reflection of the green wings fluttering around you; they filled with emerald tears, falling gently on to your hair and shoulders. The greens glimmered and gleamed about you, creating an almost ethereal quality against the red of your dress. It was the most beautiful thing I had ever seen.

The room remained in shock and then you opened your mouth and sang. A clear, pure sound that I recognised, picturing the iconic video of Sinéad O'Connor's face.

The room was held by your voice, as you sang that it had been eleven years and sixteen days since someone took their affections away. You looked at me with defiance, singing about going wherever you chose to go. I was mesmerised by the tone in your voice, the way that you put all your passion into the lyrics. I watched as you gestured with your elegant hands, acting out the song, showing you could go out whenever you wanted, your voice gentle yet determined; tentatively, you stepped in my direction. I believed every word you sang. I could picture you dining in expensive restaurants. With a shake of your head and lowered eyelashes, you raised your gaze to meet mine before the melody took your voice to the title: 'Nothing Compares 2 U'. You stared into my eyes as you continued, as though you were begging me to help you. As you sang about a bird missing its tune, your tone became vulnerable, lilting. You made little nodding actions with your head when your soft voice became exasperated with the fun-loving doctor and you rolled your eyes before giving me a little smile; he was a fool. You moved closer to me, ignoring the expressions of confusion and amusement from everyone else in the room. I knew you were just singing a song, a song written by somebody else, but the way you sang it to me made me want to hold you in my arms, to protect you, to assure you that I would do everything I could to stop you from crying again.

You made me feel as if I really had planted flowers in our garden, as if I had a life with you, but they were just lyrics, words, describing somebody else's pain. You wiped an exasperated tear away as you explained that I was hard to live with. You made fiction feel like reality.

As you stood in front of me, shaking your head, singing 'Nothing compares 2U', you reached your hands towards me and cupped my face.

And then, you kissed me.

I could feel the butterflies in your hair falling around us as your salty tears mixed with my past, present and future.

17

Melody

I watch the muscles across his tanned back flex as he throws a brittle log on to the fire. I've lost track of time, but from the chill in the air, it must be just before dawn. The sea wind is pushing its way through the gaps around the ancient windows and the heavy white curtains corrugate against the wall. I pull the soft grey sheet under my chin as he crouches, staring into the flames, before looking over his freckled shoulder at me. He smiles. I shuffle up the bed and rest my head on the heel of my hand. My gaze is held by his until he runs his hand over the stubble on his chin, straightens and climbs back on to the bed. I shift so he can rest his head on my stomach and my hand smooths over the lumps and bumps of his head: a map of his life before and after me. There are new scars – proof of his life without me – and some I remember, like the one I'm tracing the shape of with my middle finger: the jagged silver line two inches above his right ear where he had fallen off the step ladder, putting up our Christmas decorations when I was pregnant with Flynn. I dip my toe into the ice-cold water of unknown answers and hope that the current doesn't drag us away from the warm safety of the bed.

'Where did you get this scar?' I ask gently. He reaches up with his rough, warm hand and covers my finger with his.

'In a rugby match when I was twelve.' I pull my toe back into the heat of the room, contented to stay there for a while longer. I hesitate slightly before linking my fingers with his as he pulls my hands to his lips. He's lying.

'Do you have children?' he asks. How can I tell him? How do I throw this fragile man into a life with children he doesn't know – one with behavioural problems, the other with God only knows what going on in her teenage mind – and a wife who can't walk down the street without bursting into song? He has a life here, a happy life. Is it for me to shatter it?

'No,' I lie, 'you?'

'No.' We lie: we lie there tangled in sheets, our smells, our deceptions forming a momentary barrier against the storm of unanswered questions.

'Tell me something about you,' I ask. That familiar yearning returns in the pit of my stomach. The need to find out why he left and why, it seems, he has no recollection of me or our life together.

'I don't like belly buttons.'

I laugh gently. 'Belly buttons?'

'Sinister things.' He shudders. 'Tell me something about you . . .' He lifts his head and looks up at me through his long eyelashes, his eyes gleaming with the reflection of the flames.

'Hmmm . . . my left boob is bigger than the other.'

'Really?' He raises an eyebrow. 'I'm not sure I believe you.' He starts to tug the sheets away and we tussle for a few moments – deep-throated laughter, the crackling of the fire and the crashing of the waves – the background to this perfect moment. He brushes my hair away from my eyes and kisses the tip of my nose. 'I love how your nose lifts up at the end.'

'What, like a Hoo?'

'A what?'

'A Hoo. You know Dr Seuss?' I clarify.

'Who?'

'A Hoo. Yeah.'

He laughs again. 'No, I meant Dr Who.'

'Dr Who as in the Tardis?' I start giggling at our confusion; an eruption of weightless happiness fills the room.

'No, I . . .' He shakes his head and then starts, as a loud growl from my stomach vibrates against him. I stop laughing and cover my mouth as if the noise had escaped from there.

He looks at my stomach with a look of bemusement. 'Hungry?'

As the light changes from muted, stealthy greys, the kitchen wakes: and me within it. I hold the cup of fresh coffee in my hands, its warmth percolating into my satiated body. Body parts long since dead groan and stretch. Dreams from hundreds of cold empty nights evolve in front of me. The way he scratches the back of his head as he stands still for a moment trying to remember where he has put the eggs. The tilt of his head, as he lights the flame with a match then sucks the end of his finger when it burns too close to the edge; and the way he looks at me. In the months that he had disappeared, I had replayed moments like this, wondering if I had imagined these looks. Romanticised them. I must have, or else why would he have left? And yet, there they are. The quick glances as he sprinkles grated cheese over the pan, the way that right now, it doesn't matter that I have the remains of last night's make-up smudged under my eyes or that my wrinkles have started to deepen; those looks, those smiles that let me know that . . . I am the most beautiful woman to have ever graced his world. I balance my cup on the small table next to the duck-egg blue sofa that resides at the end of the farmhouse kitchen, and tuck my knees under me.

'Worcestershire sauce? In an omelette?' I query, just as I had the first time he had made it for me; the déjà vu-ness of the situation unsettles me. He points a fork at me from the worn oak island in the middle of the room.

'Just wait.' He walks towards me carrying two plates, two forks: breakfast for two. 'You'll love it.' He passes the plate to me and looks puzzled for a moment. 'How do I know you will?' he asks, shaking his head. For a golden moment I feel like there is a chance to tell him, but then I watch his worried face and I think of his carefree manner when I saw him outside the café.

'Because I look saucy?' I say with a smirk, taking the outstretched plate. I feel the weight of his legs against me as he sits opposite, his feet crossed next to me as he leans back on a mismatched armchair. I spear my fork into the strange-looking mass of egg and cheese as he chuckles politely. I look down at his feet and try to hide my look of distaste. He stops with a forkful halfway to his mouth.

'Don't you like it?' He bites into his forkful, nodding his approval.

'Um, oh, uh yes. It's lovely . . .'

He nods again, his smile turning to concern. 'Then what's wrong?' He leans forward.

'It's well, it's . . .' I take another forkful and delay my response. 'It's your feet,' I say, pushing my lips together tightly before biting my lower lip.

'My feet?' He looks shocked. 'What's wrong with my feet?' He uncrosses them and turns them this way and that.

'Well. They're, um, God, there is no polite way to say this but they're ugly.'

He swallows his food with a gulp. 'Ugly?' I nod. 'Ugly? I have ugly feet?' He frowns and looks at them, stretching his toes wide apart.

'You see!' I point at them with my fork. 'Toes shouldn't do that! They're toes, not fingers, they shouldn't spread.'

'Huh. Ugly feet. And there I've been, all my life, parading them about in flip-flops and whatnot.' He smirks. 'If we're on the subject of weird body parts . . .'

I put my fork down noisily. 'What?' I ask as he deliberately chews his food slowly, putting his hand over his mouth and looking upwards as if apologising for taking so long. Finally and purposely he swallows.

'You have no earlobes.'

I laugh. 'I do too.' I pull on my right one for effect.

'No, you don't. They join straight to your neck, they have no wobble.'

'No wobble?' I repeat, aghast.

'No wobble.' He puts his plate on to the floor and flicks his own to show their wobbliness.

'Mine wobble.' I copy his actions, my plate clinking to the ground as I flick my own earlobes, but alas. I'm wobbleless. I pick up my plate and continue to eat.

'Are you sulking?' he asks incredulously as I scrape the last of the egg from my plate.

'No,' I reply through a mouthful, sulkily. Bursting out laughing, he stands and takes the plate from me, continuing to chuckle as he walks across the kitchen and places both plates in the chipped Belmont sink. I smile behind him, get up and loop my arms around his waist as hot soapy water fills the sink. I lean my head against his back, feeling the movement of his muscles as he washes the plates and puts them on the draining board. He turns around to face me in my embrace, lifts my chin and kisses me gently on the lips and then works his way up to my ears.

'I love that you have weird earlobes,' he whispers.

'I love that you have ugly feet.'

'Is this it?' he asks, searching my eyes. 'Is this what they talk about? Love at first sight?'

'It is . . . for now,' I reply as he takes my hand and leads me back to the bedroom.

I ignore the screams from my subconscious telling me to stop. Begging me not to lie, begging me to leave and never come back. As my legs wrap around him and we sink into the bed I scream back. I deserve to have him . . . deserve to have him back even if it's just for a day. I'll leave. I'll never come back. I will protect them all from the truth, but for now . . . please let me have him.

I lie there watching him sleep. I watch his chest move up and down. Up and down. Alive. Living. I allow myself this time to believe it, to indulge myself. Taking one last thirsty look, I extract myself from his bed. Grabbing my clothes, I creep down the stone stairs and into the lounge. I stand still looking at the pictures on the walls, the mismatched furniture that somehow manages to match. I stroke the old wooden rocking chair – how long did it take him to fix it? I wonder, as I notice the new pieces of wood that have been added like a collage. My eyes follow the wooden floorboards that rise and fall, that expand and contract with this house that lives. Hanging on the umbrella stand in the corner is my bag; it nestles in between his coats as if it's been there all along, as if it belongs. Unhooking it, I feel the weight of my betrayal on my shoulders; as I take a shaking breath in, I know with certainty that I love him too much to tell him the truth. I love him too much to stay. I close the door behind me gently and the warm sea breeze takes hold of me as I start to walk away. Against the smiling sun and the greetings of seagulls, I wipe away the tears with the heel of my hand.

When I was about five, my nan used to bake with me: always on Sundays, always with her records playing and the window open, letting out the smell of baked apples and pastry. I don't know why I'm thinking of this until I hear my voice rise and fall with the melody of a very old version of 'You Are My Sunshine' by Wilf Carter. It was one of her favourites, which she would play on her record player, the crackling of time passing under its needle, but as I hear my own voice through the cracks of my tears, I notice its tempo is slow, its tone sombre.

The wind steals my voice as I sing about how he makes me feel happy, even when the clouds are grey. I choke on a small sob as I continue. Will he ever know how much I love him? I sing, pleading that the sun isn't taken away. The sun's reflection is suffocating under the hungry waves while my phone vibrates angrily inside my bag; I ignore it. Ignore what I'm doing and ignore the life waiting for my return. I repeat the chorus over and over, telling him how happy he makes me feel and begging that the feeling isn't taken away. I lick my lips, tasting the salty moisture mingling with my tears and gasp slightly, before spewing out the rest of the song without control. I wipe my face, take some deep breaths and finally whisper the title with resolution: 'You Are My Sunshine.'

As I steer my way around the twists and turns descending the steep path towards the town, I pull out my phone and see seven missed calls from Shane. Spent, I sit on a wind-beaten bench and call him back.

'Hi, it's me.'

'Are you OK? Did you find him? Melody?'

'Hmm?'

'Did you find him?'

'Yes.'

'And?'

'And nothing, he has a new life without me and the kids. So that's it really. End of the story.'

'Are you OK?'

'Not really. I'll be home on the next train.'

'Do you want me to come over when you get back?'

'That's kind, but no. I just need—'

'Space?'

'Yeah . . . space.'

I hang up the phone and walk purposefully back to the hotel.

Sitting on the edge of the bed, I open my purse to check that my ticket is there and pull out the photo-booth picture of Flynn and Rose, which was taken last month at the end of term school party. One of the rare physical photos that I carry around with me – the rest are either on the walls of my hall or on my computer and mobile phone. I smile at the pair of them, Rose pushing her nose up with her thumb as she stands behind Flynn who is crouching down in front, holding up a sign that says 'loser' and pointing up to his sister. They are enough. They have to be. I'm lucky, I think as I stand up; how many people get to have one last moment with the loves of their lives after they have died? I slot the picture back inside, stand up and take a last glance around the seaside room with its custard walls and cheesecloth checked curtains, grab my bags and head out to the railway station.

The digital board tells me that the train is on time. I drain the last of my lemonade, throw it into the bin and look down the track. My phone rings as I notice that the train is just visible on the horizon.

'Hi, Mum . . .'

'Hi, how's your friend? Are you having a nice time?' she asks.

'Yes, um, fine, I'm . . .'

'Listen, darling, my friend Veronica has got a caravan in

Wales and somebody was due to go and stay this week, only they've let her down and she's asked me if I want it. I thought I could take the kids? I'd have spoken to you first, only they were there, you see, when she asked and they're both keen to go . . .'

'What, for a week . . . with you?'

'Well yes, today, in fact. I've won a little money on the ponies and I told them we could use some of it for spends while we're there. There's a club on the site and a pool and a go-kart thing, I think . . .'

The train is starting to round the corner towards the platform as I consider the implications of this change of events when my phone vibrates again. I pull it away from my ear for a moment to see a message sliding across the top of my screen:

'Pllllllleeeeeeaaasssssseee?? R+F xxx'

'What about their clothes and things?'

'Sweetie, they are more than capable of packing for themselves and I've got the house key.'

'But Mum, are you sure? Flynn can be a bit of a handful and Rose is—'

'Look, they've been as good as gold and if there are any shenanigans I'll bring them home. It's only two hours away.'

The train pulls up and the doors gasp open.

'Um, I . . .' I can hear Mum laughing as I hear them both shouting:

'Please!!!!!!'

I smile and bite my lip.

'Excuse me, pet?' asks a tall, greying man in Bermuda shorts and hairy legs. 'Are you getting on?' He indicates the train with his head.

'Melody?' Mum asks.

'No.' I shake my head at the hairy-legged man, step back and then confirm yes to my mother, as my kids cheer and sing 'Summer Holiday' in the background. I laugh, say goodbye and briskly walk out of the train station.

My hair sticks to the back of my neck as I turn the corner towards the cliff path. I put my hands on my knees and catch my breath for a few minutes, alter the weight of my backpack and bag slightly and start to jog towards him. The path twists and turns, my throat is dry and sore and the stitch in my stomach is telling me to stop, but I can't. The cottage comes into view and I push on, the wind drowning out the sound of my breathing. I try not to think about anything but reaching him, disregard the thoughts warning me that going back will make everything worse. I slow my pace as I step into the postcard view, run my fingers through my tangled hair and slow my breathing. I twist the cool, heavy, doorknob – its reassuring weight anchors me for a moment. My hand, slick with sweat, slips slightly as if in warning. You don't belong here, it says. You're not here to stay. I wipe my hands against my blue floral dress and grip it firmly . . . I might not be here for ever, but I'm here now.

I step inside; the cool colours and air embrace my heated skin as I gently place my bags on the floor. The house is still, apart from the almost silent rattle of the window panes. The sunlight bounces off the glass dangling from the ceiling, a light fitting echoing the sculptures I've seen in the gallery: delicate shell shapes casting a cascade of rainbows around the room.

'Hello?' I take off my silver sandals and loop them through my fingers as I take small, quiet steps through and into the kitchen, where the evidence of broken eggshells and cheese gratings from our early hour breakfast remain.

'Hello?' I repeat, feeling somewhere between an intruder

and a resident. Still swinging my sandals over my fingers, I take tentative steps upstairs. There is a low moaning sound coming from the bedroom and I pause for a second. My heart hammers in my chest as the sounds get louder, more urgent. The distinctive groan of the bedsprings reverberates through the wooden floor and my toes curl slightly under their complaints. He has someone else. The thought crashes through me, devastating; wicked thorns scrape at my earlier contentment. The sounds change into something more primal; my feet continue on their path, my mind unable to stop them. I watch my hand as though it belongs to somebody else, pale-pink painted nails spread against the oak of the door. I notice that the varnish is chipped on my index finger as the door moves forward underpressure.

The sheets are disordered; writhing and imprisoned in them is Tom. His face is contorted as if in agony. I stand still, not able to take my eyes away from the wreck in front of me in the same way that you can't help but look at a roadside accident as you drive past. He screams again, without realising I'm at his side. The pain I see in his face is too much to take. I reach out to gently shake his shoulder but as I touch his hot skin, his eyes fly open; he fixes me with a blank, glassy stare. I start to smile. He stares at me and then lifts his hand. Clenches his fingers into the palm. My smile falters. His perfectly formed fist punches me. Pain blisters my skin, shoots past my cheek and into my eye as I feel myself flying backwards; the back of my head snaps with a noise like an eggshell cracking as it hits the floor. I lie for a moment as the pain throbs outwards from my cheek to my eye, to my head, to my neck, to my heart.

'Oh my God! Mell!' He scrambles from the bed and kneels in front of me. The glassy stare is replaced with concern and remorse as he cups his mouth with his hand, the knuckles slightly red from their impact with my face. 'Are you OK? I'm sorry . . .' His eyes fill as he gingerly holds my chin and turns my face so he can assess the damage. 'Are you OK?' he repeats.

'Everybody . . .' I try to speak but my lip feels tight. Cautiously, I touch my lip with my tongue and taste blood. He winces. 'Everybody hurts . . .' I reply.

'Let me get an ice pack. I'm sorry, I have dreams, nightmares, I . . .' but I stop him short as I'm filled with the mournful introduction from REM. I tell him that I know that feeling when you've had plenty of this lifetime and yet . . . you have to carry on. He motions that he's going to get some ice but I grab on to his arm.

'Don't go,' I say to him. 'We all cry and we all suffer . . . at times.' He sits down and wraps his arms around me, stroking my hair as I look up at him; I can see he's searching my face, my words for forgiveness. I sing to him, telling him that most of the time, things in life do go wrong and then I laugh and nudge him, encouraging him to join in, and he does. He sings the part about how your days can become your nights and that sometimes you feel as though you should give up, but instead you don't let go. Feeling suddenly exhausted, I reply to him, letting him know that he's not on his own. We finish the song together as he rocks me in his arms and I realise that they were right when they said 'Everybody Hurts'.

18

Tom

I wrapped my arms around you as we sat on the warm sand. Your head was under my chin and I kissed the top of it as if I'd been doing it for years. You were chattering on about how when you were little, you used to make mud pies. I can imagine you, eyes bright and mischievous, dirty grazed knees and sticky fingers.

'Did you make them?' you asked. 'It seems kids lately don't do things like that, too much worrying about E. coli, I suppose . . .'

This was where I made the decision to tell you. To tell you that I wasn't what you thought. We'd spent the last two days together and already I couldn't imagine being apart from you. I think you sensed that I wasn't telling you the whole truth about myself, and you seemed to be holding back too – waiting for me to show you that I trusted you, perhaps? This thing that we had was something that I always thought was a myth. A fairy tale. How can you fall in love – wholly and unconditionally – without really knowing a person? A thing of sonnets and Shakespeare; of ballads and Oscar-winning films: I knew you felt it too. You must have. When I woke and saw your head fly back, your look of shock replaced with understanding showed me that you did.

'I don't know.'

I watched your hand drawing spirals in the sand. 'I mean I can't remember.' Your hand stopped moving for a moment before continuing its expanding circles. 'I can't remember a lot of things.' Your back tightened slightly but then you relaxed your weight into me. I stared out at the sea and then dove in, head first into the truth. 'I can't remember anything about my life until eleven years ago.' You stayed quiet for a moment.

'What do you remember?' you asked without surprise, just curiosity. I undid the piece of white lace that was tied over your hair bobble. The wind had loosened it, twisting it around and around.

'My earliest memory isn't like yours or anybody else's for that matter; I don't remember a childhood or a home. I don't remember parents or school or college. I don't know if I went to university or what my first job was . . . My first memory is of being kicked in the gut in an underpass in Worcester.'

'Worcester?'

'Yeah. From the state of me I reckon I must have been sleeping rough for a while by then. Maybe I always had? I don't know.' I retied the lace in a bow around your ponytail.

'How did you survive?' You turned your body to the left and leant the side of your face against my chest, pulling my hand to your lips.

'Begging, stealing – only food – but . . . I've done things that I'm not proud of, I had no choice. Then, Georgie found me: gave me a job, somewhere to live – a life.'

'Do you remember anything? Anything at all about your life before then?' you asked and as I stroked your cheek I could feel fine sand against it.

'Nothing. I often wonder, though . . .'

'Yes?' you asked, almost hopefully.

'I have this nightmare, this nightmare and in it there is a

boy. It's probably nothing, but in it, half of his face is missing? Like blurred out?'

'Do you have any other dreams like that?'

'It's not a dream. It's a nightmare. He's twisted and always clawing at me . . . more of an animal than a person. I dream about a tree as well. That's why I made *Stability*. This tree? It's always got a red rose growing out of it, but even that becomes evil, it grows over me sometimes, suffocating me.'

'Did you ever try to find out who you are?'

'I'm Tom. I'm an artist and I live here. I know who I am.'

'I'm sorry, I didn't mean to . . .'

'Sorry. I just, I made a decision a long time ago to just let the past go. I'm in a good place. I've never been happier, and besides, I might find out things that I don't want to know.'

'I can understand that. Shall we go for a walk?'

'Shall we go for a walk?' I chuckled. 'I tell you that I could be an axe murderer and you say "Shall we go for a walk"?' I shook my head in disbelief as you dug me in the ribs.

'I could be an axe murderer too . . .' you replied and I realised that you were right. I didn't know anything about you other than you sang when you were upset, you made mud pies when you were little and . . . that I loved you.

I was shampooing your hair as you lay in the claw-footed bath which I found in a house sale in Truro. I remember that there were bubbles on top of bubbles.

'They don't know. The doctors. After the accident, I had a scan and they found, like, an abscess on my brain but it wasn't dangerous or anything, I just had antibiotics for a couple of days and that was that. I've seen so many different ones but they just don't know why I sing. They've said it has traits of Tourette's, but . . . anyway, on to more important things. The eighties. I'm not sure it's a bad thing that you missed them, to be honest, although there were some classic films . . .' Your accent became stronger when you were relaxed, I'd noticed, it had a slightly Brummy twang to it. Not quite Frank Skinner – your accent was softer – but it lifted and fell in a similar way. You were wiggling your toes under the dripping tap when I saw it. I saw your toes wiggling under a tap but for a second the bath was green and your toenails were painted red. I felt sick for a moment and then the room seemed to tip. I blinked and everything was back to normal.

'Do you paint your nails?' I asked, as I dipped my hands into the water and reached for the white enamel tumbler.

'I'm telling you about all the amazing films of the eighties; I give you *Top Gun* and you want to know if I paint my nails?' You laughed.

'Sorry, I just . . . it's nothing.'

'Oh no . . . don't tell me you're one of those men who like their women to do their nails for them, are you?' You looked at me over your shoulder and I couldn't help but smile, 'Because I'll tell you, Tom, I really don't think I could take it. Axe murderer is fine but cross-dresser I think I'll struggle to cope with.' I tipped the cup of water straight over your head as you spluttered and waved your hands for a towel.

'Serves you right,' I said as I passed you the towel. You looped the towel around my neck and pulled me towards you, kissing me deeply before pouring a mugful of water over me. You grinned at me and I stroked your face, wondering what I had done to deserve having you there, your bruises still clear; mine still hidden.

I watched you as you chopped the anchovies; I watched the way your tongue poked out of the corner of your mouth when you concentrated. You wiped the blade on a cloth as you hummed. I'd noticed this about you. You hummed when you were contented and sang when you were upset. You hummed in your sleep too. I opened the kitchen door to let some cool air in as you fried garlic and chillies. I wanted to ask you. But I didn't want to hear the answer. Would you stay? I knew I needed to ask but I couldn't; I was afraid of the answer.

'When do you go back to work?' I asked tentatively as I poured a glass of red wine and passed it to you. You wiped your forehead with the back of your hand and then took the glass from me, taking a large sip.

'Jo, the woman I work for, her mum is ill at the moment so I'm not really sure. Her soon-to-be-ex-husband, Shane, might ask me to do some things around the house, though.' I watched the colour rise on your cheeks at the mention of 'Shane'.

'Do you get on with him? Shane?' I asked, jealously making the words of my question run into each other.

'Um, yes, he's—' the corners of your mouth lifted, 'nice.' You tilted your head at me and smirked. 'Are you jealous?'

'Hmmm?' I asked as if I hadn't quite heard you properly. You threw the tea towel at me. 'Why? Should I be?'

'Well, let's see: he's good-looking, funny, kind . . .' I felt my face fall as I recognised the genuine tone of your voice. You started chopping black olives, occasionally looking up at me through your long eyelashes. 'But,' you added, 'he's not you.' You threw the olives into the pan, added some chopped tomatoes and stirred it with a wooden spoon, clamping the lid on and turning off the heat.

'Were you together? Before . . .' I point to you and then me.

'No. Nothing like this.' You picked up your glass of wine and came over and sat on my knee.

'I'm afraid you're going to leave,' I said into your neck. Either you didn't hear me or you chose not to answer, because the next thing you did was kiss me. It was an hour later before we ate the meal.

I leant forward and wiped the tomato sauce from your chin as you slurped your spaghetti. We were sitting on the porch, the sun was dipping into the sea and the waves below tossed and turned in their slumber.

'I love it here,' you said.

'You don't have to leave,' I replied. You nodded briefly and then busied yourself with putting your plate on the floor, picking up your wine and nudging your way under my arm; laying your head against my chest, which seemed to be where you felt most comfortable.

'I can hear your heart beating.'

'It doesn't belong to me any more. You've stolen it.'

'Makes me sound like the wicked witch in *Snow White*,' you giggled.

'Did you know that in the original fairy tale it wasn't her heart that she wanted? It was her lungs and liver?'

'Ew.'

'Grim fellows, those Grimms. The ugly sisters tried to cut off their feet too.'

'What?!'

'It's true, in the story they tried to cut off their toes so they could fit their feet into the glass slipper.'

'Blimey. How do you know this stuff if you can't remember your name?'

'I don't know. The mind is a curious thing . . .'

'It certainly is.' The mild wind played with the hem of your dress.

'I can play the piano,' I announced.

'I always said you had pianist fingers.'

'When did you say that?'

'Wh-when I, you, picked up my things when we first met . . . at the, um, café.'

'Huh.'

'I thought to myself, what beautiful hands you had: like a pianist. Do you have a piano?'

'Not yet. I'll find one soon.'

'Shall we go looking tomorrow?' You sat up eagerly. 'You can show me where you go to find all of your treasures.' Your eyes were clear and excited.

'OK. There's a market that's open on Thursday that we can go to, but I'd better get some work done tomorrow and Wednesday. I've got another exhibition due in November.'

We were holding hands as we bustled our way through the crowded marketplace. Our life that week had found its own rhythm. We talked most of the night – neither of us were big sleepers – and then as the sky lightened we slept fitfully, our limbs tangled and possessive. As I lay awake, the warmth and familiarity of you creeping into my soul and into my heart, I tried to make sense of my emotions. How could I feel this way about somebody I hardly knew? Apart from Georgie, I had never trusted anybody, never loved anybody. How is it that I could trust and love you so fiercely and so immediately? I tucked a piece of your hair away from your cheek. I had no explanation for the way I felt, but strangely, no fear either. The only fear I had was that I might lose you. Every time I saw you smile, every time you laughed, every time you looked at me, I dismissed any rational thoughts of self-preservation. I didn't know it then, but my body knew why; the synapses in my brain may have been overgrown, may have been suffocating beneath the scar tissue of amnesia, but they were there, deep down, gasping for breath; holding on to you.

In the mornings, I would make us breakfast, while you

showered. You'd taken to sitting on the porch with the sea air drying your hair while we drank coffee and read newspapers. I knew you so well, and not at all, in equal measure.

It took us an hour to get there, an hour in the heat and discomfort of public transport, but amongst it all we are a couple. I've never been in a couple before. Not in the sense that I now understand it means. I paid, you found the seat. I nodded towards a coffee stand, you steered us in that direction. Little things that seem so natural to other people but to me have always seemed strange. How do they communicate without speaking? But you made me see how easy it is. Your eyes lit up as you saw some reclaimed furniture, your nudge to the ribs told me so. I squeezed your hand in response. We stood amongst the chests of drawers and battered, neglected garden furniture. You let go of my hand and started looking and scavenging: moving teapots and china cups, old computer desks and half-assembled bedframes, and then you spotted something out of my view. It was a mirror. Nothing special, but you were staring into it, mesmerised. I watched you for a moment, the way you shifted from one foot to another, like an excited toddler. You clapped your small hands in front of you and then touched the sides of the frame in wonder. As I got closer I still couldn't understand what hold it had over you. Its frame was chipped in places, probably from being transported from one place to another without due care. There were swirls in the corners of the teak frame. The glass itself was mottled and aged. I looped my arms around your shoulder and you leant into me.

'It's just like the one my grandma had when I was little. I smashed it playing hide and seek with my friend when I was nine,' you said. I looked at our reflection and noticed a small crack that ran across it diagonally, almost splitting us in two. Your smile faded as you looked into my eyes.

'It would look nice in our hall . . .' I said. We swayed together as we watched our fractured reflection. You were wearing a lemon blouse, your top button was open and your collarbone was gleaming slightly with the remains of the suncream that I had watched you squirt on while I was making breakfast that morning. Your bruises were hidden by the pale make-up you'd applied and your hair was loose, clipped to the side by a hairgrip with a daisy on it. I fitted your body, like the two pieces of the mirror. I wished I could fix the reflection's flaws as well as the ones hidden beneath. I still do.

'Can I buy it for you?' you asked. 'Please?' There was a tone to your voice that I didn't recognise.

'I'll get it.' I took my arm from around your shoulders and went to take my wallet out of my pocket.

'No,' you said firmly. I raised an eyebrow at your command. 'Please?' you said in a gentler tone. 'Please, I'd like to.' You picked it up carefully and took it to the balding, short man wearing a brown leather bum bag.

We sipped our drinks contentedly outside a harbour pub; the smells and noises of summer were all around us. The mood between us had shifted. It had a weight behind it; there were words I knew needed to be spoken but we danced about them with comments about the view, about the weather.

'Tom . . .' you started to say, reaching your hand forward, 'I—'

'Don't.' I stopped you, 'Please. Don't say it.'

'I have to, I have a life, away from here.'

'So leave it.'

'I can't . . . there are things that I can't tell you, things that—'

'You can tell me, I don't care about whatever it is that you think you need to keep hidden. I've never felt like this.' I smiled and stroked the inside of your palm, 'At least I don't think I have.' I gave what I hoped was a wry smile. You shook your head as if you were shaking away a voice whispering in your ear.

'I can't tell you this,' you said with finality. 'Let's just enjoy this for as long as we can. I've got another night until . . .' Your lip quivered and I could tell you were fighting the need to cry. You lifted the glass of wine to your lips.

'Marry me.' You spluttered on your drink and then pushed your sunglasses on to your head. 'Marry me,' I repeated.

'I, I can't.' You looked uncomfortably around us as our conversation had been overheard by other pub-goers.

Without thinking, or possibly thinking too much, I had an idea. I dropped to my knee, much to your shock and embarrassment, and started singing. I needed to show you that I wasn't embarrassed by your condition and I wanted you to know how I felt. I cleared my throat and invoked the great Percy Sledge: 'When A Man Loves a Woman'. I remember thinking how true the words were, I couldn't think of anything else but you, and I knew, deep down, that I wouldn't swap how I was feeling for anything else. You leant your head towards me and bit your bottom lip as I carried on singing. I saw nothing but love reflected back at me, even as I stumbled over the words. You laughed quietly and acknowledged the attention we were getting with a grin while gently shaking your head. I added a bit of gumption when I sang the title again, begging you not to do me any wrong. The small crowd gave me a round of applause as you offered me your hand and pulled me to my feet. You put your arms around my neck and kissed me, much to the delight of our audience. It was only later, when you were lying in my arms, that I realised: you never said yes.

I couldn't sleep. The wind was blowing fiercely and you were singing in your sleep. I turned on to my side and watched your face as it frowned and expressed the words of 'Without You'. At that moment, you were verging on screaming the lyrics like one of the contestants on *X Factor* when it's the sing-off. Something was wrong. I knew it in my gut. I knew it as we walked home and I rambled on about how we could redecorate the cottage, add some of your favourite things. At the time I had been so full of optimism for the future that I hadn't really noticed your comments. They were all urging caution and even though you were cheerful, there was an edge to your voice. I suppose I was just caught up in the moment and the bottle of champagne that I had ordered. Thinking back over the journey home, I'm not sure you said much at all, even as we hung the newly claimed mirror at the bottom of the stairs on the wall next to the front door. I smoothed back your hair from your forehead and crept out of the room. The windows were rattling slightly and I could hear the spray of light rain against the windows. Despite the storm, it was warm inside and I felt stifled. My head ached from the afternoon drinking and the restless, heavy sleep that followed. I opened the kitchen cupboard and looked for some painkillers but there was nothing inside but an out-of-date packet of flu remedy. I opened a few more cupboards and then noticed your bag tucked behind the kitchen sofa. Without thinking, I opened it; you had taken some painkillers when we got back so I knew you had some in there. I fumbled about past half-eaten packets of mints and tissue packets until I found them. I pulled the cardboard carton which was snagged on your purse, clicking open its clasp. Coins flew out and I smiled as I scratted about on the floor trying to chase them, remembering that in your eagerness to buy me the mirror, you hadn't even closed your purse properly. I grabbed the remaining ten pence from the floor, stood and opened it properly, dropping the change into it. A piece of paper was sticking out from the note section and

I tried to tuck it back inside but it didn't quite fit properly. I pulled it out. It was a photo. Of a boy. Half of his face was scarred. Without a doubt, he was the boy who had haunted me for years.

19

Melody

I wake to feel his weight on the end of the bed. My throat is raw, and as I try to speak, I can barely make a sound and it's then that I know. I have to leave him.

I know what you must think of me. How can I deceive him? How can I lead a man – so clearly vulnerable – on a journey we could never complete, to a place that he could never stay? I have no answer for you other than I was being selfish. Indulgent. To have him back in my arms is addictive. The feel of him, the smell of him is like one more drink to an alcoholic. Just one more taste and I'll go, but the more I have, the more I want. To begin with, one little sip was enough, a glance, a graze of the fingers, but not any more. I need to hold him, touch him, hear the sound of his breathing. The need has become more demanding. Less satiated. Until – as I lie here now – I realise that I have to force the cork back in before I do more damage to myself and to him.

I sit up. He is sitting at the edge of the bed, still and facing away from me.

'Do you know that I've never felt happier than I have in this past week with you?' His tone is guarded, a whispered warning of things unspoken. 'I have never felt like I've belonged to anyone. This house is the closest I've felt to belonging. The way I know its sounds and flaws . . . but with you, I feel like I'm home. Crazy that somebody who cannot trust anyone can somehow trust a complete stranger, isn't it? And yet I did. Until I saw this.' He turns to me, his eyes green, no longer their natural blue. He throws the picture on to the bed and I struggle to breathe. 'Who are you?'

'Tom, this is, is – this is why I can't stay.'

'How do you know that boy?'

'I can't . . .' I plead.

'Just answer me one question . . . is your name even Melissa?' He narrows his eyes and I'm reminded of the way he looked before he hit me during his nightmare and for a moment I realise that I don't know Tom either. I don't know what effect these years have had on him. Living on the streets, no story, no history, no love.

'No,' I answer him. He nods and then leaves the room. I flinch as the front door slams, shaking the structure of the house, and I hear the newly hung mirror smash into a thousand pieces.

I should never have stayed, I know that now. I knew it then too but ignored the voice of reason. I pull on my jeans, my top, scrape my hair into a ponytail and slip my feet into sandals.

I've changed my mind.

I'll chase after him and explain. Maybe he'll forgive me? Maybe he'll want to know the kids? A glimmer of hope surges through me like a flame, and then as quickly as it ignites, the cool realisation that I've lied to him in the worst way, that I've betrayed his trust, asphyxiates it with a sigh. Grabbing my few belongings, I throw them into my bag and rush downstairs, the need to escape overcoming me so much that I move like greased lightning – yes really, the dance moves and pelvic thrusts accompanying the 'Huh! Huh!' parts would make Danny Zuko proud. I take an apologetic look around, as the sounds of broken glass crunch beneath my feet and calm descends upon me. Robotically, I retrieve the dustpan and brush, methodically clearing away the shattered pieces, as if one by careful one, the swipes of the brush will eradicate the damage I have caused. Staring at my shattered reflection in the contents of the pan, I pour the shards into the bin and grab my handbag from the kitchen island. In a dream-like state, I take out my lipstick and stand in front of the frame with its cardboard skeleton exposed and write 'I'm sorry'. The two words frown back at me with shame. Is that all you can say? they mock. I sit on the bottom stair, rolling the lipstick between my palms. What have I done? He deserves to know the truth, but at what cost? He'll be hurting – yes, he's been lied to – but his life will go on here. If I stay, if I tell him about the kids; if I throw him into our chaotic lives and all that having my condition entails . . . my thoughts are interrupted by the vibrations of my phone.

'Melody? Oh Melody!' My mum's voice cracks and she starts to cry. My veins fill with ice; my body freezes.

'Mum?' There is no answer, only uncontrollable sobs. 'Mum!' I shout. I can hear Flynn's voice – gentle yet commanding – as I hear the muffled sounds of the phone being passed over.

'Hey. Look, Mum, you need to come to the hospital. In Aberystwyth. Now.'

'What's happened? Is it Mum? Is she hurt?'

'No, Gran is fine. It's Rose . . . she's, she's tried to kill herself.'

The sway of the train does nothing to help me. The chatty passengers who try to make conversation do nothing to help me either. The pain that I feel is a strange sensation, one that I've never experienced before. Guilt comes hand in hand with motherhood, we've talked about that before, but this feeling? This helplessness, this angered blame is something new. I lean my head against the pane of glass and concentrate on the 'ch-ch-ch, puh-ch-ch-ch, puh . . .' sound. I try to clear my head, hearing only these sounds: 'ch-ch-ch, puh-ch-ch-ch-puh . . .' My body moves gently with it; the low moan of the horn is the only other sound I allow in: 'ch-ch-ch-puh . . .' The green hills outside become darker; limes turn into sage, sage sinks into olive, olive crumbles into aircraft grey and aircraft grey into oblivion. I feel my body shake, my eyes – gritty and sore – open to face uncomfortable stares, protective arms around teary toddlers.

'Miss?' A ticket collector shakes my shoulder again. My cheeks and jaw ache and once again my throat is parched and dry.

'I'm sorry, Miss, but you have been . . .' He coughs uncomfortably.

'Screaming like a banshee,' an affronted lady with a helmet of grey curls adds. I clear my throat and apologise, and everyone returns to their pre-crazy woman state. My headache manifests with a thud above my right eye and I root around in my bag for some painkillers but can't find any. I stretch my neck from side to side and continue the uncomfortable journey in uncomfortable silence.

'Excuse me, but . . .' A busy nurse puts up her hand to hold my enquiry, before rushing off somewhere else. 'Excuse me, could you—?' Again another 'I'll be with you in a minute' look from a porter. 'If you could just . . .' I try again, this time to a tall man with a name tag pinned to his shirt who may or may not work in the hospital. My mind and body are becoming less tolerant. There is chaos all around: wheelchairs, trolleys, doctors, nurses, drunks, babies with ear infections; the noise is too much. I can feel myself unravelling, my head taking regular blunt punches behind my eye, until I explode.

'Heeeellllllllppp!' I scream. Oh Christ. The Beatles again. Who knew I was such a fan? OK, so here I go again but this time it's different. I'm desperate. I need to see Rose, so when I start to tell people that I want someone, anybody, I'm not singing it in the wobbly-head, foot-tapping way that we've all seen the lovely lads from Liverpool perform. I'm singing it in a way that I'd imagine Danny Dyer would sing it. Even though – I tell the startled-looking nurse who tries to pull my hand from her collar – that 'I depreciate her being found,' I can feel my face singing it with aggression. I let her go and push her, before screaming at the two security guards who have appeared from nowhere to put my legs back down as I'm unceremoniously carried down a corridor. My feet are placed back on the floor while my hands are restrained behind my back. I'm still pushing and shoving at this point, begging them to come to my aid, but they just hold my arms tighter. I try to tell them that when I was a youngster, I didn't really need their help in any manner but that right now I'm not so sure. I start to feel myself getting more and more frustrated as I desperately try to control my voice: but it just won't stop.

I'm still struggling to twist and turn out of their grip, trying to tell them that I need to get to Rose, but all that happens is I that I leave the four boys from the sixties and instead try to explain my predicament with Rage Against the Machine's 'Bullet in the Head'. I'm not really a fan of this band but Flynn often played them when he was having a particularly bad day, so I end up with a kind of mix of my limited knowledge. Right now, I'm screaming that they should be doing what they've been told. I've no idea what I'm going on about apart from that I end up screaming the eff word, telling them I won't do anything they ask and spitting into the security guards' faces. Mortifyingly, I notice two policemen/ex-Welsh rugby players walk around the corner and I realise that I'm not going to get to Rose. I'm not going to be able to help her for a long time. I'm still screaming at them, 'fuck you!' and reiterating that I'm not going to do what they asked me to; over and over I scream at them, and then to my absolute shame I say the worst phrase associated with the eff word: I scream at them calling them all 'mother fu—' well, you can fill in the gaps, followed by something about killing and names. I can see the policeman's mouth moving, making sentences, but I can't hear him above the profanities vomiting from my mouth. I presume I'm being read my rights. Roughly, I'm handcuffed and forced out of the hospital, kicking a chair on my way through in true rock-style fashion, before being bundled into the waiting police car.

My body is shaking; a nervous energy is surging through me and I can't keep still. The headache is all-encompassing and as we arrive outside the police station I feel as though I'm trapped, entombed inside this body. The lights inside the station sear my skin, every part of me feels sensitive, the guiding hand at the bottom of my spine feels like needles and the fabric of my top scratches my skin. My legs ache and my body feels too heavy for them to hold. I stagger a little. They ask me questions but I can't speak. My mouth is glue. My teeth clamp and my throat closes. I'm bundled into a cell but they needn't have bothered. I'm in my own prison. It's never been this bad before. I try to stop the images of Rose. Try not to think of her because if I do, I will never get out. I lie down on the hard bed; the scrape of the grey blanket rakes across my cheek. I close my eyes and try to concentrate on the sound of the train from before: 'ch-ch-ch, puh, ch-ch-ch, puh . . .'

I concentrate on my breathing but then an image of a deathly pale Rose – still and dead-eyed – rips through me and I start again with the swearing and anger until eventually I start banging my head against the wall. Gently at first.

Thud. Thud. Thud. Until the thud starts to sound more like a crack and then there is still, dark, peace.

When I wake up, I'm restrained by thick Velcro straps and in a hospital. It takes me a moment to recall where I am and why I'm here. My eyes are grit, red and angry. My heavy eyelids stretch against their weight and I lock on to a stern-looking policewoman in the far side of the room. My forehead feels tight and I gather that I must have some sort of dressing on it. She hasn't noticed that I'm awake and I take a moment to calm myself. The image of Rose's blood drains my body, but before I let my emotions take hold, I need to speak to this woman. She isn't a friend or a foe. She doesn't know me and I've no idea if she has children or if she likes her job. This woman is of no importance to me and at the same time, the most important person in my life. If I'm going to get to Rose I need her help. She has a solid frame, not overweight but broad and firm. She has thick-rimmed glasses and her dark blonde hair is held tightly into a ponytail. Her fringe needs cutting and she flicks it away from the rim of her glasses with annoyance. She's writing something official, tapping the chewed lid of her biro as she stares out of the small window.

'Hi,' I smile. She turns her head to me and raises a disapproving eyebrow. 'Could I . . .' I try to gesture to the jug of water on the bedside cabinet, 'have a drink of water, please?' My voice is hoarse, like I've got tonsillitis. She rises from her chair as if she's never wanted to do anything less in her entire life. She holds the beaker to my dry lips and lets me drink.

'Slowly,' she adds. Her voice holds the threat and promise of what is to come. The softer lilt as she cautions me not to struggle against the straps offers me hope, but the bluntness of her 'OK?' is a command rather than a question.

'What time is it?'

'A little after half-eight. I'm afraid you've missed breakfast.' Again, the soft tone with a blunt delivery confuses me. 'What is your name?' The voice is all business.

'Melody King. Please, if I can just explain—'

'Date of birth?' The no-nonsense manner, leaving no need for interpretation.

'Fifteenth June, 1979. I'm sorry about the way I was at the hospital. Am I in Aberystwyth? Could I, am I—' I gesture my restrained hands around, 'Can I explain why I behaved the way I did?' She exhales loudly but doesn't decline my request. 'I had an accident some time ago which damaged me, somehow. There is no explanation for it, the doctors have tried but they can't find out why I do what I do . . . I sing. When I'm anxious.' She furrows her brow in confusion or disbelief, I'm not sure which. 'It used to be just singing but it is spreading into my motor skills now and I can't seem to stop it.'

'What, so you're telling me that you had no control when you . . .' she pushes herself back on her chair, grabs a note book, flicks back a few pages and says, 'spat at the security guards' faces?'

'No. Or when I was, oh Lord, saying the eff word.' I close my eyes momentarily in shame.

'So, you were anxious?'

'Please, listen before . . .' 'I Shot the Sheriff' is playing quietly at the back of my neck. It's dulled at the moment, like a closed front door on a house party. 'I might, start again. My daughter Rose has been admitted to the hospital, she's, she's—' I gulp as the party door opens and shuts, leaking a little of Bob Marley's confession and absolute denial about the deputy, 'tried to commit suicide. I wasn't there, you see, she was on holiday with my mum. Nobody would help me at the desk and I need to see if she's OK.' I start to turn my head left and right.

'OK, OK . . . Melody?' I'm still trying to look around to see if I can glimpse past the blue curtains around my bed. 'Melody?' Her voice is strong and in control. 'I need you to breathe . . .' she pushes the nurse button by the side of the bed, 'in through your nose, out through your mouth.' She pushes it again. A garden gnome in doctor form arrives. 'Could you give her something to calm her down, please? Will that help, Melody?' I nod. There is some activity beside the bed, a sharp scratch and then cups and paper plates are thrown into bins, thanks and promises to do this again soon are spoken, empty bottles are thrown into the recycling and then finally the party is over and the host slumps on to the sofa, falling into a deep, dreamless sleep.

Distant sounds: laughing; wheels of a trolley; metal hoop on metal rod; drawer open and shut; beeping machines; chesty coughs; urgent messages; requests for coffee and opening scratches of sweet wrappers . . . my head is full of the activity of the hospital but my eyes remain closed. There is blood in her hair. There is blood in her mouth. There is a gun, there is a razor blade. There are Tom's green eyes. There is a balcony, there is a gas oven, there is the sea, there is Rose and then there is nothing.
'Melody?'
'Mum?'
'Melody . . . can you hear me?'
'Mum?'
'Why isn't she answering?'
'What are you talking about? I am answering!'
'It will take a little while for her to come around. We've had to give her a strong sedative. She became very distressed while she was resting.'
'When will she wake up?'
'Hard to say. Within the next hour or so, I should think.'

'How often does Melody's condition manifest?'

'I don't know really, a few days a week maybe?'

'It's more than that, Gran.'

'Flynn?' I will my eyes to open but they remain nailed shut. A heavy lid on my invisible coffin.

'Does she often get upset when she sleeps?' a man asks, deep, rich, sharp, like a sapphire. Flynn's voice is heavy and tired.

'Yeah, I guess. She sings most nights, sometimes it's the same song, but lately it's just a scream. No wobble, no change of scale, just a very long, very horrible scream that breaks when she needs a breath and then it starts again.'

'That must be very difficult for you and your sister,' the sapphire observes.

'Sometimes,' Flynn grumbles, 'but we're used to it.' I sense the shrug of his shoulders.

'Oh Flynn,' my mum answers.

'It's nothing. Everyone has their shit to deal with.'

'Don't say shit,' I croak.

'Mum?' It takes me a moment to adjust to the slice of light that is expanding until I can see properly.

'Rose? Is she OK?'

'Mrs King, I'm Dr Banks.' I turn my head towards him. He has a sharp, hook-like nose, eyes so dark and small that I can't see where the pupil stops and the iris starts. Ginger hair stands up in tufts all over his head and his face is half hidden by a patchy ginger and brown beard. He reminds me of a chicken.

'Is Rose OK?'

'Rose is stable, yes.' I look at Flynn and my insides shrivel. He has been dwarfed by the magnitude of these events. He looks shrunken, defeated and so young, but as I meet his gaze, he fixes me with the stare of a much older person, a person who has had to deal with a lifetime of troubles.

'What happened?' I ask him.

'She cut herself . . . has been cutting herself.'

'What? How did I not know?'

'You mustn't blame yourself,' Mum interjects.

'Who else is there to blame?!' I shuffle up the bed and realise my restraints have gone. I look around for the policewoman but realise she isn't there.

'Where is the policewoman? Am I under arrest?'

Flynn passes me a drink of water. 'You've been de-arrested.'

'Eh?'

'Because you're a loon, you're under the care of the hospital, at the moment.'

'Oh.' I feel a small amount of relief. 'Tell me what happened. Did you know what she was up to?' I ask Flynn, who shakes his head.

'I knew she was, you know, not great. I mean, school has been rough for her and, well, when we found out that Dad was, you know, alive and that he left us . . . she's been down but when we were on holiday she seemed loads better. She had made friends with a group of ordinary kids, not like that bunch of emos at school. Also there was a boy.'

'A boy?'

'At the caravan park. He seemed to be into her and she was, you know . . .' He rolled his eyes and pulled an uncomfortable face.

'She was, you know, what? Was she sleeping with him?' I ask hysterically. My mum has put her hand to her throat and begins fiddling with her pearls.

'Ugh and like, how would I know? But I think she'd kissed him. Anyway, that's not the point,' he rushes on. 'Yesterday I saw him with his tongue halfway down another girl's throat, the one she'd been hanging around with.' He rubs the back of his neck. 'I shouldn't have told her.'

'Flynn found her, Mel. She was unconscious, there was blood everywhere, all over the shower curtain.'

'Gran.' He stops her mid-sentence. 'I shouldn't have told her,' he repeats.

'Oh, Flynn. It's not your fault. Has she done this before? This self-harming thing?'

'That's what the doctors have said. There are old scars at the top of her arm apparently.'

Then I remember the red stain in the bathroom at the B&B. How I had thought that it just hadn't been cleaned properly. The missing gauze from the bathroom cabinet. How could I not have known this was happening? I try to remember the last time I had seen her in a vest and I can't. I picture her. Her face when she found out Dev was alive, her reflection in the glass door in the train station, her face when I had walked into the school office . . . when was the last time I'd heard her laugh? How could I have not noticed how sad she had become? How distant. I was so wrapped up in trying to find Dev that I had lost sight of Rose.

'Can I see her?'

'Melody, I need you to stay here and rest for the rest of today and this evening,' Dr Banks says in a headmaster tone.

'You are NOT keeping me from seeing my daughter!' I explode. 'She needs me, what kind of mother am I if I don't go to her when she's hurt?'

'Mum, calm down—'

'I will not calm down. I want to see Rose now!' I throw back the covers and start to flap about.

Oh holy hell.

I'm flapping about because – as I see Flynn's face light up with amusement and my mum trying not to laugh – I've started humming and dancing to 'The Birdie Song'. I'm currently tweeting my hands, flapping my bent arms and wiggling my bum.

'With a little bit of this and a little bit of that and shake your bum . . .' I warble before linking arms with Dr Banks and swinging him around.

For crying out loud, novelty songs of the eighties have got a lot to answer for.

20

Rose

They all know. Mum, Nan, Flynn, the people at the hospital. They all know.

I just want to make something very clear. I was NOT trying to kill myself, OK? I wasn't. I'm not suicidal. I know that sounds weird when I've cut myself so deeply that I almost bled to death, but honestly I'm not. This is how it is.

Life is crap. My life. Our lives are just crap.

It started a while back. I can't really remember why I did it, I just took a paperclip, unfolded it and scratched the surface of my arm. It felt so pure; I felt calm afterwards, like I'd taken something. The Goldfish, Rose King, dork, ginger freak, none of that mattered. No, that's not true: it all still mattered but it mattered less. It didn't matter as much, that on my last physics test, I only got 90 per cent. It didn't matter as much, that I can't even get a pair of shoes with my mum without looking like a freak show and it didn't matter as much that Dad left us. He didn't die, didn't go missing, he just left.

I can cope with some of the crap because of this. I cut myself and I can cope. Even knowing that it was wrong, that I was wrong, mattered less because of it. It is just my way of coping. I don't take drugs, I don't smoke like a load of the kids at school, I don't drink; is it really that bad?

I'm not stupid, I know I took it too far and for that I'm sorry. Sorry that I had to put this on Flynn's shoulders, as if he doesn't have enough to deal with; I just couldn't stop.

Things were better. Have been better; I haven't cut myself for almost a month. Being friends with Lisa has helped. Accepting myself for who I am and not having to pretend that I'm the girl I was when I was friends with Megan, has helped, and a week without Mum has helped too. I know that sounds horrid but it was sooo nice to be able to be a normal family on holiday. It was nice to make friends with girls who wanted to hang out with me, who didn't know about Mum or about how well I do at school, who just wanted to do normal stuff. Go to the beach, play rounders. Go on body boards. It was just so nice. Then there was Alex. He came on Tuesday and knew Courtney . . . they've both got vans on the site that their families own and have known each other for, like, ever. He is, just, well, good-looking, like Bieber good-looking, and he was so easy to talk to. We were all sat at the beach talking about that vine with the cat and he started covering my feet with sand.

'You have ugly feet,' he said and I burst out laughing.

Our gang grew and by Friday there were seven of us. Me, Courtney, Alex, George, Dylan, Katie (who looks like a mini Katie Price – all drawn-on eyebrows and pouty lips) and Ella. But inside the gang were me and Alex: we sat next to each other a lot; went off to get ice cream and body-boarded . . . it always seemed to be the two of us. He twisted my hair around his finger a lot and then on Friday afternoon, while we were sitting in the dunes, he kissed me. It was kind of gross at first but then I got into it. Anyway, the next day he was in the dunes with Katie.

It's not like I thought he was the love of my life or anything,

I'm not stupid, but I thought he really liked me at least. Flynn was going to smack him one, but I just laughed and told him to chill out. It's not like I wouldn't do the same if someone hotter came along, I said. I waited until he and Gran had gone to the supermarket to get some supplies, locked myself in the shower room, and that was that.

Anyway. Like I said, they all know now, so the question is, what happens next?

21

Melody

Home. I stare into the darkness of my garden through the kitchen window and listen to the sounds of home. Such a small word that means so much. Look for its definition and you see words: *'The place where one lives permanently as a member of a family or household. A place of residence, accommodation, property, a roof over one's head.'* I remember helping Flynn with this definition when he was ten. Home – *'an institution for people needing professional care or supervision, a place where something flourishes, is most typically found.'* He had been confused by the definitions, asking me why it doesn't talk about the feeling of going 'home' in the sense of safety.

'I don't get it!' He had thrown his pencil across the table.

'What don't you get?' I had asked, trying to find the light-bulb moment where everything would become clear. It would always take that little extra something to help Flynn make sense of things, and then he would give a half-raised smile and say 'Oh . . . why doesn't it just say that?'

'A place where something flourishes.' I play this over in my mind. This is our home. Are my children flourishing? Am I?

Rose is asleep upstairs; she has been asleep for most of the day and Flynn and I have been tiptoeing around. Around the house, the home, each other. Neither of us wanting to talk about it, neither of us wanting to crack the thick layer of ice over the bitter chill of what has happened.

The washing machine finishes and I crouch on the floor, pulling out a school shirt from the bottom of the laundry bin; the only white T-shirt that Flynn owns; a pair of cream combat trousers, a blouse, knickers and a bra; all of it tangled up in a piece of white lace. I push away the feel of his hands as he tied it in my hair, the soft sand running through my fingers, the smell of his skin and the warmth of his breath on my neck. It doesn't belong here amongst our things. It's an intrusion, an imposition. Sitting with my legs apart, I start trying to untangle the lace but it's wrapped around a button, twisted around a zip, enlaced amidst our lives. I start yanking the clothes free but the harder I pull and try to release them, the more caught they become.

'Ughhh!' I shout, then stand up and yank open the kitchen junk drawer. Grabbing the scissors, I sit back down and begin chopping the lace into tiny pieces, the clothes billowing back on to the floor, unrestricted and free.

Closing my eyes, I try to slow my breathing down, taking deep breaths lest I break into another hit from Black Lace. It's only when I'm confident that I'm not about to do the conga that I open my eyes and realise that I've cut my finger. Slowly I unfurl my hand, stare at the bloodied lace and wonder how something that was pure, beautiful and crafted with love is now just a soiled rag.

The bubbles rise in the glass as I fill it with cold water. The weight of the two pills lie heavily in my palm. Fluoxetine. I've been down this route before, the side effects of feeling tired and sick, of not wanting to eat, but this time I have no choice. I can't help Rose if I'm not helping myself. I pop the tablets into my mouth and swallow them down.

'Mum?' She stands sheepishly in the corner of my

bedroom. I pull back the covers of the bed and she hesitates slightly before jumping in. I lift my arm and she lies on top of it, the well-honed position of childhood, of nightmarish dreams and high temperature-fuelled nights. I run my fingers through her heavy hair.

'Are you OK?' She sighs. I don't know what else to say. Is it my fault? I want to ask her.

'Are you going to keep asking me that?' she answers, but I can hear a smile in her voice.

'I don't know what else to ask,' I reply. I've spent hours trying to find out how to handle this 'episode' and the only thing that I can find is to be honest. We've always coped with whatever life has thrown at us if we've been honest with each other. I wonder now, at what point did we stop?

'Ask me about what I want for tea tomorrow.'

'What do you want for tea tomorrow?'

'I don't know. Fajitas?'

'OK. Shall we have a movie night?'

'Sure.'

'What shall we watch? Something funny or a thriller maybe?' I ask.

'How about a slasher?'

'What?!' And then she starts laughing. A deep down, in-her-belly laugh. I feel her whole body relax and shake with giggles. It's contagious and I can't help but join in, even if our humour may seem inappropriate to the rest of the world. Flynn pokes his head around the door.

'What's so funny?' he asks, dragging his hand through his hair and looking confused.

'Just choosing a film for tomorrow night,' and we start again.

'What about, what about . . .' Rose can barely speak, '. . . *Scarface*?' The political incorrectness of this whole conversation is taking over and we can barely breathe through the snorts and tears. Flynn sits on the edge of the bed shaking his head.

'You know that is emotional abuse, Mother, right?' I'm trying to say sorry but I'm laughing too hard.

'*Moulin Rouge*?' he adds with a smirk. 'No?'

'*Evita*?' Rose bursts out.

'*Big Momma's House*?' Flynn adds, at which point I stop laughing.

'That is just taking things too far, Flynn,' I say, slightly distressed. 'My bottom is not that big.'

'If you say so,' he smirks. 'Shall I stick the kettle on?'

'Go on then, I was going to try and sleep but I got invaded by the ginger nut.' I nod my head against Rose's.

'Can I have one too?' Rose asks. Flynn rolls his eyes.

'Kay.' He shuffles off the bed.

'And a couple of digestives!' I add.

'Are you sure about that, Mum? What with the size of your—' I silence him with a swiftly aimed pillow.

'Missed.' He sticks his tongue out and hurries out of the room as Rose throws another cushion at him. The light-hearted feeling plummets as the sleeve of her nightdress rides up and I see the bandage around her arm: covering the pain, the disgust, the unknown. She sees my face change and pulls her sleeve back down.

'Don't,' I say gently. She looks up at me through her golden eyelashes. 'Don't feel like you need to hide that.'

'But—'

'You have nothing to be ashamed of. Nothing.' I stroke her cheek. 'This,' she tenses as I pull her sleeve back, 'means that you've had a shitty time and that you've dealt with it. Maybe not in the best way, but you've still survived,' I kiss her forehead, 'you're still here. We're still here.'

There is a small moment where her face is open and I see her as a little girl. That beautiful toddler who would sing 'Santa

Claus is coming, tooooooo tooooowwwwwnn!' at the top of her voice and then demand 'Clap, Mummy, clap!' Unable to resist, we always would, and then she would take a small, grand bow as though she had just performed at the Royal Albert Hall. She would do this over and over again; each time we clapped, the louder and grander her performances. The more she would giggle, the more she would overstate the words to the song until she finally climbed up on to my lap and snuggled. Sucking her tongue and twirling her hair. I wish all I had to do to make her happy now is clap.

We drink our tea, eat our biscuits and I read to her. It's an old book of fables and fairy tales from when she was little. It seems such a natural act, lying on the bed reading to my child. When did the bedtime stories stop? I read until the warmth and moisture of the tea has left and my arms and hands have pins and needles. I read until her breathing slows, becomes heavy, and gentle snores rise from the back of her throat. Gingerly, I ease myself away from her and lie on my side, quietly closing the book and looking at the myriad of characters on the cover: characters from long ago, now reinvented by Disney or Pixar; my heart quickens.

'I can hear your heart beating.' I close my eyes. I can hear the waves crashing, the tingle from the chilli in the spaghetti sauce on my lips.

'It doesn't belong to me any more. You've stolen it.' I hear his voice as though he's in this room with us.

'Makes me sound like the wicked witch in Snow White . . .' I open my eyes, stroke the front cover and then put it on the bedside table. I lie on my side and watch Rose sleep, thinking of him, thinking of the cottage with only him in it. Cooking his meals alone, the bed made, the porch empty. How is he? What must he have thought when he returned and saw my ridiculous apology? Did he wonder where I was? Does he even care? I stroke Rose's delicate face, her skin almost translucent. Tiny blue veins, pulsing under her skin. Veins that she ripped open. I did the right thing protecting him from this, but did I do the best for them? I picture his face as he got down on his knee, his smile first thing in the morning. I close my eyes, drape my hand over my Rose's waist and drift into a deep sleep.

I wake with a start and for a deliciously confused moment I think I'm still with him. That I'm going to turn over and see his sleepy smile. Hear the wind whistling its gentle tune as it eases its way through the ancient cracks in the sea-beaten window frames. That Rose and Flynn are happy on holiday and that everything, for once, is good. But then I see the bandage, hear the bin men talking outside, not a crashing wave or a seagull calling. I squint at the clock on the wall and realise that we've slept for ten hours. Nausea fills me, urges me to stay still, but I can't. We've got a meeting with the psychiatrist at eleven. I shake Rose's shoulder gently and she groans about the time – just like every other teenager – and pulls the duvet over her head. I shower and try not to think about him. I try not to think about him as I push away my toast, try not to think of him as I swallow more pills. Try not to think of him as I choose an outfit that won't make me look like a failed mother. But he's here. He's here with every stroke of the hairbrush, with every bowl of washing-up, each time I walk down the stairs and every word I speak. He's here with every breath I take.

Oh shite.

'Mum, that is a really creepy song,' Rose says as she spits out her toothpaste. 'Are you really going to be watching me all of the time?' I roll my eyes as I warble my way through the end of the song.

'Of course not,' Flynn adds as he appears with bed hair and pillow creases on the side of his face. 'Did you sleep?' he asks. She nods.

'Loads. You?'

'Yeah. No midnight sonnets?'

'Nope, the tablets must be working.' I flap my arms in disbelief at them as they continue to have a full conversation about me as though I'm a song on the radio on the kitchen side.

'Christ, this song goes on a bit, doesn't it?' I nod and stomp down the stairs, still confirming that I will be Rose's stalker for the foreseeable future.

'Stop fidgeting,' Rose tells me as we wait.

'Sorry.' I knit my hands together.

'Rose King?'

We both get up and follow the smiley nurse into the room and sit down. It's just like any other doctor's office that I've been in before. I'm not quite sure what I was expecting to be different, to be honest. Big leather sofa perhaps? Oh, that's a psychologist, isn't it?

'So, Rose . . .' I jump slightly as a tall, greying horse of a man walks in. He canters his way across the room, all stiff upper lip and teeth, then leans back in his chair. 'How are you feeling?' His voice is soft and doesn't match the way he looks at all. I was expecting a booming town crier tone but his is soft, gentle.

'Um, OK I guess.' He smiles and I resist the urge to dig into my handbag and give him a bite of my apple (Flynn's comments about my bottom have not gone unattended).

'She's doing really well.' I rub her arm firmly and then pat it. She looks down at my hand and pulls a weird 'what are you doing?' face.

He doesn't say anything for a while. Rose and I exchange a raised eyebrow and shrugged-shoulder silent conversation.

'Rose . . . it's a pretty name. Such beautiful flowers, aren't they? Such delicate petals . . . but then you have to be careful of those thorns, don't you?' He smiles again. 'Do you think you're more like the petals or the thorns, Rose?'

'The thorns.'

'Do you think you're beautiful, Rose?'

'No.' She says it without hesitation.

'But you are Rose, you're—' I begin.

'Mrs King, it's at this point that I'm going to ask you to leave, if that's OK with you, Rose?' He has a way of saying this that doesn't offend me. I wonder if, with a voice like that, he could offend anyone.

She nods. A short, quick confirmation. This isn't a shock. I was told that most of these sessions would be just for Rose.

'Of course,' I say, trying to emulate his tone, but instead, end up sounding like a phone-for-sex girl. Again, Rose looks at me with the 'what are you doing?' face. I close the door behind me and try not to think of the heart-breaking conversation that is going on inside.

'Are you OK?' I ask as we carry the shopping into the kitchen.

'Will you stop asking me if I'm OK?!' she yells, drops the shopping bags – containing the fajita mix and movie night goodies – and runs up the stairs. I put the bags on to the kitchen table and follow the sounds of someone American, shouting excitedly about something, into the lounge.

'You need to back off a bit,' Flynn mumbles through a mouthful of toast as he sits staring at a YouTube video on his phone.

'I meant was she OK because the bag was heavy. Not because I thought she was on the verge of slitting her wrists.'

'Oh.'

'Are *you* OK?' I ask, at the risk of being shouted at.

'I, my dear mother, have a hot date.' A gentle, teasing smile pulls at the corner of my mouth as I watch him brush off the crumbs from his top and on to his black jeans. I sit on the arm of the sofa.

'Well, well, Casanova, do tell, who is this beauty of whom you speak?'

'Jesus, Mum, you're weird. Why are you talking like that?'

'No idea. Anyway, come on then, who is she?'

'She's the girl from the train.'

'Oh God. The Girl on the Train?' He rolls his eyes at me.

'The one from your "Don't Stop Me Now" performance.'

'Oh. Ooooh, she was pretty.'

'We've been fb friends for a while now.'

'Fb friends?' I ask, aghast. Fuck buddies?! How has this happened without me knowing? Oh arses. How do I tell him that that kind of relationship will never work? Someone always gets hurt.

'Flynn, I'm pleased that you're, um, sowing your, um, oats and that you're into this whole,' I start to make hand movements that resemble some kind of lopsided windmill, 'no ties, um, thing, but this never ends well. You can't,' I do a few uncomfortable thrusts to demonstrate my point, 'without having some kind of emotional investment.' He's looking at me like I'm vomiting on his shoes. I carry on regardless. 'There is always one person in the relationship who feels more than the other. But well done you, for getting on the um, horse.' I tap him on the shoulder.

'Mum?'

'Hmmmm? Oh, and make sure you're using—' I mimic opening a condom wrapper and stretching it like a balloon – quite why I'm doing this action, I'm not quite sure; I'm fairly certain that I've never stretched a condom like a balloon before – 'precautions.'

'Mum!'

'Yes?'

'What do you think fb friends means?'

'Well,' I make a circle shape with my thumb and middle finger and then poke the Peter Pointer from my other hand through the centre of it, 'without, you know, being . . .' I mimic inverted commas, '"exclusive".' Isn't that what the Americans call it?' His eyes widen and then he bursts out laughing.

'Oh Mum,' he stands up and ruffles my hair. 'You're so sweet . . .' he laughs again, 'but the idea of me being someone's fuck buddy is a bit ambitious even for you. I'm hoping I'll get to cop a feel before she gets too close to my face if I'm honest. But thanks for thinking that she might want to . . .' and then he imitates my early thrusting action. He continues to chuckle his way upstairs.

'I'm meeting her in Wolverhampton; she lives in Birmingham!' he calls over his shoulder.

'What does fb mean then?!' I shout up after him.

'Facebook friend!' he shouts back.

Oh.

I hear him gently knock on Rose's door and then close it behind him. Standing at the bottom of the stairs for a few moments, I listen to the deep rumble of Flynn's voice and then the chime of Rose's laugh in response.

I switch the kettle off, my stomach heaving at the idea of coffee as my laptop whirs into action. I fumble inside my bag and dig out the paper which Rose had handed to me when she left the psychiatrist's office, and open the self-help page. After Rose had had her session with Dr Osborne, he had invited me back inside, explaining that he didn't feel that Rose needed medication just yet and that he wanted to try cognitive behaviour therapy first and something called 'mindfulness'. He's told me that she will be involved with CAMHS – Child and Adolescent Mental Health Services – and that a tier-three worker will be visiting us about once a week. I click on the 'mindfulness' tab and read about it. My mind is blown for a few moments as I try to understand the basics of what it is telling me. To be mindful means staying in the moment, I think. Being aware of your surroundings and noticing everything that is here and now rather than what there is to worry about. OK, got it. I feel the warmth of the laptop under my hands. I feel the hard wood of the chair beneath my bottom. Right. What's next? Ooh, breathing techniques. I like these, I've tried them before to help with my blues if you'll excuse the pun. Oh. I've got to concentrate on my tummy – I'd rather not – but I'll give it a go. I focus on it expanding and contracting, concentrating on the whole breath: in and out. Shit, am I still supposed to be mindful of the chair? I continue with my breathing, trying also to be mindful of the chair and my bottom which is becoming numb. I have a numb bum, which is on the hard, wooden chair, I ride my breathing in and out and concentrate on my stomach going up and down. Damn it, did I put the chicken in the fridge? Doesn't matter, stay in the moment, be aware of the numb bum, the chair, the breathing, my tummy. Blimey, this is hard work. Stop it, back in the moment, numb bum, warm laptop, breathing all the way in, all the way out. I need a fart. I'm aware that I need to fart. I'm aware of my stomach going in and out but I need to tense my stomach or I will fart. I'm mindful that I have a numb bum, that I need to fart and that the chair is hard and the laptop is warm – oh and that I'm breathing in and ooops. I've farted. I'm mindful that I've farted and that I have a warm numb bum. I'm mindful that there is an unpleasant smell in the kitchen. I breathe the unpleasant smell in, and gratefully, back out. Back in . . . OK, that's enough. I need to open the window and I need to move my numb bum. Standing up, I rub the base of my spine, try to ignore the light-headedness and nausea as I open the window.

'Sorry I stormed off,' Rose mumbles as she walks past me, pulls open the fridge door, grabs a can of Coke, and opens it with a crack of tin against tin.

'It's OK.'

Her face screws up. 'What is that smell?' she asks.

'Never mind that, come here.' She leans into my embrace and it's only then that I realise that the whole time I was being mindful, I hadn't thought of him once.

22

Tom

So, where was I the last time we spoke? Oh yeah, I was home alone.

Georgie was shouting, 'Tom? Tom?! God, this place is a mess.' I watched her start to pile dirty plates up and turn the tap on. She was shaking her head and sniffing one of the plates suspiciously.

'Hi.' She spun around and I could see in her face that I was not looking my best. Not by a long shot.

'Oh Tom.' She turned the tap back off, went to wipe her hands on a tea towel, thought better of it and wiped them on her pristine jeans instead. 'This isn't just a touch of flu, is it?' I pushed the dirty laundry off the sofa on to the floor and slumped down. 'When was the last time you slept?' I closed my eyes and rubbed the back of my head, stretching the muscles in my neck to the right, to the left. I opened my eyes; they felt hot and sore. I squinted at her; the concern was written across her face.

'Honestly? I don't know.' My voice was cracked, weak; beaten.

'Right, go upstairs, take a shower. Shave, brush your teeth. I'll clean down here and make a pot of coffee.'

'I—'

'Just do it. You're worrying me.' She turned her back and

started looking for washing-up liquid. Sighing, I heaved myself from the sofa and went upstairs.

The water was hot and powerful but it barely registered. The noises of Georgie in the kitchen had made me feel on guard, alert. I didn't want to feel alert; I wanted to remain numb. I realised that I didn't want her there. I stepped out of the shower dripping, without a towel, and walked into the bedroom. Clothes were all over the place. I'm not stupid. I knew that I was a mess, I knew that I wasn't in a good place, but I really didn't care. A kitchen cupboard door slammed and I flinched. She needed to leave. I didn't need rescuing; I needed to be left the fuck alone.

As I went downstairs, the noises were deafening: the washing machine clanked and slurped, the coffee machine hissed and dripped. Georgie had the radio on, the shouts and laughter of the DJ booming around the house. I tried to focus on one thing at a time but it was everywhere, the noise, the intrusion. I covered my ears but even the rustle of a bin bag crackled inside my head.

'Enough!' I screamed at her and then she tilted. The room tilted and then there was nothing.

'Ouch,' I flinched as she held an ice pack to the side of my face. My top lip was swollen and my arm hurt like hell.

'Shhhhh.' She held the ice pack firmly and looked at me as though I was a stranger.

'I'm fine. Honestly. You can go.' She laughed a cold, hollow laugh.

'You're not fine, Tom. You're anything but fine. I've called for the doctor again.'

'What? I don't need a doctor. I just need some peace and quiet.'

'No, you don't. You need to talk to somebody, and besides, he's retired so you can't use your usual excuse of it being too complicated. He's a bored old man who doesn't care if you aren't a real person on paper or not.' I pushed the ice pack away and stood up.

'What do you know?' I looked at her carefully. 'Do you know who I am?'

'Tom—'

'Do you?' I shouted.

'Tom, calm down, if you just—'

'My name isn't even Tom!'

'Calm. Down,' she said, holding her hand up as if talking to a child. 'I know who you are. You're a kind, gentle man who has been dealt a tough hand in life. You're an amazing artist and a wonderful friend.'

I threw my hands up in exasperation and got up off the floor. I started walking around in circles, trying to find the words to explain to her.

'I met someone. The woman from the exhibition. I knew her. Kind of . . .' I scratched the back of my head in frustration. 'It's hard to explain, but I just, we just, fit. Mel, she was, is, perfect. We laughed at the same stuff, stupid stuff but it just felt real, right. I knew something was a bit off but I guess I just ignored it? Pretended everything was, you know . . . fine. I've never believed in love at first sight but this felt like it, like what I'd imagine it to feel like anyway. I asked her to marry me.' At this she raised her eyebrows. 'Don't look at me like that. I didn't want her to leave. I knew she would go, but I . . .' digging into my jeans pocket I pulled out the photo, 'I found this.' I passed it to her and watched as the implications of the photo sank in. Of course, Georgie knew all about my nightmares, we'd talked about them often, especially when I started to create *Stability*.

'Who is he?'

'I don't know. Her name isn't even Melissa.'

'What is it?'

'I don't know. I left. I was angry, I didn't expect her to just leave.'

'What? Vanished?'

'She left a note, sort of.'

'What did it say?'

'Sorry.'

'That's it?'

'Yep.'

'Are you going to go after her?'

'I can't.' Raising my fingers, I started ticking them off, 'I don't know her name, I don't know where she lives except that it's in Shropshire somewhere. I know that she made mud pies when she was little but I don't know her phone number. I know that she thinks my feet are ugly but I don't know her surname. Oh Christ, George . . . I know that I love her but I don't know who she is and I don't know why she didn't tell me about the boy.' The floor felt hard against my knees as I knelt down. 'Who is he? What if, what if I did something to him, before I lost my memory? What if I gave him the scars?'

There was a knock on the door and she got up to let Dr Rider in. There was the usual offer of a drink, the shuffling about as he put his bag down, comments about the weather before he sat down and looked at me over the rim of his glasses.

'When was the last time you fainted?'

'A few months back.'

'Right, and how long were you unconscious for?'

'It's hard to say. A while, I suppose, because I woke up in a hospital.'

'Hmmm. What happens before you pass out?'

'Noise.'

'What do you mean by noise?'

'Well, last time, I heard a shop shutter being drawn and that was it, pft.'

'And today?'

'The same, I suppose. I've not slept for, I don't know, but when I don't sleep, too much sound is hard to deal with. I'm fine now, really. I just need to rest and I'll be right as rain.' I smiled.

'Hmmm. Well, I think maybe trying some herbal sleeping tablets from the chemist would help. I'd like to see you again in a week. See if having a bit more sleep helps.'

Ignoring the calluses in the palms of my hand, I continued with the sculptures. Your eyes stared back at me in three deconstructed dimensions. The arch of your eyebrows, the way your eyelashes curled to the right. Hammering the steel, I squinted in the dimming light, making sure that one edge was thinner than the other as I twisted it into the curve of your eyelid. Concentrating on the fleeting memory of you looking up at me the first night we slept together; the wonder in your eyes – as if I was the most special thing you'd ever seen. I added a thin piece – the curve of the crease of your eyelid, deep and heavy. The top of my shoulders was starting to burn and my hands were beginning to jitter. I needed to stop working, yet I couldn't seem to help myself. The smell of the soldering iron, the feel of the metal and the weight of the tools: the only sensations that had ever felt part of my past. I knew it deep down. I put the sculpture next to a few old pots of paint that I kept there in the shed, then curled my hands into fists before releasing them, trying to get some control back, and then I saw you. Like a bolt, like lightning, the image of you with yellow paint in your hair which was long – down your back long – and you were laughing. The image was so clear that I lost my balance slightly and then you were gone. Closing my eyes, I tried to bring the image back, but I couldn't.

I'd downed tools for the night. The house seemed empty and cold without you. I turned on the TV and flicked through the channels but my mind wouldn't quieten. Who are you? Why did you come here? Who is the boy? Was it all a lie? I turned the TV off and headed upstairs. I ran myself a bath, wincing as I reached to put the plug in. I reached for some form of bath gel, my back reminding me that I was no longer as young as I once was. How could I go through half my life when half of my life didn't belong to me? Did you know me? Did you meet me by accident? Did you come looking for me?

Kicking my clothes into the corner of the room, I eased myself into the bath, trying not to think of you lying in there, talking about the eighties. My eyes prickled behind their lids when I closed them and my body tensed against the warmth of the bath until it finally released some of the tension beneath the surface.

Red-hot pain shot through my nostrils and I coughed and spluttered. The bath water was tepid. I'd fallen asleep. The water filled my throat and my heart struggled to beat regularly. Panic and confusion filled me, emotions I hadn't felt for a long time. Feelings that I wished I didn't have. Shivering, I climbed out of the bath and caught my reflection in the mirror. My ghostly past reflected back. I couldn't do this again. I couldn't go back to that place and yet I couldn't move forward either.

Enveloping my body amongst the sheets, I buried my head into your pillow. I could still smell your hair, your skin, and even with the bitter tang of betrayal, it still smelt like home. My body heaved with racking sobs, dry sobs without tears: just a physical release. Feeling sorry for myself has never been my thing. Life is shit; you make what you can of it. That's how I'd coped for the last eleven years. You can drive yourself mad by wanting greener grass; the glass is half full has been my way since I could remember. So I couldn't remember my past? I had a friend, a career, a place to call home. Self-pity is one of those things that I can't see the point in, but right at that moment, as the sobbing slid into whimpering tears, I allowed myself to question: what did I do in a past life to deserve all of this? Of course, this could have just been sleep deprivation taking its vicious toll, but behind the positive thinking, I knew that the boy with the scar was the reason. The reason that karma needed me to atone for.

When I woke, the midday sun was hot on my skin and I smelled of sweat. I rolled out of bed, looked around at the mess and was shocked for a moment. The staleness of the room was rank with depression. For God's sake get a grip, I told myself. I pulled open the curtains, pushed open the windows and felt the fresh sea air flow through the room, sending dust mites into confusion. I stripped the bed, grabbed a pile of dirty clothes and headed downstairs.

For the first time in days I felt hungry, not only for food but for answers. I put the kettle on, fried some bacon and sandwiched it between two pieces of slightly stale bread, making a mental note to go shopping later. I leant on the island and propped the photo up in front of the salt and pepper and ate my bacon butty. There must be a clue in it somewhere. I stared at the girl in the wizard's cape for a while too, wondering if she was his girlfriend maybe? Nah, she looked a bit too young for him. Friends, perhaps? I looked at the 'loser' sign and noticed that the corner was slightly ripped. I slurped down my tea and scrutinised the photo for clues about where it was taken but I couldn't find anything. I tipped the dregs of my tea down the sink and then I had an idea. Those photo booth things at parties were a fairly new craze, weren't they? I wondered how many there were in Shropshire.

I drummed my fingers impatiently on the side of my laptop as I waited an age for it to warm up and turn on. It took a while to log on to the Wi-Fi there too but it didn't normally bother me because I very rarely went on it. Georgie handled all of that side of things. Eventually, I clicked on Google and searched for photo booths in Shropshire. Shit. There were loads. With a sigh, I grabbed one of my sketch books and started writing a list. I started to click on a few. Some were vintage photos, so with some satisfaction I scribbled them off my list. I picked up the photo again; the props didn't look that great, so I was thinking it was one of the lower priced companies. After an hour or so I'd whittled it down to five possible matches. Now what could I do?

I wrote a quick and concise email to all the companies, explaining that I was on a tight budget but had seen one being used at a teenager's party and was interested in hiring a booth for a friend's daughter, who was turning sixteen. I left my contact details but before I pressed send, I added a quick PS asking if I could see the range of props that they used so I could assure her that they were age appropriate. I closed the lid and pressed send.

The next few hours I spent cleaning the house and then went for a walk. The wind was vicious, light white clouds racing past the heavier grey counterparts, and the sun had to battle for its spotlight. I followed the coastal path, green geometric squares sandwiched between two blues merged together in organised chaos. The front cover of a children's book popped into my mind: an elephant with patchwork colours. I shook the image away and concentrated on the conversations we'd had, pulling each one apart, hoping that I would suddenly find clarity and an explanation.

'I always said you had pianist fingers.' I slowed my stride for a moment. There had been something defensive about your answer. I stopped still for a moment and placed my hands

on the wooden fence bordering the footpath and looked past the green of the hills and down into the waves crashing below. You'd stammered.

'*Wh-when I, you, picked up my things when we first met . . . at the, um, café.*'

'*I suppose that was the first thing you saw of me.*'

'*It was and I thought to myself, what beautiful hands you had . . .*'

You knew me, didn't you?

I replayed the conversation again. Focusing on the tone of your voice, the way you had hesitated slightly before rushing in with an answer. My fingers gripped on to the wood and I could feel the indentation of the hammer that had driven the sea-rusted nails in. The cracks in the beaten planks, the cold, smooth texture that the elements had crafted. There was no hesitation in the last part of the conversation and your tone was steady – was that part the truth? Was that the first thing you noticed about me?

I let go of the fence and carried on walking up the steep path, fast enough to feel my breath catching slightly and my calves burn. I wished I'd never seen you and I wished that you had never left. I approached the top of the cliff but didn't stop to look at the view; I carried on. The sun had lost its battle and the sky was darkening. The lace of my walking boots had come loose and I bent down to tie it. I saw a flash of your face when I proposed, the love in your eyes. Was it real? Following the path down I started to think about that day, the reflection in the mirror as we'd stood together, the feeling of belonging that I'd had, the way you'd insisted on buying it and the determined way that you looked for it. Looked for something special. You were going to leave anyway, weren't you? I think I knew it then, deep down, but I'd been caught up in those feelings. Intoxicated by you, by us. Could I let you go? I couldn't ignore the past as I had so many times before; I couldn't accept who I was and carry on. There was too much to hide and forget. You knew who I was. I was certain of it. But . . . I didn't know who you were.

The rain was sliding down the windows in angry sheets. There was no gentle pitter-patter, just huge sprays that slammed against the panes. The beginning of autumn was hammering against the walls, knocking on the door, waiting to be let in. I speared a chip into my mouth from the microwavable box, clicked on my inbox and waited for it to open. I took a swig of beer, and then leant forward. There were two replies. One telling me that the firm was now out of business and going on to grumble about the economic climate. The other was more promising. It gave a list of available dates and at the end said that they had had lots of success with young adult events in the area and that they looked forward to hearing from me. I took another swig from my beer. What did I do next? Another email pinged into my inbox. It had an attachment. I swept the bottom of the salt from the box with a chip, and finished my beer as I waited for it to download. The picture appeared in fragments while the weather took its toll on the connection, but when it finally downloaded, poking out from under a pair of giant sunglasses was a 'loser' sign. A loser sign that was ripped at the corner.

'But what are you going to do when you get there?' Georgia asked impatiently as I threw clothes into a green holdall. She had turned up just after I'd wolfed down some breakfast, to check that I'd slept.

'I'm going to find her. Or him.'

'Tom, do you know how crazy this sounds? You only knew her for a week and she's obviously been keeping secrets from you, she could be anybody!'

'Doesn't matter,' I said as I looked around my bedroom for my shaver.

'Tom, just stop for a second.' I ignored her, turning in circles trying to find the charger for the shaver. 'Tom!'

'What?!' I stopped still and looked at her confused and worried expression.

'I'm just worried about you.'

I went over and hugged her. 'I know, but I have to do this. I can't go back to how I was, just ignoring where I came from, living in the moment, I can't. I'm not that person any more.' I put my hands on her shoulders and leant her away from me. She looked up at me with concern.

'But what if you find out something you don't want to know?' she asked quietly.

'Then I guess I'll have to deal with it . . . I love her, George. I have to find her, she's the only real happiness I've ever known. I'm pushing forty, I reckon; I can't spend the rest of my life not knowing about the other half.' She nodded in defeat.

'So,' she picked up my charger and passed it to me, 'what is the plan when you get there? Birmingham? Can't you just do it on the phone?'

'No, I need to go, I need to do something. I'm going to go to the photo booth place and see if I can find out where the photo was taken.'

'And then?'

I scratch the back of my head and then shrug.

'See what I can find out, I suppose.'

'What about the exhibition?'

'It's all ready.'

'What? All of it?'

I didn't meet her eyes.

'I haven't been sleeping much.' I took a quick look at the clock on the wall. 'I'll show you.'

The light flickered on in the shed and I watched Georgie's face as she tentatively started to touch the sculptures.

'Tom, these are . . .' She turned the eye, which was suspended from a wire. Each dimension on a different level, figuratively and physically. The eyebrow was made of a heavy tarnished piece that I found at the skip; the eyelashes which hung below at a forty-five-degree angle were made from stretching the metal fibres from the inside of some thick leads that I found on the beach. I wound them so that each one was arched to the same shape as yours. '. . . exquisite.' She walked towards the large sheet which stood like a dress-maker's mannequin. It was bent to the smooth curve of your stomach, your belly button winking with a shard of beach glass, a nod to my aversion to them. 'It's her, isn't it?' she asked as she glided her finger along the edge of your parted lips, a delicate tongue just visible at the corner, made with wire mesh.

I nodded. She looked at me and smiled with understanding. 'You'd better get a move on or you'll miss the train.' I gave her a quick kiss on the cheek and then I left. I went to find you.

23

Flynn

For once in my life, things are going well for me. I've got a place in college doing what I want to do. No crappy lessons about algebra or how to complain about a radio breaking in French (like, when am I ever going to need to do that?). I'll get to spend every day painting, drawing. Doing what I want to do. I've started to find my place. I'll be away from the arse wipes that have been on my case for years. Things for me are good, and I've met someone: her name is Kate. When she messaged me I thought she might have been having a laugh but since then we've hung out on Skype a few times and she comments, a lot, on things I put on Facebook. She seems to get me, finds the same things funny and likes the same stuff on telly. We've got completely different taste in music, but we kinda take the piss out of each other for it. I feel guilty, though. Guilty when I think about Rose. And Mum.

There was so much blood. It only took a few shoves of the door with my shoulder to get in but I knew I had to, it was seeping under the door in the caravan. A puddle of it. I knew she was in an arsey mood a lot of the time but I thought it was, you know, just girl stuff. She was slumped against the wall by the window, the room smelt of mildew, that kinda damp smell mixed with Imperial Leather soap that caravan shower rooms seem to have. Her legs were splattered with blood. She always looks pale, that almost see-through skin that gingers have, but this time she was grey. For a minute, I thought she was dead until she gave me this smile. She was out of it but the smile was just like, I dunno, just like an oops, look what happened . . . silly me. Not help me, look what I've done. It was just . . . oops. That's what I'm worried about. Not that she's ashamed of what she's been doing, but that she isn't afraid of it. I see her trying to hide it from Mum. I know she's still doing it, at least I think she is. When I went into her room the other day after she yelled at Mum for asking if she was OK, there was a smell in her room . . . it's hard to explain what smell exactly, but it was there. I want to scream at her, tell her she's fucking stupid, but I can't. I have to watch what I say because it was my fault that she did it in the first place. Well, not my fault that she's an idiot but my fault that she found out about that knobhead.

I'm meeting Kate on Saturday. She lives in Birmingham so we were gonna meet halfway in Wolverhampton, but she's got to work now. She works in a shoe shop but doesn't start until after lunch – a stock-take or something. I've managed to save some money from what Gran gave us on holiday so I can pay for my train ticket and grab a Maccy D's. Not exactly romantic, is it?

I have this image of Mum, half asleep, making a cup of tea and holding a note, smiling. A Post-it note with Dad's loopy handwriting on. I'd asked what she was smiling about. It just seemed odd to be smiling when she'd only just got up, hair all messy and yawning. Dad wasn't there, I remember that, because his shoes weren't at the bottom of the stairs. He would always leave them there, nice and neat. She said it was poetry and chuckled. There are other memories of the Post-it notes too, stuck in random places like the bathroom mirror, and she would always be laughing or smiling when she noticed them, saying things like 'silly sod' or 'daft bugger'. I can't remember Post-it notes after my accident, though. I don't know why I'm thinking about them, I suppose it's since I've started seeing Kate that I've started to think about how Mum was when he was about. I guess I would like to be able to make Kate smile the way that he made Mum smile.

I'm nervous about meeting up . . . what if she sees me and then legs it? Oh well, only one way to find out, I guess.

24

Tom

Digging in my only decent-looking jeans pocket, I pulled out a tenner and paid for the takeaway coffee and warm panini – adding a flapjack as a second thought. I jogged across the road and crouched down in front of the middle-aged shadow of the man I used to be.

'Here.' He looked up through a bruised, swollen eye; the smell of desperation filled the air. With shaking hands, he took the cup. His pallor changed as though he was filling up with heat; he took a tentative sip. I laid the panini and the flapjack next to him as he watched me without suspicion or judgement while I – with a permissive glance – covered them with the edge of his threadbare blanket. I remember that feeling. The feeling that you want to cram everything you can into your mouth. The hunger that eats at you from inside, when you can no longer think of anything but food: but hunger is a trickster. It invades your thoughts while you're awake and devours you while you sleep. The hunger I describe is not the rumbling sensation you may know, not the 'I should have had breakfast before I left' feeling. This is all-consuming pain and joy entwined. Sometimes it tricks you into feeling like you never need to eat again. You feel sick from it. It is your friend. It is your enemy. You want it more than anything but then – when satiation comes – your body can't handle it, so you expel it. I was once so hungry that I almost ate my own vomit. I could see the remains of a half-eaten sausage that I'd found in a bin. I had been so hungry that I hadn't even chewed it properly.

I left quickly, knowing the danger of anyone else noticing my generosity. I could have offered him money, but sometimes having money on the streets is more dangerous than not having it. As I walked away, I wondered what his story was. Did he know who he is? Had he lost his mind or did he sit there knowing everything he had lost and everything he wanted?

As I walked away, I caught my reflection in a shop window and I thought about how far I'd come. My hair was longer than it had been for a while, the waves were just starting to show, curving over the collar of my black shirt. The front of it was starting to show a cowlick, all stuck up on one side. Sometimes when I touched my hair, I expected to feel the weight of its length run over my fingers; the habit of tucking it behind my ears was never far away. I looked away from the two women walking towards me, arms linked as they tottered on heels and skinny jeans, their glances leaving me no need for interpretation. I've never cared much about the way I look. I've always studied myself to examine my features for clues rather than for vanity. My eyebrows always seem to be tidy and I wondered if I had plucked them once. Did I used to be the type of man who had manicures and had his chest waxed? I'm attractive, I suppose I know that, but I'd never really thought about it other than wondering if I'd inherited my eyes from my mother and my smile from my father; perhaps my 'ugly' feet came from my grandfather. But maybe I didn't have a family any longer. No one had found me. Maybe no one had searched for me at all. I had no distraught mother, no stoic colonel of a father standing by a fireplace nursing a whisky, with a stiff upper lip. Don't get me wrong, I've had a few one-night stands and I never found it hard to find someone to spend the night with when I didn't want to be alone, but the confident approach of city women has always unnerved me.

I stopped outside McDonald's and examined a street map. Pushing my sunglasses back on top of my head, I traced my route so far with my finger. The sky darkened for a minute and the breeze held the bite of autumn as it nipped at the tails of summer. For a minute, I felt as though someone was watching me. I looked over my shoulder but it was only my reflection in the window, hiding the mass of Saturday lunchtime fast-feeders. The sun came back out and I took out my phone to turn on the Sat Nav. One of the photo booth companies had told me that their booth was being used in town that day as a promotion. The company was a small one and the owner was there, trying to drum up some business, so they said. I couldn't find the name of the street on the map so I spent a few minutes cursing my inability to work the technology in my phone, before finally seeing the little blue arrow pointing me in the right direction. I felt like a twat holding my phone in front of me, like a tired old man holding on to somebody's arm, someone guiding me along the right path. It took me about five minutes to find the right street (I'd looked at the map on the phone and figured it out from there). The smells and sounds of Birmingham's city life attacked me. It was just so much; so loud. I walked past a group of what looked like students bellowing at the top of their voices, laughing, shouting. They were not even a metre apart; their volume could have filled a football stadium. Had I been like that as a teenager?

I was suffocated by loud giggles, deafening exclamations about make-up, lipgloss and boys from a group of teenage girls nearby and I tried to block it out as I made my way towards a stocky, friendly-faced man sitting on a collapsible chair behind what looked like a wallpaper pasting table. On it, were a range of props: an empty gilded picture frame; reading glasses of all shapes and sizes; a sailor hat; moustaches on sticks and finally – as I knew there would be – signs with various insults and declarations. He reminded me of a cartoon mole – little eyes, glasses perched on the end of his nose and a kind-looking face.

'All right, mate,' he greeted me, 'what can I do you for?' His accent was thick but there were lilts and lifts that I recognised from yours. I'd forgotten that Georgie used to take the micky out of my own accent in the early days of our relationship. She would put on an exaggerated, almost Liverpudlian accent. 'You speak like you've got too much spit in your mouth,' she had said once. I guess I've lost a lot of that now.

'Yeah, I was hoping I could find out a bit about what sort of events you do?'

'All sorts, mate, weddings, parties . . . I even did a wake a few weeks back,' he laughed with his whole body, 'school discos sometimes, summer fayres, that sort of thing.'

'School discos?' I asked, my heart beating a little faster, my breath a little shorter.

'Yeah, did one a few months back in Telford— excuse me.' He picks up a feather boa that one of the girls has knocked off the table. 'Careful with the stuff, girls.' He smiles good-naturedly.

Telford.

'Do you mind if I . . .?' I indicated towards the table with a nod of my head. I flinched at the shriek of a chubby girl with long dark hair as she put the oversized glasses on her nose. Sorting through the eclectic mix of props, I stopped still when I rested my hand on the sign. I didn't want to seem rude or worse, creepy, so I asked him for a flyer, shook his hand and left after an empty promise to be in touch.

Slipping my hands inside my pockets, I pulled out my headphones, attached them to my phone and chose a classical music radio station to listen to. I needed to protect my senses. I didn't feel like I was going to faint but the smells – fried onions – the sounds – a steel band – still unsettled me. I'd never been one for huge crowds; the seaside throngs were about as much as I could take. I just didn't like being around lots of people. As I headed out of the city centre, I kept my head down and blocked out the shouts of 'Dad!', the screams of grumpy toddlers and the sounds of the busy Saturday afternoon around me. I didn't know how long I'd been walking when I glanced up and saw a building. It was how I'd imagine a wedding cake would look like if I'd sculpted it. It was three square tiers in ascending order, each one covered in what looked like wire circles. I tilted my head upwards and marvelled at the construction. Could I have been an architect before? I shook my head: idiot, I can't even add up my shopping without a calculator, let alone work out the measurements and complexities to design a building. The sign pointing towards it told me that it was the library.

I walked towards the magnificent structure and stood in the centre – glass curves surrounded me, old and new styles combined at every corner. It was busy and noisier than I would have expected of a library, but still I felt solace within its walls. I passed shelf after shelf of books, my hand gliding over the escalator handrail as I rose to another level and began my search. I'm not sure what I was looking for really. I didn't know anything about Telford apart from the fact it had a shopping centre that I'd seen advertised a few times . . . I remember thinking that there was a bridge there, something to do with the industrial revolution. Half an hour later, I'd found the section on local history and read about the Iron Bridge. It was named after Thomas Telford, who designed bridges around the River Severn, but more importantly, I'd learnt that there were only fourteen secondary schools there. There were a few grammar schools too, but I was guessing from the budget-priced photo booth that it probably wasn't one of those. I was writing the names and addresses down when I had that feeling again: as though I was being watched. I looked over my shoulder but all I could see was the hustle and bustle of the nameless crowd, each wrapped up in their Saturday afternoon to-do list.

My stomach growled. I'd not eaten since breakfast and my head was starting to ache. Packing up my things, I threw away a few notes that I didn't need into the bin, put my bag on my back and decided to head back to the hotel for some room service, a shower and a lie-down.

It was dark when I woke up and I was momentarily disorientated. I reached for the glass of water by the side of the bed. I had dreamt about you. I could still feel the pressure in my hand where you'd gripped it hard. Your face had been contorted with pain, red and sweaty. In the dream, I wasn't worried about you; in the dream, I was telling you to keep going. Your eyes were bulging and I could hear the pain in your voice as you begged me to stop it. To stop the pain. You looked different, younger.

My phone told me that it was half-five in the morning. The city was starting to wake: sounds of coughs in the adjacent rooms; low voices of hotel staff; and the hum and hiss of buses on their early routes leaked into the room. My feet padded their way to the bathroom. I turned on the shower and stood under the hot jets of water. I closed my eyes but the images of the dream were already fading. And then I remembered, you weren't calling me Tom, you were using another name. The powerful streams of hard, urban water pummelled my back as I tried to grasp the name. But it evaporated like the steam surrounding me. As I dried my hair with the stiff, white hotel towel, I squeezed my eyes tight, trying to force my broken brain to work, to fill in the gaps. And then I see your hands; I see the rings on your finger, a single small diamond solitaire with a silver band and a wedding band of the same colour.

'*I'm allergic to gold.*'

It was just a dream: my brain attempting to make sense of the thoughts in my head. In the dream, you were begging me to stop – but you were only my subconscious telling me I was crazy looking for somebody who didn't want to be found. The rings I saw on your finger were nothing more than a jumble of memories, of hopes, of my proposal. The silver – just a recollection of a conversation we'd once had. I shrugged off the feeling that it was something more. We've all had dreams like that. Maybe a dream about an argument with someone that seems so real or that feeling when you wake up with your heart hammering in your chest as you run away from something in the shadows. Dreams are powerful things.

After breakfast, I went back to my room and looked at the list of schools. What was I going to do now? The schools were still on summer holidays for another week, I thought, and a quick search on Google confirmed this. It wasn't as though I could start hanging around school gates like a pervert, was it? But try as I might, I couldn't think of what else to do. Grabbing a pencil and notepad from my bag, I started to scribble down a list of things that I could do to find you. The list was small. Apart from the school, I had no other leads. And, even if I found him, it didn't mean that I was going to find you, did it? I drew a mind-map of all of the things I knew about you and hoped that something, some clue would jump out at me. I dug out the photo again and stared at the boy's face. He looked happy. A teenage boy. Not the villain my nightmares had portrayed him to be. He was scarred but a good-looking boy nonetheless. He had long fingers, like mine, I supposed.

'I always said you had pianist fingers.'

What exactly was I looking for? But then I laughed. How had I missed it? Just where the girl was holding up her arm, there was the tiniest part of the pocket of a school blazer, and on it, in the bottom corner, there was a glimpse of a bright red motif. Just the curve of a line, but surely that would be enough to be able to identify the school? The adrenaline fuelled my impatience as I searched school after school in the Telford area until – with almost disbelieving eyes – I found it. The red curve of a bridge: Summerfell Academy.

There was nothing more that I could do until the start of term and even then, I was still unsure of my plan. I began gathering my things; I checked the times of the next train home and then closed the door behind me. I was right to go to Birmingham because I was closer to finding you, and I suppose, closer to finding myself.

Waiting behind a gaggle of hen-party bound women to check out, I handed over my key and bent down to pick up my bag.

'Oh, Mr Simmonds?'

'Hmmm?' I looked at the tiny receptionist who could barely see over the counter. She had pixie short blonde hair and was immaculately dressed in the hotel uniform: eyebrows perfectly shaped and raised in a friendly question mark.

'You have a message.'

'A message? You must be mistaken.' I smiled back at her.

'Room twenty-seven A?'

'Yes, but—'

'A letter was left for you yesterday evening.' She typed something into the computer. 'Ah, we tried to alert you but your phone was on do not disturb.'

'Oh, yes, I was tired and wanted— never mind.' She handed over a folded piece of paper. 'Do you know who left it?' I ask. Anxiety was starting to creep up my spine.

'Sorry, no. David was on shift yesterday, I'm afraid. Have a safe journey.' She smiled her dismissal and welcomed an elderly couple who shuffled forwards. I stepped to the side, holding the letter tightly, and made my way to the restaurant. I sat down as the hotel staff took away the remains of the later breakfasters: the hungover weekend-breakers who want to get their money's worth even if they feel like nothing more than lying down in a quiet room.

I put the letter on the table and stared at it. It wasn't in an envelope, just a folded piece of paper. I picked it up and recognised from the feel of it that it was cartridge paper from a sketch pad. Taking a deep breath, I opened it.

Dear Mr Simmonds,

   I know who you are and what you are trying to do. She doesn't want you in her life, we don't want you in our life. If you ever gave a shit, just leave us alone.

   Please. If you ever loved her, stay away.

Every hair on my body was standing on end. I looked around me, expecting to see someone there watching me. My mind was reeling. The handwriting was scruffy but strong and the message was clear.

I know who you are.

Again, I had that feeling of being watched. I grabbed my things, left the hotel and started pushing my way through the streets. I suspected every glance, every person holding a newspaper, every individual talking on their phone. Was it you? How many people were watching me? I felt violated; nothing felt right. Nothing felt real. I started to run.

If you ever gave a shit.

'Watch it!' a man in a suit shouted as I knocked him with my shoulder.

'Hey!' yelled a woman holding a coffee. I ran to the train station, jabbed my ticket into the barrier machine. I needed to get home. I was wrong to go there. Wrong to try to find you.

When I got to the platform I was breathing heavily and I felt sick. Sitting on the edge of a bench, I leant my head forwards between my knees and tried to bring my breathing under control. My pulse started to slow.

Please, if you ever loved her . . . I let this sentence flow through me. *Please* . . . and then it became clearer. The message. It wasn't a threat. It was a request. A request to stay away. Whoever wrote that letter knew you and was trying to protect you. Maybe it was another man, someone you were committed to . . . but, my question was, why did you need to be protected from me?

And then I saw your face. I saw you, eyes wide open in shock as I hit you, your face from the dream, in pain and begging me to stop. What kind of a man was I?

25

Melody

The first day of term is here. I hate it when the kids go back and I hate making lunch boxes. I throw a pack of raisins into Rose's lunch box and then take them back out. Is she too old for raisins now? Should it be designer dried fruit or . . . Christ, when did this become such a minefield?

'Ugh, raisins.' She peers over my shoulder, answering my questions with her disgust.

'But you like raisins.'

'Yeah, when I was, like, seven.'

I take them out. 'Oh. Well, what would you like instead?'

'Just an apple is fine, Mum, honestly; a wrap and a chocolate bar will do. I hardly get a chance to eat it all anyway.'

Here we go again. My body aches with fatigue as I dissect her sentence and look for hidden meanings. Why doesn't she have time? Is she busy locking herself in the toilet cubical with a razor? Snorting cocaine? I can't quieten the mistrust I feel towards her. I never would have thought that she would have self-harmed, so now I'm standing in a field of what-ifs: I look one way and there is the 'What if she has been taking drugs?' I look the other way and there is the 'What if she's been smoking?' It's everywhere I go. What if she's been sleeping around? What if she's being groomed?

'S'up?' Flynn walks in, bulky black headphones around his

neck, 'Ooh, raisins.' He grabs a box. His lunch is now just in a plastic bag – lunch boxes are no longer considered cool. He gives me a stubbly kiss on the cheek and leaves with a 'Later.'

'What time are you home?' I shout.

'About half-one, free period this afternoon!' The door thuds shut behind him.

'It's so not fair. How come you get so much free time at college?'

'You'll be there soon enough.'

Will she? Will she go to college or will she be in an assisted living building? I shake the wool from inside my head and sit down. I feel so tired lately. Bone-achingly tired.

I miss him.

'So what have you got today?'

She stops with her spoonful of Weetabix hovering near her mouth. 'English, biology and RE,' she answers then shoves the dripping spoon into her mouth. 'Do you want some breakfast, Mum?' Lifting up the cereal box up, she shakes it at me.

'Nah.' The wave of nausea fills me.

'Are you on some weird diet?'

'What? No! What makes you think that?'

'Well, you never seem to eat much lately.'

'It's the tablets.'

'Oh.'

She adds another Weetabix to her bowl, splashes on milk and then heaps sugar on top.

'I'm always hungry,' she explains with milk escaping the corner of her mouth. 'I just eat food and don't get full.' She shrugs her shoulders and smiles at me, her cheeks full.

'That's being a teenager for you.'

'I s'pose.' She looks up at the clock. 'Shit, I'm late!'

'Don't say shit,' I add with defeat, rubbing the tops of my

legs, which are throbbing. In a flurry of blazer, bag and body-spray, she leaves. I start to make patterns with my finger in the spilt sugar. Round and round: sweet grains rolling beneath my fingers. It's no use trying not to think about him. He is in my thoughts every minute of the day and most of the night as I toss and turn, sleep always just beyond my reach. I've started to allow myself time to think about him. Try to compartmentalise each part of the day so I can cope with him not being here; this is my fifteen minutes. I close my eyes and for those fifteen minutes I'm in his arms, holding his hand on the beach – watching him cook. I suppose I have always known that our relationship was special.

I knew that it was different to a lot of our friends. I heard it in the way they would talk about their husbands with a roll of their eyes and an exasperated sigh. It was in their slight distrust when their significant others had a trip away, their fears veiled by a joke. It was there in the way he looked at me when I first woke up, when I put on my mascara (he would always unknowingly open his mouth as he watched me, propped up in bed with a cup of tea in his hands . . . asking me why do I do that?). It was there in his jokes and in my laugh even when I'd only had three hours' sleep because Flynn was crying through the night. It was there in the way I would look at the clock with anticipation, knowing he would be home in ten minutes, filling me with contentment. And even after he had died . . . my feelings never changed. It was still there.

When my time is up, I clear up the mess. My brain is foggy and I find myself standing in the lounge wondering why I've come in here. There is a smudge on the corner of the mirror so I wipe it with my sleeve; I look older, thinner – miserable. I don't know how long I stand there, tracing the sharpness of my face and the deeper lines around my eyes, but eventually my vision blurs slightly.

Right. I need to do something. I'll cook a proper meal for tea tonight and force it down. Rose is right, I'm not eating, I'm not sleeping and when I do the dreams are vivid and disturbing.

It's starting to show.

I open the laptop. Heavy clouds cover the sky and the cobalt blue from outside is replaced with the artificial blue glare from the screen. I know what I'm looking for; I've researched the early symptoms before: the sickness in the mornings, the fatigue, the vivid dreams, the constant lapses in concentration. I can feel it growing. How long has it been there? A tiny form that swells and grows as it feeds from me. Of course it could be a million other things: the anti-depressants for one, the constant worrying about Rose, or the grief that I once again find myself cloaked in.

I can't keep hiding. I have to get a grip. Taking myself in hand, I phone the doctor's and make an appointment for this afternoon. Perhaps they can give me something to stop the nausea at the very least and then book me in for a scan.

I flick the TV on and Teletubbies wave back. I remember Flynn, sat on his blue plastic chair, always balancing on two legs and sitting side-saddle: chubby feet sticking out from under his fleecy, train-patterned pyjamas; huge blue eyes above plump red cheeks as he peered over the back of the chair at whatever wonders Dipsy and her hat were up to – a half-chewed piece of toast clutched in his hands. I remember the feel of his warm, podgy, sticky fingers, hear the slurp of his chocolate milk from his beaker, the dense sweet smell of his wispy hair.

'Again, Mommy, peeeeeease?' he would ask.

Again. Again.

The supermarket is quiet and the hustle and bustle of the school holidays, and the last-minute dash for new school jumpers and shirts, is over. Only pre-school children are in the aisles, strapped into trolleys or manhandling the fruit and veg. My trolley is full of fresh ingredients for the lasagne I intend to make. The act of shopping soothes me; the gathering of sustenance to nurture my family gives me a much-needed sense of protectiveness. On a whim, I decided to grab one of their favourite puddings. I head towards the bakery to where one solitary festival gateau sits on the shelf. It is a strange-looking thing. A bright green dome of fondant which covers a light sponge filled with fresh cream – I don't remember when we first had it – but we had renamed it the green bomb. It seems right for the way our life is going at the moment. Bombshell after bombshell, but at least this one I can control.

A blonde girl of about three with ringlets falling down her back roughly grabs the last one from the shelf; this bothers me more than it should. The little girl is innocent; dressed as a Disney princess from the film *Frozen*, her crown is slightly askew, and her face somewhat grubby from the chocolate buttons that she has just devoured – the discarded wrapping lies next to her on the floor. But, by taking that cake, she is no longer innocent: she threatens the peace of my carefully constructed evening ahead. I'm standing by her side, looking down at her. She gives me a cheeky grin: a grin that tells me she is used to being the centre of the world. A grin that speaks of a protected childhood with indulgent parents and pink bedrooms. Walk away, I tell myself, but I find that I'm rooted to the spot. Why should she have it? I'm filled with a sense of injustice that I know I shouldn't feel towards this little princess but I can't help it; I want that cake. My children deserve it. They deserve it more than this spoilt little angel, with glitter on her sticky cheek and shining silver shoes.

'Let it go,' I tell her. Anxiously, I look over my shoulder

and am relieved to see that the mother – who is sporting designer jeans, tucked into her expensive boots – is busy swiping the screen of her massive smart phone. The princess smiles at me.

'I'm Elsa,' she beams.

'Let it go,' I repeat and then . . . and then I start. You knew it was coming, I'm sure, but I hadn't even thought it was in my memory banks. I start singing about mountains and prints in the snow and something about a 'king in iced creation'. The little girl starts twirling in her dress, joining in, declaring that 'she's a queen'. Looking around panicked, I continue to warble about wind, nobody being around and not caring about what I'm saying. The little girl jumps up and down shrieking about the snow not bothering her 'in a way'. Finally she puts the cake back down while bowing to the small crowd that has surrounded us. The mother, I notice, has filmed it all – as she has no doubt filmed every minute of this precious pre-Madonna from the moment she first opened her eyes – every milestone, from the first bite of baby-rice until the starring role in the Christmas play at nursery. After a fleeting round of applause, the crowd disperses and with the princess now absorbed in the screen of the phone, I grab the cake and make a hasty exit before I'm enticed by the need for snowman building.

The doctors were optimistic as I knew they would be. I've been put in for an early scan. I can't do anything more, other than reassure my children – for the short term at least – that everything is OK. Chopping the onions draws out the tears that I have hidden away. I spend longer than I need to, enjoying the sting and the release the tears bring. I throw the onions into the olive oil and stir until their innocuous bitterness becomes golden and sweet. I add the minced beef, garlic and oregano, and by the time Rose slings her school bag on to the table, there is a pot of bubbling tomato sauce.

'What's for dinner?'

'Lasagne. Do you want to help?' She shrugs.

'OK.'

'How was school? Can you grab the dish?' She shrugs again and pulls out the glass oven dish, puts it on the kitchen side and opens the packet of lasagne sheets.

'All right, I guess. Shall I start piling up?'

'Yes, but be careful, it's really hot.' I tear open the packet of cheese sauce with my teeth and start adding the milk to the pan.

'I had a free pass thing given to me so if I start to feel upset,' she spoons the minced beef mixture into the dish, 'then I can leave class and go to see Mrs Ford.'

'Mrs Ford? The new Learning Mentor? She seemed nice. That's good then.'

'I guess.' She puts the pasta sheet on top. 'I don't really need it, though.' I continue stirring the cheese sauce.

'Oh?' I try not to sound too interested. Too much attention and she will clam up.

'Well, I'm busy at school so I never felt the need to, I never . . .' She ladles more sauce over the pasta. 'I never did it, you know, at school.' Giving my full attention to the cheese sauce, I begin to whisk it forcefully. 'How many sheets?'

'Hmmm? Oh, as many as you think. Make sure they've got a good covering of sauce, though, or it'll be stodgy. Do you think you need a hobby then, something to keep you busier at home? Would that help?'

'Dunno. I guess.' I stand by her side while I pour the sauce. 'Shall I grate the cheese?'

'Yes, please.' As she opens the fridge, I try my hardest to stop asking her questions. This is the most she's opened up to me in a while.

'I've, um, how much?'

'Keep going.'

'I've started to— is that enough?'

'Keep going, I'm in a cheesy mood . . .'

'I've written a few, um, stories. You know, like short stories? I've been using the old laptop from the garage.' My heart is pounding.

'What, that old one of Flynn's?'

'Mmhmm.'

'I'm surprised it still works.'

'Well, it only runs Word, I can't get on the internet or anything.'

'I didn't know that you liked writing. Why did you start writing stories?'

'I dunno, we did a lesson in school where we had to watch this short animation and write our version and, I guess . . . well, the lesson went really quick and I felt a bit disappointed when the bell went.'

'Ah. The wonders of the education system.' I smile.

'So I was wondering, as it's my birthday soon, if I could have a new laptop?'

'That's enough cheese. Um yeah, I mean you'll have to show me which one and it might have to be an older model,' she throws her arms around my neck and I'm caught off balance for a minute. I hold her tight, breathing in the smell of school and hair conditioner. We stay that way for longer than is necessary for a thank-you hug.

'You smell nice,' she laughs.

'Thanks, it's a new body spray.'

'No, I meant you smell of garlic!' She kisses me on the cheek and leaves the room chuckling to herself.

I put the dinner into the oven and smile. The first genuine smile I've had for a while.

*

When I wake up on The Day of the Scan, my sheets are wet with sweat. Predictably, my throat is dry so I know I've been up to my usual night-time antics. I'm up way before the kids so spend longer in the bath than I would usually, take extra care with my make-up and hair, and try to prepare myself for the news that I know I'll receive. The phone rings as I wipe my mouth after my early morning date with the toilet bowl, and it continues to ring as I rinse my mouth with mouthwash.

'Mum! Shane is on the phone!' I wipe away the smudges of mascara from beneath my eyes, run cold water over my wrists, wipe myself down and straighten my posture.

'Hi, is everything OK?' I ask after clearing my voice.

'Hello yourself. Are you OK? You don't sound well.'

'Sore throat. So, what's up?'

'Nothing, I just, I just thought it would be nice to catch up. You know, fill you in on how Flynn is getting on in college. I would have been in touch sooner but I've been working in Birmingham over the school holidays delivering a post-grad training programme.'

I wonder if this is the truth or if, like me, he has been feeling as though we needed to put some space between us. As I listen to his voice, I notice how my reactions have changed. I no longer feel the need to check my appearance in the mirror in case he makes an unannounced visit, which had become more and more frequent the weeks before Cornwall. We had fallen into a routine of sorts. He would arrive with biscuits and I would provide coffee. I would burn the pizza, he would make salad; I would lean against him, he would let me. We had become relaxed in each other's company. I worry that now I feel differently, I may lose him.

The idea of Tom, before I went, was something so much more abstract than when I saw him: found him. I wonder if Shane has sensed how my feelings towards him have changed. He had come over a few days after Rose had been discharged. Did he notice how my body became rigid when he hugged me, his eyes searching my face with concern, or had he just thought it was because of what I was going through with Rose? Could he tell that my feelings for him had tipped on to their side, had switched allegiances, had crossed the border from attraction to friendship?

'Ooh, get you,' I answer and smile at the embarrassed pride that flows from his tone.

'It sounds more exciting than it is, I promise you.'

'It's no problem, I wouldn't expect you to be in touch over the holidays. He seems really happy, settled. Is he? Is everything OK?' I start to panic; have I taken my eye off the ball with him? Focusing too much time with Rose in mind?

'Yeah, no, yeah. It seems to really suit him. I wanted to, you know, check that you are OK, after . . . your trip. You didn't say much about it, what with everything with Rose going on.'

'I'm fine.'

'You sure? Only Jo says you've not been to hers since you got back.'

'I've not been feeling too great and, well . . . I didn't feel like I could leave Rose. Flynn tells me he's spoken to you about it?'

'Yeah. I think it's on his mind. I think he has a lot on his mind, to be honest.' I think about the scan and how they're going to cope when I have to tell them the news. Maybe I should speak to Shane first, see what kind of state of mind Flynn is in. How would it feel, I wonder, to unburden the thoughts trapped inside my head? I sigh, suddenly, feeling very old and tired as I realise that I really could do with talking to somebody. No, not somebody. Shane. I can trust him and he knows Flynn and what is going on behind those dark eyes, probably better than I do.

'When were you thinking?'

'I'm free later today? About one-ish?'

'OK. Do you want to come here?'

'Sure. See you later.'

As I hang up the phone, I see Rose and Flynn batting their eyes at each other. Flynn flicks back his hair and Rose twirls hers, looking doe-eyed.

'When were you thinking?' Rose says in a sultry tone. Flynn bats his eyelashes at her and puts on his 'girl' voice.

'Do you want to come here?' Then they both burst out laughing.

'Ha, ha. Very funny.'

'Honestly, Mum. Just ask him out already.' They snigger as Flynn nudges Rose in the ribs.

'We're just friends,' I tell them, and hope that what I'm going to tell Shane won't change that.

'Whatev's,' Rose says, shrugging her shoulders. My wonderful children. How will they feel when I break the news to them? How will they cope?

Throwing the second empty bottle of water into the bin, I stand outside the hospital, watching the gentle slide of the doors. People in. People out. Each one with their foot wedged into the mountain that looms over us throughout our life, elderly couples almost at the summit, wobbling toddlers just starting to get a steady foothold. The ever present shadow that drags behind us, getting longer and longer the closer we get to the light. I tuck my hands into my jeans and fiddle with the bottom of my flowered blouse with my thumb. Oh well. Let's get this over with. Let's find out how far gone I am.

I'm strangely calm by the time Shane is due to arrive. I've studied my reflection and everything seems the same. My hair, my eyes, my height. All of it the same and at the same time, everything is different. Vulnerable. Exposed. The water I pour into the kettle comes from the same pipes, the same water tank, and yet it is different. Is it contaminated? Should I buy a water filter? The coffee I spoon into the cup – I've not given it much thought before now – it's just regular supermarket brand coffee, but now I'm looking at it with suspicion. Should I have been drinking decaff all this time? What unknown damage has it caused? I can smell the decay coming from inside the bin, the stench of over-ripe fruit and half-eaten bags of crisps. I empty it, spray the lid with anti-bacterial spray and then stop, looking at the nozzle. Should I be using it, breathing in its fumes, could that be the ring-leader? The General leading toxins into my susceptible body? There's a knock on the door and I'm glad that I asked him to come. Glad to be able to talk to someone before I drive myself insane.

'Coffee?'

'Please.' He sits at the kitchen table, puts a packet of chocolate-chip cookies down, as I try to ignore the sense of him studying me. Can he tell?

'So,' I put the cups on to the table. 'How is he getting on? Really?'

'So far, so good. I've spoken to his form tutor and she says that he's eager; he listens to advice and works hard.' He smiles. 'When I told her he may find the transition difficult she was genuinely confused, said she couldn't see any signs of behavioural problems at all. Says he can be a bit aloof but that's because he's so focused on his work.'

'Good. That's good then. Maybe all he needed was to get away from that school?'

'Let's not jump the gun . . . it's only been two weeks, but yeah,' he rubs his chin, 'college seems to really suit him.' He takes a sip of coffee and looks at me in a way that makes me think this is not the end of the conversation. 'How's he been at home?'

'Fine. You know, just, well, Flynn. He grunts, he makes jokes, he, well, he's just him. He's on the computer a lot, but that's par for the course, right? Messaging his new girlfriend. Has he told you about her?'

'Yep. She sounds nice. Good for him, good for his self-esteem as well. I don't know what it is, but I just think there is something else going on with him. He worries. About you and Rose. And I—'

'Well, he's going to. He found her half-conscious and covered in blood. It's normal for him to be worried.'

'Yes. Absolutely, but he worries about you.'

'Me? I'm much better. I'm taking the anti-depressants, I'm sleeping a bit better—'

'He feels responsible for you, for taking care of you and Rose, and I wonder if it's too much. For him.'

'So what do you suggest? What is your . . .' I lean back and cross my arms, sarcasm sliding into my mouth, 'professional opinion? Please enlighten me, because I thought that I was doing a pretty damn good job considering my daughter is self-harming, I'm a lunatic and his dad is . . . well his dad is—' I throw my arms up and bite my bottom lip.

'What happened? When you went to see him?'

'He doesn't know who I am.'

'What do you mean?' I stand up and turn my back on him, looking out into the garden, noticing that the first leaves are starting to fall.

'He's happy. He's funny, he's everything that he always was, but he doesn't remember me or us. He has no memory of our life or his childhood.' I wrap my arms around myself.

'Did you get to talk to him then?'

'Yes, I talked to him.'

'So did you tell him?'

'Tell him?' I let out a dry laugh. 'No. I didn't tell him. I didn't tell him that he has two children. One who self-harms. And one who has to deal with both his anger and the responsibility he feels to look after his family. I didn't tell him that I've spent the last eleven years screaming for him in my sleep and learning to live with his death. He has a life, a safe life. He's incredibly vulnerable, Shane, he's created a life for himself out of nothing. He lives in a cottage that he's essentially built himself.' I close my eyes and I'm back there, the sea breeze moving the curtains. 'You can hear the sea from the bedroom and you can—'

'The bedroom?'

My eyes fly open as his voice brings me back here. 'Yes. The bedroom.'

'Melody . . . how much time did you spend with him?' I wipe away a stray tear with irritation. 'Melody?' I can hear apprehension in his voice. 'How well did you get to know Dev?'

'Tom. His name is Tom. Dev is dead.'

'Melody?'

I take a deep breath and then I tell him.

I face the window as I tell him about the way Tom looked at me when we first met outside the café. The way I felt cheated that I had found Dev yet lost him all over again. I tell him about the sculptures, how I know that Tom must remember us deep down. I tell him about going home with Tom, how it had felt like completely the wrong thing to do but also completely the right thing to do.

I wait for a moment, listening to Shane breathing. I know I should turn to face him. Are my words hurting him? Or did he always know that I wouldn't really ever be his; that I would always belong to Dev? I tell him about the days spent in Tom's arms on the beach, the nights talking and watching the flames. I tell him about the proposal and how Tom had found the photo, how I had left.

And then I turn to face Shane. He is sitting with his head leaning against his knuckles; he looks sad but not angry. I sit opposite him and he reaches for my hands; he covers them with his own and rubs his thumb up and down mine.

'I'm sorry,' I say, 'I never meant to——' I don't finish the sentence. I don't really know what I was going to say anyway: sorry that I led you on? Sorry that our messed-up lives have pushed their way into yours?

'You don't owe me an apology.' He leans forward, his forehead against mine. I close my eyes, feeling his strength, his warmth. He brushes a tear away from my cheek as I straighten up.

'Are you going to tell them?' he asks.

Years ago, when Pauline and I had been close, she had said to me that you never really know love until you have children. At the time, I was pregnant with Flynn. But I love Dev, I'd pointed out. She poured herself a glass of wine and shook her head. It's not the same, she had argued. 'Once you have children, if say, a madman with a gun asked you to choose between your husband or your child, you would find yourself saying, "Shoot my husband," I guarantee it.'

After I'd accepted that Dev was dead, I remembered this conversation; I remembered her words. I love my children more than I could ever say, but if I'd been faced with the madman, I wouldn't have chosen my kids over Dev. I'd have said 'shoot me'. I love Dev just as much as my children and I need to protect him as much as them. I want the best for all of them.

I explain this to Shane.

'But you're not protecting him, you're not giving him a choice! You're not giving them a choice. Just think about what it would mean to them, to know that they weren't abandoned.'

'But what would that fix? They know he left. They've accepted it and moved on.'

'You don't know that. Think about what knowing he lost his memory and didn't just leave could mean to them.'

'Think about what that would mean to him! You have no idea how fragile he is, no idea what he has gone through to make a life for himself. Knowing what has happened to us, all that we have had to deal with without him, that he was partly to blame, could destroy him. He's not a father, he doesn't know anything about being a father, about teenagers, about self-harming and behavioural problems.'

'So tell them, let them choose whether to get in touch with him. Give them the choice.'

'No.' I shake my head. 'Curiosity will get the better of them. It's best for everyone if they just hate him. He lived on the streets, Shane.' I picture his face as he hit me. 'A father who doesn't know you exist is a stranger. They don't need a stranger in their lives right now. They've got enough to deal with.' I take a deep breath and say, 'There's something else.'

And then I tell him about the scan.

26

Flynn

So, my meeting with Kate didn't go quite according to plan. I mean, meeting Kate was perfect. She is perfect. When I got off the train, she was waiting and I could see her fiddling with the cuffs of her pink cardigan. Pink makes it sound like she is one of those hair-swishy, giggly girls, but she was wearing a pair of denim dungarees under it and a scarf thing in her hair. She just looked cool; she is cool. But she was nervous. When I walked up to her, I kept my eyes on her red Converses. They were scuffed and knackered, not like some of the girls at college who you can just tell spend hours whitening them or otherwise making them look well worn (even though you know their rich parents have just bought them the twentieth pair that month). They were, you know, just normal.

'Hey,' I said to her feet. My voice came out like a squeak and I felt like a right dick. I pulled myself together and looked up. She didn't say anything, she just stared at me. I remember thinking that she was going to do a runner; I cleared my throat.

'I'm Flynn.' She moved her mouth but no sound came out. 'Do you want to grab a drink?' I asked and then started to garble my words a bit, going on about the journey and about this couple who had been arguing the whole way there.

She put her hands in her pocket and smiled at me, which I took as a signal to carry on talking. I could feel her staring at me as we walked which made me talk even faster about absolute bollocks. Seriously, by then I was surprised that she was still walking with me. She stumbled – halfway through me going through the entire McDonald's menu including the festive choices – so I caught her arm without thinking, and she went bright red. A rash that, like, started on her neck and spread to her cheeks. Her nails were digging into me – they were painted pale pink, short and square-shaped. She licked her lips and did this thing that was like a whistle.

'Th-Th-Th . . .' Her eyes closed for a moment, 'thanks,' and then I knew. I knew that she wasn't this perfect, pretty, blonde girl. Not perfect by a long shot. The stutter had almost crippled her, I could see it in the way she was looking down – like she was waiting for the ground to open up.

'No problem.' She smiled at me. Properly looking at me, but I didn't look away like I would normally. It's like her stutter had evened the field. Like, we've all got scars, it's just that everyone can see mine.

Later, when we were eating (she had a fish-thing) I was asking her why she would miss out on a Big Mac. Her stutter had eased off by then; it seemed like the more she got used to me the less it happened, but when, like, she ordered, it happened again and I watched the woman behind the counter squirm and catch the eyes of the girl working next to her. Once we had our food and were sitting down at a table, comparing burger fillings, I looked around for a moment and that's when I saw him. I wasn't sure at first and I don't know why I even noticed some old bloke looking at a map. But it was him. My face must have given something away because Kate stopped eating and asked me what was wrong.

'Grab your food,' I answered and we grabbed our stuff. She was still slurping her milkshake when we got out on to the street. Kate knows all about my dad. I haven't told her about Rose or anything and, well, she's seen Mum's thing up close. It was one of the first real conversations we'd had over messenger. Her dad is a loser too.

'Wh-Wh-What is it?' I was scanning the streets, right, like a nut job. 'Flynn? What's wrong?'

'I think I'm either going crazy, or I think I've just seen my dad.' Her eyes went wide.

'What makes you think it was him?'

Why did I think it was him? 'It's hard to explain, something in the way he had his head tilted while he looked at the map and, I dunno, he just seemed so . . . familiar.'

The streets were busy but I could see him as he went around a corner. Grabbing her hand, I pulled her and her milkshake along the path. We lost him for a while and we slowed down, finally standing still. I hadn't noticed – not really – that I was holding her hand, I was still searching the streets, my good eye darting all over the place trying to get a glimpse of him.

'He's gone.' The disappointment in my voice must have made an impression because the next thing I knew, she was pulling my hand to her lips. She had lipgloss on and I could feel the sticky little stamp her kiss had left on my knuckle as we turned and started walking the other way. It must have been about ten minutes after, when I caught sight of him again, and without thinking, I shouted.

'Dad!' I'm not sure what I was expecting. That he would turn and wave; apologise for being late? I noticed that he had earphones in anyway, so he wouldn't have heard.

'What are you going to say? If we catch up with him?' she asked as I held even tighter to her hand. I slowed my pace. I had a clear view of him now and he wasn't walking that fast.

'I don't know.'

'Do you want him back? In your life after he just left?' My heart was beating hard and I could hear the concern in her voice. 'Flynn, just slow down a bit. You said you hated him, that if he hadn't left that th-th-th-th-things would be different.' I clenched my jaw and nodded. 'Do you want him back? Does your mum?' My thoughts were muddled. Seeing him after all this time – after all of the time we spent trying to find him – was taking over any rationality that I had. And then I thought of Rose – how would she cope if she knew he had been this close to us and not bothered getting in touch, and Mum . . . fuck, can you imagine the playlist?

'Let's just see what he's up to and then I'll decide what to do.'

We carried on following him at a distance until he went into the library.

'So . . . what now?'

'We go in, I guess.'

'What if he sees you? It's one thing following him out in the open, but in there?' She was right, I knew she was, but I needed to know what he was doing there. I couldn't stop thinking about whether he lived there, just a half-hour train ride from us.

'I'll go in,' she'd said. 'You stay out here and I'll watch what he gets up to. It'll be fun, I'll be like . . .' she pulled her long fringe over one eye and I laughed at her impression of me, 'undercover.' She winked and it was like I'd known her for years. 'I'll text you with updates.' She gave me that smile again, the one that shows her dimple in the one cheek, and without overthinking it or losing my nerve, I went to kiss her on the cheek, only she turned her head, so her lips met mine.

'Gotcha,' she whispered and then turned to walk into the building.

It seemed like I'd been sitting on the bench for hours. The

texts kept coming; it was surreal. She sent funny messages like 'he's scratching his nose', 'he's sat down', 'he's stood up', each one interrupted by her selfies overexaggerating that pout thing that all of the girls do on their profile pictures. It was weird to think that he was in there. My dad. My actual dad. 'He's on his way out', the blue bubble on my phone screen told me. I got up and turned my back a little, so I could see him as he came out, but I kept my head down so he wouldn't see me. Kate followed quickly after as he put the headphones in and walked past. He was about half a metre in front of me. I could have spoken to him, touched him, but I remained rigid.

'He was looking in the local history section, here.' She passed me a screwed-up piece of paper and it felt like I'd been punched in the stomach. It was his handwriting, the same handwriting that I'd seen on the Post-it notes all around the house.

He'd written out a list of schools. Schools in Telford. He's looking for us, for me and Rose. But why? Why now and why doesn't he just come to the house? It's in the same place as it's always been. He doesn't want to see Mum. What kind of a coward stalks his own kids rather than face up to his wife? His wife that he just left – you know, the opposite of right – left without an explanation and left her searching for him thinking he was dead. We don't want this. We don't need this in our lives.

Eventually, we follow him until he goes into a hotel. Again Kate follows him in and listens from a distance.

'Room twenty-seven A,' she announced with a grin when she came back out, with her hand on her hip; then she looked at her watch. 'I've got to get going, Flynn. Mum will be stressing if I'm back too late.'

'Sure, I mean, yeah, course.' The sinking feeling in the pit of my stomach was new to me; I didn't want her to go. 'I'll just leave him a note, telling him to stay the fuck away.' She looked at her watch again. 'Let me help you and then I'd better leg it. I'll be in deep shit if I don't get the next train and then God only knows when I'll be allowed to see you again.' I smiled at this. She wanted to see me . . . again. I dug out my sketch pad and wrote a note.

As I'm writing it, I can see the blood on the floor again. We go into the hotel, leave the note and then run, hand in hand, to the train station.

27

Melody

'Jo?' Placing the keys on the hall sideboard, I roll up my sleeves and amble into the kitchen, ignoring the dull headache that is hovering over my right eye.

'Be down in a min!' Smiling at the organisation of her cleaning cupboard and stockpiling of various products, I pull out the bin bags (various sizes for each bin, extra-thick and scented) and start my journey around the house, emptying them as I go: even her rubbish is tidy. Following the trail of her perfume, I find Jo in her upstairs office, surrounded by paperwork.

'Oh hi! Sorry, I got sidetracked.' She gets up and gives me a brief hug. 'Are you OK? How's things?'

'Oh, OK, thanks. How's your mum?'

'Oh, much better, she's coming out of the hospital tomorrow.'

'I'll get on, you look busy,' I say as I gesture at the piles of paper in various heaps.

'It's Mum and Dad's stuff. Honestly, I tried to get things ready for when Mum gets home but their idea of being organised is getting to the chippy before the Friday night rush.'

I empty the bins, give everywhere a quick dust before I feel the need to sit down. Feeling shaky, I pour myself a glass of water and take tentative sips, hoping as I do that I'm not about to bring it straight back up again. Looking at the clock, I'm disappointed that it has only been half an hour since I arrived and yet I feel ready to have a nap. I can't keep this to myself for much longer. I'm going to have to tell them soon, but every day, I find a reason not to: Rose has a science test in the morning or Flynn is meeting up with Kate and I don't want to ruin his good mood. Our life has slipped back into a calm routine, muted and mundane: a snow-covered morning when everything looks quiet. Still. Shrouded. Safe, before you try to start the car to get to work or dig out the long-forgotten boots and bag of grit hidden in the depths of the garage. The purity of it soon turns into muddied slush and treacherous ice.

'Goodness, you look dreadful, are you OK?' I hadn't noticed her arrive in the kitchen.

'I'm fine, just a bit of a bug.'

'You shouldn't have come, Mel, when you're feeling rough. Honestly, the cleaner is back from her holiday next week.'

'I'm fine, really,' I try to reassure her.

'Well, if you insist on staying, you can sit down and help me sort through some of this post.' Gratefully, I follow her orders as she strides from appliance to appliance making me a cup of peppermint tea. She chats easily as she starts opening her post, handing it to me to shred or to put into a plastic folder if she needs to file it away later. She's talking about the village where her parents live and I'm thankful for the stream of chatter that keeps my mind in the here-and-now and not in the future with its barbed-wire promises.

'Fuck. I'd forgotten about these.'

'What are they?' She's holding up tickets as her shoulders sag. 'I'd bought Mum and Dad a trip in a hot air-balloon. Shit, it's the day after tomorrow. Too late for a refund and there is no way Mum's health would cope with it.'

'Oh, what a shame. Maybe they could go next year, when her health is better?'

'Maybe. Here, you have them.' She pushes them across the table.

'What? Don't be daft,' I laugh.

'They are going in the bin if not, and before you offer, I don't want anything for them. Look, it's for three people, I got it as a day trip for all of us. Take the kids, they'd love it.' A smile is tugging at my mouth.

'Really? Oh my God. Really?' I ask again. Christmas morning excitement is bubbling through me. One more day and then I'll tell them, oh, but what a day it could be.

I've been up since four, feeling energised with the apprehension and excitement that the day is going to bring. I've already brought up my first cup of black coffee but the second seems to be staying put. I brush my teeth, and then finish putting together the picnic that we can eat once we're safely back on the ground. There is a thick layer of mist outside but the forecast says it will shift, hopefully leaving clear skies.

His dark room smells of socks and deodorant and I almost trip over a stray, toast-crusted plate as I walk over to the mass under the duvet.

'Flynn.' I shake his shoulder, his mouth open wide and hair sticking up at various angles. 'Flynn? Wake up.' He screws up his face and throws his arm over his face.

'Mmnnnughhh.'

'Wakey, wakey, rise and shine, my boy . . . I've got a surprise.'

'Gnnkkkmm.'

The door to Rose's room creaks; the pale morning light, creeping into the room from a crack between the curtains, paints the walls a soft, warm grey. I clamber over the assault course of nail polish, hair straighteners and discarded outfit choices, until I reach her: curled up into a tight ball, sleep heavy across her peaceful face.

'Rose,' I smooth her hair back from her face and smile at how perfect she looks, 'sweetie, wake up.'

'Mmnnughh.'

'Time to get up, I've got a surprise.'

'Gnnkkmm.'

'Put something practical on, we're going on a trip.'

'What kind of trip?' is her muffled response.

'A fun one. Wear layers.'

I'm fussing about the kitchen by the time they arrive, looking grumpy and confused in equal measure. Rose is wearing a dark-green hoody over skinny jeans and Flynn is wearing a navy-blue hoody over a green and black checked shirt, the bottom of which is poking out above his black jeans. I clap my hands together.

'Perfect. Are your phones charged? You'll need the cameras.' Flynn gives a slow smile at Rose and she raises an eyebrow.

'Where are we going at half-six in the morning?' she asks, a tiny hint of anxiety clipping the softness of her tone.

'Wait and see.' We hear the parp of a horn outside. Jo had arranged for me to do some ironing for one of her neighbours whose husband is a taxi driver, so I'm being paid with a car ride to the site, which is only twenty minutes away.

Throughout the journey, I watch my children trying to hide their emotions with headphones and Facebook status updates in between whispers and hushed guesses. Their faces change and headphones are ripped from their ears as they notice where we are going; hearing the tick-tock of the indicator as we turn on to the dirt path that takes us to the launch site. Mist still covers the field which is surrounded by a small but dense forest.

'No, fucking, way?' Flynn asks me, his face incredulous

but at the same time guarded. 'Are we, um, here to watch them?'

'Mum?' Rose asks and I notice she is gripping on to the pocket of Flynn's jeans.

'Yeah, we're here to watch . . . from the air.'

And in that moment, as I watch the fear and worries of teenage life fall away from their faces and sheer, innocent joy form into laughter and shrieks of excitement, I know I did the right thing to wait, because today was about flying, about rising above all of the world and its problems and leaving everything else behind.

We are asked if we want to watch the balloon being inflated and are led to the space where the basket is lying on its side, the expanse of nylon leaking from it in a vast lake of billowing red. Rose tucks her hand into the crease of my arm and holds on tightly as we watch huge fans begin to whir, with the sound of a dozen hairdryers, as they blast the air into it. We stand mesmerised as the fabric comes to life like a sleeping dragon, stretching and yawning: its tail and wings being pulled into shape by the three men that busy themselves around it – taming it – until it is safe enough to stand and show its full magnificent self. In a half-state of wakefulness, the dragon begins to roar: fire spewing from his mouth as the men hold on to his reins, keeping him in check. Slowly he rises, angry growls still bursting from his mouth until he admits defeat and lazily rises, pulling the basket along like a shackle.

Flynn orders us to stand beside him and face his phone for a red-cheeked, wind-blown selfie, before we are taken aside and introduced to our pilot, Timothy. He shows us how to climb into the basket by putting our feet into the footholes, and goes through a few simple safety tips: don't grab branches or leaves as you pass over them; don't throw anything outside the moving balloon and don't ever attempt to disembark while in motion. Above us, the patchwork sky is wakening and as we finally climb into the basket, the sun has arched its back. The noise and heat from the burner is louder than I expected; I can barely hear what Flynn is saying but it is along the lines of 'awesome'. Rose isn't saying anything, her smile and iridescent eyes speaking enough for all of us.

We'd been told that we'd be heading west and as we start to rise, I know that this is one of the most memorable moments of my life. Gradually we begin to leave the ground, the few spectators and other early morning flyers waving us goodbye as the flames throw us higher. The balloon grazes the tops of the deep green wood, leaves caressing the sides of the basket as birds in their nests continue their chorus. I can smell the earthy scent of the ground below and the gas from above; everything feels brighter, clearer, as though I have been half awake most of my life and only now can I see the real, clear colours and smells of our amazing world. It is the strangest sensation. I expected to feel a strong breeze but as we travel on the wind everything is still: magnificently so. It isn't until the burner stops and we are hit with utter silence that I notice I am singing.

'Seriously, Mum? Westlife?' I must have been going for a while because I was already on the second verse; singing about the faces of my children and the eyes of my lover. Flynn and Rose stand next to me (Timothy behind us, either pretending not to notice my singing or just giving the most-private experience he could), and all of us holding on to the edge of the basket. I continue singing about wingless flying, as we float over the Shropshire countryside, rising higher over a dual carriageway, but anxiety creeps on to Rose's face as I finish my tribute to Ronan and the boys.

'Are you OK?' I reach for her hand, her fingers grasping the basket, her knuckles white.

'It's just so high . . .'

'Mum, this is so weird,' Flynn chatters away, oblivious, 'I can, like, hear those people talking.' Rose and I turn our heads towards where a group of farmers are sitting on the back of a stationary tractor which seems miles below us, vibrant yellow rapeseed surrounding them. The colour has drained from Rose's face and I can see that she has started to panic.

'Sing.'

'What?' she asks with confusion.

'Sing. It'll help, I promise.' I look down and can see the River Severn twisting and turning, flanked by fields of dewy-green grass and golden corn; ancient trees are standing guard in militant lines. Flynn watches Rose for a minute and then (in a dramatic, hand-gestured, operatic voice) begins singing, 'You Raise Me Up'. Rose bursts out laughing and then joins in. I, for once, am the spectator as I watch the bond between my children gleam in the early morning sun, which shines on their faces, turning their skin buttery yellow and filling their eyes with optimism. My smile uncurls across my face as they sing about standing on mountains and walking across stormy oceans: the grand gestures become more and more theatrical as they hit the final notes, telling each other that they will become more than they can be . . . and I know. I know they will survive this. As I watch the shadow of our balloon lean over the corn field I feel a sense of relief that they will survive the news that will soon send them free-falling with only each other to break the fall.

We glide through the air for about forty minutes, watching the colours of the horizon bending with the irrigation lines of the fields. We can see the world at work, the hectic lives passing below us as we travel in this bubble of silence, of stillness; of peace.

As we start to descend, so does Rose's anxiety, but she seems in control of it this time and I notice her taking deep breaths, murmuring something to herself. She is using the mindfulness techniques that we have been practising and, as we approach the landing site – a rough patch of farmland adjacent to the main road – I can hear her whispering:

'I can feel the roughness of the basket, I can feel the strength of my family, I can hear the cars from the roads . . .'

The basket tilts only slightly as the winds are so light, but we hold on tight regardless, as it bumps on to the ground and gradually comes to a stop. I suppose I should have been watching the view outside the basket but all I could see was their faces, Rose's apprehension giving way to calm and Flynn's look of awe at the wonders that life could hold for him.

Still shaking slightly from the adrenaline that is still alive and coursing through my body, we are driven back to the launch site and to a small picnic area with wooden benches spread with red-checked tablecloths, held in place with plates of breakfast pastries, ripe fruits and glasses of buck's fizz and orange juice. Tumbling over each other's sentences, we sit down. Our breakfast table is engulfed by the English countryside, as three more balloons, one multi-coloured, one deep blue and the other the same red as ours, float in various stages of their own hour of splendour. I pick at a pecan and apricot pastry as Flynn and Rose predictably grab anything that contains chocolate, both still talking about the way they could hear things from far away even though we were so high up, which leads on to a conversation about Superman and then on to the familiar argument we've all been having since Rose was seven and Flynn was ten: which superhero is the best. Condensation trickles down the side of the glass flute as I pick it up and lift it to my lips. The smooth weight of the glass is shining in my grasp as I slowly tip it to my lips. I look upwards and watch the other balloons sailing further away as the sweet bubbles fizz over my tongue and the tartness of the oranges hits the back of my throat. Holding the glass in front of me, I watch the tiny bubbles rising to the top. My heart is beating a steady thump, thump. Another cluster of bubbles floats and fizzes to the rim of the glass: thump, thump. Pop. I stare mesmerised as the little bubbles continue to rise, their short, golden life a struggle from the bottom of the glass to the summit, as they ascend – in tiny glory – before breaking free and settling on the top of the amber liquid: thump, thump. Pop. A perfect moment when they can rise from the depths and taste freedom, taste a moment of calm after the exertion of their short journey: thump, thump, before – pop. They are gone for ever.

'Mum?!'

'Get her in the recovery position.'

'Mum?'

'Step aside, please.'

'Mrs King?'

'What's her first name?'

'Melody.'

'Melody? Can you hear me, Melody? I'm just going to turn you slightly.'

'Could somebody call an ambulance?'

'No,' I rasp. The smell of damp grass and cigarette smoke causes me to retch as I shrug off the coat reeking of nicotine that has been thrown over me. I'm on all fours, my mouth filling with sweet bile before the acrid burning taste of vomit explodes from my mouth. I hold out my hand to stop the well-meaning rub of my back, as the sound of my gag reflex shatters the honey-sweet setting. My hands are sinking into the dew-stained grass, my nails soiled.

I take the tissue that has been offered and wipe my mouth, sitting back on my haunches and giving the small crowd an apologetic smile. Flynn and Rose are standing off to the side,

Flynn's arm wrapped protectively around Rose's frail shoulders. I meet his gaze and give him a look that is meant to convey that they are making a lot of fuss over nothing but his expression is indecipherable. I can't read his face, which is still and sceptical. Instead, he looks away from me and whispers something in her ear. She digs into her pocket and retrieves her phone as I bend over again, retching the last of my dignity out of my body.

It takes me some time to convince the on-site first aider that I don't need an ambulance. Too much buck's fizz and excitement on an empty stomach, I assure him. No, no, really, I'm fine. Goodness, isn't the view spectacular? I enthuse. We really must come here more often; watch the balloons. Really? Rare birds, you say? That sounds just perfect. If I could just trouble you for a glass of water and then I'll be as right as rain. I hear this, I speak these words, but I'm not here. I'm a host. A custodian. Forced to care, to nurture, to protect. My thoughts are slow and thick, my head filled with treacle. Trying hard to focus, I look over to where Flynn and Rose are standing, Rose with her hand protecting her eyes against the sun as she looks towards the dirt track. Flynn is leaning against the trunk of a tree watching me. I try to catch his eye but he is intent on biting the skin around his finger. I want to stand, to go to him, but my legs are shaking beneath the denim of my jeans and I'm worried that I may stumble. Rose starts to wave at a car that is heading over the bumpy track and I realise with a sinking heart that it wasn't a taxi that they had called but Shane.

He climbs out of the car, pushes his sunglasses on to the top of his head and gives a single wave. He's wearing a pair of beige combat trousers and a fisherman's knit, white turtleneck. It's much smarter than his usual attire and I wonder where he had been going. On a date, perhaps? With sadness, I acknowledge that I know very little about him really, whereas he knows almost everything about my life . . . and my children's, come to think of it. A field separates the two of us, but I can sense the concern written across his face, the worry in the crease between his eyes and the anger that simmers just below the surface.

The day I told him about Tom, Shane had made it clear that he thought I should tell Rose and Flynn about him. 'What right do you have to keep their father away from them?' he had asked me. My words, my explanations hadn't managed to sway him towards my way of thinking. He didn't know the struggle that Tom had gone through to find himself, to feel like he belonged, and he didn't understand the betrayal he would have felt when I decided to leave that day, without an explanation, without reason. He was even more frustrated with my decision when I told him about the scan, throwing his arms up in disbelief when I told him I didn't need any help, that I could handle it on my own. He had said that I was relying on my children too much. 'They're only kids, Melody,' he had said, reaching for my hand and pleading with me.

But here in this field, as I watch Flynn pulling himself up from the tree and striding over to Shane, I know that they have to be more than 'just kids'. They turn their backs to me and Rose hangs behind them slightly, letting Flynn take control of the conversation.

Moments later, digging her hands into her pockets, she walks towards me, head down, red ponytail swinging.

'Don't be cross,' she says.

'I'm not cross.' I tap the space beside me for her to sit down. 'You didn't need to call him, though. Honestly.' I grab hold of her cool hand. 'I'm fine. Really.' She looks up at me through her mascara-coated eyelashes, a layer of darkness snuffing out her precious, natural light.

'No, Mum. You're not.' She leans her head on my shoulder and we sit there with the animated chatter and smells of gas and grass surrounding us, neither of us wanting to take the next step towards the end of the conversation. Keeping my gaze down, I wait until a pair of brown walking boots and black Doc Martens appear.

'So.'

'So,' I answer him, looking up to meet his I-told-you-so frown with defiance.

'How are you feeling?'

'I'm OK now, thanks. Just too much excitement. I'm feeling much better . . . have you ever seen a hot air balloon being inflated? There's one about to go up over there . . .'

'Are you sure you don't want to go home and rest?' He crouches down in front of me and I smell his shampoo; his hair is still damp.

'Not yet . . .' I look him straight in the eyes. 'It's such a beautiful day and look, there's all this food to eat. When am I – are we – ever going to get the opportunity to see this again?'

He fills his cheeks with air and puffs out, shaking his head at me before smiling.

'OK, but I get to eat the last croissant.'

The nights are drawing in, I notice, as we bundle into the house. Flicking the light switches as I go, I can't help but enjoy the banter between the three of them. Conversation has returned to the superhero debate and Shane is arguing Captain America's case.

'No way! He's not even a real superhero.'

'OK, so what defines a superhero then?' Rose – ever the rationalist.

'You're overthinking it, Rose.' Flynn unzips his hoody and chucks it over the back of the kitchen chair.

'I'm not. Come on, give me, let's say, three features that define a superhero.'

'They have to be an alien.'

'No way, you can't have that!' Shane scoffs as he throws his keys on to the kitchen worktop.

'He's only saying that because he says Superman beats them all.'

'What about Spiderman? He's definitely a superhero and he's not an alien.'

'How about they have to have to get their powers by accident?' I add as I grab cups from the cupboard, throwing tea bags into them.

'Nice one, Mum, that blows Captain Arse Wipe out of the running,' Flynn laughs. My eyes are dry and sore. My convex reflection in the stainless steel kettle confirms my suspicion that I look as bad as I feel. Distancing myself from the conversation, I rummage in the junk drawer for some painkillers. I know I shouldn't take anything stronger than paracetamol, but I almost sag with relief when I find the co-codamol. I knock them back with a swig of the half-filled bottle of lemonade from the fridge, the cold temperature sliding down my throat and into my chest. I excuse myself and go upstairs to the loo, closing the bathroom door and leaning against it. Closing my eyes, I allow the tears to run freely; the sound of laughter fills the cold tiles with warmth and I smile through my watery vision. Happiness and fear tilt the scales inside, pulling me off balance. I know this is it. I know this is when I have to tell them: this was the 'one more day', and as I pull the roller blind down on the day, I acknowledge that my time is up.

Waiting. Waiting is a verb. A doing word. I am waiting, we are waiting, we wait. I wait until the end of the film; curtains are drawn and the cold dregs at the bottom of teacups and broken biscuits litter the lounge. A yawn, a stretch. How do you start a conversation like this?

'So . . .' I begin as I turn off the telly and then sit cross-legged on the lounge floor. Rose and Flynn are in their respective spots on the sofa, leaning away from each other, elbows against the arms, heads cradled in their palms. 'About today.' They fidget, pulling themselves more upright as they wait expectantly for me. 'It's going to be no surprise when I tell you that I haven't been feeling myself lately, that I've been feeling unwell . . .' Their eyes gravitate towards each other and then to me. The words I need to say are lodged in my throat, barbed and gritty.

'I'm . . . I'm, well, the thing is I . . .'

'What is it, Mum?' Rose asks.

'I, well. I have cancer.'

28

Melody

Cancer can take many forms, like the water sign with which it shares a name. Water can be dripping from the tap: a nuisance but resolvable – a firm hand, a twist – and then the problem is solved. Water is calm; at peace with its mirror-tight skin. But a lump – a mass – plummets into it, ripples: small circles that grow and grow, expanding, never stopping, never ending, growing in power, consuming energy until it finally crashes over you, destroying everything in its path.

People born under the sign of Cancer are said to be highly domestic, aggressively maternal; they take pleasure in protecting their home. But to achieve this, they can often be manipulative, vindictive and, just like the crab, quick to withdraw back into their hard shells . . . hiding.

That is what my tumour has been doing.

Hiding.

The day Flynn had gone on his first date with Kate, I had gone to the doctor's to find out my results. It was the strangest feeling sitting there in the doctor's office. Her look of embarrassed sentimentality as she sat, surrounded by pictures of her children and husband. The door was covered with poster-painted, finger-printed art. The door, which let in a woman without cancer, and evicted one with it, out into the world: a different world from the one before that twenty-minute consultation. As she told me, I couldn't help but look at the canvas of the beach sunset on her wall. I could almost smell the early evening barbecues, the tired wet sandy towels wrapped around us: sunburnt shoulders, sandy feet, as seagulls called from overhead, the rolling waves coloured blood-red. A tranquil scene, but I couldn't help but wonder . . . how many others had remembered happier times as they sat here staring into that sky filled with fire, as it descended into the waves, extinguishing its glory?

I hadn't cried; I'd nodded, listened attentively as she tried to explain and justify how it had been missed after so many tests. About how it explained what had long since been diagnosed as a mental problem was, in fact, more to do with the growth in my brain. I listened while she told me that the findings were remarkable and how they could see elements of Tourette's syndrome which – if founded – could change the way Tourette's was being researched. The bump to my head, the accident, was nothing more than a nasty case of concussion. She talked about the scan: the tissues they could see, the mass; she talked about a biopsy; about being realistic and preparing for the worst, but all I could hear was the 'C' word.

As I closed the door behind me with leaflets in my hand, my senses became heightened. It's a strange thing being told that you're probably going to die. Of course we all know it will happen one day. That fear that comes across us as a child when we suddenly realise that Mummy or Daddy might not come back. That gut-wrenching fear when you, as a child, look up to your parent in a supermarket only to discover the person standing next to you is not your mum but a stranger. The sudden fear that it is possible to be left alone. Yes, death has always been inevitable, but knowing it's going to be soon is something else entirely. The bronze door panel to the waiting room suddenly seems iridescent. The lights glare a little brighter. You notice the love in the eyes of a tired mother as she chastises her little girl for lying on the grubby floor. You ignore that the child looks scruffy; instead you notice the mischief, the passion bubbling behind the clear blue eyes. Outside, the world is suddenly in high definition. Birdsong is more melodic, its notes sweeping and soaring above the trees which nod and sway, complementing each other, the perfect accessory to an ancient outfit. My steps are filled with awareness, the smooth feel of my black nylon tights slipping in and out of the soles of my knee-high boots. The smell of my perfume, more floral than I'd noticed before. The way my eyes are blinking: tiny stop motion films that happen every day and yet we don't notice it – the marvels of the human body. A bus passes me: dull, bored faces staring out of the windows become faces planning a birthday surprise, a face remembering how they made love with a new lover, a face choosing what to cook for dinner – a meal that will please the whole family. Everything is more precious; everything is more sacred.

The kids are being more withdrawn. It's what I expected. I'm having to watch Rose's every move; check Flynn's hands for signs of fights. We had stayed up that night as I answered their questions and tried to explain what the doctor had told me. Life is going on, much the same as before. The first stage of my road to recovery is surgery. Brain surgery. I can't say it without laughing, it sounds so serious. So ridiculous. Things may change after that. I flick off the breakfast TV as Flynn comes down the stairs.

'I'm quitting college,' he says as though he's just asked what's for breakfast.

'No. You're not.' I stand and kiss his head. This is a conversation that we've had several times and this is why

Shane keeps insisting that I get in touch with Tom. Can you imagine how that conversation would go? Hi, it's me. Melody, that's right, the one you thought was called Melissa . . . Well, the thing is, we're actually married, mmhmm, yep, we have two children, one of whom was blinded in a car accident when you were driving . . . yes, that's the one, the boy you've been having nightmares about. Oh, and watch your daughter – Rose – she might start cutting herself at any moment . . . oh . . . and by the way, did I mention that I've got a nasty case of cancer? Yep, brain tumour. I'll be going in for surgery soon, so if you don't mind running the house while I'm gone? You know, pop the washing on, run the hoover around? That would be great.

'Flynn, we've talked about this, let's just see what happens when the treatment starts.'

'Have you slept?'

'Yes,' I lie.

'Liar.' He gives me a sad smile.

'How's Kate?' Steering the conversation towards Kate is the most powerful weapon in my arsenal. 'Tea?'

'Yes, please. She's good, thanks.'

Flynn's relationship had taken a more serious turn last week when he'd asked if she could come over.

'. . . and stay over,' he'd said, looking me straight in the eye when he'd asked, making his meaning clear. I had worried about my decision. Was it the right decision? One of those decisions that could have other parents up in arms? Should I have insisted that she slept in the lounge? No. I trust him and let's face it, if they're going to do it, at least it would be in the safety of our home.

'Just make sure,' I'd added, 'that she asks her parents first.'

She had stammered her way through a takeaway pizza with us all, blushing every time I had asked her a question, but the minute Flynn talked to her, even if it was something as simple as if she wanted more Coke, then she answered smoothly. When I watch them together, it is clear that they have something special and rare. It's in the small things, the sideways glances, the graze of an arm, the squirt of salad cream with pizza because he knows she likes it, each little piece adding to the strength of their relationship. When you hold your baby boy in your arms, baby-blue sleepsuit swaddling crinkly, delicate skin, you never think of what it will feel like to see the man he will become . . . One minute he's pulling himself up on the sofa, the next he's drawing inventions in his notebook; then before you know it, he's looking for shaving cream.

As first sleepovers go, I think Rose and I handled it quite well. We stayed downstairs until late watching the latest romantic comedy, made sure we kept the sound up high and tried our very best not to look up at the ceiling whenever we heard a creak. Of course, it was a little less comfortable at breakfast the next morning when I started singing 'Like a Virgin' by Madonna.

'I'm going over to hers tonight if that's OK?'

'Oh. Um, OK.'

'Her parents are away so . . .'

'Do they know you're going over to stay?'

'Yeah, they're quite cool about it. She's got her own room at the back of the garage with a downstairs loo next to it so it's not like we'll be in the main part of the house much anyway.'

'And they're OK with, well, with you sleeping in their daughter's room?'

'I guess.'

'Oh. Good. Just make sure you behave and be polite . . . and make sure you're careful.'

'What *do* you mean, Mother? That I wipe my feet before I go into the house?' He laughs.

'You know exactly what I mean.'

'Thanks a bunch,' he says, laughing.

Arses. I'm singing 'Teenage Dirtbag' by Wheatus.

'She doesn't like rock music, Mum.'

It's at this point that Rose appears in the kitchen, Superman shorts and vest with a long, tatty blue cardigan hanging off her, red hair piled in a messy bun. She looks at me then at Flynn, shrugs her shoulders and joins in with me, singing about what she could be missin' as we lean back-to-back, air guitars in hand, begging each other to listen to a mediaeval torture device.

'Ooooooh, yeah-errrrrrr . . .'

We continue to sing about getting tickets for a concert, reiterating that she doesn't know what she would be missin' . . .

We finish in a fit of giggles.

I poke my head around Rose's bedroom door and watch her sitting on her unmade bed as she glides her finger across the screen of her phone, eyebrows furrowed in concentration. There is the inevitable mound of clothes on the floor, the gentle hum of her hair straighteners. She hasn't noticed me standing there and I enjoy being able to watch her. Her sleeves are rolled up, which is huge progress in itself; she snorts at the screen and smiles – dimples sinking into her cheeks. Looking up at the clock I realise that I need to get a move on; I've got a consultation with the surgeon this morning. My heart sinks but I allow myself a few minutes more, enjoying these moments, precious moments that would normally be tinged with a moan about the damp towel on the floor, about getting a move on or she'll be late for school as I rush downstairs, cross with myself for forgetting that it's PE that day.

'Rose? Time to go. The taxi will drop you off on the way to the hospital.' She nods and her face becomes serious again and I wish that I'd left her smiling at whatever Vine she was looking at on her phone.

'Mrs King?' A portly, purple-permed porter calls my name and I follow her waddling behind down the hospital corridor. I'm shown into a room and a false-toothed smile tells me to wait.

I sit and look at the bed with the curtains pulled tidily to the side. A young man in his early twenties comes in pulling a trolley behind him and I'm weighed, my blood pressure is measured and they take some vials of my blood. Then I'm left with nothing but a small piece of cotton wool plastered to the top of my arm and a sense of dread. Eventually I'm herded into another room where I wait for the neurosurgeon consultant, Mr Rudd.

'Sorry to keep you.' A softly spoken man in his early thirties walks into the office eating a packet of nacho-cheese flavoured tortilla chips. He screws the packet into a ball and throws it towards the waste-paper bin – and misses. This does not fill me with confidence. He heads over to the small sink and washes his hands before sitting down behind the desk. 'Mrs King? I must say, you've got us all quite excited.' He smiles at me over the rim of his thin wire-framed glasses. Fabulous. A brain surgeon that needs glasses. I raise my eyebrows up at him and he checks himself.

'I can't say that I'm particularly excited about having cancer, I'm afraid.' I know I'm being rude but it's just one of those days when I can't seem to help it.

'Of course. Yes, well, shall we go through your notes right from the beginning? So you had an accident back in January 2013?'

'Mmhmm.'

'And from that it was discovered, through a CT scan, that

you had a brain abscess which we treated intravenously here for three days which seemed to solve the problem . . .'

'The brain abscess, yes, but not the singing.'

'No, no, quite . . . and it seems that we then went down the route of it being a psychological problem rather than a neurological one. After that, I see that you've had a number of referrals and that you have attended many sessions with Dr Ashley?'

'Yes, although I haven't been for some time.'

'Why did you stop?'

'Because it wasn't helping. It seems to be triggered by stress and so I have been trying different ways of coping with anxiety, and the ones that worked were the things I thought of myself.'

'I see. I also see that you did not attend three MRI scan appointments and so you were referred back to your GP.'

'My son was having a very difficult time at school and I was going to the therapy sessions, which seemed to be helping at the time, and I had already been told that the problem wasn't with my brain, so no, I didn't go.' I bite the inside of my thumbnail like a naughty schoolgirl.

'OK. Right. Let's talk about what we have found out since you were admitted into hospital in August.' He sits quietly, flicking through the notes inside a large brown folder, before double-clicking his mouse and staring at the computer screen. 'You were admitted under police custody; can you tell me about the circumstances that surrounded that?'

'My daughter had been found self-harming while she was on holiday and, as you can understand, I was in a very anxious state. By the time I got to the hospital I was finding it very hard to contain . . . my condition, and ended up singing "Help" by The Beatles. Unfortunately, that then progressed to some more aggressive songs. I ended up screaming at the police and I had to be restrained.'

'So the songs match your mood?'

'Yes. Most of the time they do, yes.'

'Interesting. How do you feel when you sing?'

'High.' He nods.

'When you were having your MRI you were singing until you were calm. The scan shows that you had excess dopamine at that point.'

I look at him blankly.

'Dopamine is the happy hormone, which would explain why you feel high when you sing.'

'Oh. Right. And is that to do with the tumour?'

'We think so, yes, we'll be able to find out more after the operation. The exciting part, from our point of view, is that your symptoms show a remarkable resemblance to Tourette's, which normally manifests early on in life. We've never had a case where it has developed later on and certainly not caused by a tumour. The high rates of dopamine have been connected to it, but your basal ganglia—'

'My what now?'

'Sorry, I'm getting ahead of myself.'

'Could you, um, I'm rather worried about the cancer aspect. If you could . . .'

'Of course, of course. My apologies. As you know from the scan you've had, the tissues that are visible showed that there is a very high chance that your tumour is cancerous.'

'Sorry, but I was told that it *is* cancer, are you saying that it might not be?'

'Mrs King, I think that it is important for you not to have false hope. The scans were very clear. A biopsy will give us an absolute definitive answer, but given what we have seen, we're almost certain. What we need to do now is find out what type it is and if we can remove it.'

'Yes, that's what I've been told, and that it's in a difficult spot to remove?'

'Let's take it one step at a time. The first step is to find out what kind of tumour it is and then we can take it from there.'

'OK.'

'So what will happen on Thursday is—'

'Could I just ask . . . how was the tumour missed when I had the CT scan? It's just that my children are having a hard time understanding it, they have so many questions . . .'

'We think it is possible that the brain abscess was a small tumour, which unfortunately on a CT scan can almost mimic a brain abscess. It would have been more easily identifiable on an MRI.'

'Which I didn't go to.'

Inside, I can feel the spring winding, tightening and tightening. A jumble of notes flutter, it seems, through one ear and out of the other.

'OK then, so Thursday?' I try to be mindful. But being mindful of sitting in this room, being mindful that I'm sitting opposite a neurosurgeon, and being mindful that I'm talking about my brain tumour, is not helping.

'It's a fairly straightforward procedure.'

I stand up, give the doctor a 'couldn't-care-less' shrug of my shoulders. Mr Rudd tilts his head and narrows his eyes in concentration as I begin head, shoulders, knees and toes – not to mention my eyes, ears, mouth, as well as my nose. I do the entire, full-length version with little 'mmmm' sounds when I begin to miss out parts of the body in succession until I end up putting my hands on my head, shoulders, knees and toes, knees and toes in silence until I hit the chorus again. I'll give him his due, he didn't bat an eyelid until I had sat back down.

'Under an anaesthetic,' he continues, as if I hadn't just been bending over touching my toes for several minutes, 'I will drill a fairly small hole into your skull so I can take a piece of the tumour out with a very, very thin needle and from that,' he points his fingers together and leans back in his chair, 'we'll be able to see where we are from the results, and how to proceed.'

'Will I need to stay in overnight?'

'Yes. We could do this in a day appointment but given your other symptoms, I would suggest that you stay in.'

'Oh. OK.'

'Will that be OK?'

'It should be, yes. I'll have to ask my mum to come over from Wales for a couple of days . . .'

'Melody,' he leans forward, 'tackling cancer is a long road to recovery and with a brain tumour, the complications can be vast. You will need support at home.'

I push the conversations I've had with Shane to the back of my mind and give him a firm nod.

Pouring the bubble bath into the running tap, I watch the swell of bubbles stretch across the top of the water and then try to call my mother for the third time since I came home. Still no answer, so I wipe off my make-up with a cotton wool pad and undress. As I sink into the warm water, my phone rings and I wipe away the foam from my hands and swipe the screen. She sounds breathless, which is to be expected; my mother never stops moving.

'Sorry I took so long, silly old fool that I am, I've broken my ankle.' My heart sinks and I lower myself further into the water. 'How are you, my darling? How did you get on with the consultant?'

'OK . . . but I need to go in overnight. Will you be able to come over?'

'Oh Melody, you know I would in a heartbeat, but I can't drive with this ankle all strapped up and what use would I be? Surely they will be OK on their own? Flynn is seventeen and Rose is a sensible girl.' I roll my eyes at that and resist the urge to say 'was'. 'And she's got Flynn looking out for her, and you've said yourself how much better she is doing now . . .'

'Yes, yes . . . I'm sure they'll be OK.' Tears of frustration fill my eyes. 'Anyway, I've got to go, Mum, someone's at the door.' We hang up, and I let out a throat-scratching scream as I throw the phone across the room, hearing it shatter with a metallic smack against the white tiles. I submerge myself under the water and block out everything except the fluid filling my ears.

29

Flynn

It was weird hearing Mum arguing with Shane. Almost like I'd imagine it to be in normal houses. You know, the kind of thing that normal couples argue about like, I dunno, not putting the washing out or . . . man, what do normal couples argue about? Their kids? Money? Anyway, I did what I reckon most of us would do. I listened in. It took me a while to understand what they were talking about and then I got the gist. Mum has met him. I get why she would, I mean, when you've been searching for someone for years and you thought they were dead then of course you would go and see them, but I don't get why she didn't tell us. It explains a lot. Like why he was trying to find us. I feel a bit shit about the note I left him now. I sat on the bottom stair trying to piece together the conversation and what it meant. She kept saying she couldn't do it to him, tell him about us, and I felt like saying thanks, Mum, but then she would get really angry with Shane and say that he didn't understand. That Dad or Tom, whatever, wouldn't be able to cope . . . that he didn't know anything about us, so I guess that means there is something wrong with the guy's memory. Huh, and my English teacher said I was no good at inference.

Mum said that she loved him too much to tell him. That was dead strange to hear. When she started crying I slammed the front door loudly as if I'd only just got home and went up to my room.

I've Googled brain tumours. Of course I have. Nasty fuckers, aren't they? Me and Rose have got to step up, I guess. Mum's going to need taking care of. Nan is no good. I mean, she's OK when we're with her, but she won't want to keep coming over here, she's got all of these groups that she goes to, she's on, like, the parish council and shit like that, got her own life. She's always been a bit like that. It's like Mum is an old friend that she really likes, but it's like when we were in the hospital last time? She kind of made it all about herself, like, what would her friends think if they knew her grand-daughter had cut herself and in her friend's caravan no less, and you should have seen the look on her face when they told her Mum had been arrested, I mean, shit, the first thing she asked was would it be in the news, not, 'Is my daughter OK?'

I know what I have to do, whether it's fair on him or not. I don't really give a fuck if I'm honest, Mum has survived on her own for long enough and if he loves her, or at least cares for her, which I'm guessing he does, then she needs him.

I wasn't surprised in the least when Mum told me that Gran couldn't make it over. She goes into hospital on Thursday, which kind of sucks because me and Rose have got teacher development days then and we could have just hung about the house, but she's asked Shane's ex if we can stay there, the night too, which is just weird. I mean we don't even know her. Mum must be desperate. Shane can't do it, something about it not being professional because he still works with me and stuff, so that's it. I've got to find Tom slash Dad. I might not know the guy but Mum does, and right now, she needs all the support she can get. Who knows? He might even make her happy, he might even turn out to be the man we've been looking for. According to his Facebook page he lives in Cornwall and is working on his next exhibition, so I figure that that is the best place to find him. The problem is leaving Rose. Kate says I should tell her what I know, but I dunno . . . what if he turns out to be a complete wanker and tells us to sod off? As if things aren't bad enough with Mum and the big 'C'.

OK so, Kate got really mad when I said that I wasn't going to tell Rose, it was quite sweet actually. I've never really seen her mad before, she had these two pink spots that appeared on her cheeks, anyway she reckons that, if it was her, she would have felt even worse later that neither Mum nor me trust Rose enough with the truth . . . I wouldn't have thought of that really, but she's right; I guess she would have felt even more isolated if I didn't, so I did. I told her about overhearing Mum first of all and then I told her I saw him. She was frickin angry that I hadn't told her, called me a 'complete wanker' and then cried a bit but then she started asking me question after question, like, does he look like us? What was he wearing and stuff and you don't want to know what she called me when I told her about the note that I left. She didn't speak to me for a few days because of that. God help the man who takes on my sister, she can make sulking an Olympic sport. Anyway, she's sort of stopped giving me the cold shoulder now that I've told her that I'm going to go and find him.

Saying goodbye to Mum this morning was not one of my most favourite things to do. I could feel that she was shaking when I hugged her goodbye, with her usual requests that we 'Don't swear' and 'Be polite'. Rose was better than I expected her to be, but I think it's because she knows we have a plan to fix things. That's what she needs. Control over something.

That's when things for her turned into a bloody (hah!) mess . . . once she hadn't got finding Dad to concentrate on.

Man, this house is like a museum. Mum is always going on about it and stuff, about how nice it is and how she would love to have a house like this someday but it's just, I dunno, dead. It's got no personality, no damage to the doors where someone has lost their temper and given it a good kick, no scratch in the wallpaper where a kid has tried to skateboard inside because it was raining out, and the whole place stinks of plug-in air freshener or those reed thingies. Joanne is OK, I guess. She seems a bit edgy but has pretty much let us get on with it. She let us order whatever we wanted from the pizza place for lunch, which was cool because we never have the extra sides or the puddings, and she's got all of the movie channels. I'm going to fake a headache in a bit and go to bed (the spare rooms even have their own bathrooms!). Rose is going to cover for me (she's going to drop a few comments about the need for teenage boys to slink off to their rooms once in a while . . . hopefully that will make her stay out of the room and not check on me) and then I'm out of here. A hundred and fifty quid a ticket it is. Fuck. I hope the Ass-hat is worth it.

So . . . this is what happened. Kate was waiting for me at the station when I got there. I had this huge lump in my throat when I saw her. We hadn't planned to meet up; I was going on my own. She gave me this smile that she does and kind of looks at me through her eyelashes. It feels like someone is pulling at my gut. I know it sounds wet but she is so beautiful . . . I can't believe I'm allowed to kiss her, let alone anything else.

'Hey,' I managed to squeak out.

'Hey.' She reached into her pocket and flashed her ticket

at me. I nodded and smiled back at her, not trusting myself to speak. The lump in my throat was even bigger and I was worried that she would be able to tell that I was almost about to cry.

'How did you . . .?' I managed to ask in this weird, high-pitched voice. She shrugged.

'Savings.'

'But—'

'I don't w-w-w-want you t-t-t-t-to go on your own. He might be a—'

'Wanker?'

'Axe-murderer.'

The train pulled up and she bent down to grab her backpack. It looked like she was about to climb a mountain it was so full. 'Be prepared,' she laughed at my confused look.

We found an empty table, sat down next to each other; I let her have the window seat and then she started faffing with her bag, pulling out family-sized bags of Frazzles and peanut M&Ms. I grabbed a litre bottle of Coke from my backpack. We smiled at each other and then she slumped herself down into the seat and we leant into each other, heads resting against heads. I didn't really know what we were going to do when we got there. I was hoping that the gallery would still be open – the last train was supposed to get there at ten and there was a private viewing of some local painter until eleven. The journey was long and at some point I must have fallen asleep because the next thing I knew, she was saying my name, shaking me awake.

'Flynn?'

My mouth felt dry and the side of my face was hot and itchy.

'We're almost there.' I sat up and took a swig from the flat Coke. It was dark outside and our reflections stared back at us from the mirrored windows. My phone was nearly out of battery so I sent a quick message to Rose to let her know that we'd almost arrived and then I turned and plugged it into my portable charger. Finally, our stop was called and we got off. The sea air hit us as we got off the train. Kate had her navigation on her phone turned on and we followed the directions down the quiet seaside streets. She held my hand tightly and for the first time in my whole life, I had someone who trusted me. Inside I felt sick. What if the gallery was closed? I hadn't worried too much about that before, when it was just going to be me, I was gonna, like, sleep in a bus stop or something, but now that I had her tiny hand in mine, I was starting to panic. The sea was crashing against the shore and we had to battle against the wind. We kept taking steps forward, she didn't say anything even though she must have been scared. We turned another corner and then we could see lights on, on both floors.

'That m-m-m-m-m, that, mmm-m-m-m, must be it.' She squeezed my hand and we started to run towards the building just as the lights upstairs were turned off. I banged on the door. The sign said closed but there must have still been someone there cuz there were still some lights turned on. I hammered my fist against the door again until the shadow of a woman came towards us.

'We're closed!' she shouted through the door. I don't blame her for not opening it, I had the hood of my jacket over my head and I was all in black.

'Please, if you could just give us a moment of your time?' I tried to sound like Rose when she wants to get her own way, like the way she had spoken to the police that time.

'Come back tomorrow,' she answered warily through the door.

'Please, I just need to find someone, a family friend . . . his name is Tom Simmonds?'

'What do you want with Tom?' She came closer to the door.

'I'm . . .' She opened the door, took one look at my face and her expression changed from curiosity, I guess, to . . . I dunno, horror? Her reaction threw me. It's been a while since somebody has openly looked at me like I'm a total freak. 'I'm his son.'

'You'd better come in.' She opened the door to let us in and we stood awkwardly, but I couldn't help looking at the artwork that was everywhere. I let go of Kate's hand and stepped towards a picture of one of his sculptures. It was the tree. The tree from the accident. It looked like the photo had been taken there, in the gallery. Squinting at it, I felt goosebumps running up my arms. There was a rose . . . he must remember us then.

'It's called *Stability*,' the woman explained.

'It's the tree from the accident,' I turned my head to Kate, 'and look . . . there's a rose.'

'A rose?'

I turned to the woman. She was attractive for an older woman. She had thick blonde curly hair that looked like it must weigh a ton. 'It's my sister's name.'

'Christ.' She gripped the front of her hair in her fist and sighed. 'You'd better follow me.' She took us upstairs and poured herself a large glass of red wine from an open bottle that was left on the table. 'Help yourselves.' She gestured towards the bottle and the half-eaten remains of a buffet. I shook my head and waited for her to stop gulping down the wine. 'Take a seat.' She pointed to a couple of arty-looking chairs, I wasn't sure if they were exhibition pieces or not to be honest, but we sat on them even though they were cold and hard and full of angles.

'Tom doesn't know who you are.' She refilled her glass. 'He doesn't remember anything from his life until eleven years ago. He was homeless, penniless and a complete wreck when I met him.

'But—' She held up her hand to stop me from talking. 'He has . . . dreams. He has dreams about a boy with half his face missing . . . I'm guessing that must be you.' She tilted her glass at me.

'I, I guess so. I dunno, are you his, you know, girlfriend?'

She laughed then, a deep, throaty laugh. 'No, no. I'm Georgie, we work together, I'm an artist.'

'Oh right. Cool. I'm Flynn and this is my Kate.'

'Your Kate? Sweet.' I was blushing; I could feel the heat in my face.

'How did you two get here? I mean, it's pretty late.'

'The train – can you take us to him? Sorry, I don't mean to be, you know, rude or anything, but I need to talk to him about Mum.'

'Mum? Melissa?'

'No.'

'Huh.'

'She's called Melody.'

'Melody? That's funny – I mean, not ha-ha funny, but – never mind. Look, it's pretty late and he lives, well, it's quite hard to find in the dark. Where are you staying?'

'We-w-w-w-w-I have a sleeping ba—'

'We were going to just—' I look away from her.

'Oh shit. Does anybody know you are here?'

'Not exactly.'

'What does that mean? Not exactly?'

'Rose knows.'

'And your mother?'

'She's, well, that is why I need to speak to him. Tom. Dad, whatever.'

'Right. Well, I can't very well leave you to sleep outside, can I? You can stay at mine for the night.'

'We'll be OK, we'll just—'

'Flynn?' I nodded. 'Do me a favour. I'm knackered, my

feet hurt and I want a bath. Tom is a very, very special friend and we have been friends for a long time, but if I leave his son, even if he doesn't know he has one, on the streets? He would kick my ass from here to China, so, get your shit together and let's go.'

Kate was trying to hide a smile.

'OK, keep your hair on,' I smirked at her.

'Christ, you look just like him.' She shook her head, drained her wine and flicked off the light switches along the way.

30

Rose

'Where is he?' Jo turned on the bedroom light and I covered my eyes with my arm. This is how my day started.

'Who?'

'Don't play games with me. I may not be your mother but I am responsible for you both until tomorrow. Do you know where he is?' She was standing in her designer skinny jeans, long white sleeves poking out of her navy-blue body warmer. It was past midnight and she still looked like she had stepped out of a Marks & Spencer catalogue. All that was missing was a pair of oversized sunglasses perched on her shining, swinging ponytail. I shrugged. 'Has he just gone to his girl-friend's?' I nodded. 'OK, I'll just go and Facebook message her parents, just to check, then . . .'

Friggin' Facebook. It must have been so much easier to get away with things when the internet didn't exist.

'OK, OK . . . he's not there.'

'Where is he then?'

I sat up and bit the corner of my nail. 'I can't tell you.'

'No, Rose, that's not the truth. You can tell me but you're choosing not to.' I looked away and stared at the curtains, which had birds flying on them, all expensive shabby chic; not just shabby like our place. 'Fine. I'll ring Shane.' She stormed out of the room, perfume following her like a cape in a Disney film. I went to the loo and stayed sitting there for a while. This is when I miss it the most. It would have been so easy to feel the release, the control of the cut. I shook my head and started the mindfulness process. It does work: it's hard to do it but by the time she came storming back in, I was calm and in control.

'Has he gone to find your dad?' I tucked my hair behind my ears and pulled down the sleeves of my PJs. She tried not to stare at my arms but I could feel her looking, checking. Then she pretended to sneeze so she could go into the en-suite for some 'tissue' – it was so lame and fake that I started to laugh. She came back into the room with a really pissed off look. 'Look, Rose. I don't know how I've landed myself into this life of yours but I'm in it. If you don't fuck about with me then I won't fuck about with you. Deal?' I was a bit shocked by how she spoke to me but I gave her a quick nod. 'Good. Roll up your sleeves.'

'What? No!'

'If you are in any danger at all, I have to ring an ambulance. I don't want my career fucked up because I didn't look after you properly, OK?'

'Fine.' I rolled up my sleeves to my elbows and raised my eyebrows at her. 'Happy?'

'All the way up, or you can change into one of my vests if you'd prefer?' She raised her eyebrows back at me.

'Jesus. Satisfied?' I asked her as I turned my arms this way and that.

'Good. Now . . .' she sat on the edge of the bed, 'tell me where he is before I have to call the police.' I rolled my eyes and sighed.

'Cornwall.'

'How the fucking fuck has he got to Cornwall?!'

'The train.'

'But that would have cost him——'

'He used his birthday money.' Her face sort of softened then. 'Right, grab your stuff and we'll get going.'

'What?'

'To Cornwall. I presume you know where he was going?'

'Kind of, but——'

'Come on, get a move on.' She stood up and looked around, then held her chin in her hand with a worried expression. 'Do you need, you know, snacks and stuff? And toilet breaks?' I clamped my lips together to stop myself from laughing. She looked lost for a moment; the hard-faced businesswoman façade had slipped.

'I'm sure I can survive for a few hours.' She smiled then, almost as if she was looking forward to driving for several hours in the middle of the night with a moody teenager that she hardly knew.

The first hour felt a bit awkward. She kept asking me lame questions about school and talking about her tiny school in Wales and that she never had the stuff that all of the other kids had. She said she remembered putting cardboard inside her shoes one day because they had a hole in them and it was raining outside, and after that, I started to relax. We stopped for petrol and she let me have whatever I wanted from the shop and it turned out that we liked a lot of the same things. She wasn't as uptight as I thought she'd be about the mess in the car. I dropped a half-eaten packet of smoky bacon on the floor at one point and she just waved off my apologies and said it was due for a clean soon anyway. We got talking about clothes and stuff and then we ended up talking about her wedding and how her elderly aunty hadn't taken her medication so she could drink at the reception and ended up throwing sugared almonds at everyone. I told her about how Mum sings in her sleep and then, I don't know why, maybe it was because she was driving and not facing me, or that she wasn't, like, forcing me to answer questions, but I started talking about things I don't normally talk about. I told her about how it felt when we found out Dad was, like, living a different life and that he'd left us. She told me about how she had wanted kids but that she couldn't have any. About how horrible it felt every time she saw a negative pregnancy test. It was like we were in this little bubble of, I don't know, trust? Five hours in a car is a long time to be with someone. She told me about how Shane had tried to pretend that it didn't matter when she knew that it did and that she would get so angry with him for trying to be happy all of the time when they both knew that they weren't; about how she hated him telling her about the kids that he was working with, that it felt like he was punishing her for not being able to get pregnant. She said that of course that wasn't true, but that it had felt like it at the time.

Then she told me about her job and how it feels to be in charge, to be responsible for your own income and how amazing it is to be able to walk into a shop and be able to afford something special and realise that it was all down to your own hard work. Yours and nobody else's.

'I'm a bit disappointed in you, Rose,' she said as we parked in an uneven, potholed car park.

'Eh?'

'Well, you haven't asked if "we're nearly there yet" once.'

I got out of the car and stretched. The sun was only just starting to rise and I could hear the seagulls calling above the sounds of the crashing waves. It was only half-six but we could smell fresh bread baking. There was a small bakery across the road and it looked like it had a café attached to it. We crossed the empty road and stood outside and, of course, the sign said closed. She knocked on the door.

'What are you doing?' I asked, feeling embarrassed. 'It says closed.'

'Rule number one. Challenge everything.'

A tired-looking woman pulled back the sign and unlocked the door.

'Yes?'

'Hi there, I'm so sorry to bother you and I know how busy you must be, but we've been travelling for hours and—'

'We don't open until eight.'

'Of course, of course, it's just that my daughter has diabetes and her blood sugar is a bit low . . . never mind, I think I saw a vending machine further up, oh, but I haven't got any change! So sorry about this, if you could change a fifty? We can be on our way.' The woman's face suddenly became a little more alert. 'So sorry about this, you must be rushed off your feet.' Jo put on this 'we must be brave' and yet sympathetic face.

'Well, I was about to put the coffee machine on anyway, I suppose I could make an exception.'

'Oh, no, no it's fine, if you don't open until eight, we wouldn't want to impose . . .'

'No, no, it's fine really. I can make a hot chocolate – would that help with the diabetes, or perhaps a croissant? I can put a batch in early?'

'That would be . . .' pause for dramatic catch of breath, 'just perfect. Thank you, really you're too kind,' she added as we walked into the warmth of the café. 'I bet this is one of those places that is famed for a special bread or pastry, Rose . . .'

'Oh, yes. We're well known for our pecan Danish pastry.'

'That sounds amazing!'

'Oh they are, if you don't mind holding on for half an hour, I can rustle one up if you'd like to try it?'

'Oh no, I didn't mean for you to—'

'It's no bother, really, I need to make some anyway.'

'You really are too kind. I see what they mean about this place, the people are just wonderful,' Jo added as she placed a gentle hand on the woman's arm. As the woman turned her back to us, Jo winked at me. 'You see, challenge everything.'

It was as I finished the last of my hot chocolate that I noticed a local newsletter pinned to the cork board. There were various local business adverts on it, but something caught my eye. I got up and took it down. It was the logo of the gallery. Sitting back down, I placed the newsletter on the table between us. Dad smiled up at me.

'Look,' I pushed the paper towards Jo, 'it's him.'

'Ohh, he's nice-looking.'

'Gross.'

'Sorry.' She wiped the crumbs from her jeans as .she scanned the paper. 'It says that he's been offered an exhibition in a gallery in London. Wow. Sounds like he's doing well.'

'And?'

'Nothing, I just think that, look, if it was me and I was doing my own thing and becoming a success, well,' she took a sip of her coffee, 'it's going to be a lot for him to deal with, that's all.'

'Wouldn't you rather know, though?' She shrugged her shoulders. 'Anyway, that's not his choice now. Mum needs him. He's our father. He needs to know.'

'But she didn't want him to know.'

'Do you think we're doing the wrong thing? Telling him?'

'I don't know.'

My phone whistles.

'Finally!' I text Flynn back and ask him why he hasn't had his phone on, and then I tell him we're here, that I had no choice but to tell Joanne.

Fuck was his reply.

They were standing outside the gallery when we arrived. Flynn apologised to Jo as soon as he saw her; I was glad about that. She called him a deceitful little fuckwit but then smiled and said that it was all water over the bridge or something like that. Dad's friend, partner, whatever, was really pretty. Like that perfume advert with all of the gold . . . something like adore? Anyway, she looked a bit like her. It made me feel a bit worried, you know, for Mum. I mean, Mum was pretty and everything, but she's not, like, model pretty. Mum was more, cute, I guess.

'So how are we going to do this?' Georgie asked. 'I think it would be better that I go and speak to him first. He's not great with surprises and as far as surprises go, this is a pretty big one; he might need a few minutes to adjust.'

Flynn scowled slightly, then looked at me. I looked at Jo, who nodded.

'Yeah, I think that would be best.' I straightened myself up.

Flynn wasn't looking great. It's situations like this when his temper blows up. I fixed him with a look. A look that I hoped would mean 'calm the hell down'. Kate linked her arm through his and looked up at him. 'I know you want to get home quickly, but you have to handle this in the right way.' She smiled at him.

'Jeez, get a room,' I mumbled as we all headed for what I presumed was Georgie's car. Joanne was texting while we walked.

'Your mum is out of theatre. Everything went well and she's sleeping.'

'Does Shane know where we are?' Flynn asked.

Jo nodded. 'He says to tell you . . .' She smiled at the screen. 'Shane never managed to lie to me without me knowing about it, so . . .' She passed the screen to him where there was an emoji doing a high five. Flynn laughed.

We pulled up at the side of a lane just behind an old cottage. It was quite high up on a hill and the back garden dipped downwards away from the house. It had an old building in the garden, with one of those wavy tin roof things. Georgie went inside the building and told us to wait where we were. Once she went in, we all got out of the car and wandered over to the edge of the hill, looking down into the sea. It was pretty, even with the grey clouds. I turned around and looked at the house. It reminded me of something you'd see on an American show, one of those ones that you see with an old wooden hammock swinging on the porch outside, only this building was covered in the white plastery stuff like Christmas cake icing. Rubbing my arms, I stood next to Flynn and put my head on his shoulder.

'Can you believe he's in there?' I asked him.

'Yeah, he's in there and Mum is in hospital.'

'I know, but if what Georgie says is true, he didn't ditch her, did he? And it's kind of your fault that he didn't find her.'

'Thanks for that.'

'Well, it's true. Just don't go in there like a dick.'

'I won't. It's just,' he checked his phone, 'it's almost eight already and Mum will be out this afternoon. We can't not be there when she comes home.' He looked over his shoulder at the shed. 'How long does it take?' he asked, the last of his patience prickling his words. He bent down, picked up a stone and threw it over the edge of the cliff. We all leant forward and watched it plummet into the sea but we lost sight of it before it hit.

'Will she have a patch of hair missing, do you think?' I asked nobody in particular.

Kate picked up another and passed it to him and that's how we passed the time until Flynn got tired of waiting.

'Enough of this shit.' He threw a final stone over the edge. 'We can't afford to waste any more time.' He turned to head towards the house, so I turned to follow him.

31

Tom

I want you to know that even then, I hadn't given up on you. I want you to know that I never stopped thinking about you and that I never woke up in the morning without missing you, the warmth of your skin, the curve of your back against me. Things hadn't changed for me since I last saw you. When I finished my pieces of work inspired by you, I entered a competition . . . I didn't win but I had a call from an owner of one of the bigger galleries in London and they had agreed to exhibit my work. I'd already sold *Stability* for a tidy sum and I knew that if I sold a few of the other pieces too, well, it would make things easier. Financially. And that would mean that I could show you the person I had become. A success. Not some loser with no past and no future. I would be able to show you how I could support us and that whoever that person was that you had to run away from, he didn't exist any more.

That day, I had been up since five in the morning; I'd started running in the mornings. I've started that again, by the way, it's one of the things the doctor recommended to help with the insomnia. It was working – most of the time – and I'd made some changes to my diet. Making sure that I didn't just survive on caffeine and microwave food. That morning was the first time that I'd had to turn on the fluorescent strip light in the shed, a sure sign that winter was approaching. Its buzz was soon covered by the noise and sparks from the grinder as I sharpened my tools, ready for a full day of work. As I turned the metal, the sparks fell over the tips of my fingers and another fleeting memory passed of a bonfire: red gloves holding a sparkler and the smell of hot dogs. This is a childhood memory, I'm sure. I tried to capture it, examine it for clues, but all I could see were the sparks and the glove; nothing more. The muscles in my neck were aching again but every time I felt like taking a break, the more I'd think of you. With every piece I sculpted, every callus on my hand, I knew I was a step closer to becoming the man you deserved. The wheel slowed and I put the sharpened chisel to the side, the smell of hot dogs replaced with the metallic smell of steel.

'Tom?' Georgie closed the shed door behind her as I wiped my hands on my battle-scarred jeans.

'A bit early for you, isn't it?' I flicked on the kettle, which balanced on the plank of wood that kidded itself into believing that it was a counter at the back of the shed. I examined one of the mugs. My grubby fingerprints marked the handles and there was a brown tea-stained ring inside about a centimetre from the bottom. I shrugged and tipped some instant decaf coffee into it. 'Coffee?' I asked.

'Yes. I mean no, I, Tom . . .' She was standing still by the door, wringing her hands. It looked like she hadn't quite decided if she was going to stay or not. Steam plumed from the kettle and I distracted myself by pouring the water into the mug.

'Shit, I don't know where to start . . .'

'The beginning?' I leant back against the counter; she paced a bit, still wringing her hands.

'Two kids showed up at the gallery last night.' I immediately felt my stomach drop. If we'd been burgled, I'd need to rethink my plans. The money would have to go into the gallery, of course it would.

'The boy,' she looked at me for a moment, 'the boy has a scar down one side of his face, and he's blind . . . in the one eye. Tom, he got the scar from a car accident. A car that smashed into an oak tree.'

The room tipped like the horizon on a ship going over an angry wave.

She pulled the chair over to me, took the mug from my hands and told me to sit down. Holding my hand in hers she started to talk.

'Did I . . . did I do it?' The smell of the cheap coffee and the steel dust scraped the back of my throat.

'Yes, Tom, you were driving the car he was in.'

'I was driving . . .'

'Tom,' she opened my palm and rested it in hers, drawing small circles with her thumb over the dirt-filled creases in mine, 'Tom, you were driving because you're his dad.'

'His what?'

'You are a father, Tom.' The grit in my eye mixed with the memory, the room that I had dreamt about, the room with you in it, only this time I could see a baby. A baby bloodied and blinking, wrapped in a white towel, and being passed to me . . . '*You're a father.*' Everything in the room stilled. I could hear our breathing, the seagulls outside circling the shore; the hush of the waves far below.

Georgie's words were simple. *You're his dad.* How can three words affect you so completely? It was as if a giant hole had been ripped open inside me, and the only way to fill it now would be to find out everything about this child. My child. I'm no longer just me. I read somewhere that the population of the world increases by four births per second. Think of that. 'You're a father' – four times per second. All over the world: A father in Italy rushes into the hospital where his wife, her long dark hair in a braid which he had watched her plait that morning, is matted against her smiling, sweaty face. There is oil smudged across his skin as he hears the words *'Sei un padre'* and the tiny bundle is passed into his open arms. A French woman is crouching down, passing a startled-looking baby, wrapped in a red cardigan, to a stricken young couple whose birthing plans have gone awry as the baby makes an early arrival in a pub car park instead of the hospital: *'Vous êtes un père.'* A tired widow of a British soldier stands looking at the headstone as grief rips through her: 'You're a father.' Those three words are being uttered around the world in six thousand different languages – 'You're a father' – starting a Mexican wave, crashing into lives, sending ripples of euphoria and fear. Those words are being spoken about tiny babies all around the world, but it feels different for me: my baby is grown up.

'I have a child?' I asked.

'You have two, actually.' There were tears in her eyes as she searched my face. 'You have a daughter too . . . Rose.'

'Rose. And the boy?'

'Flynn. He looks just like you when he smiles.'

'Huh. Flynn and Rose.' I scratched the back of my head. 'Is their mother,' I was afraid to ask and yet desperate too. I hoped with every inch of myself that it was you. It had to be you. 'Is it . . . her?'

Georgie gave a little sniff and started nodding. 'It's her. Melody.'

Melody. The sound of your name bounced around the room, bringing light into dark corners. I have a family. We have a family. I'm not alone.

'Mel—' and then I started laughing. Georgie looked uncertain for a moment and then joined in, but I soon stopped because walking through the door was the face that had haunted me for years, less scary, less menacing and a lot like me.

My feet walked towards him without my instruction, he took a step back but then seemed to will himself to stand his ground. I stretched out my hand and he held it. The hole inside began to fill as I felt the warmth in his palm, the feel of his skin, still soft and untouched except for the callus on his right index finger. The hole drank in his smell, slightly musky and rich, its thirst insatiable as I noticed the colour of his eyes, the texture of his hair, the broadness of his shoulders. It was a formal greeting, but it was also so much more. Then, he almost seemed to lose his balance as he leant forwards; he was a stranger to me and yet it had never felt so natural to hold another human; to have his gangly frame inside my arms as the word 'Dad' caught in his throat. Over his shoulder I saw a girl walk in. She was fragile; pale, but with red hair that cloaked her shoulders, and I knew in an instant that she was my daughter, another part of me that I didn't know I'd lost. It was in her hooded eyes, the rise of her cheekbones and the full lips that have often smiled back at me from my own bathroom mirror. Her eyes filled with tears and she looked down where the toes of her baseball trainers kicked at the ground. Flynn stepped back, his eyes unable to meet mine.

'This is Rose . . .' His voice was deeper than I expected, more of a man than a boy. As her brother said her name, something in her changed; her back straightened and there was a spark in her eyes. She walked with a determined stride towards me and put out her hand to me. I was taken aback by the formality of her stance.

'Pleased to meet you, Tom,' she said without a tremor. 'We've come to ask for your help.'

'Rose . . .' Flynn turned to her.

'I believe you met our mother? Melody?'

'Rose!' Flynn snapped. She glared at him and I could see in the rise and fall of her breathing that she was not as calm as she was letting on. I surreptitiously watched the way they looked at each other, their posture, the way they were having a hidden conversation, my gaze switching from one to the other.

'Let's, um, is there somewhere we can go . . . to talk?' Flynn asked me.

'Yes, let's . . . go into the house, I'll put the kettle on.' I dug my hands into my pockets and led the way. 'Do you like, um, tea?' I asked as we walked towards the house, the wind almost swallowing my words. My son following behind me. My son. It should have sounded alien to me but instead it felt as though, throughout my life, I had been saying the word without pronouncing it correctly, as though I'd been dropping my 't's', until now. Son. I smiled.

It was starting to drizzle – small droplets were falling on to the cars parked in the lane. I noticed another teenage girl and a slender woman leaning against a silver Audi.

'Yeah, I like tea,' he answered, raising his voice above the sounds of the sea and wind as he followed my look towards the car. 'That's my girlfriend.'

'A little old for you, isn't she?'

'Not that – oh!' When he saw the look on my face he realised I was joking. 'That's Mum's boss, kind of.'

'Is she here? Your mum?'

'No,' Rose answered from behind us. I looked over my shoulder at her and she met my eyes with a fierceness that forced me to look away. What had it been like for them, not knowing where I had been all this time? The way Flynn held me answered all my questions about the kind of man I must have been before. The way he clung to me indicated his relief. But the expression on Rose's face told an entirely different story.

'Would you like your friends to come inside?' I asked Flynn. 'It can get pretty blustery out here.' He nodded and then beckoned them over. My hands were shaking slightly, I noticed, as I opened the door. Standing back to let them in, I watched how they moved: my children. Flynn sort of ambled – still does – but Rose was striding, yet she still seemed to keep her head and eyes lowered. I watched her as she reached towards the flowers I'd put out on my window sill. Her face softened as she touched the red petals of the roses in the vase. But as she looked up to meet my gaze, her face hardened.

'I'll make us some drinks . . .' I stammered as Georgie put her hand on my arm.

'I'll do it, it's probably best if you—' She nodded towards where Flynn had slumped down on to the sofa; I noticed that his hands were clamped in between his girlfriend's. Rose sat on the arm next to her brother. Jo went with Georgie and I busied myself by throwing another log into the burner, hearing Flynn's angry whisper to his sister asking her what the hell was wrong with her. Rubbing my hands together, I perched myself in the armchair opposite them. For a moment there was silence.

'Shall I start?' I asked. My voice sounded more in control than I felt. Flynn nodded and Rose shrugged her shoulders. 'So . . . my name is Tom Simmonds, but you already know that, and I, um, I lost my memory eleven years ago. I don't know my real name, I don't remember my parents or my childhood. Erm, I'm an artist – a sculptor – this is my home: the only home I have ever known.' Rose flashed Flynn a look at that. 'Georgie found me living on the streets and gave me a place to stay, gave me a job, and that, well that's about it . . . until a few months ago when I met the most amazing woman, who carried a photo of a boy I've had dreams about, and then left me without telling me her real name or where she lived . . .'

'So you *do* remember Flynn?' Rose asked.

'Not exactly. I've had dreams about a boy with half of his face damaged, and I had dreams about a tree that had a rose growing from it, so I guess I remembered you too, in a manner of speaking.'

'You don't remember Mum at all?'

'No . . . but I've had a few, well, I think they're memories, of your mum . . . Does she know? That you're here?' They looked at each other: a conversation of widened eyes and raised eyebrows. Rose shook her head at me. 'Did she tell you about the time she spent here?' I asked and again, Rose gave another little shake of her head. My shoulders sagged and I sat back in my seat. 'Do you want to tell me your side of what happened?' It's an amazing thing to watch: two siblings, who look so different, communicating without words and depending on each other so openly. Flynn spoke first.

'OK, Tom? This is what we know . . .' Flynn and Rose told me everything – about the accident, my disappearance, and how you searched for me . . . until the day you gave up and accepted I was dead. Rose filled me in on your trip to Taunton, and everything you learnt about me, assumed about me, after that. And Flynn told me you didn't want me to know about them – he said you thought it wouldn't be fair on me.

'Why would she not want me to know?'

Flynn looked uncomfortable but then sighed.

'She said she loved you too much to tell you.'

'Well, now I know.'

'Now you know,' he confirmed.

'There is one thing you haven't told me, though . . . what's my name?'

Rose smiled then, a real smile that made her dimples sink into her cheeks. Up until that point, Rose's face had been stern, she hadn't made eye contact. As I spoke, telling them the story of my life after the memory loss, it had felt like there had been a radio on in the background. A radio that wasn't quite tuned in properly. But, in that moment, when she smiled at me, it felt like the dial had been turned, the words finally crisp and solid.

'Devon, Dev for short. Your name is Devon King.' She beamed at me, like the sun breaking through the clouds.

'And . . . are you Kings as well?' I chewed my bottom lip as they both nodded.

'So we were married? Melody and I?' They nodded again and I started laughing. 'Talk about history repeating itself.'

They looked confused until Georgie interrupted: 'He asked her to marry him. When she was here.'

Rose and Flynn looked at each other with stunned faces.

'But she was only here a week . . .?' Rose questioned.

'Haven't you ever heard of love at first sight?' I could feel happy tears filling my eyes. Flynn scratched the back of his head as he shook it. 'So, let's go.' I clapped my hands together. I had everything I had wanted for so long. I knew who I was, I had a family, I belonged, and I had you. You loved me.

'She loves me too, though, right?' They both nodded in exactly the same way and I laughed as I stood up. 'She loves me, and now I know who I am and, Jesus, is this what it feels like? To be . . . normal?' Rose and Flynn exchanged concerned looks.

'Our family is anything but normal . . .' Flynn murmured but exhilaration seeped into my body, filling me with euphoria that I couldn't contain, I needed to go to you. I dismissed his comment with a wave of my arm.

'I'll just go and grab a few things and then, God, I can't wait to see her. You don't know what it's like to love someone so much and for them to just leave. It's . . .'

'Unbearable,' Flynn and I said at the same time. I wish I'd

chosen my words more wisely – of course they understood. I looked at the hurt behind his eyes and realised that what I had been through was just a drop in the ocean compared to what he'd been through.

'Tom, there is something else, something you need to know.' The tone he used was sharp, like the scrape of a bullet being put into the barrel of a gun. 'Look, just sit down for a minute, and then we can leave, OK?'

I glanced at the door. I knew I was being irrational; I knew that I was acting like a fool, but all that I could think of was the need to get to you.

'You can tell me on the way,' I said slightly breathlessly. 'If we leave now . . .'

'Dad!' Rose stood, the word sounding as alien to me as it did to her; she licked her lips as if tasting it for the first time. She corrected herself, her skin growing red with embarrassment. 'Tom . . . please sit down. This is why we've come.' Georgie appeared at my side; her hand was on my shoulder and she applied the smallest amount of pressure and I collapsed under it. I watched Kate's thumb stroke Flynn's and the way that his knee was bouncing up and down. Rose took a breath, looked at Flynn and then began.

'If Mum was here for a week, I'm sure you would have experienced her—'

'Singing? Yeah, she sang "Nothing Compares 2 U".' I smiled at the memory of your red dress, the green butterflies and the taste of your kiss.

'Yeah. Her condition. Did she tell you what caused it?'

'The slip on the ice, yeah, but—'

'Well, something has changed. We've found out that the bump to her head was just concussion.'

'Oh. So . . .'

She swallowed and I watched her fingernails digging into her palm. Flynn slipped his hand away from Kate and placed his hand over hers. She looked up at him and slowly released her fingers. He raised his eyebrows as if questioning her if she was OK and then looked at me.

'There is no easy way to tell you this . . . Mum has a brain tumour, and right now she is in hospital, recovering, as they had to stick a needle into her brain and take a piece of the tumour out.'

I closed my eyes for a moment as I let her words trample over my thoughts. I remembered the way your hair felt as I tied it with lace, the way it smelt of apples, and how you sighed with happiness as I washed your hair in the bath. But as I thought of you, my mind replaced my memory with the image of a scalpel, your hair matted with blood, your sigh a scream. The question I needed to ask swelled in my throat as I tried to form the words.

'Is it cancer?'

'Yes . . . she's going to have to have a lot of treatment and . . .'

I pictured your hair falling to the floor in clumps as I brushed my hand through it; I saw you lying there in a hospital bed, reaching your arm out towards me.

'She can't do this without help,' Rose added. 'She can't do this without you . . . we can't do this without you.'

There was no hesitation in my reply. I knew what I needed to do.

'So, what are we waiting for?'

Standing in my bedroom doorway was Georgie. She was smoothing down her hair and watching me as I threw things into my bag.

'You know I have to go,' I said to her without meeting her eyes as I grabbed a day-old pair of socks from the floor.

'I know.'

'But?' Hastily, I pulled open a drawer and lifted out a stack of T-shirts and laid them on the bed. I looked at the bag and then hunted under the bed for a suitcase that had been there when I moved in.

'A case?' She raised her eyebrows at me. 'How long are you going for?'

'I don't know.' The image of you on an operating table almost winded me.

'But what about your exhibition? You can't just leave, for God's sake! You barely know these people!'

'They are my family.' I turned to her. 'What would you have me do? Say it's nice to meet you, I'm sorry your mother has cancer but I've got work to do?'

'Well, kind of, yes. You're not that man "Devon", you're Tom. You belong here.'

I thought of all of the things that she had done for me and how happy my life had been because of her. Gently, I put my arm around her shoulders and she leant into me as I told her I had to go. Even if I hadn't found out about the children, I still would have gone to you.

'Teenagers are supposed to be a nightmare and Jo says that this pair can be a handful.' She sniffed and I realised that she was crying.

'They're my children, Georgie. And it's not like I'm leaving the country . . . I'll be back. She might take one look at me and kick me out.'

'Pffft. Fat chance,' she sniffed.

'I'll ring you tonight, OK?'

'Just . . . remember who you are. Don't let them change you into someone else, because Tom Simmonds is the best of them.' She wiped her face with the back of her hand, smudging her mascara, then kissed my cheek.

As they all piled into the car, I turned to look at the cottage – my home – with Georgie standing with her arms crossed in the doorway, her hair flying around her face in the wind, and held up my hand to say goodbye, before I folded myself into the front seat of the Audi.

32

Melody

I'm safe. I feel sheltered, locked inside my world. I'm walking through a field full of calf-high daisies; it's summer. The smell of cut grass and the sound of far-off bumblebees fills me with optimism, like the first day of summer when you open the curtains, open the windows and enjoy the relief that it's finally here. There is a hum: a teeth-vibrating hum. I look up towards the sky and shield my eyes against the glimmering sun. My skin smells of warm lemons, my feet are bare and I can feel the tickle of grass between my toes. Searching the sky, I try to find the source of the humming. In the distance I can see a machine; it looks like a harvester, blades turning, the sun reflecting their sharp circular edges. It's moving towards me. I look down and see the flowers bowing away from the noise. The hum is louder but above it I can hear screaming; it's the flowers, thousands of them screaming in pain, all at once, all high-pitched. I start running towards the harvester to tell him to stop; to tell him that the daisies are alive. Urgently, I cover my ears against the squeals as I run. My voice is blocked in my throat; I try to pull it out, but every time it starts to form it bursts and retreats, like bubble gum. The feel of the grass has turned into mud and as I look down I see that the sludge is red. The flowers are bleeding but the machine keeps coming. I'm stuck, my feet imprisoned in the blood-mud, as the screams get louder and the hum vibrates through my body. On the horizon I can see the carnage, the once clear sky becoming dusty; petals – torn from their stems – float up: the lucky ones that are escaping. The sun shines on to them as they turn from petals into golden musical notes that fill the sky, flying higher and higher, glowing brighter until I have to close my eyes.

'Melody? Melody? You're in the hospital. Deep breaths now, your surgery went well . . .'

The sky cracks and the harsh light of the hospital pulls me away.

The nurse moves me into a ward and as I slip in and out of sleep, I hear the hustle and bustle that the sick bring: the assertive voices of the nurses with the more obstinate patients; the kind, softer tone employed with the more vulnerable. My head is sore and I drift back off to sleep with the next round of painkillers.

When I wake, Shane is sitting by the side of the bed.

'I hope it's OK that I'm here? The kids . . .'

'I told them not to come. It's nice that you're here.' My voice is croaky. I shuffle myself up the bed as he passes me a plastic blue cup of water. 'I didn't want them to be in the hospital, with me, again. It might have upset Rose, reminded her of last time.'

'You look like an extra in an American civil war film.' He gives me a lopsided smile. Tentatively, I reach up and feel the bandage wrapped around my head. A stunning-looking woman with a velvety Jamaican accent appears at his side. Her dark skin seems almost luminescent: a picture of health.

'Melody . . . It's nice to see you again. I'm Dr Malone, I assisted Mr Rudd. There was some swelling, so we've upped your steroids a little, but other than that everything went smoothly.' She smiles, her teeth perfectly straight and her lips full. 'We were able to move you from intensive care on to

Ward Eighteen a few hours after surgery, which is always a good sign. We'll see how you go overnight and then you should be able to go home. The piece of the tumour has been sent to the lab, here in the hospital. The pathologists will have a closer look under the microscope and then we'll know what type of tumour it is.'

'How long will it be until I know?' My open question doesn't need any clarification. The Question: The Question that leaves me breathless with dread and The Question that gives me hope. Once it's answered, that hope will be gone, but still, I can't help but crave it.

'Not long. A day or so.'

She scribbles something on her chart, gives me a catwalk smile and tells me to rest. Shane sits at my side as I drift in and out of sleep: giving me clues to crossword puzzles; gossip from magazines. The next time I wake, he has gone and the lights on the ward are dimmed. My mind drifts to that week with Tom. I close my eyes and try to feel the sun on my face, his hand – rough and calloused – in my palm, the feel of his hard shoulder beneath my temple as we watched the waves rolling closer and closer towards us. I think of Rose and Flynn, lying side by side on the sofa, nudging each other, laughing the same way, tilting their heads identically, and then I drift back into a sedated sleep.

The next morning, I feel alert and impatient to get home. The noise of the hospital seeps into every part of me and I yearn for quiet. Absolute quiet. This scares me. It's something I hadn't really thought of. The idea of cancer scares you in so many ways; you think of the hair loss, the pain, the frailty, but you don't consider the irritation of the hospital ward. When I was in labour with Rose, I had been on a ward with women on either side of me. One woman had talked so loudly that I knew every moment of her own pregnancy woes. Her swollen feet, her morning sickness, the whole epic story. As I had breathed through my early contractions, which had become more and more aggressive, her prattle continued. On the other side of me I had a woman in mid-pregnancy who would constantly be sick, then feel better and stuff her face. I could hear the rustle of crisp packets, the exclamations of joy when the food trolley arrived and then, inevitably, the smell and sounds of her regurgitating it all back up. I'd forgotten about this part of the story, remembering only the pain later, the joy when Rose was born, so somehow, this part had been blurred into the background; now I remember. I remember that coping with the annoyance of the sounds of other people's lives encroaching on my concentration, on my coping methods, was almost as bad as the labour itself.

Shane arrives looking dishevelled and I wonder which troubled teen he has been helping this term; he seems distracted and unsettled, as if he has somewhere else to be.

'You didn't need to come, Shane, I'm being released—'

'Back into civilised society?' he grins.

'Ha, ha . . . I could have got a taxi. My legs work fine.' I wiggle my toes to prove my point.

'Don't be daft. I was on my way home anyway. How are you feeling?'

'Fine. A bit groggy from the meds but OK . . . I can't wait for a bath.'

'Feel the urge for a bit of Agadoo, eh?' I stick out my tongue at him and he laughs, with a smile that doesn't quite reach his eyes, and again I worry about what he is dealing with at work. 'Do you mind if I go and grab a quick coffee? I've had a manic day.' He's passing his mobile phone between his hands repeatedly, as if he needs to check some urgent message but doesn't want to do it in front of me.

'Sure. You can get me one too, please, if you don't mind?'

'Latte?'

'Please.' He passes his phone between his hands a few

more times and then leaves. The smell of him lingers for a moment, heavy and male, until the smell of freshly squirted hand sanitiser extinguishes it.

We pull up outside my house; he's been quiet for most of the journey, anxiously tapping on the steering wheel and huffing under his breath at the slightest of traffic infractions. We sit for a moment as light drizzle settles on the windscreen; the ticking of the engine cooling down fills the silence like pins and needles. Jo's car is in the drive, which has been left empty for over a year.

'Is there something wrong?' I ask. He takes his hands from the steering wheel and sighs. Anxiously, he looks towards the house and back at me.

'What?' I ask. 'Are the kids OK?'

'The kids are fine, it's . . . let's just go in.'

Chatter is behind the door like bubble wrap; it protects my steps and sharp apprehension, then pops as I close the door behind me. Flynn appears from the lounge, looks briefly at my head and then in two strides swallows me in his embrace. I can feel his collarbone against my forehead, the muscles in the tops of his arms the way I used to feel the dimples around his knees, the smell of baby shampoo long gone and the smell of manhood just holding my attention long enough for me to nod in recognition. He kisses the top of my head and then holds me at arm's length.

'Don't go mental, OK, but you've got a visitor.' I look up briefly to see Shane looking away, unable to meet my eyes, as he joins Jo who is giving me a shy smile from the kitchen. 'You've brushed your teeth, right?' Flynn asks me with a smile.

'What?' Fleetingly, I wonder if the visitor is my dentist as I step into the lounge.

He fills the room. Every part of it. That missing piece of

furniture you've always needed, the room has always missed: the framed mirror that you hang over the fireplace; the nest of tables in the corner of the room; the throw blanket over the back of the sofa or the thick pile rug placed in the middle of the room. The room looked fine before, but that final touch makes it feel like . . . home.

He's sitting on the sofa. Rose is sitting next to him and for a moment I'm utterly floored. They look so alike. How have I never noticed it before? I look down at his hands; there's a plaster around his ring finger.

'You've hurt your finger.' My voice is steady. Slowly, I meet his gaze as he stands up and walks towards me.

'You've hurt your head.' He reaches out and touches the bandage. As I stretch up to link my fingers through his, I wonder how I have managed to stay alive all of this time without him. From the tips of my toes, tiny vibrations start to take hold; the slow tempo and synthesised note throbs through my body.

'Stay,' I say. Shakespears Sister . . . whatever happened to them? I start to sing, holding on to his hands in front of us. I touch his face as I tell him I'd go everywhere with him. As I sing, I warn him that he shouldn't leave me on my own, because I wouldn't understand; I want him to stay. I hold this note and then repeat it. I know how this must look. Corny, to say the least, but my warbling voice begs him to stay. Over and over again. He pushes a stray piece of hair away from my face. My thoughts are battling against themselves. I desperately need him, desperately want him, but then I think about the world that he has, that I'm tearing him away from. Images of Flynn fighting flash before me, Rose covered in blood. And then there's me. With this sickly thing inside me. I twist my face into something a little more sinister and start telling him that he had better keep praying that he can go back to his old life. I push his hands away from me, my voice now bitter. I think of him tossing and turning when he sleeps; I think of the way he cries out when nobody is there to hear him. Maybe that would be better. For him to be on his own. Can I bring that into my children's lives? Do I want my children to hear his screams in the night? I begin to sway in time with the music inside, the instrumental part that only I can hear, and then I panic because I know that at any moment I'm going to try and hit a window-shattering, high-pitch note, which is most definitely not in my range. I put my fingers in my ears and try to give an apologetic look to everyone as, here I go:

'Iiiiiiigghhhhhhhhhhhhhhhh!'

Luckily, there are no windows smashed, just squinting eyes and ears being covered. Thankfully, the rest of the song is just pretty much me grovelling over and over again. I let out an exasperated sigh through my lips and give him a shrug of the shoulders that says, this is me. Are you sure?

'OK,' he says, 'just warn me next time you think you're going to have to hit that note again.' I lean my head against his chest and he folds his arms around me just as I hear the front door softly close. When I turn my head, I notice that Shane and Jo have gone and I'm left with my family. All of it.

'Tom? Do you take sugar?' Rose asks tentatively from behind the door.

'Um, no, I'm trying to cut back, thanks,' he answers. We're sitting on the sofa and I smile as I feel the vibrations of his voice through his chest and into my cheekbone. Flynn barges through the door, his arms full of biscuits and his teeth holding a packet of tortilla chips. Unceremoniously, he dumps the lot on the coffee table as Rose follows with mugs of tea.

'May as well have supplies, I reckon this conversation is

going to go on a bit.' Flynn noisily slurps his tea, slumps on to the small sofa and then tears open a packet of chocolate digestives and dunks one in.

'Pig.' Rose, standing beside him, scrunches up her nose in disgust and delicately nibbles the side of her cookie.

'Do you recognise anything, Tom?' Flynn asks as the end of his digestive drops into his tea. 'Shit.'

'Don't say shit,' I mumble.

'I wish I could say that I do, but, no, sorry.'

'Weird.' Rose shoves Flynn over with her hip and then sits by his feet.

'Could you tell me a bit about what you remember before the accident, Flynn? If it isn't, you know, if you'd rather not . . .'

'No, it's fine. You were, well, fun . . . you were mint at Lego.'

'Mint?'

'Teenager for good,' I explain from under his arm.

'You danced.' Rose smiled up at me. 'You and Mum, you danced a lot.'

'Huh, what like *Strictly*?' Flynn almost chokes on his tea and Rose bursts out laughing.

'Jesus, no. You just . . . I know! Shall I put the DVD on?'

I feel my body tense. 'I don't know if that might be a bit much just yet, Rose.'

'There is a DVD?' He leans his head down and I look up at him.

'Yes, but . . . I know. How about I get some photos? You know, break you in gently?'

I'm chewing the inside of my cheek as I watch his face drinking in every photo, every scene from a different world to the one he knows. We've agreed to take this trip down memory lane in chronological order; at the moment, we're just on our early life together. He holds one up, of us holding bottles of beer outside a small club, and shakes his head, looking up at me.

'What?' I ask, trying to hide my smile at the uncomfortable look on his face.

'What was I thinking? The hair!'

'I loved your hair! We were about to go and see a rock band that night . . .'

'But it's so . . . big! What was the band like?'

'They were awful.' I shake my head at the memory.

'Never mind the hair.' Rose leans against him. 'Look at the sideburns.'

'Hmmm, yeah, you have a point. I wasn't so keen on those.' I laugh.

His face lights up as he comes to the next one. It's of me leaning out of the window of our first flat, a golden Chinese lucky cat waving from the takeaway below.

'Did we live here?' he asks excitedly. 'Did we paint the lounge yellow?'

'Yes, we did, do you remember?'

'I had a flash. Not a whole memory, just I guess a bit like a photo but with smell.'

'What, like a scratch and sniff?' Flynn asks.

Tom laughs a slow, lazy laugh. 'Yeah, I suppose. I could see you up a ladder with yellow paint in your hair and I could smell Chinese food.'

'So it's in there somewhere.' I knock on his head gently with my fist, yawning as I do.

'Shall we leave it for tonight? You need to rest,' he says, concern spreading into a frown.

'No, it's fine, we can—'

He puts his hand against my cheek. 'You need to rest.' Flynn and Rose swap smug glances. Looks that say, we did the right thing. Flynn gives an over-exaggerated stretch and

Rose gets up, grabbing the last chocolate biscuit before Flynn's hand gets to it.

'Hah, too slow, Jo.' He snatches it from her hand.

'Hey! Mum, he just—'

'Flynn, give it back to your sister.'

'But—'

'Now,' I add as I stand.

'Fine.' He starts to pass it back to her and then shoves the whole thing in his mouth and runs off.

'He's such a—'

'Rose . . .' I warn.

'Fine.' She throws her hands up. 'Whatever. Night.'

'Night,' Tom and I reply. I turn to him with a 'kids will be kids' look and meet his eyes. Eyes that are not reflecting the humour in my own, eyes that appear to be like they belong to a person looking down over a cliff before they are about to jump off.

'Are you OK?' He begins to clear up the crockery and nods, not looking at me. 'Tom,' I place my hand on his arm, 'are you OK?' He stands up, holding the cups, looking at them as if he can't remember how they got there.

'It's just . . .' he swills the cold tea at the bottom of the mug in slow, circular movements, 'I have no idea how to be a father.'

'That's exactly what you said the first night we came home from the hospital with Flynn.'

He looks up at me through his eyelashes. 'And what did you say?'

Kissing the end of his nose, I reply, 'You will.'

33

Melody

We hold hands at the threshold to my bedroom. Our bedroom.

'Should I carry you over?' He's nervous. Tom is quick to crack a joke to ease tension. Dev would pause and think carefully and then perhaps make a joke; more often than not, though, he would know how to fix the problem: take away the tension, like cutting a taut piece of string. I link my fingers through his and open the door. My bed glares at me. Who is this intruder? it asks. Momentarily, he pulls at my hand. 'Should I sleep downstairs? I wouldn't want to upset the kids.' I laugh at this.

'You'll find that my kids,' I correct myself, 'our kids, are a lot more . . . I don't want to say mature, but, well yeah, mature.' I turn on the bedside lamp. 'I see them around others of their age and I see how different they are; how much more established in their skins. It's good, I suppose, that at least there has been something positive to come out of the hardships they've faced.'

Wearily, I sit down on the bed and tap the space next to me. Watching him glancing around the room fills me with so many emotions that I feel immobile. He's trying not to show his desperation for information, for answers. His eyes – blue today – stop darting for a moment and he seems to still. The muscles in his face relax and the creases around his eyes turn upwards as he sees one of his earlier sculptures. It's the dove he had made in that very first class, where I had watched – transfixed – as his hands had twisted and turned, making something beautiful out of nothing. Tentatively, he gets up from the bed and walks over to the corner of the bedroom.

'You never forgot that part of you. If you had, I would never have found you.'

He pushes the wing gently. 'Are you glad you did?' he asks, watching it turn and catch the light.

'Yes and no,' I answer truthfully.

'No?' He tilts his head.

'Selfishly, yes, I'm glad I found you. I've never felt . . . whole since you left. The world was never quite bright enough, like watching a film on a video player rather than watching it in high definition, I suppose . . . does that make sense? But then I look at you, I look at you and I know how much you're going to have to change to become part of this family, part of this life, and I think you might have been better off if I hadn't found you.'

Letting go of the dove, he comes and kneels by my feet. 'If you hadn't found me . . . I'd never have seen high definition at all.'

'Tom, there is so much I need to explain, the kids have things going on, problems . . .'

'Melody?' He pauses. 'Let's keep this until tomorrow . . . for tonight, let it just be us.'

I nod, not trusting myself to speak, then I remember. 'I have something for you,' I say, reaching over to the bedside drawer, my fingers closing around the cold brass of the bell. He tilts his head and watches my hand as I open my palm, his eyebrows rising in shock. He looks up at me, his lip wavering as he tries to keep his emotions in check. He stretches out his arm and I gently link the bracelet around his wrist, closing the clasp; the bell singing its Melody as it is returned to its rightful place. Slowly, he stands, pulls me to my feet and gingerly undresses the bandage from my head. Every part of me is aware: the hush of the bandage, the hairs rising along my forearms and the static in my hair as he smooths it down. I lean against him and he circles his arms around me and for one split second I feel safe. All the troubles around me are kept away by his body: a barrier keeping all of the bad things out. A split second of naivety before I remember the biggest threat is inside his arms, inside me, inside my head.

I wake to find the bed empty. The clock tick-tocks its way past eight as I reach to find the other side of the bed cold. Downstairs I can hear voices. It seems strange to hear a duo of bass tones this early in the morning. Sun leaks in through the curtains, a puddle of it landing in my open palm from where one of the curtain hooks has fallen off the rail. I close my fingers around it, but of course it won't be contained; instead the light flows over my knuckles, over the slight dip in my skin where my wedding ring used to be. Sometimes, on days like today, I would think about what normal families would be doing. During the last two years, I have avoided the whole Family Day Out scene, scared that I would offend some stranger with an offensive song or embarrass the kids unnecessarily, but today, with my family downstairs, I feel an almost confusing pull towards normality, towards A Day Trip. I stay still for a moment as Rose's laugh dances up the stairs and I swallow down the nausea. It's not too bad today. Most days it's eased off by eleven-ish. Trying not to move too quickly, I swing my legs over the edge of the bed, flex my toes and then search for my clothes, smiling as a brief flash of the night before pops into my head.

The smell of coffee makes me gag as I tiptoe down the stairs.

'Is she your first girlfriend then?' Tom asks.

'Well du-uh,' Rose replies, 'like he's going to have seen much action with a face like that!'

I cringe as she says this. I know she's joking. but I worry that to Tom she might sound cruel.

'Whatever, ginge,' is Flynn's response.

The kids are sitting at the breakfast table, Flynn biting a doorstep of toast and Rose nibbling at an apple. Tom is still wearing yesterday's jeans and grey T-shirt, which is still crinkled from where it lay on the bedroom floor; his back is towards me as he spends a few moments trying to work out how to ignite the hob. With a click and a whoosh, the blue flame licks the bottom of the frying pan. I stand back and watch him as he swills the oil around the pan and then cracks an egg into it. Eggs again. Sensing he is being watched, he looks over his shoulder at me and smiles. He turns back to the pan, splashes some oil over the yolk and then slides it on to the waiting piece of bread, which he cuts into two triangles. Walking towards me, he holds the plate with great pride, offers it to me and then asks if I'd like a cup of tea. Sadly, the answer remains unspoken as I vomit all over his feet.

He steps back involuntarily as I retch again.

'You could have just said no.' He shakes his head and then wipes the corner of my mouth with his thumb. 'Rose, would you mind going up and running your mum a bath and I'll clean this up.' He rummages in his back pocket and passes me some chewing gum. 'Do you need a glass of water?' I nod, speechless at the ease with which he's dealing with the situation. He guides me to the chair, as Flynn slides a glass of water across the table at me like we are in a Western.

'Thanks. I'll be OK in a bit, it's not too bad today.' He

bites into the sandwich, chews it thoughtfully and then looks down at his shoes.

'I don't suppose you're a size eight, Flynn?'

'I am, yeah. I'll go and grab you a pair of old trainers.' Tom's face cracks into a huge grin and I realise that he's happy . . . even though he's standing – eating a cold egg sandwich – with sick all over his shoes.

I giggle as Tom shouts up the stairs.

'Mel? Where is the mop?'

'In the cupboard under the stairs!' I shout back. This is so weird. I turn the hot tap back on with my foot and then wash my hair. We have decided to take the kids out to the park for a picnic and then to see a film in the new open-air cinema, which is a lot less scary for me as I can walk a short distance away if I start singing. The Things that need to be discussed are put on the back burner. Tomorrow will be the day that we will face The Things that we will find out at the hospital and The Things that we will have to learn about each other. The Things, we have decided, can wait for one more day. I get out of the bath, wrap the towel around me and then rummage through my wardrobe. As I dress in my jeans and black polo neck, I ignore the headache that is creeping up my scalp and instead enjoy the sounds and smells of a house full of life. The thud, thud, thud of Flynn's music, the declarations and giggles as Rose talks to Lisa on her phone, and Tom humming beside me as he hangs up his clothes in the once empty wardrobe. I spray a brand of perfume on that I haven't dared to take out of its box for several years. It's the last gift that he ever bought me, the same brand that I always used to wear and the same brand that I haven't been able to smell without feeling my heart being ripped from my chest. Today is different, though, and as I spray it, I can feel a thousand memories spiralling around me: the box that he tried to gift-wrap so carefully even though it had still looked like a toddler had done it, a shopping trip to buy our first pair of curtains, neither of us knowing whether we needed to measure half of the window or the whole thing, an argument when I threw a jam sandwich at him which missed and hit the kitchen window and his bemused stare as we watched it slide slowly downwards.

'You had a red-and-black checked skirt with a missing button on it.' I turn to see him tilting his head towards me, leaning slightly forward as if he is off balance.

'I did.' My eyes fill. 'You broke it actually.'

'How?' He tilts his head in that way that makes him look as though he's considering the formula to a complex mathematical problem.

'In the heat of passion,' I gasp seductively then laugh at his raised eyebrows. 'You put it in the washing machine with my fluffy cardigan and it got caught . . . I suppose you were thinking it was better to ruin the skirt than my poorly cardigan.'

'Why was your cardigan poorly?'

'It was the cardigan I always wore if I was ill, dummy, it was—'

'Green! Dark green and fluffy?'

'You remember my cardigan but you don't remember your children? What kind of sick weirdo are you?' He grabs me around the waist and pulls me on to the bed kicking, wriggling and laughing.

'Mum? Can I borrow your straighteners?' Rose walks in, her face inevitably staring at her phone screen. She looks up and her face contorts in disgust.

'Uh, gross. At least close the door.' She shakes her head, grabs the straighteners and walks out of the room, closing the door behind her with a hidden smile.

*

Today is a good day. The sun is out and it's unseasonably warm; as we approach the local park, there is a sense of freedom amongst the parents that are sitting on benches chatting, their hands holding takeaway coffees. Long queues snake away from the ice-cream cabin, children enjoying the last threads of a summer that should have been long gone. The basketball court holds the athletic teens in their bright trainers and branded clothing; skateboarders flip at the top of the ramp while groups of teenage girls stand at the side watching, either trying too hard to look interested or too hard to look nonchalant. The kids are walking ahead – Rose's ponytail swinging and Flynn's ever-present flick of the head to position his hair so it covers the left side of his face – steering our course towards the lake. Tom's hand holds mine and his thumb is running up and down my index finger. My mind wanders to where it shouldn't; wondering if this is the last time I will walk through this park in the sun. My head is pounding again. I try to ignore the little voices inside that tell me that I may as well not even bother hoping that the results will show something unexpected, that I'll be given a reprieve from the constant hurdles I'm always struggling to jump over. My vision sways and I hold on to Tom a little tighter, holding on to the here and now. We are on a patch of grass beside the lake; a group of Pilates-perfect women are stretching by a tree to the right and a winding path towards the shopping centre guides couples with swinging bags and irritated children away from us. I shiver slightly as the notes of 'Feeling Good' trickle over my skin, Michael Bublé and Nina Simone versions battling with Muse. My senses become alert as I watch the birds soaring up and I start to sing, my voice starting low and then rising through the octaves as I ask them if they understand how I'm feeling. I ask the sun too, as well as the wind that drifts past. I lift my chin and stare up at the sky, acknowledging that it's the beginning of an original day, an original life and then the song title explodes from my mouth as I truly do, in this minute, feel good.

I stop still and smile at Tom and the kids who have turned around and started to unpack the blanket that we have brought. With a shrug of the shoulders, Flynn slumps down with Rose beside him and they start clicking their fingers, Flynn adding, 'duuuumm . . . dum-duuuumm . . . dum-duuuums'. Tom is facing me holding both of my hands in his, as I start swaying in time to the finger clicks, talking about fish and rivers, buds on trees, and again I really do feel good. He grins and starts swinging his shoulders back and forth with me as Flynn starts parping like a saxophone in the background. I shake my head at the ridiculousness of the situation. Rose has a look on her face that is part embarrassment, part pride as she continues to click her fingers and tap her foot, and by the time I have hit my last declaration of the feel-good factor, they have all joined in. We're all laughing as Tom and I finally sit down, and my headache is momentarily dulled as the endorphins filter through my body, pushing the anxiety aside.

Rose digs around in her backpack as we start opening packets of sausage rolls and crisps and produces another photo album.

'The baby years,' she announces as she crosses her legs and tucks a stray strand of hair behind her ear. I nestle myself between Tom's legs and lean into him as he holds the photo album in front of us.

'Blimey, we didn't wait long, did we? How old are you?' He's referring to the photo of me seven months pregnant with Flynn, standing on a bridge in Shrewsbury eating an ice cream. I'm wearing a pair of leggings and a blue denim shirt that is billowing over my tummy. 'How old are you there?'

'Twenty-one.'

He traces the photo with his finger. 'We're already married?'

His thumb rolls over where I'm holding the ice cream, my wedding ring clearly visible.

'Yep. We'd already been married a year by then, that's the week before we moved into the house.'

'The one you're in now?'

'Mmhmm.'

Flynn brushes off the pastry from his jeans and then leans over and turns the page.

'Behold the ugliest baby known to man,' Rose announces as I give the camera a tired smile; a very wrinkly-looking Flynn with a pink face and a very bald head pokes out from beneath a baby-blue blanket.

'I dreamt about that, about you being in labour with Flynn.'

'Really?' Flynn asks, a quietly pleased look on his face.

'At least I think I did, I don't know if it was a memory, though, or just a dream.'

'What can you remember from the dream?' I ask.

'Not much, you had a red top on?'

'I did. It had little Scotty dogs—'

'On the pocket.' He finishes my sentence.

'It did, yes . . . so you do remember.'

'I guess so.'

We chatter through the rest of the album, the pictures of a chubby Flynn first sitting up, Dev walking on a beach with him on his shoulders as I, heavy with my pregnancy with Rose, smile up at them.

'Talking about ugly babies, look at that! Jeez, you were a minger.'

Rose scowls at Flynn but then grins. 'I'll take that as a compliment, dearest brother, as that would imply that you don't think I'm a minger any more.' Outwitted, Flynn just rolls his eyes.

'She was a bundle of fury . . . red hair and an angry red face most of the time.'

Tom laughs at the next picture of me desperately trying to feed her what looks like radioactive peas. Her head is starting to turn away from me with a look of utter wrath.

Rose pulls a look of disgust. 'What are you trying to feed me?'

'Avocado, I think,' I answer.

Patchy grey clouds interrupt the constant sun as October prods us, reminding us that it's still there. Flynn checks his phone for the time, and we decide to pack up and head towards the open-air cinema, a car park really, except for a small patch of grass at the front, for days like today when the protection of a car is not needed. I swallow another couple of pills and then we walk – this family of mine. What do we look like to the outsider? Like a happy family out for the day after a long week at work? Do we look like we've never been apart? Do people envy us? I would. Look at how Flynn and Rose walk together, talking, laughing, scowling; their closeness must be apparent to the outsider, surely? And what of me and Tom? A good-looking couple? Does he look out of my league now that I can feel the tiredness creasing my skin, travelling in the bags under my eyes? Can they see the gaping holes in our relationship that we're stepping around or do they just see the love that is holding us together?

Tom goes to the booth and pays for the tickets, pride sneaking into his voice as he asks for two adult tickets and two children. The clouds are gathering closer to each other, seeking each other out, finding strength in numbers. Not even half of the car park is full: the film hasn't got great reviews, just a standard family film about a man who ends up being sucked back in time to the nineties and ends up – one presumes – finding himself able to change his own direction in life. But I don't care about the film; I care about how I feel right now. Part of a normal family. We've zipped up hoodies and Flynn has returned from the snack bar laden with nachos and popcorn. A few cars have exited halfway through the film and the clouds have started to spit. The fold-up chairs are uncomfortable and we have given up sitting on them, instead plonking ourselves on the blanket we used earlier. Flynn throws some popcorn at me and grins; Tom is quick to retaliate and popcorn bounces off the end of Flynn's nose. Rose starts laughing then, really laughing, the type of laugh that rumbles at the back of the throat and produces snorts and tears. More cars leave and the spits become rain; before long, the clouds have become one and have started to throw heavy, fat drops upon us. In moments, our hair is soaked and hanging from our heads. Rose's eyeliner pools under her eyes and rain drips from Flynn's eyelashes as we start to stand. Puddles are forming quickly in the potholes of the car park, the film is coming to an end and the final credits start rolling, to Coldplay's 'Yellow'. We pack up our things in a rush and take a short cut across the car park. We start to jog, Tom and I, but stop and turn towards the laughter and squeals of the kids as there they are – just as they were when they were infants – jumping up and down and splashing in the puddles all around them. A bubble of laughter escapes my mouth: the sight of the screen credits rolling behind them, the roll of thunder in the distance and the laughter and shrieks from my troubled teens are such a strange and familiar experience, that I'm rooted to the spot. Tom holds on to my hand, water dripping from our fingers, and then turns to me and says (over Chris Martin's declarations of truth), 'High definition.'

34

Tom

Faith. I'm not a religious man, I don't think I ever have been.
Even in my darkest moments on the streets, I can't remember
ever praying, ever asking for His help. But that day, I needed
the reassurance faith can bring. I wished for it as we walked
through the doors into the hospital and I wished for it when
we sat down and waited for the consultant. I once heard on
the radio that only two to fifteen per cent of the world's
population do not believe in God. How can that be? How
do people have such solid faith in something? What is their
secret? How amazing it must be to truly believe that there is
someone; something out there that is controlling your life for
you. How wonderful to have the reassurance that God will
guide you through your life and that even when things are
going badly, you know there is a reason for it, you just need
to find it. Find the lesson so you can learn from it and discover
the forgiveness to carry on stumbling through life with this
blind faith in your pocket. They had discussed how one report
had shown that eighty-one per cent of the Vietnamese population did not believe in God and I remember thinking that
maybe they had seen so many horrors that their faith had
been taken from them: stolen; hidden away like the Viet Cong,
waiting in the shadows. Right then as I felt you shaking beside
me, heard you humming 'Knockin'on Heaven's Door' (the

Guns N' Roses version), I wished for that faith, that we would be protected and that there would be some message that would make all of it seem clear, but as he spoke the words, explained that you would have to have surgery that had life-changing, possibly life-threatening risks, I knew that I hadn't got that faith. I haven't got faith that there is an all-powerful, all-knowing divine being. He went on to explain that the surgery to remove the tumour was more difficult than they first suspected, that the area that it was in was hard to reach, and that the chances of them taking the whole tumour out were very slim. He talked about the procedure where you would swallow a capsule containing a fluorescent dye which would light up the outside of the tumour; that he would cut out some bone from your skull so that he could operate on the brain; that he would put metal brackets to replace it and that he would then stitch the scalp back over it. I thought of red Indians with their scalps and for a small moment I wondered if he has his own collection of trophies, scalps that he'd taken. You had stopped humming. I had prepared myself for a whole playlist throughout this session but you seemed almost calm. As if you were discussing cutting out paper chains, not pieces of skull and scalp. You asked questions about the shunt they would insert to drain off fluid – where did the fluid go? Back into the body, came the answer. Do you remember? How calm you were? The word radiotherapy bounced off the walls as you asked about how often you would have to have it; you said you were lucky – lucky! – that at least you lived close enough to the hospital to make the weekly visits.

'Tom? Tom?' You held my hand still. I didn't realise that I was tapping the table hard like a jackhammer. The sounds of the air-conditioning were whirring inside my ears and the dulled noise of the hospital seemed louder somehow; my chest was hurting and I was finding it hard to focus. I'd had this feeling before, that I couldn't protect you, that feeling of not being able to fix the problem. The consultant was kneeling down in front of me, talking in slow tones, telling me that I was just having a panic attack and to try to slow my breathing, in through the nose and out through the mouth. I stared into your concerned eyes as he continued to talk to me, reassuring me that I would be OK in a few minutes and to just concentrate on my breathing. I felt like a right dick. You were the one with cancer, you were the one who might die and there I was having to learn how to breathe.

'I'm fine,' I told you.

'Has this happened before?' he asked you.

'Yes,' you answered him. 'It happened quite a lot after the accident . . .' You looked away from me.

'And you've seen your local GP, I take it? About these anxiety attacks?'

'I've seen a doctor, yes. It's nothing, I get a bit breathless every now and again. It's nothing.'

'It's not nothing, Tom, you had lots of them before you left . . . Maybe you should go to your old doctor? Now that you're back, you're still registered, I mean, you were never officially declared dead.'

'Dead?' the doctor almost shouted. You sighed and explained our circumstance in a nutshell.

'You have amnesia? And you haven't seen a practising doctor?' he asked in an exasperated tone.

'Look, I'm fine. I'm getting some of my memory back and—'

'Can I be frank here?' We both nodded. 'The next months, maybe years, are going to be very difficult both physically for you, Melody, and emotionally for you both. If you are going to be able to give her the support she needs, first you need to sort yourself out.' I nodded. 'Soon,' he added.

*

Watching you telling the kids was like nothing I've ever experienced before. The whole way home you were quiet and contained. You held yourself together, mostly, I mean after you broke out into Rick Astley's 'Never Gonna Give You Up'. Normally they were both tolerant of your outbursts, but this time I could see the muscles in Flynn's jaw tighten. Rose seemed in control, though she kept digging her nails into her palm. But when Flynn grabbed her arm, and whispered one word into her ear, she seemed to crumble. You went over to Rose and held her in your arms, and then – as if bursting from a cage – erupted into a festival-jumping rendition of The Killers' 'Mr. Brightside'. Watching you apparently enjoying yourself while singing about something killing you and taking over, was one of the cruellest manifestations of your condition I think I can remember. Flynn walked over to the window with his back to you both. I stood by the doorway feeling like an intruder. He turned around and glared at me, as you breathlessly turned on the tap and filled a glass with water.

'So, what are you going to do?'

'Well, I, I, we're all going to have to—' I could hear my voice was weak as I stumbled over my words.

'If you can't handle this you should go. Now.'

'That's enough, Flynn,' you warned.

'No, it's not. What is the point in him being here if he doesn't know what he's going to do? I mean, it's not like he stuck around last time when things got tough.' The anger in his eyes was palpable and the tension in the room was thick.

'I don't know why I left last time, but I promise you I'm not going to leave you again.' My voice didn't waver this time. 'This is not what your mum needs right now, what she needs is for all of us to deal with this, one step at a time.' He strode towards me and stood so close that I could smell the white spirit that he'd been using to clean his paintbrushes.

'Don't tell me what my mum needs.'

'Flynn,' Rose said softly, 'please, just don't.' He looked at them and then back to me before storming out of the house, the front door shaking against its frame.

You got up and wrapped your arms around my waist.

'He'll be OK, he just finds it hard to deal with things sometimes . . . Let's order a takeaway and put a film on . . . Rose, what do you fancy?'

'I'm not really hungry, but you two go ahead. I'm going up, I've got some homework to do anyway.'

'NO.' I'd never heard you raise your voice at her before and it startled me. A strange look came over her face, hurt followed by disbelief.

'Really, Mum? You really think I'm going to do something now? Do you not know me at all? Jesus!' She got up and stormed past.

'Rose, I—'

'It's fine.' She turned with her hand on the door. 'I guess you can trust Flynn to go out with his fists but you can't trust me to go to my room without—'

'Rose, I didn't mean—'

'Yes, you did. That's exactly what you meant. Don't worry, I'll leave the door open. So feel free to spy on me whenever you feel like it.'

'Shit,' you said, pulling yourself away from me and running your hands through your hair as if you were already expecting it to fall out. 'Do you know what? Let's open a bottle of wine.'

'Are you sure you should?'

'What's it going to do? Kill me?' You gave a hollow laugh and pushed past me into the kitchen.

'I didn't mean it like that, I was thinking about it giving you a headache.'

You started hunting in the cupboards; I hung back slightly, giving you some space.

'I've got a headache all of the time anyway. Red or white?'

'Um, red. Mel, let's—'

'Do you know you didn't start drinking red wine until I was pregnant with Flynn?' You twisted the lid off and clanged two wine glasses on to the kitchen side, '—and Stilton. You suddenly decided to like the two things I was craving constantly.' The wine glug, glug, glugged its way into the glasses and you took a huge mouthful, watching me over the rim. I took the other glass and followed you back into the lounge, noticing that you glanced up the stairs as you walked past.

I sank into the sofa and you sat on the floor with the bottle of wine next to you.

'So . . . I suppose now is the time we need to talk about The Things.'

'I suppose so. What are you worried that Rose is going to do?'

You took another long drink and then told me about what happened after you left me in Cornwall. About being arrested at the hospital and about the steps you had taken together to help her stay calm. I don't think you were aware of how many times you glanced upstairs as you talked, as if the need for you to check on her was almost desperate. After the second glass you climbed the stairs and I heard a hushed conversation, heard the creak of the bed as you sat down and then the click of the door as you left her in her room. The door closed behind you like a vote of confidence. You looked agitated as you came back into the lounge, tapping at your phone.

'Flynn isn't answering,' you explained without looking up.

'He's a teenage boy, don't they do this? Go out with their mates until dark?' You looked up at me from your phone as if I'd just spoken Japanese. Rose looks at me like that now too; I see you in her so much, Mel, it hurts.

'Not Flynn. I've just messaged Kate to see if she knows where he is.'

'Why not Flynn?' I asked.

'Because he doesn't really have any friends.'

'Why? He's so . . .'

'Because he has no patience and doesn't suffer fools gladly, is that the saying?' I shrugged my shoulders. 'He fights, Tom. A lot. It's a defence mechanism. He's grown up with kids teasing him about his face, and of course more recently, having a mad mother.'

'Hasn't he made any friends at college?'

'I think he's been keeping himself to himself. He's focused on his art, which is good, it distracts him. Kate is his friend, his only friend apart from me and Rose, and I'm not sure we count . . . oh and Shane, but Shane is there in a professional capacity most of the time. I'll text him and see if he's heard from him.'

'So he's Flynn's what?'

'Behavioural Support Worker. Flynn couldn't even go to the same classes as his peers by the end of school last year. Too many kids pushing his buttons.'

You said this matter-of-factly. I was trying hard not to react, knowing that you needed me to stay calm, but the questions were firing through me so quickly that I was finding it hard to focus. Upstairs the bathroom door closed. You stopped texting for a moment and looked upwards again.

'Has it always—'

'Shush,' you snapped and tilted your head to the side and closed your eyes. You waited for what felt like for ever until, with a sag of relief, you heard the toilet flush and Rose's footsteps padding along the landing.

'Rose?' you shouted. 'Can you call Flynn, please? He's not answering.'

'Kay,' she answered, sounding bored. You took another sip of wine, slowly this time, and sat back down.

'Shall I, um, put the telly on?' You looked at me with a squint that said are you really that stupid?

'No, it's probably best if . . . are you hungry? I could make us an omelette?'

'Christ, no. No more eggs.' Your phone vibrated and you answered, talking in exasperated tones to someone I presumed was Shane. You walked out of the kitchen, rubbing my arm as you did, and I was left standing in the centre of your lounge but not in the centre of your life. Not knowing what to do with myself, I wandered upstairs and into your bedroom. It smelt of you, not a perfumed version but something more primal. It was there as I sank on to the end of the bed, a smell that's hard to describe, a bit like clean laundry mixed with rain. There are studies to show how people are attracted to each other by smell. Pheromones, I think they are called, that somehow attract us, to help us find genetically compatible mates. Maybe that's how I knew you were the one?

'Tom?' I looked up to see Rose, anxious and pale by the door. 'Can I come in?'

'Sure.' She sat beside me and pulled at the end of her hoody.

'Has Mum told you? About me?' I nodded and tried to meet her gaze, but she looked down. 'Does it make you want to leave?' She looked up at me, tentatively at first, and then with an almost challenging stare.

'No.'

'Why? Why would you want this?' She threw up her hands and then raked her fingers through her hair.

'I don't have a choice,' I answered with a clarity that I'd only just started to understand myself. 'I love her.'

'But how can you know if you don't remember your life before?'

'I don't know. I just know that I'd rather a life with my

family, and everything that goes with it, than a life without you all.' I put my hand on my chest as I try to explain to her. 'This was empty, but since you found me, I feel . . . whole. Does that make sense?'

'But what if she dies? Will you still want us?'

And then, before I could answer, you bounded through the door, slightly breathless, and focused on her face. 'He's been in a fight.'

'Surprise, surprise.' Rose unfolded her legs and pulled her hair into a ponytail. 'Who with?'

'I don't know yet, he rang Shane. He's bringing him home after Flynn's cleaned himself up.' You bit the corner of your thumb. 'He split the other kid's lip apparently.'

'Well, that's Flynn for you. Hit first, think later.'

'It's not really his fault, he's upset about me and—'

'Why do you always do that? Defend him? It is his fault, Mum.' You looked stung by her words, physically pulling your face back. 'He chose to hit someone, he always chooses to do it, and he needs to stop, because, if something happens,' her voice caught in the back of her throat, 'if something happens to you, then how is he going to cope? How am I going to cope if he's in jail, Mum?'

'It won't come to that,' I said. Even as I spoke, I could feel how alien my words sounded to you both, how much of an outsider I was. 'It won't come to that,' I repeated. 'I'll be here, I'll help.'

'He might not listen to you.'

'Maybe not, but he doesn't seem to be listening to you either.' I worried that I'd overstepped the mark; said too much. Until you started nodding.

'You might be right, maybe he'll listen to you . . . He always played up more for me when he was little.' You gave a sad smile and then leant your forehead against mine as you looped your arm around Rose's shoulder.

'We'll be OK . . .' you said quietly, but neither Rose nor I replied, choosing to believe – for a moment – that what you were saying was believable.

'I know that I've been . . . away,' I pulled back from you both, 'but I knew you, and that must have come from somewhere deep within my core and like you said, I'll learn to be a parent. How does he normally react when he comes home after something like this? I might not know how to be a dad yet but I do know what it's like to see people at their worst, I've seen what they can do when all logic and sense passes them by. I might not be able to protect him but I might be able to understand him.'

It was late when the key slid into the lock. You'd fallen asleep on my chest as I watched muted TV and Rose had gone to bed a little while ago, kissing you on the head before she left, like you were the child and she was the adult.

'Flynn?' you asked groggily the minute the door closed. You got up, rubbing your eyes. He was standing by the door, still with his hand leaning on it. Quickly and clumsily, you walked to him and took his hands in yours, turning them over to inspect the damage to his knuckles. There was dried blood on the leg of his jeans and I wondered if it was his or the other boy's. 'Oh Flynn. What happened? What did they say?' He shrugged his shoulders and I felt an unfamiliar surge of anger towards him. Your brow was furrowed and I could tell that you had a headache from the way you were squinting slightly. You should have been upstairs in bed, feeling safe and rested. You should have been concentrating on feeling better, not having to deal with a temper tantrum from an almost fully grown man.

'Nothing.'

'Well, they must have said something. Who was it?'

'It was nothing. I just – I needed to – it was just an argument about a phone.'

'What about a phone?'

'Ryan said that the app I was using to download music was shit so—'

'You hit him over an opinion about an app?' I asked. I could hear the irritation I felt scraping my voice.

'He often says things to wind Flynn up,' you jumped in, quick to defend, 'even before the accident . . .'

I was finding it hard to keep all my thoughts and feelings inside. Trying to battle The Right Thing to Do. Should I act like a father? Put my proverbial foot down? Threaten to . . . what? Ground him? Or should I act like an outsider, leave you to sort this out privately? They came to find me, travelled a long way, for what? So I could do the shopping and clean the house?

'Enough,' I said quietly but firmly. You both looked at me with confusion. 'Enough,' I repeated, looking at Flynn. He squared his shoulders, the alpha male; we began the dance that has been played by wolves and gorillas, lions and tigers, fathers and sons for centuries. The show of dominance and submission. I took a step towards him.

'You need to let her rest, take some time, Flynn. Why don't you go to your room, listen to music, paint, draw . . . but go to your room and sort your shit out. Now.'

'Don't tell me what to do.'

'I'm not telling you what to do, I'm suggesting that you let your mum rest.' His shoulders lowered, his eyes dropped and then he climbed the stairs.

The next morning, he came into the kitchen as I was on the phone to the doctor's.

'Yes, please, today if possible.' I held up a cup at him and flicked on the kettle as he gave a short nod. I opened the wrong cupboard looking for the tea bags; he passed me the cream ceramic container that had the word 'tea' written on it. A smile; a thanks. 'My name is . . . Dev? Um, Devon King.' I looked away from Flynn, feeling as I said the words that he had caught me: the imposter. 'Date of birth?' I repeated the receptionist's question. Flynn opened the kitchen drawer and passed me a copy of one of the missing people reports that Rose had shown me the day before. I scanned the information and read out my date of birth. 'The second of March, 1975,' I said. I poured the boiling water into the cups and accepted the next appointment for later in the afternoon.

'Thanks,' I said to Flynn as I hung up the phone and poured the milk into the cups. 'How's your hand?' I asked, not looking at him but instead concentrating on stirring the tea. Behind me, he was busy pouring corn flakes into a bowl. I turned to pass the milk and he took it from me; his knuckles looked swollen and there was a slight graze on his third finger. He saw me eyeing it and looked away.

'I know I shouldn't have gone out,' he said quietly in a low mumble, 'it's not like you can tell me anything I don't know already.'

'OK.' We sipped our tea in silence. 'Could you come with me this afternoon?'

'What, to the doctor's?'

'Yeah. Do you have a free session on Fridays?'

'Um, yes, but won't it be a bit, you know, awkward?' He flicked his hair to the one side.

'I just thought that it might help to have you there, you know, to help with the details that I don't know. Mel is tired, she needs to rest before the operation on Monday. I think she's going to watch chick flicks all day.'

Rose walked in, attaching her ID badge to her blazer jacket. She looked up at us and then scowled at Flynn.

'Well done, dick. That really helped with things yesterday.'

He stuck his middle finger up at her. 'Is this yours?'

'Funny.' She walked over and grabbed his hand firmly but gently and turned it over, just as you had the night before. 'Not too bad, didn't go for a wall as well then?' He shook his head then said sorry to her. She chewed her bottom lip and shrugged her shoulders. 'Who was it?'

'Ryan.'

'Great, his sister's in my French class, she'll be a joy to be around today.' She grabbed a brown speckled banana from the fruit bowl and peeled it while holding open the swing bin lid with the foot pedal and then threw the skin in. She grabbed her bag and paused briefly and awkwardly by my side, then lifted herself on tiptoes and planted a swift kiss on my cheek.

'Laters,' she shouted as she closed the door behind her.

'OK,' Flynn answered, 'but I'm not kissing you on the cheek.' He grinned and shoulder-bumped me as he grabbed his bowl of cereal and slouched out of the room.

35

Flynn

It was weird watching him fill out the form at the doctor's. He looked up at me and asked if he'd spelt his middle name 'Sebastian' right and to double-check our address. Small things that we all take for granted were a big deal to him. As he looked over the details, his face had this expression on it, a bit like Mum's when she reads one of Rose's reports.

We sat and waited quietly. I tried to give him some space and put my headphones in, hoping it would make sure he didn't feel the need to make small talk. But I didn't have any music on . . . It was a good job, really, because when they called his name he was just sitting there. I pulled out a head-phone and nudged him. He sort of jolted when he saw the name sliding across the screen: *Devon King – Room 2*.

We sat down opposite Dr Grey. You know when a cartoon character or a superhero has a name that suits their person-ality like, I dunno, The Flash or Dr Doom? Well anyway, his name suits him. Dr Grey. He just looked . . . grey. He was pale and – what's that word Rose uses about her counsellor? Insipid. Yeah, that's it, like he could have done with being steam-cleaned. His breath stank of coffee and even I could tell that he needed to pluck his nostril hair and change into a clean shirt.

'So Devon . . . what can I do for you?' I raised my eyebrows at Tom and waited for him to try to explain the shit that has been going on in our family.

'It's a bit of a long story,' Tom started.

'These appointments are scheduled for ten-minute intervals; perhaps you could give me the highlights?'

I shook my head. I felt bad for him – Tom, I mean, this was a big deal for him, he's only just found out who he is after all this time and he's supposed to just give the 'highlights'? Man, adults can be such twats.

'OK, well, I've had amnesia for the last eleven years and until recently I didn't know my own name.'

Grey blinked a bit and I could see he was wishing he hadn't given him the five-minute warning.

'Amnesia is a very strong word to use without a diagnosis.' Dick.

'I guess so . . . what would you diagnose a person with if they can't remember anything before the last eleven years?' Nice one. Dr Grey leant back in his seat and then rubbed his hands together, the way that some men do when they're told what's for dinner.

'But you remember now?'

'No, I mean yes, I remember bits, 'like flashbacks, but sometimes I don't know if they're real or dreams. My family . . .' he says this word the way that actors say 'Oscar', 'found me. They are filling in the blanks about who I was before I disappeared.'

'I see.' Dr Grey leant forward and started tapping on his computer. 'So this is your . . .?'

'Son.'

'What do you remember about your father, before the disappearance? Anything that may have triggered him to run away?'

'We'd had an accident.' I lifted my hair briefly to show him the scar. 'He wasn't himself after that.'

'What kind of accident?'

'A car crash.'

'Did your father suffer any head trauma?'

'No. I was the only one injured . . . I wasn't wearing a seat belt.'

OK, so I know that we should have told Tom a bit more about the accident, but, to be honest, I don't like talking about it. It's like the accident is the one thing that people hear about when they meet me. It's the question that I know is asked by every new teacher that I've had, every friend of Rose's . . . Christ, it's in the faces of strangers in the street: 'What happened to that poor boy?' Like I said, I don't like talking about it.

'Who was driving?'

'I was,' Tom said, squaring his shoulders as he did, like he was about to have a fight. It's the first one of his mannerisms that I recognised as my own.

'Do you remember the accident, Devon?'

'Tom, my name is Tom. I don't remember being Devon, not yet anyway, and no, I don't remember the accident, but I must do somewhere in here . . .' He knocked his fist against his head as if he was knocking on wood.

'Why is that?'

'Because I created a sculpture that was a tree with a rose growing out of it.'

'A rose?'

'It's my sister's name.'

'And I've had nightmares about the tree that I hit.'

'Hmmm, do you have any other symptoms?'

Tom started telling him about the panic attacks.

'OK. Well I can print you some leaflets about how to deal with anxiety for now. If it continues we could try some anti-depressants?' Tom nodded. 'But in the meantime, I think that I need to refer you to a psychiatrist.'

I snorted. I couldn't help it. I'm the only one in my messed-up family who doesn't go to one.

'We should have a group membership,' I said under my breath.

'Sorry?' Dr Grey asked as he slurped his coffee from his mug.

'Nothing,' I answered.

I wasn't feeling great by the time we got back. I popped my head around the door to Mum's room where I could hear some cheesy declarations of love from whatever film she was watching, but she was asleep. After I turned the telly off, I stood there for a while watching her. It was like she'd shrunk. And it was only then that it really hit me, that my mum was ill. I mean, I knew what the doctors had said and I knew that she'd had all of these weird symptoms, but only then could I actually see it. Her skin wasn't the right colour it had a grey tinge to it and her lips looked pale. I hadn't really noticed that she'd lost weight until I went to pull the blanket up over her, and I saw that her shoulders had slipped out of the neck of Tom's shirt she'd been wearing . . . My mum. I leant in closer. Her snores had stopped and she was singing quietly, something about sugar and honey and being a handy girl? Something like that and it made me smile to think that she was dreaming about nice things.

Thinking that you might lose your mum is a feeling that creeps up on you and stabs you when you're not expecting it. Memories fly into your head when you're putting toast in the toaster or looking for your socks in the washing bin. Like when she would always buy me a comic if I was poorly and make me treacle milk before bed . . . I remember getting into a fight at school about that. It was the answer I'd given the teacher when she had asked what makes us feel safe. This gobby little shit, I can't remember his name now, told me I was a freak and a mummy's boy. I think his parents moved him shortly after that. His black eye had been one of my best. I think I was about nine at the time. Then there are the memories of when I was little, her sleepy face by the side of the bed when I was in hospital, the way she would always stroke my hair back from my face and kiss my eyebrow before she left. The way she would smile when I stood up in a school assembly, proud of me talking about my rubbish painting of a leaf, as if I was standing in the Tate Gallery, not the school assembly hall.

I stroked her hair and kissed her on the eyebrow, and I had to quieten the sob that had lodged itself in my throat. I couldn't stand to feel like this. If things go wrong in our family we can normally fix it, do something to make us all feel better, but I couldn't fix this. I could feel the muscles across my shoulders aching with tension and my stomach felt hot inside. I knew that the last thing anyone needed right now was for me to get into a fight but I don't know what else to do with myself when I feel like this. I tried hard not to slam my bedroom door behind me, when every part of me wanted to rip it from its hinges. Punching the bed a few times did little to stop the tears rolling down my face. I was crossing my bedroom over and over again, trying to breathe through the anger I felt at the world.

There was a knock on my door and Tom walked in before I could say anything. I know how I must have looked, crying and stomping around. I know I must have looked like a kid having a tantrum, but he didn't say anything, he just sat on the bed and pulled some wire and a pair of pliers out of his bag. He started clipping and bending, as I clenched and opened my fists. It's something that Shane had suggested I do a while ago, to try and release some of the tension that I was feeling. Open close, open close. Digging into his bag, he pulled out a sketch pad and a pack of well-used pencils.

I got what he was trying to do but I didn't feel calm enough to draw. Open close, open close went my fists as I walked up and down the small room. I couldn't help but watch his hands working; he was creating what looked like a face but I thought that the forehead was too high. My breathing was still fast and I could feel my pulse racing through me. Eventually, I was irritated enough by the elongated forehead of the face that I spoke.

'The forehead is too high.' I grabbed the sketch pad and drew a rough sketch of the face that he was creating and reduced the size of the forehead. Tom didn't say a word apart from, 'huh,' then changed the dimensions of the face.

'You know, I never could get the dimensions of a face quite right without looking at a photograph or a mirror. I can do your mum's, though.' He smiled, grabbed his stuff and left, propping the face against the space-rocket lava lamp that has been in my room since I was eight. The room was going dark and I went to draw the curtains but facing me was my reflection. I stared at it for a while, the urge to throw something through it tearing through me. Without thinking really, I grabbed the sketch pad and started drawing. My lines weren't steady, the anger making my hands shake slightly. I tore away the first page, it was crap, and I started again. I didn't notice the time pass; page after page I shaded under my eyes, the outline of my jaw, the jagged edge of the scar and the way my one eye always seems slightly hooded. I stretched and rolled my head from one side to the other, releasing some of the tension, and continued to study myself in a way that I never had before. The reflection from the window wasn't sharp enough so I closed the curtains and turned on the bedside light, grabbing the mirror that I use if I need a shave. I crossed my legs, changed pencils and started again, my edges becoming crisper. I smiled for a moment as I remembered Kate kissing the dimple that shows when I do that and I did a quick sketch of myself. It felt weird to be smiling at myself, but if I'm going to be a half-decent artist I need to be able to adapt my techniques, at least that's what my tutor says. I was lost in the sound of the pencil scraping against the paper and the now steady beat of my heart.

My door creaked open and Mum was standing there holding a plate with a tower of ham salad sandwiches, a packet of bacon crisps and some Coke. She put them on the bedside table and sat by me, picking up one of the earlier sketches which she passed to me. My face was ugly, my lips in a thin line. The strokes were thick and heavy where I had pressed too hard with the pencil and my eyebrows, creased above my eyes, were scowling. She leant back against my wall and watched as I flicked back to the beginning of the pad. My face was contorted with anger, my cheeks wet on the first two. I licked my finger and turned the next page. In this one my face had relaxed slightly, the lines more accurate, and in the next one, my muscles were completely relaxed but my forehead was furrowed in concentration. My expression was different again in the following one. I didn't look threatening: I looked calm; my head was leaning to the right as if I was trying to see myself from a new angle. Then there were the ones of me smiling like a knob, I could see that the one side of my face looked good. I covered the other side with my hand, grabbed the mirror and placed it in the middle of the paper, giving a complete me without the bad side. Mum was shuffling papers behind me then put her hand over mine and pulled the mirror away. She put the first drawing over the top of the last.

'It's not the scar that makes you look bad, Flynn.'

And when I looked at it again, I didn't like what I saw.

I knocked on Jo's door and waited. Jo opened it and tried to hide her surprise.

'Hi, um, sorry to bother you, but I need to get hold of Shane and he's not answering my texts, I wondered if his phone is broken?'

'It is, I, well, I washed his jeans and it was in the pocket.' She pulled a face, half apologetic, half like a naughty school-girl. 'He's upstairs actually, come in . . .' She pushed the front door open and as I walked in I noticed that the house smelt different, the smell of last night's dinner like when we've had fajitas and left the dishes on the kitchen side overnight. It was good, I'd rather that than air freshener any day.

'Shane! Flynn is here!' She looked different too, a bit more relaxed? I dunno, her hair didn't look as perfect as it normally does. 'How's your mum? Coffee?'

'She's OK, I guess, tired. She goes in tomorrow for the big op. Yes, please.' She pulled this metal thing that twirls and holds loads of these capsule things.

'OK, so I've got cappuccino, latte, caramel latte, macchiato?'

'Er—'

'Or I've got hot chocolate? Mocha?'

'Um, just a black coffee? Please.'

'Americano. OK. How is she feeling about going in?'

'Nervous, I guess.'

'She must be . . . and you and your sister? How's things with Tom? I'd imagine that must be a bit odd?' I watched her awkwardly as she dashed from cupboard to cupboard getting cups, sugar and then biscuits. 'And how is Kate? She's so pretty, isn't she?'

'She's fine, away this week visiting family.' I scratched the back of my head, trying to stop myself from grinning like an idiot every time anyone mentioned how pretty my Kate is.

'Hey.' Shane walked in with wet hair, smelling of shower gel. Jo gave him this weird smile and then turned around to take the coffee cup from the machine and added another capsule for Shane. 'Everything OK?'

'Yeah, kind of, I guess . . . I, um, I need your help with something.'

'OK . . .'

Jo put the coffee in front of us and then made some excuse about having to go upstairs to sort out some clothes or something.

'I need to stop fighting.' He laughed and then took a slurp of his coffee, wincing slightly.

'Ugh, caramel.' He pushed it away as if it was poisonous. 'So where have you got this strange idea that fighting might be a bad thing to do?' He smirked at me. Not in a condescending way or anything, he was just being sarcastic. One of my other 'workers' had explained to me that they were not supposed to use sarcasm as it 'gave the wrong message'. I remember thinking that was a load of bollocks at the time.

'I've had a good look at myself, and what with Mum and everything . . . She doesn't really need my shit at the moment and, well, let's be honest, she might be ill for a long time and I know I need to change; I just don't know how. It's like a mist comes over me when I lose it and I don't know how to stop it.'

'We've talked about ways to control your anger before—'

'Yeah, but then I didn't really try it.' He raised his eyebrows at me and tutted. 'I mean I did try it but I never really *tried* it, if you know what I mean.'

'OK, so tell me what you've used.'

'Hmmm, I tried the counting to ten thing.'

'And?'

'Well, I just counted really fast.'

'OK, what about the tensing your fists?'

'Yeah, that works, kind of.'

'What about the balloons?'

'I'm not blowing up and letting go of balloons, dude, I'm not a complete knob.'

'I think you need to find out what helps you. What about writing a journal to help you work out what your triggers are? Write down how many hours of sleep you've had, what you've eaten, how you react to different situations.'

'Yeah, I need to work on being, well, normal.'

'Why would you want to be normal? It's dull. Why not just try to be a better you?'

When I got back, I could hear Mum and Tom talking quietly in the lounge. By the stairs was a small suitcase – packed, I guessed, for tomorrow. Rose was sitting at the top of the stairs; she put a finger to her lips in a 'shhhh' position. I climbed up and sat next to her.

'You OK?' she whispered.

'Yep, I am . . . I will be. I'm going to try, Rose, really I am.'

'Good. I need you, here, with me. I'm struggling too.'

We leant towards each other like we used to when we were kids.

'Have you started doing it again?'

'No. But I've wanted to.'

'That's good then, that you wanted to but haven't . . . Why are we whispering?'

'Listen . . .'

I could hear Mum's voice, soft and relaxed.

'When Rose was three I saved up enough money so we could go to Borth for a week. The weather had been awful most of the time but I'd put on their wellies – Rose's were pink with little flowers on them – and we went for a walk. Out of nowhere the weather changed, the sun came out and we spent the next few hours on the beach . . . Rose ended up in her pink knickers and a T-shirt that had white lace around the bottom, which got soaked as she jumped over the waves. Flynn was into his scouting stuff at the time and was scaling a pile of rocks nearby, scavenging for bits of old rope and driftwood to start a fire with. I remember Rose's laugh – she had such a cheeky, throaty one – as she fell into the water. I looked up and Flynn had made a flag out of a stick and a piece of fishing net, and he was laughing and waving it at us. It was the first time after you left that I had felt happy without you, but even then, I pretended you were standing behind me, arms around my waist, watching our perfect children . . . the best of us.'

'I'm sorry I wasn't there.'

'You kind of were, to me anyway . . . I'm scared, Tom.'

'I know.'

'What if something goes wrong in the operation? What if I never get to see them enjoy the beach again?'

'You'll be fine.' Tom's voice was muffled like he was talking into her hair. 'You'll be fine,' he repeated.

Rose and I looked at each other.

'What if she's not?' she asked, her eyes filling with tears.

'Then we will have to be. Otherwise everything she's done for us will be for nothing.'

36

Rose

19th October

I opened the curtains even though I knew it wasn't quite morning; the sky was dull and heavy and it was drizzling. I always think that is such a shit word to describe the rain. I mean, if you use the word drizzle in *Bake Off* it sounds all nice and indulgent. Lemon drizzle cake – sticky, delicious icing – salad with a drizzle of dressing, suddenly even salad becomes something more exciting. But when the rain drizzles over us? All we feel is damp and cold; there is nothing indulgent in that at all.

Mum went into hospital today.

I swung my legs over the edge of my bed and leant down on my palms, pushing down hard to help relieve some of the tension. After a few minutes, I traced the scars with my finger. I pressed down quite hard on these too; it might sound stupid but it's almost like I'm getting a quick fix. The scars have become little silvery lines now and in an odd way, they look quite pretty, almost like a tattoo. That's how I like to think of them now, tattoos. It makes me feel less of an outsider, I mean, loads of people get tattoos that they wish they could get rid of, right? Drunken nights out with mates or the names of boyfriends and girlfriends that have long since become exes. These are my little mistakes, my love affair that was good while it lasted but now it's over. That's not to say that I don't crave it, just in the same way that I bet older women wish they were back in . . . where did people go in the noughties? Magaluf? Ibiza? Anyway, I bet when they're dragging their kids around the supermarket, that there is part of them that wishes they were off on a drunken holiday with their friends or having a final fling with a long-lost love.

Today is the day I might lose her. I know I shouldn't have looked but I couldn't help it, couldn't help but Google brain tumours and what happens when they try to remove them. The possible – no, not possible, probable – side effects are endless, even from the dye that they put in her which can make her sensitive to light; that can make her liver pack in and make her blood pressure plummet, and that's before you even get into the actual surgery. I looked at the clock and saw it shining with its luminous arms, stretching to half-five. I wanted to creep into her room and snuggle up to her like we always have, but I couldn't because Tom is here. I could hear the hushed noises downstairs, the rattle of the water running in the pipes as the kettle was filled up and the flick of the switch as it started to crack and groan with the effort of heating up the water. Scraping my hair into a ponytail, I sighed and looked around my room, wishing that I wasn't so untidy. I crept past the closed doors and nipped to the loo, brushed my teeth and listened to Mum's soft snores from the other side of the wall. Her bedroom door was open a bit and I pushed the door slightly, realising that it must be Tom downstairs. I didn't want to wake her but I didn't want her to go to the hospital either. My stomach felt like it was about to hit the floor as I thought that this could be the last time that I ever see her asleep, the last time that I might have the chance to cuddle up to her. The bed was sinking slightly as I crawled across the duvet and climbed under it. The sheets smelt slightly of Tom, which was weird but not horrible; as I dropped my arm around Mum's thin waist, though, I was filled with all of the smells that are unique to my mum.

In biology, we were told that a baby can recognise the smell of their mother's amniotic fluid just a few days after birth, and that they can tell the difference between the smell of their mother and that of a stranger. At first I thought that must be a load of crap, but then I started thinking and I thought, well, yeah, I suppose I would recognise my mum over another woman with my eyes blindfolded. I closed my eyes and tried really hard to remember Mum's smell, because if something happens to her, I'll be able to look at photos and videos and stuff but I won't be able to smell her.

It's funny, I used to wonder what Dad would smell like and now I'm surrounded by his smell but might lose hers. I stayed really quiet while I lay there, just closing my eyes and listening to her snoring, thinking about stuff like when I first met Tom. When I saw him standing there with his arms around Flynn, I'd felt this hatred, this anger towards him, which is just, like, bizarre considering I'm the one who has been obsessed with finding him all these years, but when I saw Flynn's face almost crumple like a little boy who has just grazed his knee, I was just so furious, you know? Like, how dare he hug Flynn now after he had disappeared from our lives for so long? I hate seeing my brother upset but I hate him looking desperate even more . . . but then he started telling us about how he had no memory of us and when I talked about Mum? The way his face changed? It was like in the films, you could really see how much he loves her. I know it sounds a bit naff but it's true.

'Oh, hey,' he whispered as he walked in carrying two cups of tea. He put one cup down gently on the bedside drawers next to Mum's side and walked around to the other side of the bed and deposited his own drink. 'You OK?' he asked me as he sat down with his back against the headboard. I shook my head slightly. 'No, I don't suppose you are.'

'What will happen, when she goes in today?'

'It's just like we talked about, they'll put in the dye and then after a few hours they'll do the surgery . . .'

'Will they shave her hair off?'

'Only a small part.'

'She'll look weird with just part of it shaved off.'

'The chances are that she will have to have chemo after the operation anyway, so—'

'I'll be bald,' Mum murmured before she stretched and shifted so she could kiss the top of my head. 'Good morning, what time is it?'

'Quarter to six. There's a cup of tea for you there.' Tom smiled.

'I can't have it, nothing to eat or drink, remember?' His face fell and he looked as though he'd just accidentally run over a toddler rather than made a cup of tea.

'I'm so sorry.' He got up from the bed.

'It's fine, Tom, honestly.' Mum shook her head at him and rolled her eyes with a smirk on her face as he took the cup away from her side of the bed. He looked at it as if it was about to detonate at any minute and put it on the window sill, then got back into bed, giving it a final suspicious look as he pulled the duvet over him.

'Are you OK?' she asked me.

'Are you?' I answered.

'Scared.'

'Same.'

'What is with that word?' Tom asked. 'Same?'

Mum laughed quietly. 'Teenager talk. It means "I agree".'

'Well obvs, durr.'

'Obvs?' Tom raised his eyebrows but he was smiling at me. Sometimes I catch him watching me, not in a creepy way or anything, he kind of looks, I dunno, like he's pleasantly surprised. I don't mean that in an 'I'm so amazing' way but, look, it's like when you wake up and think it's a school day but then you remember it's Sunday? That's how he looks at me, like he's just remembered it's Sunday morning . . . does that make sense?

'So bald, hey? Are you going to get some weird scarf things or are you going to go for the nude look?' I propped myself up on my arm and twisted a piece of her hair around my finger.

'I don't know . . . we could have some fun with wigs.' She smiled but it didn't quite fill her face.

'You can pull off the bald look, I reckon, you've got nice eyes.'

'You've always said my eyes make me look like an alien, Rose.'

'Yeah, but a pretty one.'

She stroked my hair. 'Maybe I should try being a redhead?'

'Nope,' I said abruptly. 'Nope, nope, nope . . . you have to go through a rite of passage to become truly ginger. We redheads have to earn our ginger status. You have to have tolerated many years of sarky comments like "Quick, get the fire brigade! Her hair's on fire," or "Don't worry, it'll go grey when you get old," or "Back in the biscuit tin, ginger."'

'Ginger ninja,' Tom added.

'Ginger minga . . . the list is endless.'

'OK . . . purple?' she asked, smiling, and then looked at the clock, realising, I guess, that our lazy morning chatting in bed was almost over. Tom took a sip of his tea and tried to ignore the signs. She didn't even really try to contain it this morning. It took me a moment to recognise the first few lines; the tempo was quite slow and the notes started off fairly low. She sang about staying up and not sleeping so she could listen to me breathe; she looked at Tom and sang about watching him smile while he sleeps when he's in a deep dream, and then I recognised it from that really old film *Armageddon*? The one when they send a bunch of oil miners up into space to save the world from being destroyed by a meteorite . . . Did you know that apparently NASA use that film for training? They have to try and spot all of the mistakes. I know it sounds like I'm trying to distract myself by talking about NASA, but sometimes when she sings, you can see that she just wants to get the song over and done with, but then there are the times when she really means the lyrics. Flynn had come in and had lain down horizontally across the bottom of the bed; even after he had curled up a bit, his big hairy feet still stuck off the end. She had hit the chorus by then and she was crying as she was singing about never wanting to shut her eyelids, about never wanting to go to sleep because she would miss us and she didn't want to not be here for things. When she had finished she had said, 'sorry,' and left the room, shutting herself in the bath-room. We all stayed where we were, still thinking about the lyrics to the song and hoping that she wouldn't have to.

'I have an idea,' Tom said, scratching the back of his head. Flynn sat up and crossed his legs, watching Tom jumping up off the bed through his fringe.

'What?' I asked as he started hunting around the room, opening and shutting drawers until he found it. He stood in front of the mirror, plugged it in and flicked the switch of his hair clippers, raising his eyebrows, and with one quick motion, shaved straight down the middle of his scalp. Flynn snorted and shook his head as we watched Tom's hair fall all over the floor. When he had finished, he rubbed his hand over the short stubble.

'Nice but it's easy for you, your hair was short already.'

Tom raised the clippers up at Flynn, his expression challenging. Flynn almost shrank away from him. I looked from one to the other. A knot was in my stomach as I watched Flynn. I don't think Tom realises what a big deal Flynn's hair is. He uses it to hide behind; it is – and always has been – his way of protecting himself. He flicked his hair and then looked at me and then back to Tom.

'Do it,' he said, pushing his hair back from his face.

'Flynn, I—' I wanted to tell him not to, that it was a ridiculous idea, but I couldn't find the words. Tom suddenly looked uncomfortable.

'Mate, I was just kidding,' he chuckled as he unplugged the clippers and started wrapping the lead around them.

'I'm not, do it,' Flynn repeated.

'Have a think about it first,' I said but I knew I was fighting a losing battle; Flynn has always been determined. Once he's made up his mind, he very rarely changes it.

'I said I was going to change, didn't I?'

'At least call Kate, see what she thinks?' It was the only thing I could think of that would stop him.

'Why? Do you think she's with me for the way I look?'

'Well, it's not your charming personality.' I gave him a sarcastic grin. He got up and stood next to Tom, looking in the mirror. I glanced at the wall where I could hear the shower running, then back at him. He turned, looked at himself and scraped back his hair with his hand.

'I think we should – I should – check with your mum.' Tom sounded nervous, like he was regretting this whole conversation in a big way.

'Why? You're my dad, right?' Flynn asked as he let his hair go and opened the drawer where Mum keeps the scissors and tape and emergency birthday cards. 'Right?' he asked again, looking Tom straight in the eye.

'Yes, I am.'

'Good, then you can protect me from Mum, because she's going to flip when she comes out of the shower.' And with that, he held up his fringe and cut it. I made this weird little gulping sound and then started laughing, the type of laugh that is slightly hysterical as I watched clump after clump of his hair falling to the ground. Tom unwrapped the lead to the clippers again and finished the job.

'Fuck,' Flynn said as he stepped forward, rubbing his head the same way as Tom had fifteen minutes ago.

'You're supposed to say, "Don't say fuck",' I chastised Tom.

'Oh, um, don't say fuck.' Tom put both of his hands either side of his own face; he reminded me of that character from that horror film *Scream*. 'But, fuck.'

'Is it that bad?' Flynn asked his reflection as Tom stood behind him.

'What? No! We just look so alike . . . it's mental,' he laughed. I got up from the bed and stood next to them; they do look just like each other. I mean, there is no hiding Flynn's scar now, or his eye, but it honestly doesn't look as bad as I thought it would and then I realised I was the odd one out again. Again. I don't really remember thinking yes I'm going to do this, or what will happen when I get to school or how stupid will I look . . . I just picked up the scissors and cut it. A huge chunk out of the middle of my scalp, right where Mum would be having hers.

'Rose, no!' Flynn went to take the scissors from me but it was too late; once I started I couldn't stop. Tom looked like he was going to throw up as my red hair floated down in huge clumps. I barely noticed the sound of the shower being turned off as I cut and, oh my God, it felt good to cut: the weight of it falling away; all of the horrible comments I've had, the teasing, the 'Goldfish' comments, all of it just slipped away. I registered the sound of Mum retching in the bathroom before I put my hand out to Tom for the clippers.

'I'll do it, you can blame me then,' he said nervously, glancing over his shoulder towards the bathroom before he shook his head and the whir of the clippers started again.

We stood and stared at our reflections, like three people lined up outside a concentration camp.

'I'll be glad when I'm not throwing up every— Aaghhhh!' We all turned to Mum. Her hand had flown to her mouth and her eyes were wild and wide beneath her towel-turbaned head. 'What have you done?!'

'Um . . . showing our solidarity?' Flynn ventured.

'Sol-id-arity?! I don't know what to say, you all look so, so . . .'

'Bald?' I offered.

'Well, yes, but Christ . . .' and with that she ran back into the bathroom and was sick again.

We were all sitting around the kitchen table, simultaneously eating our bowls of cereal and rubbing our sheared heads. Mum walked in and slowly looked from one of us to the other and then started laughing, eye-streaming, hiccup-inducing laughter. It was contagious and soon we were all at it, in fact I laughed so much that the milk from my cereal shot out through my nostrils, which only added to the hilarity. It took us some time before we could all talk again but then, as it always does, time caught up with us and we were forced to accept that in ten minutes' time, the taxi would arrive and Mum and Tom would be going to the hospital and Flynn and I would be going to school and college. We went about the business of clearing the dishes; Mum double-checked her bags and pestered Tom about having enough stuff to read because the surgery took at least four hours and he would be bored. Tom's phone vibrated and we all stopped and looked at him as he told us that the taxi was here. He went to the door and spoke to the driver who got out and opened the boot for Mum's case. The three of us stood awkwardly at the door while Mum's eyes darted around anxiously as if she was looking for something.

'Ready?' Tom asked her and she gave a quick nod and then started singing this song about it being 'the final countdown' she kept singing 'did-do-der-dooooh-di-doh-duh-do-doooh' and then there were 'dum, du-du-dum, der, dum, bedudump-pum-pum-pum-poooooom!' She looked really upset when she was singing it, like she wanted the moment to be something other than eighties soft rock. When she finished she started hugging us and kissing the tops of our bald heads before – with one final kiss – telling us she loved us and that everything would be OK, then she turned and followed Tom to the car. We stepped out and walked through the garden and stood by the side of the kerb. I don't know how to write how I was feeling: seeing her get into the car. All of the bad things I had read, all of the risks that I knew she was going to face, came rushing at me – all at once. I started to think that maybe it would be better if she didn't risk having the surgery – what if she just had chemo? Surely that would be less of a risk than having her scalp cut open? The door closed with a soft thud as I watched her fidget and attempt to click the seat belt into place. Her hands must have been shaking because Tom leant over and plugged it in for her. She turned to look at us then; her whole body looked scared, right down to her nostrils which were slightly flared; she tried to give us a reassuring smile but her hand was reaching towards the door handle as if she was having second thoughts and wanted to get out, but before she could, the car started to move away from the kerb. Through the back window, her head was turned towards us and before I could stop myself, I started running after her. Flynn tried to grab my arm but I shook him off; I vaguely remember him shouting my name. My feet were bare and I could feel the gravel digging into my soles as I chased after the silver taxi. I couldn't keep up, but after a minute it stopped next to the flat-roofed council houses, propped up by malnourished chain smokers and pregnant teens. Mum got out, pulling me to her while I sobbed and begged her not to go: the concrete prisoners watched and then turned their backs, returning to their life sentences.

Thinking about it now, I couldn't have handled it worse really. Anyway, I was calmer once she got back in the car, like I'd had my final farewell properly. Flynn had caught up with me by then and had his arm around my shoulder as the car pulled off again.

I'm glad it happened because I felt almost numb by the time I got to school. I didn't even really feel nervous about what people were going to say when they saw me. I heard laughs and saw nudges but as I walked through the corridors to assembly I didn't care what they were saying or doing. All I could think of was that I might never see my mum again.

The assembly was about road safety, ironically, and I had tuned out from the monotone of the Deputy Head as he talked about looking both ways, blah, blah, blah; he'd then gone on – again – about uniform when I realised he was saying my name. The whole school seemed to be sniggering and I could feel my cheeks going red.

'Rose King, I hope you're listening!' he said, frowning and rocking forwards and backwards on his heels like a Weeble. 'Extreme haircuts is just one of the things we have addressed recently and as stated in the recent newsletter, it will not be tolerated. Please go and stand in my office.'

I stood with my legs shaking; as I'm writing this, I can't really remember being there at all . . . I guess I was in shock or something, but for whatever reason I stood still and said, 'No.'

'I beg your pardon?!' he shouted. All the heads in the front rows turned towards me and the staff around the side of the hall were looking at each other with shocked faces.

'No,' I repeated; my voice was clear and strong. 'This is not an extreme haircut.' I looked around at the smirking faces and moved my eyes to as many as I could, like I was addressing each and every one of the people in that hall. 'My mum has cancer. Cancer. It's not a swear word but it's not a nice thing to say. I'm sure that, at some point in your lives, you will be affected by it. My mum is in hospital right now having her skull cut into, they are digging around in her brain to try and take it out,' the smirks had turned to concerned, sympathetic or pathetic – I'm not quite sure which – looks, 'but the chances are they won't be able to, which means she will have chemotherapy, which means that she will lose her hair. That is why I have this,' I air quote the words, 'extreme haircut. Because I wanted to do something to support her, I wanted her to feel less of an outsider . . . If there is anyone who wants to tease me about it, or call me names, then feel free, because if there is one person who thinks that cancer is funny, something to laugh and joke about, then I can honestly say that I couldn't care less what they have to say. It isn't a joke, and it isn't something that can be laughed away.' As I said this last part I could feel my legs jittering and I was afraid that I was going to fall over before I could sit down, but as it happened, I didn't need to because Miss Singh started clapping and then stood up . . . as did the rest of the staff and then, OK, so some of the kids had an arsey look on their faces when they did, but they stood up too, until I was surrounded by the school clapping and smiling at me.

After school, Megan caught up with me and asked if I wanted to go to KFC on Tuesday; she said that she had missed our chats. I told her I'd like that but I wasn't sure just yet if I'd be free. I wanted to say yes straight away but there is still that little part of me that is hurting from when they all ditched me. Lisa told me I looked like a nutter but she said it in a nice way and told me that everyone was talking about how cool I was telling Mr Greene off in front of the whole school. Sorry for going on a bit but I'm trying to ignore the time, we're waiting to hear from Tom. Oh, my phone's ringing!

It was Tom. They couldn't get it all.

37

Melody

When I woke up in the hospital, I was alone. It's a funny word, alone; it can mean so many things. There is the alone when you put your kids to bed and open a bottle of wine: the feeling of peace and calm and the relief and indulgence that comes with it. There are the times when you're alone in the bath with a good book, your body relaxed and content; alone in the car with your favourite song blaring out of the radio as you sing at the top of your voice. Then there are the moments when you're alone and yet completely surrounded by people: the first day of school as you let go of your mum's hand and go through the classroom doors; that awkward alone when you're on a training course and you have to introduce yourself; or that tired and grubby feeling of alone when you're on the train coming home from work. As I lay there, in a hospital filled with hundreds of people, I don't think I have ever felt more alone. I knew. Of course I did, that they hadn't been able to remove all of the tumour; I knew because I was singing about being alone from yet another eighties classic by rock goddesses Heart. I knew as I sang about the clock ticking and nobody answering the telephone and – as my internal backing track struck a power chord – I gave a heartfelt explanation about how until recently, I had always got by, by myself, and that I didn't care until I met Hugh (Hugh?) and how it chilled me to my bones. As the curtain was drawn back by a tired-looking nurse (who I was sure couldn't be much older than Rose) I continued to question her as to how I would get her on her own.

Since then, time has passed by, and my body has been caressed by the warm rays of radiotherapy, its energy changing my cells, trying to destroy the cancer and leave my healthy ones alone. I lay still, wearing a Perspex face mask – making me look like I was about to go fencing – while the waves of radiation washed over me; I resisted the urge to say 'en garde' at the beginning of each session.

I managed to keep my hair for a while, but as soon as it started to come out in small clumps, I joined the rest of my crazy family and shaved it off. You should see the reactions we have when we go out in public.

We went to watch a show at Flynn's college as they have a really gifted performing arts section and Flynn had been involved in some of the artwork for the set so suggested we all went for a cheap night out. As we waited in the queue, through the college canteen with its anti-drugs posters next to the adverts for meal deals, we couldn't help but overhear the conversation behind us. A couple – in their late forties at a guess – were talking about us. We heard someone saying Flynn's name in murmured tones before, much louder, 'Well, what do you expect when the whole family looks like a bunch of hooligans? It's the parents I blame.' I went to turn around but Flynn just rolled his eyes at me to show he wasn't bothered by the comments. Tom, however, didn't notice Flynn's dismissal and turned around to face them.

'Have you always lacked social etiquette or is it a middle-aged thing?' he asked. Rose, Flynn and I all looked suitably impressed by the double whammy of insults in his opening sentence.

'I beg your pardon?'

'So sorry, should I have spoken louder?' He cleared his throat and spoke in an exaggerated voice, 'SHE HAS CANCER, WE HAVE SHAVED OUR HEADS TO HELP HER FEEL BETTER ABOUT HER HAIR LOSS,' to which heads started turning, making me feel awkward. 'THERE IS A CANCER RESEARCH CHARITY BOX IN THE ENTRANCE HALL IF YOU FEEL GENEROUS ENOUGH TO MAKE A DONATION WHICH WOULD GO SOME WAY TO APOLOGISING FOR TEASING A DYING WOMAN.' They shifted uncomfortably under the disgusted glances launched in their direction, and my awkwardness was soothed by their ashamed expressions. Apparently, after the show they donated fifty quid.

Then there are the exact opposite reactions, like when we were in the supermarket and a little boy of about four started pointing in our direction asking his mummy why we all had no hair. The mother had crouched down and said that it was because we were all very poorly; she had then looked up at us and said through a barely contained emotional breakdown that we should all 'stay strong'.

Rose had been furious about that and swore that she would never wear nude lipstick again if it made her look like she was dying.

I didn't feel much different in the first few weeks of radiotherapy but my condition worsened, apparently because of the swelling in my brain. Without rhyme (excuse the pun) or reason, I started singing songs from musicals, from 'Don't Cry for Me Argentina' (while I was trying to drain some spaghetti) to 'Jesus Christ Superstar' (the 'came around the corner on a Yamaha' version) in the middle of a garden centre. The kids and Tom looked more exhausted than me during that first week, which isn't surprising when you've got 'The Music of the Night' from *Phantom of the Opera* being sung badly for hours on end. I'd asked Jo if they could stay there in the end.

Shane had been there too when I arrived, and I could tell by the sheepish looks they were giving each other and the not-so-secret smiles, that their relationship had changed. It was endearing the way they had looked at each other as they told me that they had decided to give things another go, almost like they were telling their parents that they were 'going out' with each other. After a while, Shane had left and Jo immediately switched into gossiping teenager mode, telling me how they had just 'fallen for each other again' and that they had talked all night the day I had come home from the biopsy and (with blushing cheeks) told me they hadn't been able to keep their hands off each other since. She had seemed so much more relaxed than the woman I had first met; she looked like she had put a little weight on too, and the softness suited her. They had been more than happy to let the kids sleep there for the week until my symptoms started to go. As it happened, it was only another week before the music started to slow down so the kids were able to sleep at home again, but then the other side effects started.

The nausea was helped by tablets although they never quite got rid of the 'travel sickness' feeling, but the tiredness was – is – what I'm fighting.

Now, it's almost Christmas and in the words of Wham!, it will be my 'Last Christmas'.

The treatment isn't working. The tumour is too aggressive.

'Mum?! Where are the tree decorations?' Rose relays Tom's message from within the depths of the attic.

'By the—' I search for the word but I can't find it. It's square and brown and has the words 'school books' scrawled across it but I can't remember what it's called . . . I feel the letters slip away, a piece of paper that has been cut up into bits that are now floating away on the breeze. I close my eyes and try to grab them, I catch a 'b', before struggling for the other pieces. My eyes spring open, '—box! The box with the school books in.'

This is happening a lot lately: I keep forgetting things, losing time. Yesterday I was in the kitchen peeling a potato, and then, suddenly, I was asleep on the sofa. I can't remember the transition between leaving the kitchen and falling asleep.

I haven't told them yet . . . it can wait.

This is the first Christmas that Rose will remember having a whole family. Flynn can still remember little bits of Christmases with his dad but Rose was too young. There are two weeks left until the big day and I intend on enjoying every moment, every smell of pine and fir, every shimmering snow scene on the fronts of cards, every excited child in the street dressed up as a shepherd or a king.

Fighting cancer is the biggest struggle you can ever face in life. It devours your body, your thoughts, but the most exhausting part of it is the hope: it dangles hope in front of you. It's there when you wake up; it's there when you're being zapped with radiation and it's there when you're so tired even lifting your arm to scratch an itch leaves you feeling drained. It whispers in your ear, you need to rest so you can get better, you haven't been sick today, that means it's going, see how awake you are this morning, it must be shrinking. But now that hope has been taken away, I feel like I have won. Now I don't have to waste my energy hoping for myself, I can hope for the future of my family and that is a whole lot more enjoyable.

I won't be here for the birth of their children or their wedding days. I won't be here to see them graduate or to see Tom grow old. We won't be the elderly couple who still hold hands in public and sit in companionable silence on their favourite park bench, but . . . I can plan for these occasions.

The good thing about having a terminal illness is that it is very difficult for people to refuse (said with brimming eyes and quivering lips) your dying wishes. Which is why I've asked Jo and Shane to come over this afternoon while the others go Christmas shopping to finalise my list. So far, I have written gift cards for each of the kid's birthdays until they are twenty-one. I've tried to get them things that will make them smile, normal things, not something naff like naming a star after them or anything, but, for example, for Rose's eighteenth, I've ordered her my favourite twelve novels for her to read, one for every month of her eighteenth year. She reads a lot – it's all vampires and teen spies at the moment, but I'd always planned to share my favourite novels with her when she's a bit older. For Flynn's eighteenth, I've booked him driving lessons (I've checked and he can still drive, even if he only has the sight in one eye apparently) and for that Christmas, three laps in a Formula 1 car. The more sentimental gifts come with the big milestones. For the birth of their first child, I've had a cot-sized patchwork quilt made up with parts of their first baby clothes (Flynn's first outfit was soft beige with little rabbits on and Rose's was lemon with duck lings on it). I've asked for the lace from my wedding dress to trim it. When Rose moves into her first house, she is to have all of my cookbooks (stained with chocolate cake and Christmas dinner) . . . she thinks I've thrown them away and had a massive strop that we wouldn't have the recipes for her favourite cakes. And for the night before their wedding days, I've recorded a DVD telling them my most cherished memories and just, you know, mum stuff.

Rose comes into the room, flashing Christmas stocking earrings below her auburn stubbled head, carrying the decorations. Flynn is selecting a Christmas soundtrack and Tom walks in, his face and body hidden by parts of the fake six-foot Christmas tree that we bought when we were first together. I'm filled with emotion when I see him carrying it in, remembering the way my stomach used to knot in the first few years after he disappeared. The way I would try so hard to make sure putting the tree up was fun when all I wanted to do was cry and scream.

'What's wrong?' He kneels down by my feet, bits of fake tree left on his shoulders. Last year a whole arm had come off but I didn't want to part with it; we'd just turned it against the wall so you couldn't see the gap.

'Nothing,' I wipe my eyes with my sleeve, 'it's just so nice to see you here, with the tree.' He furrows his eyebrows. 'We bought it the first year we were together and I always found it so difficult, putting it up without you, but now you're here.' I laugh through my tears then. George Michael's dulcet tones fill the room as he 'whooooo-hooooos-oooooh-ohhhhhhh-hu-hooooos . . .' Flynn holds up a bottle of mulled wine and goes about the business of chopping up orange and pouring it into the slow cooker like we had the year before. Rose hunts for the cinnamon-scented candle oil and lights it, instructing Tom that he is not, under any circumstances, to start putting on the tree decorations until – the three of us say in unison – 'The house smells like Christmas!'

He gently pulls the arms apart and assembles the tree as I sip at the warmed wine. Flynn is untangling the red tinsel and I close my eyes for a moment, taking in the sounds, smells and tastes: holding them deep within so I can bring them back to life when I need them. I'm not a saint, I know I'm telling you of all of the positive things about accepting the inevitable, but I'm scared too. I know there is going to come a time in the not-too-distant-future when I will become weak; that I won't be able to take care of myself, and I know that I will, with absolute certainty, die.

I don't fear death itself. I'm not a religious woman and for that I'm grateful. The idea of judgement day would scare me, like the time I took the kids away for the weekend and didn't remember to feed the hamster and it died – would I be on my way down into Dante's nine circles of hell for the manslaughter of a rodent? And what about the time I fancied my PE teacher in secondary school? That's lust if I've ever felt it; I sometimes still think of his thighs. What else is there? Gluttony, greed, anger – I can do all of those on a Friday night when I eat an entire tub of ice cream and still get cross when I finish it all. I think the only circle of hell I could probably argue a case against would be violence, but then I remember all the spiders that have met their squishy doom under my slipper and I decide that I would definitely be on my way down. I'm sure there is fraud and treachery in there too – does lying about your age to get served when you're under age count? I did that on several occasions when I was a teenager, so I think that just leaves me with heresy; does fancying Prince Harry more than Prince William count as heresy? Regardless, my point is, I'm glad I'm not religious because these are the sorts of thoughts that could be going through my head, and I don't want to be thinking about the things I've done wrong in life, I want to savour all the good things right up to the moment of my death. I don't want to be floating around as a ghost seeing everything and not being a part of it. I don't expect to see a white light and a line of long-lost relatives waiting for me with open arms when I die; I expect there to be nothing. Which is why I want to enjoy every minute of the time I've got to live and I want to go knowing that even if I'm gone, I can still do things for my family that will put a smile on their faces.

'This one is from when we went to Wales for Flynn's tenth birthday and it rained the entire time,' I say as I pass Tom the tree decoration of a sheep with Merry Christmas written on it in Welsh. 'And this one,' I stroke a glass ballerina, 'was when Rose performed *The Nutcracker* when she was six, and this one,' I reach for an old-fashioned Santa with an elongated beard, 'was the first one we bought together . . . it cost five quid, which was a lot for us back then.' I smile at the memory and pass it to Tom who handles it gently and hangs it on the tree.

'And this one?' Tom holds a polystyrene bell with a green pipe cleaner sticking out of it and sequins glued in a chaotic pattern.

'Flynn's first masterpiece.' Rose giggles. I lie back down and sigh with contentment. The wine has made me drowsy and the fire whirs quietly while the electric lights and fan conjure up the impression of a real fire and I feel happy before I drift off into a deep sleep.

When I wake, the room is completely decorated. The branches with pine cones and holly are lying beneath the fireplace, the fake candle arch sits on the window sill as the novelty Santa stands guard holding his saxophone in the corner of the room. My last Christmas is here.

Flynn is sitting by my feet at the end of the sofa watching *Home Alone*. Sensing that I am awake, he turns to me and grins.

'You almost missed the bit with the iron.' He nods towards the screen. I look to where he is pointing but there are big spots of the screen missing. Rubbing my eyes, I sit up a bit but there are still definitely parts missing. The blood rushes inside my ears and I can hear Flynn chuckling at the festive slapstick but I can only see small pieces of the screen. Looking around the room, my vision becomes blurred and I feel like an electrical current is firing through my body; I register Flynn scream 'Dad!' and the next thing I know, I'm on the floor. Rose is crying and Tom is on the phone talking about my body being rigid and shaking.

I'm looking around the room and it feels like I'm not really there; the festivities look garish and too bright and the smells are too strong. My leg hurts, as does the side of my face.

For the next few minutes or maybe hours I drift in and out of sleep. Sometime later I register that there are paramedics leaning over me and I'm sitting up talking. I think I must have been talking for a while, but I don't remember what I have said. Jo and Shane are here and they are clinging on to each other, which makes me laugh. I feel drunk, I feel sick, I feel . . . ill. I try to refuse when they tell me I need to go to hospital but my words are garbled. I try to say, 'It won't make any difference,' but what comes out is 'diff not'.

Once we arrive at the hospital and I've been put in a private side room I tell Tom that he needs to go home.

'No, I think I should stay,' he answers.

'I don't want you to stay.'

'The kids will be fine, Shane and Jo said—'

'I don't care what they said!' I yell. 'Your kids need you. I don't want you here!'

'Mel, I think I should stay.'

'GO HOME!' I scream and throw a plastic cup of water across the room. 'Don't you get it? You can't do anything for me here, they need you more than I do.' He gets a towel from the bag which has been hastily packed and wipes up the water, placing the cup back on the cupboard. Slowly he nods, kisses me on the forehead and leaves.

'How are you feeling, Melody?' I turn away from the soft tone of the doctor as he closes the door behind him. I don't want to talk; I'm angry. I'm angry that the cancer has spoilt my plans, has ruined my 'Perfect Day'. 'Melody? Do you understand that you have had a seizure?' I nod. 'The chances are that it will happen again. I've spoken with your consultant, Mr Rudd, and he tells me that he has explained what to expect when you stop treatment?' I nod again. I can't answer him even if I wanted to. Deep within me, the mournful piano has started and Lou Reed is whispering in my ear about a 'Perfect Day' where I could have drunk sangria in the dark, and after that, I could go home. Our duet is sweet and sad, filled with optimism and defeat. I'm glad I spent the day with them; it really was almost perfect: a perfect fun-filled weekend. It would have been a 'perfect day' but you see . . . this cancer hangs from me, clings on; steals my perfect weekend and it makes me forget who I am, turns me into someone else. It just continues to hang from me: this cancer; this growth. It can never be harvested; never cut out or cut down – never, ever taken from me.

The doctor closes the door quietly behind him as I sob into my pillow and stare at the bare walls from the depths of my white, starched coffin.

38

Flynn

College is good; my art is becoming more structured and has many 'layers to it', or so I'm told. I know I sound like a pretentious knob, but my art is helping me. It's helping me cope with what is happening to Mum.

She's dying.

When she had the first fit, just before Christmas, we still kind of thought she would get better, but once they started happening more and more and she told us that she wasn't going to have any more treatment, well, you don't have to be a genius to work out what happens next. It's Valentine's Day soon and I'm taking Kate to Dad's for the weekend, just the two of us. Part of me doesn't want to go – I mean, what happens if Mum, you know, goes and I'm not there to say goodbye? But part of me thinks what if she goes and I don't *have* to be there to say goodbye? How do you do that? Say goodbye to your mum? Some days are better than others, like yesterday, she was awake and with it for a few hours, asking me about Kate and asking me to show her some of my work, but then there are days like last Thursday when she had three fits within the time it took me to watch the last two episodes of *The Walking Dead*. Watching her go stiff and start shaking is, I mean fuck, it's well, man . . . it's just horrid. Her eyes kind of go back in her head and sometimes she has spit in the corners of her mouth.

Walking is a no-go now too, she's just too weak, so we had to get a stairlift, I mean, Jesus, a stairlift! This time last year she was normal – well, not normal but you know, healthy and now . . . she's not even really her any more apart from the little bits of time when she's awake and not dosed up on whatever stuff the nurse has given her. Having a nurse in and out of your house all the time is dead strange too, and when she's there before you've even got up, it's just plain weird.

Mum refuses to stay in bed some days but on others? I don't even think she realises she's been asleep for over forty hours at a time.

Dad is amazing with her and I guess us. He washes her, feeds her; talks to her non-stop, even when I'm sure she's not listening to what he's saying. She sometimes just stares out of the window and she is so still that I get scared to go too close in case this is it. IT. We talk about when IT happens quite a lot.

Our house is going up for sale.

When she first told us, Rose and I had been furious. How could you even think about selling our home? I asked. I'll be honest, I thought it might be the meds making her a bit loopy, but she talked to us when she was in one of her 'normal' days. It went something like this:

'When I thought your dad was dead, I had so many memories of him in this house that it made it much harder for me to cope with it. I'd look at the garden and remember his promises; I'd see a missed piece of painting behind a picture and remember that we had fallen about laughing because we had run out of paint at the last minute; how it had poured down with rain the day we had chosen the bedroom carpet and how we had rushed our choice because we were so soaked and never really liked it the whole time it was on the floor; or the fact that we had bought the table at the top of the stairs just because we felt sorry for the woman on the market stall so we had taken it, just to make her day. These were nice memories that I had, and I found that hard enough. I don't want you to look at the stain on the carpet and think that is where Mum knocked over a glass of Coke when she was having a seizure or that was where she banged her head. I don't want you to look at that stupid stairlift and remember me sliding up the wall without any hair, or stare into this room and think that is where she died. I don't want that for you.' She had held on to my hand and then stroked Rose's face. 'I want you to go and live with your dad. I want you to have a fresh start.'

Rose and I didn't say anything; we just looked at each other. She wants us to move away from our home, from our friends. Rose has been really quiet about it, I mean, it'll be the start of her GCSE year and she is just starting to fit in with her friends; and me, well, I don't mind about the college thing. I'm getting on well and I can apply to finish the second part of my course at the college in Cornwall. Dad says he'd extend the studio too so I can have my own place to work.

There will be quite a bit of money after the sale of the house. I mean, we're not going to be millionaires or anything but there will be enough to extend the studio and the house. I'm warming to the idea and Kate had already started applying to uni over there, so I guess we'll be closer than if she was going and I was staying here anyway. Yeah, I'll admit, I'm starting to like the idea; the only thing is when I picture us there, I always picture Mum there too and she won't be.

I was looking through some photos on my phone the other day, the ones from when we went up in the hot air balloon. Mum looks so different; her eyes have creases around the sides when she smiles, but now her whole face looks creased. Like when I used to forget to take my school shirt out of the washing machine until the next morning.

And her eyes, I don't know how to describe it without using the word dead but that's just how they look . . . dead, especially when she does that weird zoned out thing. I picked her up the other day while Dad stripped the bed; it was like holding a bag of bones. She must weigh as much as a five-year-old now; she barely had the strength to put her arms around my neck.

Georgie has been coming over most weekends and I'm glad that Dad has her. He talks to us about what will happen after and he asks us questions about the past a lot, like he's trying to get as much of a picture of our life before he left, before she goes. He kind of feels like our dad now. At first you could see he was trying almost too hard to say the right things, do the right things, but now it all feels so much more natural. I started calling him Dad instead of Tom when Mum had her first seizure. I didn't plan to suddenly start calling him it, it was just, I dunno . . . instinct? I was so shit scared when she slid off the sofa, all stiff and juddering, that I, well, I guess I just needed my dad. I do need my dad. I'm so glad that we found him; that we went after him. He is holding us together, and I think that Georgie holds him together. It's a good feeling having him take care of us after so many years of it being Mum and me. Even though she always tried to be the one in charge, I always kinda felt like it was my job too, to be the 'man of the house'.

I overheard him crying in the lounge when Georgie was here the other day, and I thought about how much he must try to hide from us. I wanted him to know it was OK, that we are used to having to cope with stuff, but it just seemed such a private thing that I didn't want to, you know, intrude.

I'm painting a pretty grim picture here and I don't mean to. Mum still has her sense of humour, like the other day, right, she had been awake enough to be downstairs while Gran had visited. I hate it when she comes because she just makes the whole thing seem so hopeless, I mean I know it's hopeless but she makes it feel even more hopeless, like the death of Mum will literally be the end of the world. OK, I'm not explaining myself very well, I know it is awful. The worst thing, right, is for Mum to die. We're dealing with it in our own weird way, but when Gran is here she makes it feel like the whole of mankind will be extinct and the earth will become a desolate, barren wasteland. Anyway, after she had gone, we wanted a bit of normality so out came the biscuit box and the cups of tea and we settled down to watch one of those build-your-own-house things. Mum was enjoying herself, talking about what we should do to the cottage as if she was going to be there with us. It might seem a bit, I dunno, morbid? to be talking about it but it wasn't, it felt quite normal, like we were talking about redecorating, just the same as any other family. Anyway, she started to get tired so once it had finished, Dad helped her into the stairlift and then went to get her one of those vitamin drink things. The whir of the stairlift started and then she was singing at the top of her voice. So loud that we all sort of hurried into the hall. The song she was singing was so right but so wrong at the same time that we all burst out laughing; she was singing 'Spirit in the Sky' by Doctor and the Medics.

At first she looked appalled by what she was singing and tried to cover her mouth but then she got the giggles, laughing in between each line and trying to do this weird dance with her arms which kept hitting the button on the seat. Every time she would hit the chorus the seat would sort of jolt to a halt, then go up a bit, then stop. By the time she had got anywhere near 'the spirit in the sky' she looked exhausted and Dad went to the top of the stairs to help her off the lift, but by then he couldn't stop laughing either, real proper girl laughs, all high-pitched and everything. Mum finally got it together and told him in a fake pissed-off voice that it's a good job it wasn't her time to be laid down to rest because her horrible husband was too busy laughing at his poor dying wife to be able to take her to that place that is supposed to be the best.

Anyway, like I was saying, it's almost Valentine's Day and we wanted to make it special for Mum. Me and Dad have been working on it for a while and everything should be ready for the big day and Rose has been taking care of her side of things. Mum has always told us that Dad was romantic . . . I don't know how he came up with the idea but it is perfect. It will be perfect and I can't wait to see the look on her face when she sees what we've done.

39

Melody

It's almost here . . . the end.

I'm not sad, so please don't you be. The end is rarely a bad thing. The end of a good meal where you feel satiated and full, the end of a journey when you can finally climb into your bed and the end of a good film when you stretch and think that you must recommend it to someone else. Of course endings can be bitter-sweet: the end of a turbulent relationship – good memories overshadowed by bad – or the end of a box set when you mourn the characters and setting until you find the next one to replace it with; the end of a good book when you turn the final page, desperate to finish it but reluctant at the same time.

My end is coming in sweet, indulgent dreams. My life, my memories are hiding behind my closed eyelids. I'm standing in the garden, watching Rose in her pink flowered pyjamas tucked into her wellies as she stomps around, watering weeds with her washing-up liquid watering can. Flynn – with grazed knees and a superhero T-shirt – is hanging upside down from a tree, eyes closed like a bat. I can taste the coffee from my white mug that has Flynn's six-year-old fingerprints arranged into a slightly wonky flower, and I can hear the radio in the kitchen playing Beyoncé's 'Single Ladies'. Dev comes and sits down beside me and I lean my head against his shoulder.

'They're growing up,' I tell him.

'They are,' he answers and kisses the top of my head.

'Is it time to go?' I ask. 'I feel like I need to be somewhere else.'

'Not just yet, I have a surprise.'

'What surprise?' Flynn pulls himself back up, not a grubby-looking junior but a confident young man. He steps down from the tree and Rose puts down her watering can, the pyjama legs are transformed into bo-ho shorts and her hair is plaited down her back; they are smiling at me. I turn to Dev and he is holding out his hand.

It takes time to open my eyes, precious minutes wasted on the effort of pulling back my eyelids, pulling me back from my dreams of a life without cancer.

'Wake up, Mum, we've got a surprise for you.' Rose is wearing a dusky-pink dress, which leaves her shoulders bare and is trimmed with a delicate lace the same shade. Flynn is wearing a deep green suit; for a moment I'm confused and I attempt to wade through my sticky thoughts, trying to find an invitation or newsletter that I have missed, but then my tired, damaged brain processes the words 'surprise' and I know that I haven't forgotten something. Tentatively, but with purpose, Flynn helps me move up the bed and supports me with extra cushions and Rose sits next to me, opening up her make-up case with a smile.

I can hear classical music floating towards me from somewhere in the house as she closes her lips tight in concentration. I want to ask her what is going on but it's taking so much of my energy to stay upright and awake that I'm just happy to watch her. Closing my eyes at her request, I feel the shadows of the eye make-up brush bringing life back to my lifeless skin; I taste the sweet cherry lipgloss waking up my chapped lips and the blusher brings back embarrassment to my cheeks. Flynn helps pull me up and is then banished from the room as my powder-blue nightdress is discarded and replaced by a cream soft-cotton dress. Looking down, I see it has tiny doves sitting on rose bushes tumbling diagonally across it and I know that this is Tom's design. The slush in my brain stretches and snaps, making way for sharp, cut-glass clarity.

This is a wedding dress. Adrenaline shoots through me, forcing my fading body to react, and I'm rewarded with a smile, my face obeying my thoughts for once without the bribery and concentration I usually have to apply to make this crumbling carcass obey my commands.

Flynn comes back into the room, happy-sad eyes smiling at me as he asks if I am ready. With great concentration, I nod and he lifts me into his arms in the effortless way that I have lifted him so many times in his life; the dress hushes the groan of my discomfort as he carries me on to the landing. The music is louder and the scent of – I rummage through my brain to find the right connection – cut grass, perfumes my thoughts and I suck in my breath when I see what they have done. Entwined through the bannister are fairy-lighted hedgerows; a giggle escapes me as I see the hated stairlift has been dressed for the occasion, as has the hall. My ex-council house has been transformed into the English countryside. Flynn's paintings cover the walls; at the ends of each stair there are vases filled with tall grasses, cow parsley and buttercups. The stairlift sits in front of a painting of a vintage car; the traditional wedding ribbon stretches three-dimensionally outwards. Everything I want to say comes out in a hiccuped cry but my body expresses my thoughts for me: I'm smiling and laughing as Flynn lowers me into the car-chair. I hold on to his arm and try to show him how grateful I am and how proud I am. He leans his forehead against mine and says, 'You're welcome.'

'Oh wait!' Rose dashes into her room and brings out two daisy chains. Momentarily, I wonder where she found daisies in February, but then I remember the day that we had beaten our record for the longest daisy chain that we had ever made; how we hadn't wanted to get rid of them so we had frozen them: kept them looking alive even though they were really dead.

She places one on her own head – a crown around her short hair – and then places one on mine. The weight of it presses down as though I am wearing the crown jewels, but it makes me want to hold my head up a little higher; makes my posture a little straighter.

As I make my journey down and into the countryside, more of my surroundings become clear and I take in every detail – to the mouse sneaking out of a hedgerow, which we had seen on a day out on Rose's seventh birthday – to the hot-air balloon flying over the wheat fields, its three passengers looking down at the beauty of the day. There is a beach in the distance and there is Rose wearing her wellies and holding a fishing net . . . I pass Flynn chasing frogs from the old pond outside Mum's house and through the window of our house is me and Rose, cutting out gingerbread men, just like we used to if there was a school fayre coming up. Then there are the three of us trying to fly a kite: Flynn's face a picture of concentration; Rose's face hopeful as I stand – wearing denim jeans and a blue striped top that I had forgotten I ever owned – trying to launch the kite into the sky. I continue my descent towards a water-coloured Rose who is cartwheeling along a path – I'd forgotten how she used to do that, walk normally and then without warning just break into a cartwheel. I'm surrounded by my children's childhood and I know – if ever I had been in any doubt – that I am deeply loved.

As I reach the bottom of the stairs, there is a gravel pathway leading to the lounge door which has been transformed into double oak doors. There are stained glass windows either side of them, hanging over the normally whitewashed walls, which have been replaced with the aged bricks of a church. The combination of Flynn's art with Tom's sculptures is breath-taking.

Fairy lights drip from the fir trees either side of the door – Rose's touches amongst the boys' craft.

Flynn picks me up and Rose places a delicate bouquet of cow parsley, buttercups and grass into my hands as the doors open.

Inside the room has become a church, with chairs arranged like pews and wooden hearts hanging at the end of every row. As I'm carried in I realise the room is filled with my family and friends. My mum is all in peach and is sniffing into a tissue beneath a huge peach hat; Shane and Jo are dressed in their best and are smiling at me next to Georgie and Kate and the remaining guests, my children. My children in all shapes and sizes. Flynn has created a montage against the back of the room that looks like the inside of the church with rows and rows of people – but each face shows Rose or Flynn smiling back at me. From chubby toddler faces to spotty teenagers. As I look closer, I see them in their later years too. Flynn has somehow managed to age them so that I can see them as they will be, in their twenties, in their forties: there is Rose wearing a graduation hat; Flynn holding hands with Kate; Rose with a huge pregnant tummy and then further along I can see them both holding small children by the hand. There are a few comical ones of Tom dotted about with a thought bubble above his head and question marks inside, and in his hands he is holding a map. There are images of us there together too with greying hair and jowly faces. And there at the very front of the montage is Dev and me on our wedding day. I look up towards where an altar has been constructed at the far end of the room and there he is, waiting for me as I have waited for him for so long. Flynn clears his throat and then *Ave Maria* starts as my son carries me down the aisle.

Flynn passes me to Tom and I use my strength to reach out and touch his face. I hear the voice of the Reverend at the front of the room but his words are too complicated for me to grasp and so I don't try to. Instead I spend all of my time looking at Tom's face, concentrating on the creases around his mouth, the green of his eyes, the dimple in his chin. He says the words 'I do,' and I try to repeat them. Stroking my face, he tells me that I don't have to speak but I open my mouth, enjoying the sound of those two words. 'I do.' He grins with tears in his eyes and turns me around to where everyone is clapping and smiling.

I try to smile back but speaking has taken everything from me and I close my eyelids just for a moment to regain some strength.

When I wake, the chairs have been returned to their rightful positions, and the altar has gone and has been replaced with food. I can hear the clink of glasses and quietened conversations. Tom is sitting at my feet, rolling a champagne flute in his hands, and Rose is sitting on the sofa arm next to where I am lying; Flynn is sitting on the opposite sofa and has his arm draped around Kate's shoulders and smiles as he sees me looking at him. I smile back and then close my eyelids again.

Mum gently shakes my shoulder; her familiar powdery smell brings back my own childhood memories of not wanting to let go of her hand on the first day of nursery. The feel of her putting a 'magic' wet flannel on my head when I was ill and the way she would clap her hands together if she got excited about something. I worry how she will cope with my death. She's always been an optimist; even now as she kisses my cheek and tells me she will be back next week, I don't really think she believes that I'm going to die. It's as though I've just got a nasty virus that I'll shrug off. I wish she could put the magic flannel on my head now. The thing about my cancer is, it has taken everything it could have taken. Even my last words. I want to tell her to enjoy the rest of her life, to enjoy her grandchildren. I want to tell her how much I love her and how lucky I am to have had her as my mother, but instead I just dribble, as my top lip tries to talk.

It's dusk when I wake again. The church-room is now lit with fairy lights along every surface and at the back of the room, I can hear the animated and heated discussion that comes with the choosing of a playlist.

'But that song is so depressing!' Rose groans.

'How about—'

'No, no, no! Dad, there are other songs that come from a different decade than the nineties, you know.'

'How about this one?'

'Ah, Mum loves that song.'

I'm thirsty but I don't want to stop them talking, I want to listen to them being normal. I try to move myself but I can't. My arms are no longer strong enough to lift my body and I make a horrid gurgling noise as I try to move. The three of them are beside me and their concerned faces and orders of 'lift her up' and 'get a glass of water' are like knives slicing away the normality that had filled the room just moments ago. This is where I decide that I want to die. I want to leave them all, leave them to get on with their lives, so they don't have to constantly talk quietly because I'm sleeping, so they don't have to check on me every few minutes. I focus on their faces as they move me about, a puppet with its stitches barely holding the seams together. Dribble is tenderly wiped from around my mouth as Tom pulls me into his arms.

'Let's get her back up to bed.'

I don't want to go upstairs, I want to stay in this beautiful room, surrounded by the images of their future. I try to say I don't want to go but my mouth is too busy drooling; I try to jerk my head and my arms but this just confuses them.

'Is she going to have a seizure?' Flynn asks.

'Put her back on the sofa, Dad,' Rose instructs. Tom looks from one of their faces to the other, then back down at me. I calm myself so he can see that I'm not going to have a fit. The song that they had been talking about fills the room.

It's my favourite song. Kate Bush's 'This Woman's Work'.

I must show some kind of recognition because they all laugh softly. I let the first notes of her voice soothe my tired skin as she 'ah-haaaaaaaa-ooooooh-huh-hooooo . . . ah-haaaaaaaa-ooooooooh-ooooooh-hooos'.

'Oh!' Rose slaps her hand over her mouth and then grins. 'You haven't had your wedding dance.'

Tom smiles down at me.

'Are you comfortable? Do you want me to put you down?'

I grunt what I hope is a negative sound and they all laugh. 'May I have this dance?' he asks as he strokes my cheek. I use the last bits of my energy to nod as he kisses the top of my head.

I'm going to join you all now.

As I'm being swayed in my husband's arms, I take a step out from that body that is lying with such frailty that it looks as though it is made of glass and I stand beside you all, watching this: the last scene of my life on this earth. I watch the way that Rose's head is leaning on Flynn's shoulders, his head leaning against hers, both of them with silent tears falling down their faces. As I stand by you, my body back to how it used to be, my voice obeying my commands as it once had, I watch the way that he looks at me like he's looking at the rarest, most beautiful creature on Earth. It will be hard for him, changing from just a man into a father. Sadness fills me as I watch how he's telling me that I have a bit more life in me, a bit more strength.

I could be crying now but I don't want to let my sadness show.

He's telling me about all of the words he could have told me, but he didn't say them, all the places we could have gone if he hadn't left and about all of the things that I had needed from him but he couldn't give me.

Desperately, I want to tell him that the pain of watching me fade away is almost over and he will finally have the thing that he has been searching for, for so long: belonging.

He will belong . . . to them.

Looking at the images around me, future versions of myself haunt my thoughts like past mistakes: mistakes that can't be changed – just like the future. Instead, I flick through my memories like a photo album: building a snowman with my mum; Rose screaming while I tried to put her in a princess dress – her face an angry red, splattered with glitter – and Flynn . . . fists bloody and eyes that hold regret and confusion like a magician's cloak: the same eyes that had cried sticky jam-stained tracks as I kissed away the pain of a toddler tumble, and I wish . . . that I could have just one of those days back: wish that I could live it one more time.

Disbelief crawls across Tom's face as he registers the way that my body is becoming a little more limp, and soon my chest won't rise again; my voice will never sing another song.

Looking up from my face I see his eyes try to focus on his children's faces. Rose's hand covers her mouth and Flynn looks down as they realise that 'This Woman's Work' has ended.

Epilogue

Devon

You've been gone for six years to the day.

Happy Valentine's Day, Mel.

I know what I must look like to the other grievers in this cemetery, kneeling here planting wild flower seeds in February. I mean, firstly, who plants seeds in February anyway, right? What can I say, Mel? You always liked a challenge, always fought for what you had, so this is something we do together, try to defeat the odds. When we visit on your birthday in June, we look forward to seeing which flower you have chosen to fight for. It's become a bit of a contest and we take bets on which flower will win; the winner gets out of doing the laundry for the month. Last year it was snapdragons, a whole bunch of them. Flynn won that one . . . let's see what you give us this year.

There is an elderly couple who are often here when I visit. They put a cuddly teddy next to the gravestone. I looked last time I was here, and the little girl, 'May' had died in 1957, just six years old. Sad, isn't it? They must look at me with the same pity as I do them; they must look over and feel sorry for a man in his prime spending Valentine's Day at a graveside, but they couldn't be more misplaced with their sympathy. I know it sounds stupid, but I'm happy; I like coming here.

After all this time, the kids have finally agreed that it was the right thing to do all those years ago, to sell your house and leave your ashes here in this churchyard where you used to do grave rubbings when you were little. They understand now why you left strict instructions not to be buried somewhere where we would feel obliged to visit every week, and so we make the trip up here just twice a year. I like visiting you and telling you my story; about the first time I saw you drinking from that water bottle and looking at the front of the gallery, how I felt when the green butterflies fell down, swirling around as you stood in that red dress, how beautiful you looked.

Oh, I've got some news. They've finally given me a diagnosis of, ready? Psychogenic amnesia/dissociative amnesia (the name depends on which doctor I'm talking to), which apparently is a symptom of PTSD. I know, me, the person who can't watch war films because they're too gruesome. OK, so in a nutshell and without all of the medical jargon, because I know how much you hate that, it basically means that because of the psychological stress I went through in the accident – which, I guess, was the guilt and the images of seeing Flynn flying forward and being so scared that I'd almost killed my kids – my brain suppressed my memories. They reckon it might have something to do with how I felt when Mum and Dad died too. There is loads of research about it, but to be honest, I'm just glad to know that I didn't leave you all because I was a twat, but because the fear of hurting them was too much for me to cope with. It makes it easier for me to forgive myself for leaving you and the kids, and of course it makes it easier for them to understand – especially Flynn. It's good for them to know that I left them, not because I didn't love them, but because I *did*. PTSD affects people who have seen all manner of horrors, but me? Putting my kids in such danger, I guess, was the most traumatic and horrific thing I could imagine happening to me. Now I know that, I can control the panic a bit better. If there's a noise that makes me jump or when I feel like things are crowding me, reasoning with myself and talking myself through why I feel like that helps me cope.

Let me just clean these bulbs away. No matter how many times I tell your mum that you hate daffodils, she keeps bloody planting them. She's good, by the way – she's met a man, James, he's nice . . . likes trains a bit too much for my liking but they seem happy; she came and stayed for a bit when Rose was, you know, having a hard time.

Anyway, back to my story, so, when you died . . . it was tough, Mel, I'm not going to lie. Some days we didn't speak to each other, we just kind of functioned. The funeral arrangements were all sorted – when did you do that by the way? And then there was the house sale. The kids found that really tough, and we had some proper screaming rows during that time, but, I don't know how you raised them like that but they would always end up laughing or taking the mick out of me or each other, whereas a few minutes before, they were hurling abuse at one another. That's what kept us together during that time, their ability to row and then recover with a joke or a nudge, or – I've noticed with Flynn –he will slide you a cup of tea or a can of beer. His way of making peace without having to talk, I guess.

Blimey, it's cold.

They'll be here in a bit. We've always tried to give each other a bit of space when we see you, so we each get you to ourselves for a bit, but this is the first time we've all arrived separately. A sign they're growing up, I guess, becoming more independent. Flynn is driving up after his exhibition – I'll let him tell you about that – and Rose will be here this afternoon;

she's doing much better now and she's got some really exciting news to tell you.

Moving to a new school wasn't as hard for her as I thought, what with nobody knowing about how Flynn used to be and without, well, the whole singing Mum thing – no offence, my love – she fit right in; made some new friends and started surfing quite a lot. She's a real water baby and living by the sea suits her. Do you remember I told you that she left with straight As? Where does she get those brains from, eh? The thing is with Rose, you think she's OK and then, well, you know about all of that. Last year was a tough one but she's much better now and she has found a new productive way of coping. She's managed to get a good apprenticeship with the local newspaper, and she is really enjoying it. Sorry, I'm probably repeating myself again. Anyway . . . things are good. I'm going to get going in a minute. Kate is coming to stay over tonight and the house is a bit of a tip. They'll be moving in together soon, I think; Flynn is making decent money from his sales now and Kate has just got a job with a solicitor's about half an hour away from us, so . . . I'll miss him; we work well together. He tells me if he thinks my dimensions are wrong and I tell him when his lines aren't clean enough – plus we have learnt to cook. I know, and not just eggs any more, although I do still make a good omelette. We cook together most nights and Rose cleans up. We really are doing well, Mel, you would be proud of the family we have become. They tease me about being single a lot of the time, telling me I should get myself 'out there', but I'm not ready. You see, the thing is, I'm getting some of my memories back.

It's happening most days now, I remember a little bit more and the memories are so vivid it's like I'm there again. Every day, I wake and wonder what we're going to be doing today, like yesterday, I was tying my bootlaces and there you were, as clear as day, standing behind Flynn holding both of his hands above his head, helping him take wobbling steps towards me. You looked up at me; your hair was swinging forward as you were smiling and encouraging him to walk to Daddy. I could smell the fabric softener on my clothes and hear the children's television in the background and then you were gone . . . but you don't stay away for long. So you see, Mel, for me, you're not gone, you're just waiting for me, waiting for me to remember, remember that my name is Devon King, remember that I am a good man, a good father and most importantly, remember how I was loved.

Flynn

Hey Mum. Just a sec, let me just plant these seeds. I was going to go for sweet peas this year but I figured it might give the game away, anyway, why mess with what works? Snapdragons for the win. Man . . . I can't believe you've been gone for six years. It's weird, like, it seems like you only died last year but then again, so much has happened since you died that it does seem like ages ago. I've just had my second exhibition and it went really well, I mean not on the scale of Dad's when he showed his sculptures of you, but I sold quite a few and I wasn't as nervous as last time.

Shane and Jo came. Man, she's huge! Honest, Mum, it's like she's been stung by a whole bunch of bees, but I suppose when you're pregnant with twins, you've got to expect to look like a whale. She's been here, I see, there are no smudges on the granite at all. I wonder how she'll cope keeping her house clean when the girls arrive – I told you they were girls, right? Anyway. Kate has got a job in a solicitor's. I never thought she'd have the nerve to do something like that, especially with, you know, her stammer and everything, but she has and soon she'll be earning a good wage.

We've decided to move in together in the summer. I haven't

told Dad yet. I think he'll be cool about it and I'm hoping I can still use the workshop; the places we've looked at aren't too far away so I can drive there. I'll miss not living with him, though; I'll miss the sound of your bell as he moves around the place – he still wears the bracelet, you know. You'd think it would be irritating, the jingle of it whenever he moves, but it's like it is part of him, like *you're* still part of him.

The car you got me for my twenty-first is still running like an angel. Kate says I'm obsessed with it, which I'm not, she's just jealous because I call her honey-bun whereas I just call Kate, well, Kate.

You'll be pleased to know I haven't been in a fight for over five years now. I think Dad's idea of having a punchbag and a few gym bits in the extension was the making of me, to be honest. I mean, it's not like I haven't still got a temper but working out really helps and when I have a bad day, like when I took this commission from this old woman in the village, I thought yeah, why not? She's proper old money, lives in one of the really old, massive houses just outside town. I thought it would be a landscape, you know? With my own twist, like the ones I had just exhibited, the ones with the small crack in the sky with another landscape in, I told you about them, right? They're not obvious, the cracks, you have to really look for them, so I guess that would go some way to explaining why she must have thought I was just a regular artist, but when I got there, she wanted me to paint her fucking dog, Mum. A dog. A red setter to be exact. Anyway, she offered me a fair amount of money, and me and Kate wanted to go to Italy for our holiday, which was gorgeous, Mum – you'd have loved it – anyway, Christ, that painting took . . . for . . . ever to finish. The punchbag got it full on for about a month then, but hey, better that than some poor bloke who just happened to look at me the wrong way. And besides, I used one of the less successful versions for Rose's Christmas present: I stuck her face on it. It made her laugh because it really looked like her; she has it on her wall in the office at home so she must kind of like it. She's doing much better, has Dad told you? She'll be here in a bit anyway.

Dad is good. Has he told you he's started getting his memories back? We were eating dinner the other day and he burst out laughing. Me and Rose didn't know what the hell was so funny but he said he had remembered a day when apparently you had laughed so hard at him falling over outside a concert that you farted really loudly, and the more you laughed the more you did it? Anyway, he was still chuckling on his way up to bed that night. We think he should start to get out there a bit, you know? He's happy and everything, but we worry that he'll be on his own when we start moving on, but I guess he will in his own time; it's like he's in a new relationship with you at the moment anyway.

I miss you at night. Sometimes I wake up and think I can hear you singing but it's normally just Dad snoring.

Right, I'd better make tracks. I've got to pick up Kate after I get back; she's coming over for the weekend and me and Dad said we'd cook her chilli and loaded potato wedges and I need to get it in the slow cooker.

Love you.

Rose

Hi, Mum. Just a mo, I'm just going to plant these sweet peas. There's no way I'm letting Flynn win again – seriously, washing your brother's pants is something no girl should have to do. There. Sweet peas will triumph.

It feels different coming here now. Like I understand you more than I ever had before.

Your boys are doing well. Flynn is so very different from the boy you knew; I don't think I could have coped with the past year or so without him.

I hadn't really noticed it at all – the need to feel it again, the control, the relief. I suppose I was pretending to ignore it, ignore the whispers, 'just once won't hurt', but as it happened, the choice was made for me. I was doing the washing-up and cut my finger on a knife. I'm forever telling them to not put knives straight into the sink but they never listen. Anyway, Flynn just stopped and stared at me. I'd asked him what? He fetched the plasters as I wound kitchen roll around my finger and then took my hand and put the plaster on, like I was a child. It was just plain weird and I told him so. 'You're singing,' he said, smiling. And there it was. I was singing and I hadn't even realised it. The song was one that you sang when I went through my self-harming stage so I must have known the lyrics from you. I've Googled it since and it was by Cat Stevens and it's called 'The First Cut Is the Deepest'. The feel of the blade and the sting filled me with a rush so powerful, Mum, it was how it must feel to an addict when they have one last fix, but there you were, in the room with us, calming me down just as you had when you were alive. The timing couldn't have been worse if I had started down that path again because I was just beginning a placement with the local newspaper. I understand a little about how it feels now. That gorgeous release it gives you when you feel upset or stressed. It really is like a drug.

After that day, I decided to do something positive with that feeling, so I've started writing a blog. It's for people with anxiety problems. I've mentioned you a few times, I hope you don't mind. I've tried to incorporate how we used mindfulness techniques in the early days and how singing can help to release dopamine – the happy hormone – into the brain. I dug out my old diaries and used them to help others understand the pressures you can feel as a thirteen-year-old girl and I've talked endlessly to Dad and Flynn about what they were thinking and doing during that time. I can't tell you how good it felt to be able to go through that time in my life with a purpose. Even if I just help one person out there, it will be worth it. It made me feel closer to you, going back through that time, made me understand the woman you were, how you dealt with me and Flynn and all of the troubles that we put you through. How selfish we were and how difficult it was for Dad to become our dad when he had fought so hard to find stability and a place that he could call home. He told me some horrible stories about what life on the streets was really like. I even got him to write a piece about the horrors he had to face; how worthless he had felt, how lost.

And as for me, Mum – I want to thank you. From every part of me to every part of you. Thank you.

Melody

I've talked before about what I thought would happen when I died. I told you that I thought there would be nothing, no white light, no army of ancestors, but what I hadn't thought of is my energy. We talk about having none of it at the end of a busy working week. We talk about having to burn it off when we have too much of it, we swallow drinks to give us it and avoid sugar to take it away, but what happens to it really, this energy? Einstein told us that energy never dies, it just transforms into something else, so here's what I think happened to mine. When I was living, all of my energy went into my family, my thoughts, my worries, my joy and my sadness. How can all of that just disappear? Einstein tells us that it doesn't and who am I to argue with a genius? So when I took my last breath, when I ceased to use it, did it die with me? I don't think that it could. If physics is to believed, it just transformed into something different.

You know that feeling when you're concentrating on something and all of a sudden there is a song, a melody in your head that you just can't shake? Well, there you go. My gift to you: a Melody in your head.

Right now 'I'm Walking on Sunshine' and 'woow-oooh' . . . doesn't it feel good?

Acknowledgements

Where to begin?

This book wouldn't be in front of you if one person hadn't asked to read the whole manuscript, and so a huge thank you goes to my agent Amanda Preston. I have said thank you to you a gazillion times, but it never seems quite enough, so I'll say a few more: thank you for your belief in me, for your constant enthusiasm and support. You changed my life.

A massive thank you goes to all at ILA, their hard work made my dream to be a full-time writer become a reality and has given Melody the chance to be heard around the world.

I had no idea the amount of hard work and love that goes into polishing a final manuscript and for that I'm eternally grateful to my editorial team: Jennifer Doyle for her unwavering belief and love for Melody and her family; Sara Adams and Kitty Stogdon for adding the icing on the cake and pushing me to make *The Songs of Us* the best it could be.

To all at Headline, you're amazing! Phoebe Swinburn, who will soon be my adopted sister if my mother has anything to do with it, and to Helena Fouracre whose email made me cry as she 'highlighted beautiful little snippets'. I've always wanted to have someone feel this way about my writing, thank you.

The beautiful cover was designed by Heike Schüssler.

Thank you for the thought behind the images, I love seeing Melody watching her children fly every time I look at it.

It's rare to able to honestly say that you love your job and that you love the people you work with, but for me it was true. So, my heartfelt thanks go to my amazing colleagues at Wrockwardine Wood Junior School. To Claire Ashley and Emma Jackson, who believed in me and supported me through the tough times and celebrated with me through the good. To David Kirkpatrick, who put up with me and my constant tears and frustrations through the submission process, and who made me cry with laughter on the days where I felt like my writing career was at rock bottom. To Molly Clark, for her endless grammar advice and general wonderfulness, and for proofreading my first three chapters. Massive thanks also go to Julie Henry for being the best boss in the world! To Louise Brindley-Jones for her constant friendship, Cara Leck for her enthusiasm and Alison Williams, who stayed up late into the night and came into work with tired eyes because she couldn't sleep without knowing what was going to happen to Melody. I miss you all immensely.

To my new 'colleagues': the members of The Fiction Café Writers and Readers' Group on Facebook. In particular, Wendy Clarke, Cath Deacon, Mooky Holden, Jennifer Gilmore, Kiltie Jackson, Jennifer Kennedy, Kate Baker, Sherron Mayes and Natali Drake to name but a few! Thank you for your support, your jokes and advice. I couldn't have gone through the editing process without you all.

To Bev Osborne, my friend and first proofreader, who gave me invaluable advice and encouragement, spotting my mistakes and ringing me the moment she finished it, even though she could barely talk through her tears.

Nicki Smith, my life-long friend and counsellor on all things 'loon', thank you for your years of friendship, your company and endless generosity.

Thank you doesn't quite seem a strong enough phrase to use when I think of all the things my family have done to support me, but my thanks go to my mom for being, well, my mom and for doing all of the things that moms should do, I love you so, so much! And thanks to her wonderful husband, Chris, for putting up with me! Drunken hugs to the mad, wonderful bunch that make up the Evans family but especially my mother-in-law-to-be, Jackie Evans, who is the most selfless person I have ever met. We're so grateful for everything you do, and I love you to bits. Thank you to my nan for reading me *The Twits* over and over again when I was little. To my brother, Dan, for impromptu prosecco deliveries and to my dad, aka Clark Griswold, who brings a whole new meaning to the word 'Christmas'.

And finally, Us. My children, Ethan, Ally, Max and Delilah. You make my heart sing every day. Thank you for putting up with my tantrums and tears when I've been at the computer all day, thank you for making me laugh, making me tea (Max), making me proud and making our messy home the best place on earth to be; I wouldn't want to be anywhere else. To my Russell, who is my biggest champion and harshest critic. He has supported me through days when all I have done is talked about the King family and days where I did nothing but cry at the endless rejections that flooded my inbox. You are my sunshine.

Bookends

When one book ends, another begins...

Bookends is a vibrant new reading community to help you ensure you're never without a good book.

You'll find exclusive previews of the brilliant new books from your favourite authors as well as exciting debuts and past classics. Read our blog, check out our recommendations for your reading group, enter great competitions and much more!

Visit our website to see which great books we're recommending this month.

Join the Bookends community:
www.welcometobookends.co.uk

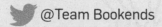 @Team Bookends   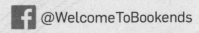 @WelcomeToBookends